P.S.: I'M INNOCENT

Steve Ruediger

iUniverse, Inc.
Bloomington

P.S.: I'm Innocent

iUniverse books may be ordered through booksellers or by contacting:

iUniverse
1663 Liberty Drive
Bloomington, IN 47403
www.iuniverse.com
1-800-Authors (1-800-288-4677)

ISBN: 978-1-4620-6934-7 (sc)
ISBN: 978-1-4620-6933-0 (hc)
ISBN: 978-1-4620-6932-3 (e)

Printed in the United States of America

iUniverse rev. date: 12/08/2011

Acknowledgements

Extremely valuable, tough, and sometimes painful critiquing by the members of Sanibel Island Writer's Group Number Two greatly improved this novel. Also of tremendous assistance to this author were workshops, meetings, and educational sessions provided through his membership in Southwest Florida Romance Writers, Gulf Coast Writers Association, and Mystery Writers of America, Florida Chapter.

Thanks to Bart and Nancy.

Comment

This novel includes a fictionalized version of slave labor conditions suffered by farm workers. For a non-fiction look at conditions on some farms, this author suggests reading *Nobodies: Modern American Slave Labor and The Dark Side of the New Global Economy* by John Bowe, published by Random House.

The Sanibel Police department is a well-trained, professional law enforcement agency. Conservation organizations on Sanibel are hard working and dedicated. Representations in this novel of a dishonest policeman and of a phony conservationist are for dramatic purposes only and are not intended in any way to represent real individuals.

CHAPTER ONE

Eggs and Guns

A sudden splash followed by crunching noises startled Lizzie Grant. Her breath caught in her throat. Lizzie loved the beach at night but felt vulnerable alone on the long, empty stretch of sand. She stopped dead in her tracks, trembling from head to toe. She wanted to run but her feet would not move. Instead, she forced herself to slowly turn, afraid of who might be approaching behind her.

Lizzie gasped relief as she saw an enormous reddish-brown loggerhead sea turtle emerge from the Gulf of Mexico. She couldn't believe she was about to see a real loggerhead dig a nest and lay eggs.

Lizzie regained self-control and ran to find cover. In her haste, she almost dropped the bag full of posts, ropes, signs, and the infrared video camcorder she carried. Not wanting to alarm the turtle, she settled behind a clump of sea oats to watch the creature struggle up the gently sloping beach, carving a trail like a tank track.

As the turtle moved closer, the faint roar of distant engines disturbed the peacefulness of Lizzie's observations. She glanced up. Far out in the Gulf, a boat with no running lights sped along the coast, the distant roar of its engines echoed in the otherwise still night. Its shadowy outline was only faintly visible in the dim moonlight. Lizzie returned her attention to the turtle. A mysterious boat was a distraction when a real living loggerhead was only a few feet away.

She felt lucky to have sighted the large sea creature. Her new job included marking turtle nests for the Sanibel Island Environmental Conservancy

(SIEC). Before escaping to Florida six months ago, it would have amazed Lizzie to be paid to save wildlife and protect nature.

But, even in her new job, seeing an actual turtle was rare. The mother turtles usually completed nests and returned to the ocean depths unobserved. Daytime beachgoers to Bowman's Beach Park would trample the turtle tracks, making nests hard to find. So Lizzie searched for them at night.

Raising her camera, Lizzie began shooting video as the turtle examined the sand, moving its large head from side to side and prodding with its flippers for a site which met its nesting criteria. Scientists weren't sure what those criteria were, but the turtle knew. Using her rear flippers she began strewing sand in all directions, digging a hole for the approximately one hundred rubbery, ping-pong ball sized eggs she would lay.

In spite of her concentration on the sea turtle's efforts, Lizzie could not help noticing the approaching long, low boat. It turned, heading to shore directly in front of the sea oats Lizzie crouched behind. After the turtle started laying its eggs, nothing could distract it from its biologically-dictated task. But Lizzie didn't want it spooked before the eggs started dropping. She also was afraid the boat might spook her. She felt very alone.

As engine sounds faded, sputtered, and died, a man leaped from the boat into the water a few feet from shore and pulled the sleek craft closer to the beach. People began disembarking, struggling over the sides and then wading through the shallow Gulf water as the man held the boat.

The people were black, all except the man holding the boat steady. The men passed suitcases and duffle bags to the beach. Both men and women flopped down on the sand beside their bags looking exhausted. They sat on the trail left by the loggerhead without noticing it. Children scattered among the boat people were nervously quiet, hugging close to their parents and looking around wide-eyed.

Lizzie became so curious about the people she ignored the turtle for a few minutes. But her job involved researching wildlife, not watching human beings on the beach no matter how unusual they were. The people hadn't seen her and didn't seem to be going anywhere right away. She told herself she must not fail in her job. Both her fear and her curiosity were less important than this golden opportunity to study sea turtle behavior. The loggerhead had already begun laying eggs. Lizzie could stand and approach without scaring the turtle away. She walked around to the beach side and shot video of eggs spewing out of the turtle into the hole in the sand.

After getting several minutes of excellent egg laying video, Lizzie turned her camera onto the people near the water. Her curiosity overcame both her fear and her work ethic. She stepped forward down the sloping beach to get a closer view of the approximately twenty black people sitting on the Sanibel Island beach at three in the morning; certainly not a normal event.

"Hey you, what're you doing with that camera?" The white man holding the mooring rope yelled at her, his voice angry. He wore a black t-shirt and blue jeans, wet from standing in the water.

Lizzie backed up. If she reached her bag behind the sea oats, she could grab it and run.

The man called for someone else to hold the boat. Then he leaned in to get something.

As Lizzie ran up to the sea oats, she looked around to see the man stomping up the beach toward her, waving what looked like a gun.

Gasping with fear, Lizzie abandoned her bag and ran through clumps of bushes into the woods behind the beach. Burrs and thorns stabbed her bare feet. Grasshoppers whirred up striking her face. Round Australian pine nutlets pushed their tiny ridges into her skin. She ignored the pain. Her heart raced. She had to get through the thick beachfront line of bushes and out of sight, had to lose the man from the boat, the man with the gun. She headed toward the dirt road which wound through the woods behind the beach.

"Hey, stop!" the man yelled.

Lizzie stumbled forward. She found the rutted dirt road and ran down it. She remembered seeing an isolated stilt house back in the woods. Probably nobody would be there off season. She had nowhere else to run.

Painfully gasping for breath, she stumbled up to the frame house with gray siding. Deserted. No lights on. No sign of life. No car was in the parking area beneath the house. The only sounds were the whirring of insects. She darted toward the tool shed under the house.

"Hey, stop."

She was too late to get away. He was right behind her. She was out of breath. She turned to face him.

The short haired, muscular man dashed to within a few feet of her. He stopped and stood looking up and down Lizzie's slender body. She felt as though he was looking right through her thin cotton shirt and tight, well-worn jeans. He chuckled and walked up to her. He held a pistol in one hand while he motioned with the other for Lizzie to relax. "Calm down, young lady, just calm down. I don't want to hurt you. I only want your camera."

Lizzie backed slowly until she was against the rough wood wall of the tool shed. She trembled, too afraid to say anything. The air seemed thick and unbreathable. Maybe she could dart around into the blackness behind the tool shed before the man actually grabbed her, and then lose herself in the woods.

The man had a glint in his eyes and a sardonic smile. "If you're not going to hand it over, I'll have to take it from you." He looked like he was enjoying himself. He held the gun up. It looked huge.

Lizzie expected to be assaulted, raped. She felt terribly alone. Even if she called out, nobody could hear her and running again didn't seem possible. She started to cry.

The man stepped forward and viciously ripped the video camcorder from Lizzie's hand. She stifled a scream. Her hand hurt. He was so close she could smell the odor of boat fuel on him.

"Please don't hurt me," Lizzie sobbed. "Please – please – don't…"

Her words caught in her throat as a man suddenly sprang from the shadows beside her. This second man came from behind the tool shed. He pointed something at the man from the boat. "Move back, asshole; return the lady's camera," growled the newcomer.

Lizzie wiped tears from her eyes and looked at her rescuer. She was amazed to see an elderly, white-haired gentleman dressed in a neatly pressed sports shirt, shorts, and white socks. He looked like he belonged on a golf course, not in the woods holding a machine gun. Lizzie realized that's what he held, a machine gun.

The man from the boat dropped the camcorder.

"Beat it," the old man grunted. Barrel-chested and of medium height, he had a hooked, Roman nose; a lantern jaw; and a bronze tint to his weathered skin. His nose was slightly bent like it had been on the receiving end of a few punches.

The boat man hesitated.

The old man waved his machine gun. "When I say beat it, I mean beat it. I can get off ten shots before you fire one. Beat it, asswipe. You don't want me upset."

The man from the boat hesitated for another second then turned and silently walked away. He disappeared down the dirt road.

The old man laughed. "That jerk almost shit his pants when he saw my Uzi. You see the macho way he walked off? Inside he wanted to run like hell. Hi, I'm Joe Caunteloupo. That's spelled different from the fruit. Don't call me no cantaloupe, I ain't no fruit." The old man reached out to shake Lizzie's hand, fumbling his machine gun out of the way.

"Uh, hi, I'm Elizabeth Grant." She shook his hand. "My friends call me Lizzie."

"They call me Joey C. I noticed you earlier doin' somethin' on the beach.

"I didn't see you on the beach."

"People usually don't."

"You have a phone? That man really scared me. We should call the police." Lizzie waved a couple of mosquitoes away from her face. She was finally catching her breath. She picked up her camcorder and backed several steps toward the road, out of the shadow of the house. Lizzie was relieved to be rescued but, still, she was alone with this old man and he was holding a machine gun and he looked like a tough old guy.

"No need for police, I called Homeland Security. I expect the Coast Guard'll be here soon." Joey slapped at his legs. "Fuckin' bugs."

"Homeland Security? Not the Sanibel Police?" Lizzie's trembling hand wiped moisture from her face.

"I got a friend at Homeland Security. Don't mention that to nobody. He ain't supposed to know me."

"It was lucky you saw what was happening," said Lizzie, as she slapped herself on the cheek.

"I don't sleep too good no more."

"That's a shame."

"Yeah, I guess it's 'cause I was always a night person up north. A lotta my business took place at night. And I was always around people. It's kinda lonely here, except for the damn blood suckers." Joey waved his Uzi around his legs to drive off mosquitoes.

"What did you do?"

"I was a consultant."

Lizzie looked at the strange weapon Joey held pointed at the ground. She gestured toward the contraption. "I was in South America once, Peru. That looks like the machine guns the soldiers carried."

"Yeah, it's an Uzi. It's sometimes handy to have a machine gun around."

"Aren't they illegal?"

"Hey, I'm on my own property. What were you doin' down there on the beach at three in the morning? Not the best time to get a tan."

Lizzie held up her camcorder. "I was shooting video of a mama sea turtle laying her eggs."

"Really? Man, that'd be somethin' to see. I'm from New York where we got just about everything. But we don't got no sea turtles layin' eggs in the Big Apple."

"Come with me and take a look. She's probably still laying unless the people scared her off. Sea turtles need to be undisturbed and there are more and more people everywhere."

"Yeah, too many. I've always said there's a lot of 'em the world'd be better off without." Joey shook his large head in disgust and glanced at his machine gun. He had a scar over his right eye.

"Come on then, come with me – please – I'm really nervous about that man."

"No, I better not. Too much law enforcement makes me nervous. I expect they'll be showin' up soon."

"Okay, well thanks." Lizzie shook his hand again. She started onto the dirt road but then turned back to the old man. "I owe you my life. If there's ever anything I can do."

"Hey, don't worry about it." He smiled at her. He certainly had a lot of wrinkles. "Go protect those turtle eggs."

"Okay – I wish you'd come with me. I'm afraid that man might still be there."

"That shit ass? He's a hundred miles away by now. The young punks don't got the piss and vinegar we had in my day. Don't worry your pretty little head none. You're now officially a friend of Joey C. My friends don't get hurt."

"I'll still be careful to make sure that man's gone. Thanks again."

"Any time."

Lizzie turned to go.

"Oh, hey," called Joey, "I'd just as soon you not mention seein' me."

"Okay, sure." Lizzie walked back onto the winding dirt roadway which ran behind the beach. She was still trembling from everything that had happened. As she went over it all in her mind, she puzzled over the guy from the boat calling her "young lady." At 32 she didn't hear that very often. She thought maybe the moonlight made her look younger.

Lizzie crept low behind bushes bordering the beach. She was afraid to return but had to retrieve her bag containing her car keys. It was much too far to walk home. She pushed a branch aside and looked up and down the moonlit shoreline. She saw no sign of the muscular man or his boat. Lizzie took a deep calming breath and stepped through a gap between bushes onto the beach.

The black families were still huddled together near the loggerhead turtle track. A Sanibel Island police officer was with them. His small, green, beach patrol vehicle sat on the sand a short distance away. Lizzie was relieved to see the policeman. She was not afraid of the families on the beach. Nevertheless, Lizzie felt tension leave her when she saw the representative of the law. She hurried toward him.

The policeman had his back to Lizzie. He was telling the families gathered in front of him: "Go about a mile down the beach that way." One of the men translated into French as the officer pointed toward the south. Lizzie had taken French in high school, but this French sounded strange.

"You'll see wooden posts with ropes marking the park exit," the officer said. "Walk up that trail to a bus. Everything will be all right. People will meet…" The policeman turned slightly and noticed Lizzie. "What are you doing here?"

"I was photographing that sea turtle over there." She gestured with her video camera toward the turtle, which was now flippering sand to cover its eggs. Lizzie shifted the camera from one hand to the other and then reached out to shake the policeman's hand. "We haven't met before. I'm with the Island Conservancy, Lizzie Grant."

The policeman ignored her hand. He had bushy black eyebrows and a thin white scar on his left cheek. The officer looked over Lizzie and her camera with an expression of uneasy hostility. "You shouldn't be here. This is police business." He towered over her. At five-foot-two Lizzie was used to that.

She looked down at the empty hand she had extended. She dropped it to her side and spoke quietly as she looked up into his shadowy eyes, "Did Homeland Security notify you about these people?"

"What about Homeland Security?" The policeman had an edge to his voice. He glared at her; like that policeman had glared several years ago when Lizzie accidentally went through a red light.

Lizzie tried to keep the tremble out of her voice. "Homeland Security was called. So I guess the Border Patrol or the Coast Guard or whoever should be here soon to help you."

"Who the hell called them?"

"Well, uh…"

"Who else knows about these Haitians? Who else was here?" demanded the officer. He had a metal name tag on his shirt reading "Sgt. Malflic." It was at Lizzie's eye level.

"Nobody," Lizzie lied. "My cell phone is over in my bag behind the sea oats."

A disgusted look spread across Malflic's tanned face. His hand went slowly to the pistol on his hip. "Are you alone out here?"

"Yes… I always…"

Some of the black men began speaking rapidly in French, seemingly all talking at once.

"You people move back over there," ordered Malflic, waving an arm toward the south end of the beach. His other hand stayed on the pistol. He turned his attention back to Lizzie. "Why don't we take a little walk up to where your phone is."

"I don't need my phone."

The policeman growled, "Up to the woods, now." He reached out toward Lizzie but froze as fast approaching sounds filled the night. A helicopter, its blades thumping, swept up along the coast. The copter's spotlight played along the beach. It paused as it lit up Lizzie and Malflic. The policeman moved his hand away from his pistol and backed away from Lizzie.

The spotlight continued along the beach until it illuminated the crowd of Haitians. It stayed focused on them.

"Shit," exclaimed Malflic. He turned from Lizzie and ran over to the Haitians. Lizzie could see the words "U.S. Coast Guard" on the side of the helicopter.

CHAPTER TWO

Breakfast With Agnes

"This guy threatened you with a gun and you didn't report him to the police?" Aaron "Birdman" Carter was incredulous. Over breakfast in his apartment Lizzie had described her encounter with the man from the boat. Lately Lizzie spent more time in Aaron's apartment than in her own, which was right next door, in the Conservancy employee housing units. Both apartments were small, sparsely furnished efficiencies.

Lizzie shrugged. "I promised that old man I wouldn't mention him to anybody."

"The guy with the machine gun?" Aaron reached down and absent-mindedly petted Agnes, who purred deeply. "You mentioned him to me, aren't I somebody?"

"I think he meant not to mention him to the police. But my story wouldn't make sense if I didn't include him; so I can't report any of it."

"You're not safe alone at night on that deserted beach." Aaron pointed down at the animal sitting between them. "Why don't you take Agnes with you next time? She'd protect you and she needs the exercise. You could let her run up and down the beach. I feel guilty keeping her cooped up in this small apartment."

Lizzie laughed as she offered a sausage to Agnes, whose large teeth took the meat carefully from Lizzie's fingers. The animal, wagging its crooked, black tipped tail, chomped down the sausage. "The police would certainly be after me if they caught me with a Florida panther on a public beach. But I know it's a problem having her here."

Aaron scratched his pointed chin. "I never realized when I helped care for her at the animal hospital that she'd become so imprinted on me she couldn't be released back into the wild."

Lizzie reached out and petted Agnes. The six foot long cat rubbed her grayish tan furred body against Lizzie's bare leg. "She'd go up to the first person she saw and try to make friends - probably scare them to death."

Aaron stiffened and almost spat his words. "More likely she'd get herself killed. Humans are the dangerous animals. I was talking with Augie about it earlier. He told me he has some slash pine land out near his Immokalee farm, said I could use it if I wanted to set up that rural wildlife shelter I always wanted. I'm going to look it over."

Lizzie smiled. "That's great, Aaron. He said you could just use his land for free?"

"Yeah."

"Well then what's wrong? You look glum, not happy."

"I've gotten used to living next to you, Lizzie. I love Sanibel Island. I love you. And we're talking Immokalee, a backwoods farming community; mostly Hispanics and a few rednecks."

Lizzie gestured around her. "But you wouldn't be cramped like here; you'd have lots of space for the animals you want to rescue. You'd be doing something that's useful and that's yours."

Aaron touched Lizzie's hand. "But I wouldn't have you. I'd want you with me. You're my favorite animal."

Agnes emitted a low growl.

Aaron moved his hand to the large cat's back. "Sometimes I think she understands English."

"No, she just wants another sausage." Lizzie reached down to offer one to Agnes. She felt the edge of Agnes's teeth as the panther took the sausage. "She almost bit me," exclaimed Lizzie.

"Jealousy"

"She does make a racket when we lock her out of the bedroom." Lizzie smiled thinking about all that had happened between her and Aaron since she arrived in Florida lost and distraught. She tapped her knuckles on the table as if punctuating a decision. "You know, about Immokalee, I might consider it. But it would be a major change. How isolated is this slash pine land Augie's offering you?"

"It's way back on the other side of nowhere."

"No other people nearby?"

Aaron laughed, "I'd have you all to myself; if there's anything left after the mosquitoes finish with you."

"I'm like a magnet to the little blood suckers. I attract them wherever I go."

"You also attract men wherever you go, like that man who parks across San-Cap Road."

Lizzie glanced toward the window. "What man? What are you talking about?"

"A man in a blue Ford has been parking on the shoulder recently. Yesterday, when you left to go shopping, he followed you. I was worried. But he wasn't around when you got back; so I thought maybe it was coincidence." Aaron leaned toward Lizzie with a questioning look. "You haven't noticed him? He hasn't approached you, said anything to you?"

"No, I have no idea who he is. What did he look like?"

Aaron shrugged. "Average looking, middle aged."

"Now you've really got me worried. It's the average looking people who turn out to be the real nut cases."

Agnes growled softly.

"I know, Agnes. You'll protect me." Lizzie petted Agnes and gave her another sausage, then looked back up at Aaron. "When are you going to check out the Immokalee land?"

"Saturday."

"I'll go with you."

CHAPTER THREE

Shallow Water

Later that day, after grabbing some sleep, Lizzie used a seine to check marine life in underwater grasses behind Sanibel. The shallow waters of the back bay held a wide variety of tiny creatures. A person looking down into the water from a boat would see only gently swaying grasses. However, when Lizzie ran her net through the grasses, she came up with baby shrimp, small sea horses, pipe fish, puffers, tiny crabs, globs of gelatin, and things she couldn't identify. She'd only been doing this for a few weeks.

Today Lizzie was wearing her green bikini, with the cheeky Brazilian bottom and the triangular top. She also wore her wide-brimmed straw hat and felt like a real Floridian. She was around the end of Butcher Point in about two feet of water, wading along just beyond the mangroves, hidden from the view of anyone on Beach Road. Lizzie found the road's name ironic. It led to a small park with no beach. There was a parking lot, a strip of grass, an assortment of large rocks, and then the water; not even an inch of beach. Without a beach, few people stayed very long.

The shrimp Lizzie caught were almost microscopic. Some people thought shrimp with their heads on were ugly. Lizzie thought they were cute. She counted the tiny creatures, then threw them back in the water. They would go offshore and grow up to be adults. In a year or so she might have some of these little fellows for dinner. She had mixed feelings about that, but not so mixed as to restrict her diet.

Lizzie took samples every few feet. She had a note pad, a pen, and her cell phone, all kept in a small wet/dry bag when not in use. The bag was held in front of her by a strap over her shoulder. She made notations in the pad about what she netted, and used the phone's camera to photograph anything interesting or needing further study.

After finishing with the benthic study of one small area, she dumped its subjects back into the water and looked ahead to where she would wade next. She finally stopped before reaching the deeper water beyond the point.

After turning and walking back past the mangroves at the point, Lizzie could again see the parking lot at the end of Beach Road. In addition to her own car, there were two vehicles in the lot, parked side by side, pointed in opposite directions. One was a Sanibel Island police cruiser, the other a black pickup truck, both with their windows down. The policeman was talking across to the man in the truck. They were too far away for Lizzie to hear what they were saying. She thought the policeman reached out and handed something to the other man.

Lizzie waded a few feet closer to the park through the underwater sea grass. The man in the patrol car suddenly looked around at her. She recognized him. It was Sergeant Malflic, who had been with the Haitian refugees on the beach the previous night. Malflic glared at Lizzie, then turned forward in his seat, gunned his patrol car out of the lot, and raced it onto Beach Road.

The departure of the patrol car exposed the side of the pickup truck to Lizzie. Staring at her out the driver's side window was the man from the boat, the short haired, muscular man who had threatened her with the gun and demanded her camera.

Lizzie's cell phone chimed *The William Tell Overture*, the theme from *The Lone Ranger*. Lizzie grabbed her wet/dry bag to get the cell phone out.

The short haired man stepped from his pickup.

Lizzie couldn't get the zipper to work on her bag. It was stuck. She pulled at it. The phone rang again: *Dump derump, derump, rump, rump.*

The man walked down to the water's edge, staring at Lizzie with an intensity she found frightening.

She pulled the zipper frantically. It wouldn't budge. The phone sounded a third time.

The man paused for a moment, and then stepped into the water. His boots and the bottom of his jeans were getting wet.

Lizzie backed up a step. The cell phone produced its musical alert a fourth time. Lizzie frantically jiggled the zipper then pulled at it again. It zipped open. Lizzie yanked out the cell phone and screamed "Hello" into it.

The man stopped.

"Hello, Lizzie, this is August Winters."

The man from last night's encounter made a fist and punched the water in front of him.

"Hello, Augie," Lizzie responded to her boss, the Chairman of the Board of the Environmental Conservancy. "I'm scared. I'm out here alone at Butcher Point and there's this man coming toward me."

The man said "shit," turned, waded back out of the water, and stomped back to his truck. When he reached the truck he turned and looked again at Lizzie, an angry expression on his face. He turned away, got in his truck, and drove off.

Meanwhile, Augie was saying, "Lizzie, are you all right? Should I call the police?"

"No, no, I'm okay. He's leaving. Sorry, Augie, I'm usually not one to panic. Last night was terrible and it seems to be continuing."

"Your being nervous is perfectly understandable; a beautiful young woman out somewhere alone and a man approaches her. In these times and after all that's happened to you recently, you got every right to be scared."

"Thanks for understanding." Lizzie inhaled and exhaled a couple times. "Okay, I'm okay now. I've caught my breath. Why were you calling?"

"I wondered if you'd have time to drop by my office later, say about four-o-clock?"

"Four this afternoon, your office? Sure, I'll be there. And thanks again."

Lizzie clipped the cell phone onto her bikini strap beside her right breast. She took one more deep breath and then turned to look out along the beautiful mangrove coastline. She wondered what Augie wanted.

CHAPTER FOUR

Augie's Auguries

"I think we should discuss your future," began Augie as Lizzie sat opposite his large desk in his small office. The Chairperson of the Board of the Sanibel Island Environmental Conservancy (SIEC) is an honorary position given to a prominent island resident. Past chairmen had been inactive, letting the paid foundation manager do the work. Augie was different. From the beginning, he threw himself into everything. He aggregated more and more power within the foundation, which owned large tracks of land on Sanibel and which conducted conservation studies on both the island and adjacent waters. His hard work resulted in Augie being re-elected to the chairmanship year after year. He became the public face of the foundation and a powerful political presence in the area. The paid manager was reduced to a mere cipher.

Augie's wife, June, basked in the reflected glory Augie's position gave her in the Sanibel Island social hierarchy. Augie made frequent trips to his Immokalee farm, the basis for his wealth. June never went there.

Lizzie had put on a short green Georgette cover-up tunic over her green bikini. She crossed her legs and wondered why Augie was showing so much interest. "My future?" Lizzie asked. "What do you mean?"

"Has Aaron told you about my offer?" Augie leaned his stocky frame forward. His loose jowls wobbled around his Burl Ives-look-alike face. At Christmas he played Santa Claus.

"You mean the land near your farm so he can set up his animal sanctuary?"

"Yes."

"He told me this morning."

"I thought he might. Did he ask you to move there with him?"

"Yes, but I haven't decided yet. I'm going out with him Saturday to look it over."

"Very good." Augie leaned back in his leather executive office chair, a chair almost too big for the small room. "You need to investigate all aspects of such an important decision." Augie adjusted a small desk display of American flags to one side so it wasn't blocking his view of Lizzie. When she remained silent, Augie continued: "But we're not here to discuss your personal life; at least not directly. I just want to make your situation perfectly clear. I've made an offer to Aaron I don't think he can refuse. He's real attached to that cat and, let's face it; we can't have a Florida panther living in SIEC housing."

Lizzie nodded. "It was only supposed to be temporary."

"Yes, but it looks to me like if the cat goes, Aaron will go too. So I made the land offer."

Lizzie smiled. "Aaron appreciates your offer."

"He should: I'm giving him free land to set up his life's dream." Augie pointed at himself. "But I also get something: increased security for my big farm. That worthless slash pine land borders one long side of my farm. Outcroppings of bedrock are all over that section. I guess you know I'm what they call a gentleman farmer." Augie sat up straighter and gestured vaguely in the direction of Immokalee. "I've got a man out there, Boss Pigott, who actually runs the farm."

"His first name is 'Boss'?"

"No, but that's what everybody calls him. So it might as well be his name. Anyway, I got off the subject. The dirt on the part I'm giving Aaron is too poor for farming. So I fence it in and your boyfriend puts his big cat there. Then I'll help him find other big cats that need a home. He's got a wildlife refuge and I've got something bordering one side of my farm that no sane person would try to cross." Augie hesitated for a second. "You know, like United Farm Worker union organizers."

Lizzie shifted in her seat. "What does all this have to do with my future?"

"You have a decision to make: either go with your boyfriend into a trailer out in the remote piney woods near Immokalee or stay here at the Environmental Conservancy on beautiful Sanibel Island."

"I told Aaron I'd think about it."

Augie leaned forward toward Lizzie. His jowls shook slightly. "I want you to know right off that whatever decision you make, I'll help you in any way I can. If you decide to go out there in the woods with your boyfriend and his cat and you ever need anything, just call on me. I'll be there for you. On the other hand, if you decide to stay here, you have a very bright future with the Conservancy."

Lizzie nodded. "Thank you, Augie; your opinion is very important to me."

"I'm glad of that, Lizzie. I've been watching you closely and I really like what I see. You're a very hard worker and you got yourself a lot of sense. I heard about that problem you had on the beach last night; something about Cuban refugees.

"Actually, Haitian refugees."

Augie blinked and tilted his head slightly. "Haitians, really? That's unusual. The Haitians usually come in on the other coast. They make good farm workers. How'd you find out where they were from?"

Lizzie gestured in the general direction of Bowman's. "A policeman was there, a Sergeant Malflic. He said they were Haitians."

Augie nodded. "Oh, so you called the police."

Lizzie shook her head. "No, not me."

Augie leaned forward. "I thought you were all alone out there with that loggerhead turtle. So who called the authorities? It certainly wasn't the turtle."

Lizzie laughed. "No, she was too busy laying eggs. Whoever called Homeland Security, it wasn't me."

"Homeland Security? Is that who was called?"

"The Coast Guard showed up with a helicopter. They're part of Homeland Security, aren't they?"

"Yes, helping protect America." Augie sat far forward in his chair as he fixed his gaze on Lizzie's blue eyes. "Anyway you apparently had the sense not to get involved and call anybody. If you stay here at SIEC you could be in line for the top position, under me that is. Someday Jenny will move on and I'll need to fill her position. That person would have to have the political savvy to know when to keep out of things that don't concern her."

Lizzie reached out and touched the edge of Augie's desk. "I've only been here six months. Are you saying I might be considered for the job of Conservancy manager?"

"Yes, definitely, if you're smart and play your cards right. Your first crossroads on this journey is the decision whether to go to Immokalee or stay here." Augie smiled his politician's smile. "As I said at the beginning, no pressure from me either way. I just want to be sure you understand everything at stake."

Augie stood up and came around his desk.

Lizzie also stood. She reached out to shake his hand.

Augie took her hand in his. But, instead of shaking it, he held it as he stepped closer and gave Lizzie a quick kiss on the cheek.

CHAPTER FIVE

Dropped Mangoes

Lizzie stripped off her green cover up and her bikini after entering her apartment. Sweating in the summer sun and the handling of marine specimens in the back bay had left odors she was eager to shed. She dumped her clothing in the wicker laundry basket near her front door but then paused, noticing an unusual smell. Maybe it was something in the laundry basket. But washing it out would have to wait. After several hours wading in the back bay and her hurried visit to Augie's office, Lizzie was desperate to get to the bathroom. She hurried from the small hallway into her living room. As she entered that room someone stepped heavily behind her from beside the entryway.

Startled, Lizzie whirled around. The muscular, short-haired man from the boat blocked her escape back into the hall. He wore blue jeans and a tan T-shirt. He was smiling.

Lizzie covered her breasts with her hands and backed away from him.

"I see you're a natural blonde." The man flicked his eyes down toward Lizzie's crotch. "I'd been wondering about that."

Lizzie moved her left hand down. "Let me get my bathing suit from the hall."

"No, I don't think so," the man laughed. "I like you like this."

Lizzie's legs shook. "What do you want?"

The man took a step forward. "I want to be absolutely certain you never tell anyone you saw me last night or earlier today."

"I won't say a word." Lizzie spoke urgently. "I swear to you, not a word to anyone. Now go away… Please." She tried to sneak back another step. He followed her. She could feel her legs trembling. She needed to pee. She hadn't gone all afternoon. She wanted to scream. But the SIEC housing was isolated in a wooded area of native Florida vegetation. Usually nobody was around until later in the evening.

"I also need the digital memory card from the camcorder you used on the beach," the man added.

"It's not here. It's at the office. I gave it to Augie. Please leave. I promise I won't show anybody the part of the video with you on it." Lizzie looked around but saw nothing she could use to defend herself.

"Do you take me for a fool? I'm serious about this." The man was raising his voice. "Your health, your life itself, my life also, depends on the destruction of that video and your forgetting you ever saw me. This isn't a game."

Lizzie felt tears gathering in her eyes. "How can I forget I saw you if you keep turning up everywhere I go? Please go away; I won't tell anybody I saw you. I don't even know who you are."

"I never introduced myself. My name's Clete." He stuck out his hand.

Lizzie reached out automatically to shake hands but then jerked her hand back over her breasts. She pressed her right hand tightly against her left breast, gripping herself, almost painfully. She wanted to scream.

Clete's eyes sparkled as he looked her up and down. "This is far more complicated and more deadly than you could possibly imagine. People have already been killed. I must be absolutely certain you don't tell anyone you saw me with Jack."

The trembling was extending throughout Lizzie body. "Jack? I don't know any Jack. Who's Jack?"

Clete smiled slightly. "Sergeant Malflic."

Lizzie backed to where her lower legs were against the front of her sofa. If she went any farther she would fall down onto it. Clete seemed enormous to Lizzie. He towered over her. She was trapped naked between him and her sofa. Lizzie couldn't think of any way to get to her bedroom where she had the small handgun in the drawer beside her bed. Any move to get away and he would grab her. She could not stand the thought of his hands on her. She must delay him, get herself more time.

Desperately, Lizzie blurted out, "How did you find me?"

Clete smiled. "It was easy. Jack said you worked for the Environmental Conservancy. Obviously, you would live in SIEC employee housing. All I had to do was check the names on the mailboxes. Easy as pie."

"You broke into my apartment to warn me? You're just warning me?" Lizzie tried to keep from yelling, tried to keep her voice reasonable. "You're not going to kill me or rape me?"

Clete shook his head, still smiling. "I didn't break in. You should lock your door."

"I haven't needed to until now." Lizzie was trembling all over. She began to cry. A little squirt of urine trickled down the inside of her left leg. She felt like she'd completely lost control of her body.

Clete put his right hand on Lizzie's upper arm. "Calm down. I won't hurt you. I like you."

"No, please, no," Lizzie sobbed.

Clete ran his hand down her upper arm. He smiled at her. "Your skin is very soft," he said in his deep, gruff voice.

Lizzie looked up pleading into his eyes. She felt helpless. She was surprised to discover his eyes were emerald green. She put her hands on his shoulders to push him back and moaned, "Please, don't. You said you were only after my camera. But you're not acting like that. You're acting like you want something else. Please, let me go get my camera. You can have it. Please."

Clete moved his hand off her arm along her hip then over onto her stomach. "Later, we can get the camera later."

"Oh no, please no. Don't touch me there. I can't stand to be touched there. I'm ticklish." This strange man had his hands on her. But what could she do? He had her trapped. If she fell back onto the sofa he would jump on top of her. That would be far worse.

"Ticklish? Where? Here?" asked Clete, flicking his fingers gently on her skin a fraction of an inch below her navel.

"Yes, there. I mean, no. It's worse than the bottom of my feet. Please don't." Lizzie felt waves of fear and revulsion surge through her body. "The camera, remember, you came for the camera"

"I know I shouldn't get distracted from what I came for. But you're very distracting." Clete tickled his fingers against her stomach.

The tickling sensation shot like electric current through Lizzie's nerves. She bit her lip trying to suppress an outburst. It was hopeless. Clete kept tickling her stomach. Lizzie gasped and began panting. She couldn't help it. She slid her left hand up and grabbed Clete's hand. She pressed his hand against her stomach to stop his hand from moving or from going down any further.

She was hyperventilating. She completely lost control and felt the warm urine flow down the inside of her legs. She was trembling all over and felt hot.

"You don't know what that does to me," she moaned

Movement distracted Lizzie. She looked around Clete's left shoulder and saw Aaron standing in the doorway to her living room his mouth gaped open.

Aaron was immobile, stunned. A couple feet in front of him Lizzie, the only woman who had ever loved him, was naked in the arms of another man. She was looking directly at Aaron and she was gasping passionately.

Screaming, Aaron tossed the bag of mangoes he had brought for Lizzie onto the floor. He threw himself across the room at the strange man holding Lizzie.

That man spun around and raised his arms protectively as Aaron slammed into him. It felt like hitting a brick wall.

Lizzie fell back onto her sofa.

Aaron punched at the man, who somehow managed to shove Aaron back and then throw one punch.

Aaron felt the world vanish around him.

When Aaron woke up, Lizzie was sitting on the floor beside him crying. She was still naked. He blinked and looked around. He didn't see the man anywhere.

"Oh, thank God. I thought you were dead," Lizzie sobbed, placing her hand gently on Aaron's cheek.

"I might as well be. Who was that man?" Aaron felt sick and dizzy.

"That was the man from the boat last night, with the Haitian refugees."

Aaron tried to get up, but fell back. "Where is he?"

Lizzie gestured toward the door. "Clete left when he knocked you out. He just ran out without saying anything."

"Clete? You know his name?"

"He told me his name just before you came in." Lizzie looked down at the liquid glistening on her leg. "God, I'm filthy."

"Yes, you are." Aaron struggled to his feet, turned his back on Lizzie, and staggered out of her apartment.

Lizzie looked over at the mangoes which had rolled out of a burst paper bag into the corner of her living room. She fell forward onto the part of the hardwood floor where Aaron had lay. She pounded the floor with her fists and sobbed.

CHAPTER SIX

Growling

The master and his mate are unusually quiet during this long ride in the big-shiny-moving-thing, thought Big Cat. Hostility shot back and forth between the two humans. The mate had not eaten the morning meal with master and Big Cat for two days. Big Cat missed begging meat pieces from the mate.

She licked her paw and glanced out through the opening at the passing countryside.

Also the master and his mate had not secluded themselves in the master's den and made strange noises the last couple nights. Both the master and the mate seemed happier after they made those noises. It must be some sort of noise-making ritual they enjoyed. Big Cat didn't understand why they refused to let her join them. She liked rituals and she could make a lot of noise.

Big Cat didn't like seeing the master unhappy. Sometimes she felt jealous about the special relationship between the master and his mate. Now she wished that relationship would return. She only wanted to see the master happy and he was not happy now.

Big Cat's thoughts were distracted by the passing landscape. She remembered this land. It was like where she grew up. No it wasn't only like it. It was it. This was where she grew up. She recognized the trees and bushes, the feel of the land, its scent.

Wait, she thought, we're passing it. She remembered being hit by a big-shiny-moving-thing right here as she tried to cross this wide trail. It was a long time after that before the master could get her to ride in his big-shiny-moving-thing. She remembered what the big-thing that hit her had done to her.

Big Cat stuck her head out the rear opening and looked back. She whined.

She missed home and they were moving away from it, taking her away from it again.

Lizzie glanced over her shoulder at the Florida panther on the back seat of Aaron's Prius. "Agnes seems upset."

"That makes two of us." Aaron's hands were white, gripping the wheel.

Lizzie shook her head. "Oh, come on Aaron, we've gone over all this. Aren't you ever going to stop being mad at me; can't you forgive me?"

Pounding his fist once on the wheel, Aaron looked over at Lizzie. His face was red. "I still don't understand if this guy was threatening you and you weren't having a relationship with him, why you pleaded with me not to call the police."

"He said it would be dangerous."

"Then you're saying he threatened you?"

Lizzie looked down at her lap. "No, I felt it was more like he was warning me."

Aaron snorted. "You have a strange reaction to somebody warning you; fall into his arms naked and start panting."

"He tickled me," Lizzie whispered.

"So all a strange man has to do is tickle you and you'll take off your clothes and dive into his arms naked?"

"No, I was already naked."

Aaron glared at the road ahead and shook his head. "Augie says I should give you another chance. But I don't know. I don't think I could take another shock like catching you with that man. That hurt terribly. I love you too much. Loving you hurts too much."

"Aaron, I said I was sorry. I'm going with you to look at the land for your wildlife refuge, aren't I?" Lizzie looked over at him and gestured ahead.

Aaron didn't respond.

"We're having a nice Saturday ride out in the country to look at the land that could become your life's dream animal shelter. Be happy Aaron."

"Don't tell me what to be. I'll be however I want to be. I'm not even sure why I let you come along."

Lizzie looked over at Aaron's long, stony face. "I might want to share your dream," she pleaded.

"If I can't trust you then I can't stand having you with me," Aaron growled.

"Oh, Aaron. Forgive me." Lizzie turned in her seat to more directly face Aaron, who continued staring ahead at the long straight roadway, lined for miles by orange groves. "I'm miserable with you being so mad at me. Try making up if it's only for today. We're going to have the whole day alone together just the two of us."

Agnes turned away from the right side backseat window, stuck her head up between the two front seats in between the two people, and turned her face so her greenish yellow eyes were looking directly into Lizzie's blue eyes. The panther made a rumbling noise in her throat.

"I meant the three of us," said Lizzie. "Sorry Agnes, I didn't mean to leave you out."

Agnes growled again.

Lizzie held up her empty hands. "I didn't bring any sausage."

"Looks like you don't have anything for either of us," grumbled Aaron, as he reached over to pet Agnes.

CHAPTER SEVEN

Slash Pines

Aaron drove his 2010 Toyota Prius along a narrow, winding road off of Highway 846. The dirt road was hedged in on both sides by a variety of thick vegetation. The soil of the rutted road was sandy and would probably be treacherous after a rainstorm. The road ended abruptly at a small clearing surrounded by tall pines. Clumps of palmettos and swaths of Brazilian pepper spread across the flat landscape.

"It doesn't look like much," said Lizzie, who was wearing True Religion designer jeans, a Save The Earth T-shirt, and Mephisto strappy sandals. Lizzie had been habituated to trendy clothing by her social climbing husband. She brought remnants of her northern wardrobe with her when she fled south.

Aaron didn't respond to Lizzie's comment about the land. He just looked around.

Lizzie and Aaron opened their doors and simultaneously exited his Toyota.

Aaron turned back to the car and opened the driver's side rear door. Agnes bounded out past Aaron and ran off into the palmettos. She disappeared behind a line of bushes about 200 yards away.

Aaron and Lizzie stared after her.

"I think you just accidentally released a panther into the wild," Lizzie said. "You may never see her again."

Aaron was briefly silent, and then said, "She'll be back. She's faithful."

Lizzie glared at Aaron for a long moment then turned her back on him and walked off along a sparse trail between palmettos. She needed a few moments by herself. Being with Aaron was painful; he was so cold and hostile.

Lizzie walked aimlessly examining the unimpressive flora. As she stepped between two palmettos, she heard a rattling noise. She stopped dead. Directly in front of her a rattlesnake rose up in the strike position. Its rattle was persistent. The poisonous snake hissed and flicked its tongue, his evil eyes fixed on Lizzie's face.

Lizzie stepped back then stepped back again. The snake's head moved forward and rose higher above the trail. Trembling all over, Lizzie turned and ran. After fifty erratic yards in and out between trees and bushes, she stopped and stood panting. She looked back, afraid the rattlesnake had followed her. No movement stirred the palmettos. Everything was silent except the sound of her breathing. The snake had vanished. It could be anywhere.

Lizzie decided to return to Aaron as quickly as possible.

A rifle shot echoed among distant trees as Lizzie tried to thread her way back between palms and palmettos.

Lizzie, worried about Agnes, stood still listening for a second shot or for sounds from whatever had been shot. She heard nothing, only the sounds of a light breeze in the trees.

Even more determined to get back quickly to Aaron, Lizzie hurried along a trail to where the car should be. She couldn't find it. All the pines and palmettos looked the same. She paused and glanced around.

A cloud of mosquitoes engulfed Lizzie. Panicking, she swatted at them and yelled, "Aaron, Aaron, where are you?"

"Over here." His voice sounded far off.

Lizzie hurried toward Aaron's voice. After working her way around several clumps of Australian pine trees, a low lying rocky area of limestone outcroppings, and some thorny bushes, she saw the car. Aaron was a short distance beyond it. He was spraying Deep Woods Off on himself.

Lizzie ran over to him. "I got lost." She took the can from him and began spraying her bare arms and around her neck. She also shot a few blasts at her jeans and shirt.

"I'm worried," stated Aaron. "That rifle shot; have you seen Agnes?"

"No."

Aaron looked around and then called out, "Agnes, here Agnes, here." Aaron's call went unanswered. The woods remained silent except for the breezes through the treetops.

Aaron walked over to where a pine had been toppled by lightning. He sat on the trunk, which made a natural bench. He leaned forward with his hands on his knees and looked down at the ground and shook his head. "It was dumb of me to let her out and expect her to stay around like a house pet, a dog or cat."

"She is a cat," responded Lizzie, standing in front of him. "She'll come back when she wants to."

Aaron didn't look up.

Lizzie sat on the log beside Aaron and gently placed a hand on his shoulder. "She'll be back. She loves you."

Aaron continued to look at the ground. "I don't know. It would be terrible if I lost her."

Lizzie massaged Aaron's neck and boney shoulders. "Be patient. It'll work out."

They sat side by side on the log talking about Agnes and about the land for another fifteen minutes. Aaron turned slightly so Lizzie could massage his neck muscles with both hands.

"A tall perimeter fence will be the first thing," Aaron was saying. "Even before a trailer." He looked up as something moved beyond a cluster of Brazilian pepper bushes. "Look over there. Is that her?" Aaron pointed.

Lizzie's eyes followed the direction indicated by his pointing finger. "Yes, I think it is."

A big cat was bounding toward them at full speed.

"That better be Agnes," murmured Lizzie.

"It is Agnes," said Aaron, standing up. Lizzie's hands fell from his shoulders in mid-massage.

Agnes ran up directly in front of Aaron. Something was in her mouth. Agnes looked up at Aaron with bright, intelligent eyes. She dropped a mushy lump at his feet then looked up at him again with adoring eyes. She purred.

Aaron looked at the lump and realized it was a rabbit.

Aaron reached down and petted Agnes. "You brought daddy a present. You're a good girl, Agnes. You're a wonderful hunter."

Agnes purred deeper. Her whole chest rumbled.

"We could make a fire and have rabbit for lunch," Aaron enthused. He knelt down to exchange kisses with Agnes.

Lizzie walked over to the Toyota. She opened the back and got out the bag of sandwiches and drinks they'd picked up earlier at the 7-Eleven.

Lunch was disturbed by a vehicle roaring through the pine woods. Lizzie, Aaron, and Agnes quickly chewed the last bits of their food as they rose from their seats on the ground near Aaron's Toyota and looked along the road. Remains of snacks from the 7-Eleven were strewn around Lizzie and Aaron. Agnes had gnawed a piece of rabbit into gristle.

The approaching vehicle backfired loudly. Agnes's eyes opened wide. Her ears turned in unison toward the sudden sound. Her jaw opened. The rabbit gristle fell out. Jumping to her feet and running, Agnes leaped over the fallen pine trunk and scrunched down behind thick bushes on the other side.

A large, noisy black Land Rover with darkened windows skidded to a stop behind Aaron's Toyota. With its fancy grillwork, intricate extras, oversized wheels, and long antennas, the Land Rover looked like something from another planet. It vibrated as it sat with its motor rumbling and its antennas swishing. The extravagantly large gas guzzler's thick dust cloud swept over the clearing.

The driver of the Land Rover did not emerge from his machine. Aaron and Lizzie, curious and choking on dust, approached the huge vehicle, trying to look in.

The door of the Land Rover slammed open. A heavy beat vibrated the air. The sounds echoed off the trees around the clearing. A large hand pounded rhythm on the steering wheel.

"Can we help you?" Aaron yelled.

The music suddenly snapped off. A muscular man hopped out of the Land Rover. He nodded toward the open door behind him, "I love that Alicia Keys. She got a mean set of pipes."

The man was gigantic. Aaron was six foot, two inches tall. But he was looking up at the man, who, in contrast to Aaron, was heavily muscled and bulky.

Lizzie thought of the Jolly Green Giant; except this man was neither jolly nor green. He wore scuffed old boots; filthy, torn blue jeans; and a cotton shirt that might have been either white or gray originally. It was hard to tell now what it had been long ago when it was new and had all its buttons.

"You'll seen anybody 'roun' 'ere?" the enormous man asked.

Aaron shook his head. "Nope, nobody."

The huge man examined Aaron, taking in his gym shoes, shorts, and Irish linen bush shirt. He spat on the ground a couple feet from Aaron's left foot. "I know who you are; you Birdman. Mr. Winters tol' me you got legs like one them herons and a nose like a beak."

"Some people call me that," responded Aaron, his upper lip curling in a distasteful expression. "I don't like the nickname."

"Well, Birdman, lemme tell ya a truth: we don't none of us always get what we likes." The monstrous newcomer snorted as he leaned toward Aaron. "And also here's another truth for you: I really don't give a shit who it is don't like something I say or do."

The huge man turned his attention to Lizzie, who stepped back behind Aaron as the man examined her with bloodshot eyes. "Mentioning getting what a man wants, Mr. Winters said you might have a bee-u-ti-ful l'il blonde with you. Man, he was one hundred and ten percent co-rect. You look like you could give a fella a good workout. No offense intended, Miss."

"Just exactly who are you?" asked Aaron, hesitantly taking a step forward.

"Sorry 'bout my manners. I be Boss Pigott." He stuck out his chest and looped his thumbs into the front pockets of his pants.

"You call yourself Boss?"' asked Lizzie.

"Everybody learns to call me Boss... Back to my original question: ya seen anybody 'roundabout here?" Pigott waved his left arm at the clearing and the woods.

"No, not recently; who are you looking for?" asked Aaron.

"Young black boy. He wearin' work clothes. Might have a gunshot wound."

"No, we haven't seen anybody," responded Lizzie. "How would he have gotten shot?"

"He was in the wrong place."

"We haven't seen any boy," said Aaron. "There's just the three of us here. We haven't seen anybody else."

"Three of you? I only count two." Pigott glared at Aaron and Lizzie, then, suddenly tense, looked around suspiciously and backed toward his Land Rover.

"He means Agnes," said Lizzie. "He counts her as a person."

"Another babe?" Pigott stopped backing and smiled. "Where she?"

"No, not a woman," said Aaron. "Agnes is a Florida panther. She's over behind those bushes." He pointed to the bushes behind the log. "Your Land Rover scared her."

"You tellin' me they's a panther back that bush?" asked Pigott, opening the door of his Land Rover. He reached in and brought out a rifle.

"No, no," said Aaron, stepping forward. "Agnes wouldn't hurt anyone. There's no need to be afraid."

Pigott, scowling, launched himself toward Aaron. He glared down, his vast belly pressed against Aaron's chest. "Get one thing straight, Mr. Birdman. Boss Pigott ain't afeared o' no man."

"Only panthers?" asked Lizzie, as she hurried up, trying to intervene between the two men.

Pigott bumped Aaron backwards and turned to face Lizzie. "Hey, little sexy one, Boss Pigott also ain't stupid. He know when to be careful. That applies to both wild cats and wild women. Ain't no little Boss Pigotts runnin' 'round I don't want runnin' 'roun.' Keep that in mind ya' ever need a real man, a careful man."

"Hey, that's my girlfriend you're talking to," said Aaron, a tremble in his voice as he worked to maintain his balance after the shove from Pigott. He hesitated then walked back up to the towering man.

Pigott smiled down at Aaron. "Yeah, that's right. I talkin' to her, not you." Pigott reached out and pushed Aaron aside. Aaron stumbled backward and fell on his rear end into a Brazilian pepper bush. Pigott turned his back to Aaron and looked down at Lizzie. "Now what was you sayin' 'bout that cat?"

"Put the rifle away and I'll introduce you to Agnes," said Lizzie, glancing over to make sure Aaron wasn't injured.

Pigott smiled. "Okay, l'il sexy thing. You introduce me."

"Put away the rifle."

"Sure, I don't need no rifle for some little animal thing that a woman ain't afeared of." Pigott strutted to his truck. He put the rifle inside and locked the door.

"Follow me," said Lizzie.

"Any ol' time," responded Pigott, smiling.

Aaron stood up and brushed himself off.

As Pigott and Lizzie turned toward the log and the bush behind it, Aaron started to join them. Pigott turned to Aaron. "Not you, little man. She be the one showin' me it. You jess stan' over there." He pointed to the side of the clearing furthest from both his truck and the fallen log.

Aaron stopped where he was. He didn't go where he was told to go but he also didn't join Lizzie and Pigott. Lizzie noticed Aaron was sweating profusely.

Lizzie knelt down in front of the log and called out, "Agnes, come here girl."

Nothing happened.

"This some imaginary cat?" asked Pigott, who stood behind Lizzie. "Ain't no such thing as a friendly panther. That's nuts. You people been smokin' funny grass?"

"She's nervous. You left your car running. The sound makes her nervous."

"I never know when I might gotta leave some place in a hurry."

"I know what to do," said Lizzie. "Ice cream. She loves ice cream. I have a couple Nestle's Drumsticks in the cooler."

Lizzie walked over to the cooler, flipped open the lid, pushed aside some ice cubes and flakes, and brought out a Drumstick cone. She unwrapped it, walked back to the log, and knelt down again.

Pigott's bulging, bloodshot eyes followed her every move. He licked his lips.

"Look Agnes, your favorite ice cream with chocolate and nuts."

Agnes's head poked out from beside a bush.

"God damn it," exclaimed Pigott, taking a step back.

Agnes saw the ice cream cone and jumped out. She leaped over the fallen pine tree and landed on all fours crouching directly in front of Lizzie and the cone.

Pigott ran back to his Land Rover. He fumbled with his keys, dropped them, looked over at the panther, scrambled along the ground for his keys, unlocked the door, and crammed himself into the Land Rover. The vehicle roared backward, turned quickly, then, spewing sand at the rear wheels, sped off.

Aaron stood with his hands on his hips trying to look through the dust cloud left behind by the Land Rover.

Agnes was rumbling contentment as she licked and slurped the chocolate covered ice cream cone which Lizzie was, with difficulty, holding out for her.

Aaron drove his Toyota Prius at a comfortable 60 mph on Route 82. The two-lane highway was the only route back to Sanibel Island from Immokalee. Traffic left over from rush hour leaving Fort Myers was still relatively thick in the opposite direction as twilight turned to night.

Shortly after leaving Immokalee, Agnes jumped to her feet on the rear seat, and eagerly looked out through the open window.

"Something interests her around here," said Lizzie.

"Probably smells something, maybe another animal," replied Aaron.

Several miles later, Aaron announced, "I'm going to accept Augie's offer."

"What about me?" asked Lizzie.

"I'll have to think about that," said Aaron. "Think about whether I can trust you."

"Oh, Aaron."

They were both silent for the rest of the drive.

CHAPTER EIGHT

Bloody Bed

Lizzie, Aaron, and Agnes arrived in silence back at Conservancy employee housing, two sets of stilted duplexes on opposite sides of a small parking lot. All three got out of the car and walked toward the stairs in downcast moods. Aaron stopped under the light at the base of the stairs and turned to Lizzie. "Did you notice that blue Ford following us onto the island?"

Lizzie looked back at the empty entrance to the parking lot. "I didn't see him."

Agnes sprang up the stairs leading to the center of the walkway between the two apartments. She paused to look back at the two humans.

Aaron crossed his thin arms and looked down at Lizzie. "You seem to have a constant stream of admirers."

Lizzie looked up into Aaron's eyes. "I have no idea who that guy is. It scares me. I need you to hold me." Lizzie opened her arms.

Aaron gave her a quick hug then stepped back. "It's been a busy day. I'm tired. I'll see you tomorrow,"

Aaron trotted up the stairs away from Lizzie, who felt like crying. She followed slowly behind him but, at the top of the stairs, turned in the opposite direction, toward her own apartment. Agnes ran back and forth between the two people until Aaron called, "Here, girl." The panther then eagerly followed Aaron into his apartment.

After closing the door to her apartment, Lizzie removed her filthy clothes and tossed them into the laundry basket.

As she entered her living room, Lizzie checked beside the door and behind the sofa to make sure nobody was there. Something about the room didn't seem right. Something was out of place.

Lizzie walked into her bedroom, turned on the lights, and froze. Her breath caught in her throat.

On the bed directly in front of her was a man's nude, bloody body. The top of his head was missing. Something was stuffed into his mouth, distending his cheeks, In spite of the distortion and all the blood, Lizzie recognized Clete.

Clete was laid out on his back. His chest was muscular. His left arm hung off the bed. His hands were open and empty. His legs were spread apart. Where his penis should be was torn flesh and masses of blood.

My God, he's been castrated.

Blood and skin and pulpy stuff, possibly Clete's brains, were scattered around the room: on the walls, on the bed, on everything.

Lizzie grabbed the doorway, leaned her head against it, and threw up. The clumpy mess that had been her supper seeped down the door jamb.

She looked at the bloody body again and then turned away, staggering back into her living room, disoriented. She collapsed onto her sofa and painfully discovered she was sitting on her telephone. It should have been on the table beside the sofa. She picked up the phone and dialed 911. No dial tone.

Lizzie ran to the front door. Half way out she realized she was naked. She stopped, torn in her panic between ignoring her lack of clothing and running on or turning back and getting dressed.

"Damn, damn, damn," she screamed, as she pounded her fist on the metal railing opposite her apartment door. The way things were she could not run naked into Aaron's apartment and tell him Clete was in her apartment, even a dead Clete. She went back, rummaged in the laundry basket, retrieved her shirt and jeans, pulled them on without underwear or shoes, and ran back out of her apartment, leaving the door open.

She ran to Aaron's, threw open his door, ran in, and screamed, "There's been a murder. Does your phone work?"

Aaron was lying on his sofa with his arm over his eyes. Agnes, chewing on something, came out of the kitchen and looked curiously at Lizzie.

"Uh, yes, I guess so. Doesn't yours?" asked Aaron.

She grabbed Aaron's phone, dialed 911, and told the woman who answered, "There's been a murder at the Conservancy employee housing."

Aaron sat up and exclaimed, "What?"

Lizzie dropped the phone, even though the woman on the other end had told her to stay on the line. She ran back to the door.

Aaron followed her.

In the doorway she turned around to face Aaron. "That man Clete, he's been killed, in my apartment."

She threw herself into his arms.

"And there's your other friend," said Aaron.

"What?"

"Look at the parking lot, quick."

Lizzie turned her head. In the parking lot directly below them was the blue Ford Aaron had told her he'd seen following her. The man in the Ford had a camera and was snapping photographs of them embracing.

She broke loose from Aaron and ran to the head of the stairs. "Hey, you."

The man dropped the camera onto the seat beside him and grabbed his steering wheel. He sped out of the parking lot, spinning his tires on the gravel road.

Moments later, two Sanibel Island police cars, sirens wailing, skidded to a stop in the parking lot.

CHAPTER NINE

Interrogation

Sanibel Island Police Chief Detective Brian Hunter ordered Lizzie to describe once again in precise detail finding Clete's body. Hunter had asked for the same details again and again and again. It was late at night and Lizzie felt sick and exhausted, emotionally drained.

Prior to the questioning, Lizzie and Aaron had waited outside in the parking lot while an assortment of police, sheriff's deputies, and forensics experts entered her apartment. The only one Lizzie knew was Sgt. Malflic and he showed no sign of ever having met her. About a half hour after the police had entered Lizzie's apartment, Aaron was told to go to his apartment and Hunter invited Lizzie to join him in her living room. He acted like her living room was his office.

Her little apartment had become as busy as a deep discount sale at the mall: investigators from the Sanibel Island Police and from the Lee County Sheriff's Department kept coming and going in and out of her bedroom.

Lizzie sat on her living room sofa. The slim, tanned, bald, forty-something Hunter sat across from her in one of the two mismatched chairs she'd bought at a church thrift sale. He questioned her for awhile, then stood up and walked outside, then came back, sat across from her again, and asked more questions. He never smiled. He acted like he doubted everything.

Lizzie was made uncomfortable not only by all the questions but also by her jeans digging into her. It felt like a metal clasp was cutting into her skin at the base of the zipper. If she sat one way it dug into her deeply; if she shifted, the sharp metal pushed against an even more sensitive area.

"Now, let's go over this again," growled Hunter.

"Could I get something from my bedroom?"

"That's still a crime scene," muttered Hunter. "What do you need? I'll see if somebody can get it for you."

"Underwear, I'm really uncomfortable."

"Why? Is your underwear dirty or something?"

"No, I'm sorry, I haven't any on. I just threw on these pants and shirt after I found the body."

"You were naked with Mr. Grimes?"

"No, I was in a hurry when I was going out. I'd taken off my clothes when I came into my apartment."

"You didn't mention that."

"It didn't seem relevant."

A slight smile played at Hunter's lips. "And no clothes were on Mr. Grimes' body." Hunter leaned forward. He was almost leering. "So you and Mr. Grimes were both naked?"

Lizzie leaned back on the sofa away from the detective. "No… I mean yes. But what does that have to do with anything?" She gestured toward the bedroom. "He was dead when I found him."

"That's what you say."

Lizzie could feel herself trembling. "Ask Aaron. We'd just arrived. I was only here a moment or two. I came in, saw the body, and ran out. All I did was find the body."

"I've already talked with Mr. Carter. He said he lay down on his sofa and may have dropped off to sleep. He wasn't sure how much time elapsed between the time he went into his apartment and the time you burst in."

"But it was only a few moments." Lizzie was desperately trying to hold back tears.

"He also said you own a gun. Where is that gun?"

"In the little table beside my bed."

"Let me check on that. Stay here." Hunter stood up and turned toward the bedroom. But before he could take a step in that direction, a red-faced man came out of the bedroom and asked Hunter to join him outside for a moment. That man held a couple of plastic bags. Hunter called, "Hey, Joe," to the uniformed policeman standing beside the bedroom door and pointed at Lizzie. Hunter mouthed something to the policeman.

Lizzie watched Hunter's back as he went out behind the red-faced man.

Lizzie started to stand. The patrolman stepped toward her. "Detective Hunter says for you to stay there."

"Am I under arrest or something?"

"I have no idea. Why don't you wait for Detective Hunter? He'll be back in a moment."

Lizzie sat back down. She couldn't hold herself back any longer. She started to cry.

Where's Aaron? He should be helping me; be here with me. I need him. But it sounds like he thinks I killed Clete. How could Aaron think that? How could he? Aaron can be so jealous. Oh my God, I don't understand any of this. All I did was find the body; that's all I did.

Detective Hunter was holding the two plastic bags when he strode back into the apartment and over to Lizzie. "Can you identify these items?" he asked, pointing at the bags. "Don't open them."

Hunter handed Lizzie a plastic bag. It took Lizzie a moment to realize the item inside was her white bikini bottom. The last time she had seen that particular bikini was several days ago when she threw it in the laundry basket after coming in from breakfast with Aaron. Now it was soaked in red and badly crumpled.

"It's one of my bikini bottoms," she told Hunter.

"And this?" asked the detective, handing Lizzie the other bag.

"That's my handgun, the one I told you was in the drawer by my bed."

"Well, that answers two of our questions," Hunter said as he sat down, "But many mysteries remain. For example: what happened to Mr. Grimes' clothes? We've searched this apartment from top to bottom; no bloody clothes, not even any clean clothes that would have fit Mr. Grimes. So: what was he wearing when he got here and what happened to it?"

"I have no idea. I wasn't here when he got here."

"How'd he get in?"

"That's easy. I never lock the door. He knew that." Lizzie was still holding the two bags. "Why are these things in plastic bags?"

"I'll ask the questions," responded Hunter, standing up and taking the bags from her. He handed the bags over to the policeman named Joe then reached into a pocket and pulled out a card. "But first I'll read you your rights."

"This is crazy. I just found him. I don't even know him."

"Please don't say any more until I've read you your rights and gotten someone to take down what you say."

Lizzie, sobbing, fell over onto the sofa.

"Please sit up," Hunter ordered.

The phone rang. It was on the table beside the sofa, right by Lizzie's head, next to where she had fallen.

Lizzie sat up and stared at the ringing phone. "But it was disconnected. That's why I ran to Aaron's. It wouldn't work."

"It looks like it's working now," said Hunter as he sat back down.

Hunter's jumping up and sitting down and going in and out was starting to make Lizzie as nervous as all his questions. She wished the man would sit still. She wished he'd leave. But that didn't seem likely.

Lizzie picked up the phone. "Hello?"

"Hello, Mrs. Grant? This is Julius Finch. I'm an attorney over here in Miami. I've been retained to represent you if you need an attorney. Are you in need of an attorney?"

"Yes, yes, the police are here now. They seem to think I had something to do with this murder. They were just about to read me my rights."

"Who is that on the phone?" asked Hunter.

Lizzie held the phone away for a second. "An attorney named Finch from Miami."

"Julius Finch?" asked Hunter.

Lizzie nodded. "Yes."

Hunter stood up suddenly. "What the hell's going on here?"

Lizzie returned to the phone. "I'm sorry Mr. Finch; Detective Hunter here asked me who I was talking to."

"And you told him?"

"Yes."

"And you want me to represent you?"

"Yes."

"Okay, I'll be there in three hours. Let them read you your rights but then don't say another word. I'll see you in three hours. No, on second thought, make it 10 a.m. tomorrow. I'll need to review the police report before I see you and you'll need to get a little sleep."

"I'm not sure where I'll sleep. I can't stay here. My bed's a bloody mess."

"I'll find you tomorrow. The police will know where you are." He hung up.

Lizzie looked at the phone in her hand and then sat it down. "He said to let you read me my rights and then not to say another word."

"Yeah, that's what attorneys say." Hunter looked at Lizzie like he was an entomologist and she was an insect. "How do you know Julius Finch?"

"I'm not supposed to tell you anything."

"I was just wondering why an Environmental Conservancy employee who probably only makes minimum wage would have a high powered Miami mob attorney calling her at two in the morning offering to represent her."

Hunter paused for a moment, like he was thinking. Then he read Lizzie her rights, concluding by saying, "Obviously, now you're not going to tell me anything. I'm reluctantly letting you go for now. We need to do ballistic tests and talk to the state attorney; get all our ducks in a row. Then we'll definitely see you again. Don't leave the island."

CHAPTER TEN

Finch

Lizzie sat in the lotus position on the carpeted balcony floor of room 238 at the Sanibel Longview Inn and Seaside Resort. It was the morning after she'd found Clete's body. Trying to sleep in the unfamiliar hotel bed, she had kept dreaming of Clete's body beside her. Finally, jumping awake, she ran out and sat on a metal chair on the balcony. She gasped the thick sea-soaked night air, slid from the chair onto the floor, and fell asleep.

Now the morning sun was on her full force. Closing her eyes, she saw bright red blood and mangled flesh. Lizzie blinked, shook her head, and looked out at the deep blue Gulf of Mexico through the jail-like grillwork of the balcony's protective railing. She inhaled and exhaled trying to settle nervous thoughts of prison. She felt lonely and abandoned. Where was Aaron? He had not tried to contact her since the police arrived and separated them. Why hadn't he insisted on being by her side?

Detective Hunter had booked the Longview room. Lizzie didn't think it was just coincidence that a Sanibel Island Police patrolman worked off duty as the resort's night watchman.

A loud knock sounded at the entrance door in the adjoining bedroom. Lizzie rushed in from the balcony, glanced at the clock, saw it was exactly 10 a.m., grabbed her short red cover up, threw it on over her nakedness, and hurried to the door.

A paunchy, balding man, in his sixties stood on the narrow walkway just outside the door. He had been looking around but directed his attention to Lizzy when she opened the door. "Mrs. Grant?"

"Yes, are you Mr. Finch?"

"At your service." The attorney bowed slightly and smiled at Lizzy. He wore a black, long sleeved Guayabera shirt, blue jeans, and western boots. A backpack was strapped to his shoulders.

"Come in," said Lizzie, stepping aside.

"No, I think it might be better if we take a walk on the beach. Less chance of 'bugs.' Some authorities are lax in their recognition of attorney-client privilege."

"Let me get my bag."

"That could be as risky as talking in the room. No, just as you are will be fine."

"At least let me get my bathing suit."

The lawyer looked her up and down. He raised his eyebrows slightly and smiled. "That might be a good idea."

When they reached the beach, Lizzie removed her cover up and tossed it onto one of the beachfront reclining chairs provided for hotel guests.

The tiny amount of fabric in Lizzie's bikini was compensated for by the attorney. Finch was overdressed for the beach in his boots, pants, shirt, and backpack.

"Take off those boots," Lizzie suggested. "The warm, wet sand feels nice between your toes."

Finch shook his head. "I'd rather not."

Lizzie breathed deeply, inhaling the salt air blowing gently off the water. She felt rejuvenated by the heat of the sun on her skin as she and Finch walked down the beach. She waded in the warm waves lapping up onto the sand. The attorney kept clear of the water.

Finch insisted they stick to small talk until they were beyond the stretch of beach in front of the hotel. He wasn't very good at pleasantries, mumbling as Lizzie chatted.

Lizzie asked Finch who hired him to represent her.

"That's confidential," the lawyer grunted.

Lizzie looked over at the man. "Even from me?"

"Yes, I've found it best with my usual clientele if they're ever asked who paid for their lawyer, they be able to truthfully reply they didn't know." The booted Finch was having trouble walking on the loose sand. He paused for a moment and faced Lizzie. "Let's just say you've got a powerful friend who'll see you through to the end for better or for worse."

Lizzie was silent, thinking about this. It sounded like a wedding vow. *Could my husband be paying for this lawyer? No, that's impossible.*

They resumed walking. Eventually, they reached a particularly lonely stretch of beach. Ring-necked gulls, which had been sleeping on the warm sand, squawked warning then flew off, cawing angrily, as Lizzie and Finch approached. Finch spoke up; "Okay, tell me everything from the first time you met this Clete Grimes character until you found him dead. I've got a digital recorder in my backpack, which I'm now turning on." Finch reached over his shoulder and did something to the side of his backpack. "Now, every detail."

When Lizzie told about the old man with the Uzi, Finch interrupted her. "You didn't mention him to the police, did you?"

"No, he told me not to and so I didn't. Also that detective never asked about anything other than my seeing Grimes on the beach and his showing up at my apartment." Lizzie noticed sweat stains spreading all over Finch's shirt. "You're sweating quite a lot. Why don't you take off your shirt?"

"No, no, I couldn't take off my shirt while at work. Dressing appropriately is important. My image you know." Finch flashed a professional smile at Lizzie. "Now back to what happened; continue."

When Lizzie described seeing Grimes meet Sgt. Malflic, Finch stopped her again. "You also didn't mention this meeting to the police, did you?"

"No, they never asked and I just wanted to get away. I only answered that detective's questions. I didn't volunteer anything."

"Good; go on."

After Lizzie described finding the body and calling 911 on Aaron's phone, Finch said, "Okay, that's enough. Let's head back."

Finch's shirt was one big sweat stain.

Lizzie looked up and saw two distinctive birds high above them.

"Look, swallow-tailed kites. They're rare here." She pointed them out to Finch.

"Yeah," responded the Miami attorney, obviously lacking any interest in birds. "We need to concentrate on this case; your life may depend on it."

Lizzie gasped. "Is it that serious?"

The lawyer nodded. "Yes."

"Oh, my." Lizzie stopped walking. She looked around with a distraught expression at the nearly empty beach. "But how can this be? I didn't know him. All I did was find his body. How can they suspect me?"

"There are a couple things you might not know," responded Finch, looking at Lizzie with an expression which would have been called pity on the face of someone less hard-boiled.

"What?" asked Lizzie, as she resumed walking. "If it involves me I have a right to know."

"I went over the police reports this morning." Finch looked around. By now they were back on the hotel's beachfront. The lawyer wiped sweat from his brow as he hesitated, making sure they were far enough away from other people not to be overheard.

Lizzie retrieved her cover-up from the chair and started to put it on as Finch continued, "You identified one item last night as your bikini bottom and another item as your gun?"

"Yes," responded Lizzie, pulling her arm through the left sleeve of the cover-up.

"I wish you hadn't made those identifications. But what's done is done." Finch shrugged then touched Lizzie's shoulder so she would look up at him. She paused half in, half out of her cover-up. Finch spoke slowly. "Your gun has been identified by ballistic tests as the murder weapon. It was used to shoot Mr. Grimes once, execution style, in the back of the head. Yours were the only prints found on the gun."

Finch paused at the look of horror in Lizzie's eyes. Then he went on: "Grimes' penis was cut off, wrapped in your bikini bottom and, together, they were stuffed in his mouth."

Lizzie dropped onto the reclining beach chair like she'd been punched.

"His penis?" she gasped.

"Yes. He'd been emasculated."

"They wrapped it in my bikini bottom?"

"Yes, and stuffed it in his mouth." Finch smiled and nodded.

"That's horrible." Lizzie slumped with her face in her hands and wept.

Finch took a deep breath as he looked down at his petite blonde client. He leaned over and helped her finish putting on her cover-up as he added, "I would not be surprised if they arrested you on murder charges later today; tomorrow at the latest. The only reasons you're not already in jail are they need to coordinate with the state attorney's office, they know you're not going anywhere, and they know you've got a lawyer who will hold their balls to the fire if they make the slightest procedural mistake."

Lizzie looked up at the lawyer. "But I will be arrested?"

Finch nodded. "It's only a matter of time."

CHAPTER ELEVEN

Augie's Logic

Finch walked Lizzie back to her room and told her she would hear from him. "If they arrest you, don't say anything. I'll meet you at the jail."

But she wasn't arrested that morning. Soon Lizzie grew restless, she felt like the walls were closing in, like her hotel room had become a prison. Having not heard from the police or anybody else by early afternoon, she called Augie to hear another human voice and to ask if she still had her Conservancy job.

"Come by my office," Augie responded

Lizzie put on a comfortable pants suit so she would be dressed modestly if the police swooped down on her to drag her off to jail.

"Hi, Augie," said Lizzie as she entered the chairman's office and quickly sat down, trying hard not to break down crying.

August Winters walked around his desk, past an American flag hanging from a pole in the corner of the room. He placed a huge hand on Lizzie's shoulder. "Be strong and trust in God. Everything will work out."

"Thank you, Oh thank you," she cried, reaching up and patting the hand on her shoulder. She straightened herself. "I'm okay. I wanted to apologize for missing my back bay work earlier today. Maybe I can do it later."

"No, that's okay." Augie gently squeezed Lizzie's shoulder then returned to the large leather chair behind his desk. He smiled. "A one day gap won't make much difference. Remember it's a long term study of the effects of pollution and so-called climate change on our ecosystem. What counts are cumulative results over weeks, months, and years."

"Yes, I know." Lizzie slid forward slightly in her chair. "Sometimes I get so wrapped up watching each individual little creature, some are so cute, I forget the study is to determine long term influences on the entire ecosystem."

"What happens to the individual organism is unimportant. It's the system that counts," Augie emphasized, spreading his hands out in front of him.

"But each individual is unique." Lizzie tentatively smiled.

Augie clenched a fist. "If you stepped on an ant and killed it, you wouldn't feel remorse. But if all the ants on the planet were killed, it would be an unprecedented ecological disaster."

Lizzie's smile vanished and she slid back in her seat. "I see your point… Anyway, I wanted to promise you I'd do the loggerhead turtle beach walk tonight if I haven't been arrested by then."

"Do you really think they're going to arrest you?"

"Yes, oh God, it's all crazy. But yes I think they'll arrest me." Lizzie started crying. She slumped forward and put her head in her hands. Her shoulders shook.

Augie opened a desk drawer and took out a box of tissues. He handed them across to Lizzie and asked, "Do you need an attorney Lizzie? Would you like me to recommend a good one?"

"No, I have one." Lizzie looked up at Augie. "In fact I'd been wondering if you'd hired him."

"No I didn't. Sorry, but I would have been happy to help."

"I appreciate that." Lizzie blew her nose.

"Where are you staying, Lizzie? Aaron was in to see me earlier. He said last night you went off without even asking for his help."

Lizzie straightened up in her seat. "How could I stay with him? He thinks I'm a murderer. And I don't know what to think. I don't know how that body got there. I'm not even sure Aaron didn't kill Clete."

Augie looked at her sharply. "You suspect Aaron? Why?"

"There're things you don't know." Desperation came into Lizzie's voice. "Clete's uh, his, uh, penis was cut off, wrapped in one of my bathing suits, and stuffed in his mouth. Isn't that what an insanely jealous person would do to send me some kind of sick message? Aaron went absolutely, completely crazy when he found Clete in my apartment with me."

"Naked," added Augie with a raised eyebrow.

"So Aaron told you about it." Lizzie carefully placed the tissue box and a used tissue on the corner of Augie's desk.

"He told me everything." Augie looked at the used tissue with obvious distaste.

Lizzie retrieved the tissue.

Augie smiled benevolently. "Aaron views me as a father figure. Growing up an orphan was difficult for him. Maybe his love for cats is a substitute for the human love he missed. Sometimes I feel a little guilty..." Augie shook his head. "But I must keep my eye on the larger picture."

Augie pulled a fresh tissue from the box on the corner of his desk and blotted at the corner of his right eye. "I'm not used to becoming emotional about things. Sorry. Anyway, this morning Aaron was very upset. But if what he told me is true he could not have murdered Clete."

"What do you mean?"

"Clete's body was definitely not in your bed when you left your apartment in the morning, right?"

"Yes, I'm groggy in the morning. But I would have noticed a dead body in my bed."

Augie smiled.

"It's not a joke," objected Lizzie.

"I know." Augie composed away his smile. "After that you were with Aaron all day and, when you got home, went directly to your apartment and found the body."

"Yes."

"So, no matter what time of day Clete was murdered, Aaron was with you at that time." Augie raised his shaggy eyebrows, and held his hands up, palms out, emphasizing the obviousness of his point.

"You're right." Lizzie smiled. "Aaron couldn't have done it. How could I have missed that? It makes me feel better."

"It shouldn't."

Her smile vanished. "What do you mean?"

Augie raised a finger and stabbed the air, like a professor giving a lecture. "The police would have two theories based on their evidence. Either the boy friend killed the new man out of jealousy or the woman killed the man. Eliminate Aaron as a suspect and you're the only one left. You could have killed him before you and Aaron went to Immokalee."

"But why would I kill him and cut off his penis? That's sick, disgusting, and obscene."

Augie raised three fingers one at a time. "Maybe he tried to rape you and you did to him what you thought a rapist deserved. Maybe you were making a comment on men in general. Maybe it was some kind of trophy. The police could come up with all sorts of theories. Women have been known to castrate men."

"But I'm not that kind of woman. I wouldn't do any of those things. I'm innocent!"

"You don't need to convince me, Lizzie. I know you didn't do it." Augie leaned forward again in his chair and placed his hands on his desk. "You need to convince the police you're innocent. You're the only suspect they have. Another alternative theory is that you and Aaron did it together. You are each other's only alibis and it would be more reasonable to conclude that two people overcame a strong man like Clete than that one tiny woman overpowered him."

"But Aaron and I weren't even on Sanibel Island. We were in Immokalee."

"So you are each other's alibis. Anybody see you out there?"

"No, we were alone."

"That's too bad."

"No, wait." Lizzie leaned forward. "That foreman of yours, the big guy, dropped by for a few minutes."

Augie smiled and nodded. "Good, he'll say anything I want him to say."

The phone on Augie's desk rang. He picked it up, listened for a second, and then spoke away from the phone to Lizzie: "Sorry I need some privacy. I'll talk to you again later."

Augie returned to the phone, "Yes, just a minute. I can't talk now." He waved for Lizzie to leave.

Lizzy stood up and hurried out, leaving Augie's office in a daze.

After getting behind the wheel of her blue 2007 Infiniti, Lizzie sat for several minutes and cried. Eventually, she didn't know how long it was, she started the car and drove back to her hotel.

CHAPTER TWELVE

Harrison

Lizzie was awakened by a knock on her hotel room door. She shook her head and looked around, momentarily unsure where she was. Then she figured out that her exhaustion from last night had finally caught up with her and caused her to doze off after returning to her room. But who was at the door? Maybe a maid. But more likely the police.

"Just a minute," she yelled as she checked her makeup in the bathroom mirror. She smoothed down her pants suit, wrinkled during her nap. She didn't want to be embarrassed at the jail.

Finally, she opened the door.

Standing immediately in front of Lizzie, wearing the sports jacket she had bought him the Christmas before last, was her husband, Harrison Winston Grant III, the asshole, social-climbing husband she had run away from.

"Harry," Lizzie gasped, "What are you doing here?"

Her husband was the last person Lizzie wanted to see. Even the police might be more welcome. She had not fully realized how miserable her life with him had been in Maryland until she discovered a new life without him in Florida.

"May I come in?" Harry asked.

"Yes, yes, sure, yes," Lizzie said, stepping aside in a daze as her husband strode into her hotel room and sat down on the only comfortable chair.

Lizzie sat on the edge of the bed and asked, "So I guess you heard I've got a problem?"

"Yes I heard."

"I didn't do it."

"I know you didn't."

"I'm glad you have faith in me."

"It's not a matter of faith." Harry sneered. "I know for certain you didn't do it. I can prove you didn't do it. So I came down to make you an offer." Harry smiled his chamber of commerce smile.

"I don't understand." Lizzie leaned forward toward Harry. "What do you mean you can prove I didn't do it?"

Harry snapped a finger. "Absolute, fool-proof proof."

"But that's impossible." Lizzie stood up. "How would you know up in Maryland what was happening down here? And how could you prove I didn't murder Clete when I can't even prove it? And what do you mean by making me an offer?"

Harry looked Lizzie up and down. "The offer is very simple: you give up this silliness, come back to Maryland, and live with me as my wife and I'll prove you didn't murder this man Clete. All this terrible business will go away and I'll have my pretty little trophy wife back. I'm tired of telling people you're away looking after your sick mother. They're beginning not to believe me."

Lizzie stared at Harry. She could feel her skin crawling under his gaze. "Harry, this is ridiculous." Lizzie began pacing the room. "You're telling people I'm away caring for my mother? My mother died years ago." She stopped in front of Harry, hands on her hips. "I left you, Harry. Can't you understand that? I left you. I know it's socially embarrassing for you but I couldn't stand to live with you any more. Everything with you was about getting ahead and impressing people. You couldn't live your own life. You were trying to live everybody else's image of what your life should be."

"That doesn't matter now, Lizzie." Harry stood facing her. "You should be happy I still want you back and have a way for you to get out of this mess you've gotten yourself into. I knew without me to look after you something terrible would happen. The starry lights in your eyes aren't necessarily a reflection of intelligence."

Lizzie took a step closer to Harry. "How can you prove I didn't murder Clete?"

"I've had a man following you. As I understand it, you can't prove how long you were in your apartment after you left that young boyfriend of yours, what's his name?"

Lizzie looked away, dropped her hands to her side, and murmured, "Aaron."

"Yes, Aaron. By the way, does he know how old you are?"

"I'm only 32." She looked up defiantly at Harry.

"Yes, and he's 26. I bet if he'd known how much older you are he'd have dumped you in a minute."

"No, he wouldn't." Lizzie put her hands on her hips.

Harry leaned forward slightly. "Does he know?"

Lizzie thought Harry smelled like mint mouthwash. She stepped back away from him. "The subject of age never came up. Besides, we have similar interests."

"I know," Harry sneered, "nature, ecology, saving the planet."

"Yes, he loves nature."

"And here he is at 26 working for minimum wage explaining bushes and trees to people." Harry grunted. "Absolutely zero potential to become a success in the world."

"Other things are important to Aaron."

"Yes." Harry suddenly raised his voice. "Like my wife."

"He cares for me."

Harry pointed to his own chest. "But I'm the one who can save you."

"You've said that. How?"

"As I've already told you I've had this man following you."

"Why?"

"To cover all possibilities: if he reported back to me that you were miserable down here, I would have tried to get you back. If he reported you were happy, I would have had him collect evidence about your affair for when you sue me for alimony."

"I wouldn't have done that."

"You took the Infiniti when you left."

"I wasn't thinking. I'll give it back as soon as I get another car. I promise." Lizzie waited through a moment of silence then asked, "What did your man report?"

"Milos reported you were happy. So I had him gathering evidence of your infidelity: pictures of you and that skinny jerk Aaron hugging and kissing; which you seemed to do a lot."

Lizzie glared at her husband. "We were happy until this happened. I can't believe you invaded our privacy like that. You still haven't said what evidence you have."

Harry smiled. "When you came back that night, Milos used his night photography camera to take pictures of you and Aaron talking in the parking lot, you entering your apartment alone, you rushing out of your apartment, and you and Aaron in each other's arms in his doorway."

Lizzie shook her head. "I still don't understand."

"All these pictures were automatically time-stamped by Milos' camera." Harry smiled his stuck-up, superior, I've-got-you-by-the-balls smile. "They prove absolutely that you did not have time to murder that guy you found on your bed. If you'll come back with me and resume being my wife, I'll have Milos turn the pictures over to the police. All suspicions will be erased. All charges will be dropped. You'll be free as one of those birds you love so much."

"Except I'd have to return to Maryland, live with you, go to social events, play the domesticated brainless wife, and smile and smile and smile no matter how miserable I felt."

Harry nodded. "That would be the deal. I would insist on you coming back as my wife."

"What if I don't want to be your wife? What if I refuse? What if I stay here where I'm happy? Will you give the police the evidence proving my innocence?"

Harry stepped closer to Lizzie. With his hands on his hips, glaring down at her, he spat out, his hot breath in her face, "If you won't come back to me you can rot in hell, fry in the electric chair. Why would I give a damn what happens to you if you don't want to be mine?"

Lizzie quickly stepped away from Harry and then turned back to face him from across the room. "For a moment I thought you might be here because you cared about me." Lizzie pointed toward the door. "Get out; I need to call my attorney."

"What do you think you're going to tell him?" asked Harry, sneering.

"That I have another suspect in Clete's murder," Lizzie returned Harry's glare. "That my husband is in town and capable of killing a man he might find in my apartment."

"But that's ridiculous," exclaimed Harry.

"Get out," yelled Lizzie. She rushed across the room and pushed at Harry. "Get the fuck out."

Harry seemed surprised by the violence and profanity from Lizzie. He raised his chin disdainfully, turned, and strutted to the door in as dignified a manner as possible with Lizzie continuing to push at him. She thought back to all those times he had told her she was afraid of her own shadow. The memories made her push even harder.

As she hurried Harry through the door Lizzie yelled after him, "I'm also going to ask my attorney if, in addition to criminal matters, he handles divorces." Several people lounging by the hotel's pool looked up at the arguing couple on the walkway above the pool. Harry noticed the people staring at him. He strode away as fast as he could.

Lizzie stepped back into her room, sat on her bed, and wept. At least she still had the turtle patrol later tonight. She would enjoy that. Her entire future beyond that was a blackness of pain and despair.

Lizzie took a quick beach stroll and had a drink at the poolside bar. She usually didn't drink. But what the hell. Then she returned to her room, removed her clothes, lay down, and fell into a restless sleep, dreaming of severed penises chasing her on little cartoon feet.

CHAPTER THIRTEEN

Pinholes

That evening, just as the sun was setting, Lizzie was again awakened by a knock on her hotel room door. She was sure this time it would be the police. She picked up her scattered clothes, dressed quickly, and opened the door.

Aaron stood in front of her shifting from foot to foot, looking uncertain. "Man, did I have an ordeal today being grilled by the police."

Lizzie stepped aside. "Come in."

Aaron stepped to the middle of the room, and then looked around, as if he didn't know what to do next. Finally he spoke. "Lizzie, it really hurt me a lot last night when you didn't want to stay with me, when you dashed off to this hotel."

"But you were so jealous of Clete." Lizzie felt on the verge of tears. "You'd been angry with me for days. I tried and tried to get close to you. Nothing worked."

Aaron spread out his long arms. "But Clete's dead now. So everything's okay. He can't come between us anymore."

Lizzie stepped toward Aaron. "You thought I killed him."

He shook his head. "No, I didn't."

Lizzie put her hand on his arm. "But you told the police you didn't know how long I had been in my apartment after we got back from Immokalee. And you told them about my gun."

"I couldn't lie to them. They asked me questions. I had to answer." Aaron looked into Lizzie's eyes and placed his hands on her shoulders. "Damn it, I love you, Lizzie. I want you with me. I'm getting a trailer moved over to those woods near Immokalee. I want you to move out there with me."

"I love you too, Aaron," Lizzie said as she wrapped herself around him. They kissed and fell back onto the king-sized bed.

"Come with me tonight," urged Aaron, as he and Lizzie lay together after love making.

"I can't. The police have ordered me not to leave Sanibel. Also I've got to do the turtle patrol. I promised Augie." Lizzie sat up suddenly. "My God, it's getting late. I need to start getting ready." Lizzie jumped from the bed and started picking up her clothes, which had been thrown around the room.

"But I want you with me," moaned Aaron, sitting up.

Lizzie paused with her panties in one hand and her bra in the other. "I have to straighten things out with the police first. Then maybe I could live in Immokalee and commute in for my SIEC work. I've finally decided to go ahead and get a divorce from my husband like you've wanted me to. He was here earlier."

"Your husband was here?" Aaron stood and pulled on his clothes.

"Yes."

Aaron stared at Lizzie as he continued to dress hurriedly. "In this room?" Aaron's voice was rising in both volume and pitch. "Your husband from up north?"

Lizzie was still immobile, surprised by the vehemence of Aaron's response. "He was here earlier today. I need to talk to my lawyer about filing divorce papers."

Aaron's eyes widened. "You have a lawyer?"

"He was here first thing this morning. His name is Finch. He's from Miami."

"He was here in this hotel room, here with you, alone?" Aaron, now yelling, waved his long arms around, gesturing at the room surrounding them.

Lizzie shrugged. "Of course."

Aaron jerked on his belt, dashed over to the door and threw it open. His face was red. He was perspiring. "I've got to get away from you for a little while to think. You've had two men up to your hotel room in less than a day."

"But it was just my lawyer and my husband."

Aaron had stepped out of the room and now stood on the walkway fastening his belt.

Still naked, Lizzie couldn't follow him.

"Everywhere you go, men keep popping up," Aaron jeered.

A loud scream came from the parking area.

"Damn you, damn you, damn you," cursed Aaron. He was shaking with anger. He suddenly stepped back in toward Lizzie. But he stopped when another scream echoed up from the parking lot. "Oh my God, Agnes. I've got to go. Agnes may be in trouble."

"Agnes?"

"I left her in the car."

"But it's hot out."

"I left the car running with the air conditioner on." Aaron looked in panic toward the parking lot as soul-penetrating screams of agony came from that direction. Aaron's skinny body seemed to be trying to move in two directions. Another scream resolved his indecision. He turned away from Lizzie and called back over his shoulder. "Maybe somebody tried to steal the car. We'll have to talk later."

Aaron ran off toward the stairway.

A moment later the screams from the parking lot stopped abruptly.

CHAPTER FOURTEEN

Arrest?

The night was warm with a strong breeze blowing from the Gulf as Lizzie roped off and posted a new loggerhead turtle nest. Screeching wind gusts drowned out other sounds. Lizzie, alone on one of the most deserted stretches of Bowman's Beach, wore her yellow bikini with the black polka dots. Her wet/dry bag hung over her shoulder.

Lizzie hummed to herself as she worked, trying to drown worries of arrest when she returned to her hotel. She was also concerned Aaron didn't really love her but considered her a possession; that Aaron was like her husband in not loving her for herself.

The sign she was hammering into the sand read: "Please do not disturb/ Sea turtle nest/ Do not place beach furniture, dig, or drive stakes within ten (10) feet of this sign. Violators subject to fines and imprisonment. Should you witness a violation, please contact the Sanibel Island Environmental Conservancy 555-2329." Lizzie used a small hammer to pound in the stake holding the sign.

"Thought I'd find you here."

The suddenness of the male voice startled Lizzie. She whirled around. Sgt. Malflic stood less than two feet away.

"What are you doing here? Is something wrong, has something happened?" Lizzie's voice trembled.

Malflic stepped closer, looming over her. "Yes, a warrant has been issued for your arrest for first degree murder."

"Oh, no," Lizzie gasped.

Malflic reached behind his back. He brought out handcuffs.

"Drop that mallet," Malflic ordered. "Turn around and put your hands behind your back."

Lizzie did as she was told. She started to cry as Malflic slapped the handcuffs onto her delicate wrists. They hurt. "I didn't do anything." Lizzie looked back over her shoulder at Malflic.

He was smiling maliciously.

"Wait a minute," Lizzie exclaimed. "Shouldn't a police matron help arrest and search me? Shouldn't there be more of you? This doesn't seem right."

Malflic shrugged. "Getting arrested never does." He continued to smile. "I knew where to find you, the rest of the department didn't."

"You could have radioed them."

The police sergeant chuckled. "I didn't want them interfering."

Lizzie was jolted by a sudden revelation and a sudden feeling of extreme fear. "You," she exclaimed, continuing to look around at him over her shoulder. "Clete was worried people would connect you with him. When I saw you on the beach you were reaching for your gun but stopped when the Coast Guard came. I was afraid you'd use it on me." The words continued to pour out as Lizzie stared at the man's hateful face. "If you wanted me out of the way then, you must have also wanted him out of the way. He was the one who could connect you to the smuggling of illegal immigrants."

Malflic tightened the handcuffs painfully.

Lizzie screamed in agony.

Malflic pulled her around to face him. He glared at her. "You stupid big mouthed bitch, you've screwed yourself real bad. When the arrest warrant came out, I wanted to grab you first to see if you're bright enough to figure out what's going on. I guess you're brighter than you look."

Lizzie continued hysterically screaming. Malflic slapped her hard across the face. Lizzie screamed louder. Malflic struck her backhanded, cutting the corner of her lip. Lizzie gasped down her screams. She began hyperventilating. "And… and when my phone was disconnected you were among the police in my apartment. You must have reconnected it."

Malflic stuck his face up close to hers. "Clete told you to keep your mouth shut. If you'd listened to him he'd still be alive. Now I'm gonna have to do you too, you stupid bitch."

Malflic roughly grabbed Lizzie's right arm. His fingernails bit into her flesh. She lost her balance and fell sideways. Malflic grabbed her by the hair and dragged her across the sand. Shells cut into her legs. Points of pain ripped through the top of her head. It felt like her hair was being jerked out as he pulled her tumbling through some scratchy bushes behind the beach. Her feet and legs cut a trail in the sand, dirt, and small bushes.

Lizzie realized if she didn't get away from Malflic he would kill her. She tried to grab her wet/dry bag. It swung back and forth as the police sergeant roughly dragged Lizzie behind him. She had a can of pepper spray in the bag.

Lizzie caught the bag in one hand and tried to use her other hand to open it. The zipper was stuck. The zipper always seemed to be stuck; cheap bag. "Damn," she cried in frustration.

Malflic spun her around again, jerked the bag out of her hands, undid the left handcuff, and threw her against a cabbage palm tree.

Lizzie gasped at the impact. Parts of the tree projected out, stabbing into her back.

The sergeant stretched Lizzie's arms around behind the rough surfaced tree and snapped the left cuff tight. Lizzie could feel the lattice-patterned thick frond bases of the tree jabbing into her skin. She remembered the bases of the broken off fronds were called "boots."

"You won't need this," said Malflic, reaching out and ripping off the top of Lizzie's bikini. The straps cut into her as they were torn away. He pulled at the wet/dry bag, trying to rip it off also. His jerking at the bag and then releasing it banged Lizzie against the rough boots of the cabbage palm. She felt like her back might break.

"God damn thing," Malflic growled as he gave a final tremendous yank. The strap holding the bag broke after cutting cruelly into Lizzie's back. Malflic threw the bag off into the brush.

The wild eyed police officer tried to rip off Lizzie's bikini bottom. It wouldn't rip. He pulled and pulled at it, hurting Lizzie, jerking the fabric out away from her then releasing it, banging her into the tree. His fingers were down inside the front of the bikini, his nails scratching her tender skin. Lizzie felt violated. Suddenly he knelt down on his right knee and roughly pulled her pants down. Lizzie's car keys, which had been clipped to the strap on the right side of her bikini bottom, fell off and vanished into the sand at the base of the tree trunk. Malflic was eye level with Lizzie's crotch. He looked and smiled.

"Step out," he grunted.

When Lizzie did nothing, Malflic jerked her pants from under her feet forcing her to lose her balance. The rough thatch of the palm boots scraped her. She hit her head against the tree, then regained her footing and stood trembling. Blood trickled down her forehead into her left eye. She could taste blood in her mouth. One of the cabbage palm boots was jabbing her below her left shoulder blade. Malflic was staring down at Lizzie's naked body. She tried to cross her legs to cover herself.

Malflic reached out and stuck his hand between her legs. "Soft skin," he mumbled as he spread her legs apart then ran his hand over her pubic area, up her stomach and onto her breasts. His touch revolted her.

"I don't understand. I thought you were going to arrest me; take me to jail," sobbed Lizzie. Mosquitoes were feasting on her.

Malflic stepped back and looked Lizzie up and down. "I can think of a lot better things to do with you than kill you."

"Like you killed Clete?"

"Yeah," Malflic responded, "aren't you brilliant."

"Why did you kill him?" Lizzie tried to catch her breath. Hyperventilation had dizzied her. She tried to concentrate her mind, calm herself.

"I was ordered to. He was talking too much."

"Ordered to? Who ordered you?"

Malflic shook his head and laughed. "I'm not as dumb as Clete. You stumbled onto something bigger than you realize. I'm just a little cog in this operation but I've got enough sense to keep my mouth shut."

"You were ordered to kill Clete and put him in my bed, to castrate him?"

"No, that was self preservation, my own idea." Malflic continued to stare at Lizzie's body as he talked. His eyes stayed below her neck. He licked his lips as he reached down and rubbed the front of his pants. "I had to find somebody to frame for his murder. His telling you too much resulted in his death sentence. So it would be appropriate to throw suspicion on you and your boyfriend; two suspects would be better than one as long as I wasn't one of them. I didn't care which of you fried; just so it wasn't me taking the one way trip to Raiford."

"How did Clete end up on my bed?" Lizzie thought if she kept Malflic talking somebody might come along to save her. The mosquitoes continued to drain her blood. With her arms cuffed behind the cabbage palm she couldn't swat them. She tried moving her body to shake them off. Blood continued to drip into her eye.

"Nice wiggle." Malflic kept looking up and down Lizzie's body. "You really are something to look at."

"I don't understand why he came back a second time or why you were there." Lizzie felt like screaming but there were no other people for miles. It was difficult staying calm enough to keep him talking, to postpone the horrible moments to come.

"I knew you were going out to Immokalee, I been keeping my eye on you, babe." Malflic gave Lizzie an obscene wink. "So, after you left, I went to your apartment and called Clete on your phone. I told him I had handcuffed you to your bed and he should come over and help me decide what to do with you. He told me not to hurt you, he'd be right over. Then I unplugged your phone to keep from being interrupted." Malflic seemed proud of his murder plan. He was actually smiling. "When he got to the bedroom doorway, I shot him in the back of the head with your gun and pushed him forward onto your bed."

"How did you know I had a gun?"

"Gun permits are on file at the police department."

"But how did you know where I had hidden it?"

"The gun wasn't hard to find. Where does a woman keep her gun? Near her bed. Easy."

"But your fingerprints weren't on the gun."

"A skin colored latex glove courtesy of the Sanibel Police Department. We've had them ever since people started getting A.I.Ds. I took the chance Clete wouldn't notice the glove, rushing in out of concern for you. He was a real Sir Galahad."

"But why did you cut off his penis?"

"To make it look like a sex crime, to deflect suspicion from myself and from the Haitian operation."

"You're sick. You're a pervert."

Malflic suddenly looked up into Lizzie's eyes. He exhaled quickly and almost screamed as he stuck his reddening face close to hers. "I'm not sick. It was a well calculated plan. I didn't enjoy cutting off the bastard's cock..." He smiled a weird smile. "Not really." Malflic shook his head emphatically. "It wasn't sick. It was a logical plan to throw suspicion on you. I'm the law. I'm smart." He pointed at his own forehead. "Even when I make a mistake, I think fast and cover it up. When we were securing the crime scene after you reported the murder, I remembered the phone was still disconnected, a small mistake. So I plugged it back in. So many cops were doing so many things, nobody noticed. I hadn't planned this but when you said the phone hadn't been working and then a short time later it rang, it made you look like a liar. I'd lucked into more evidence against you."

"But now I know you killed him, you murdered Clete," Lizzie screamed.

"So what? This ain't one of those old Perry Mason mysteries. I'm not going to break down in some court and confess my sins." Malflic laughed. "What's gonna happen here is everybody will think when you learned you were wanted for murder you threw yourself into the Gulf and drowned; committed suicide."

"I'm a good swimmer." Lizzie continued to secretly twist her wrists in the cuffs.

"It will look like you just kept swimming out until you were exhausted."

"How will you make it look like that?" She could feel the metal cuffs cutting into her wrists.

"Easy; I drag you out and hold you under until you drown. I'm a lot bigger than you so that won't be difficult. Then I just shove you into the current. They won't find you for days."

"My bruises will make them suspicious," Lizzie cried. "The handcuffs will ruin your whole plan."

"I don't need handcuffs to hold onto you, baby doll. Fish and crabs and other things nibbling at you will take care of the bruises. Hell, there're sharks in the Gulf. Probably won't be anything left of you for people to find. You'll disappear without a trace. Me and my fellow officers will have to keep searching forever for the insane castrating bikini babe of Southwest Florida." Malflic laughed and stepped over to the edge of the sand where bushes screened the small clearing from the beach. He began unbuttoning his uniform shirt.

"What are you doing?" cried Lizzie.

"I don't want to get my uniform wet while I'm holding you under." He glanced at her, smiled, and winked. "Besides I intend to have some fun with you first."

Lizzie pulled again at her handcuffs. A pain shot through her right wrist. She moaned.

Malflic folded the shirt and placed it on the ground. He then sat down and removed the short black boots he was wearing. He stood again, unbuckled, and removed his gun belt, which he placed on top of his shirt. Then he removed his pants, which he folded and placed beside the shirt. He sat down on the sand again and took off his socks. Then he stood back up and removed his underwear pants. His erection sprang loose.

Lizzie was sobbing.

Malflic strode over to Lizzie. His body other than his well-tanned arms, face, and neck was a sickly-looking pale, dead-fish white.

Lizzie tried to push herself back against the unbudging tree.

Malflic ran his hand over Lizzie's breasts. He squeezed the left one like he was checking a fruit for ripeness. Then he pushed himself against Lizzie, rubbing his stiff penis against her body. "Mmmm," he moaned.

Lizzie gasped and struggled against the cuffs which stretched her arms back around the tree. She looked up into her attacker's face.

Malflic bent at the knees and pushed against Lizzie as he reached down and forced her legs apart. His erect member came up between her legs.

Oh God no.

She tried to squeeze her legs back together.

"Oh, yes," moaned Malflic, as his body spasmed. He was not quite inside her.

Lizzie tried to twist sideways. Warm fluid spurted onto her.

Lizzie screamed as the palm frond boots cut into her back again.

"Hurts, don't it?" commented Malflic. "I need to lay you down. Once is never enough for me."

He started to reach around behind the tree but then mumbled, "I need the keys."

Malflic walked over to his clothes, reached down into his pants pocket, and brought out a small key ring. His wet, erect penis wobbled back and forth as he walked back.

Malflic stepped around behind the tree and removed the cuffs. He immediately grabbed Lizzie's left wrist tightly and dragged her over to his clothes.

Lizzie was again gasping for breath. She tried harder to concentrate, to isolate her mind from what was happening to her.

Malflic tossed the cuffs and the keys onto his pants. Then he dragged Lizzie back through the thorny bushes to the beach. She fell down and tried to dig in her heels. Malflic roughly jerked her back up and around so that she was in front of him. He suddenly shoved her forward. Lizzie spun sprawling around onto her back on a mound of sea shells. They cut into her bare back.

Standing at her feet, his penis red and erect, semen still dripping from it, Malflic looked down at Lizzie on her back on the beach, her legs spread open. She was trembling and crying. But she told herself she couldn't give up. She tried to concentrate her breathing like she had learned in yoga classes up north.

Malflic stepped over her left leg, preparing to straddle Lizzie and lower himself onto her.

Lizzie suddenly drew her legs in to her chest, shifted slightly then kicked out toward Malflic's crotch. She felt her toenails catch under Malflic's scrotum.

Lizzie pressed down under herself with her hands and arms and drew her legs back in to her chest. She thought she heard something tear as her nails ripped loose from Malflic's scrotum pouch.

Lizzie used the momentum from drawing in her legs to flip over backwards.

Holding his hands over his crotch and screaming, Malflic fell onto the beach where Lizzie had been lying less than a second before.

Lizzie rolled away, feeling the shells imprint on her skin as she rolled over them. She leapt to her feet and ran up the beach.

"No, no, no," Malflic was screeching. Lizzie looked back as she ran. The police sergeant was stumbling to his feet and turning toward her.

Lizzie ran to where Malflic had undressed. She knelt down and tried to pull his gun from its holster. It was strapped in.

"Get away from there," Malflic yelled as he ran up the beach. He was limping as he ran and was still holding his crotch. His face was red, which made the white scar on his left cheek stand out.

Lizzie pulled at the snap on the leather holster strap. It came unsnapped. She pulled out the gun. It was bigger than her gun. But she recognized it from the gun safety classes she had to take when she got her gun license. It was a Grok or Glock or Crock or something.

Lizzie snapped off the safety and looked up. Malflic was only about five feet away. He was holding out his hands and walking slower.

"Put the gun down," he was saying. "Everything will be okay. Nobody needs to get hurt. Just put the gun down and everything will be fine."

The gun was wobbling badly in Lizzie's outstretched hands. She pulled the trigger.

Malflic's crotch seemed to explode. Something flew off. Blood sprayed everywhere. A gaping hole appeared where Malflic's private parts had been. Malflic was still standing. He looked down. His jaw was hanging open.

That shot was too low.

Lizzie raised the gun and fired again. Malflic's nose and mouth vanished in a splash of red. Fragments of his face flew off. Malflic fell backwards, away from Lizzie. She stood up and stepped over beside his body. Lizzie fired three shots into his chest and two more into his head.

Lizzie looked down at the gun in her hand with revulsion.

My God, what have I done?

She threw the weapon away into the bushes. The gun seemed to float in the air before disappearing among the plants. Everything seemed vague, in slow motion, like in a dream.

Something was on the sand a couple feet from Malflic's body. Lizzie stepped over and looked down at it. The object was long and bloody. Strands of torn skin hung off it.

My God, it's his penis. The blood's draining from it, finally.

Lizzie turned back and looked at the remains of Malflic's body. His face was almost completely gone. One of his legs twitched.

The horror hit Lizzie. She trembled uncontrollably. She raised her right hand in front of her face, the hand that had fired the gun. Lizzie stared at her hand. It shook. She dropped her hand and looked wildly around, up and down the silent beach. She heard a ringing in her ears. It drowned out the sounds of the wind and the surf. It even drowned out the loud beating of her heart. Probably firing the gun near her ear caused the ringing. A storm of memories, fears and thoughts came jumbling over each other. She ran down the beach with no destination, just running to get away, just to get away. But she could not outrun the ringing noise.

Lizzie became winded after running about 50 yards. She gasped for breath. A pain tore into her side. She placed her hand onto her bare breast. The moon came out suddenly from behind a cloud. She felt her nakedness. She felt exposed. Lizzie ran up through the bushes and back into the woods. Thorny plants tore at her naked skin. Looking back behind her, she ran straight into the side of a tree. It knocked her down. She lay still for a moment then opened her eyes.

Lizzie was lying face down in a field of little yellow and purple flowers which covered an open area surrounded by thick bushes and trees. The flowers were pretty. She put her face down among them.

Oh just to rest peacefully.

A mosquito buzzed into her right ear. Lizzie slapped at it but only succeeded in hurting her own ear. She felt mosquitoes and sand fleas and other biting creatures all along her naked body. She jumped up and ran frantically back into the bushes and between the trees. She seemed to be running forever. The thorny bushes and a clump of sawgrass cut at her. She saw an opening ahead. She ran to it.

Lizzie was back on the dirt roadway behind the beach. Lizzie vaguely remembered the road had been created years ago by the Sanibel Island Police Department so it could sneak up on nudists, who used to frequent the more remote parts of Bowman's Beach.

Oh my God, the Sanibel Island Police.

Lizzie ran back off the roadway into the thicker woods and pushed herself between bushes again, struggling to get somewhere, anywhere. She went on and on. She swatted at mosquitoes. She fell down several times. Each time she picked herself back up, before the insects could settle on her, and she ran on.

She came out of the woods suddenly. In front of her was a stilt house.

I remember this house; the old man with the machine gun.

Lizzie stumbled over to the stairs which led up to the front door. Everything looked dark, deserted. Lizzie grabbed the railing and put her torn, bleeding right foot onto the first step.

CHAPTER FIFTEEN

Isolation

The wooden steps creaked as Lizzie climbed up to the stilt house's front door. Trying to make as little noise as possible, Lizzie turned the knob all the way until it clicked. Amazed it was unlocked, she pushed at the door. It opened.

Lizzie eased the door far enough inward to slip through. She entered the dark house on tiptoes. The moonlight coming through the doorway vaguely lit up a living room containing chairs, two sofas and a large television. A strange looking radio sat on an end table beside one of the sofas. She turned and quietly pushed the door closed. Reaching out and touching a wall, Lizzie made her way forward into complete darkness. She was still trembling and slightly out of breath from running through the woods. She bumped into a chair and almost knocked over a small table.

Standing naked in the middle of this strange living room, Lizzie could hear her own heart beating fast, very fast.

She took a step then stopped. She tried to concentrate on slowing her breathing, on reaching within her, on calming herself. Her chest was rising and falling rapidly along with her breathing. She felt as naked as she was.

Suddenly lights blazed on. Lizzie whirled to find herself eye to eye with the old man she'd met previously. He had come up behind her silently. He was wearing striped pajamas. He didn't have his machine gun this time.

"You ever hear of knocking?" he asked.

"I've had some trouble," Lizzie stammered, crossing her arms over the front of her body.

The old man shook his head solemnly. "It sounded like the Fourth of

July or Chinese New Year out there, 'cept I recognized it as a Glock. Was that you?"

"Uh, yes, but..."

"You leave anybody alive?"

"No, no, I didn't," Lizzie sobbed. "I'm, uh, I'm sorry to barge into your house like this."

"So nobody's following you?"

"No... No, there shouldn't be. But they'll look for me. Oh God, they'll look for me." Lizzie threw herself against the old man and started crying onto his chest.

The old man didn't seem sure where to put his hands. Finally he placed a hand on each of Lizzie's bare shoulders and gently pushed her away from him.

"You're gonna get me all excited jumpin' onto me like that. Besides, you're getting blood and sand and stuff all over my pajamas. You look like you been working the night shift at the slaughter house."

"I'm sorry," Lizzie looked down at herself. She was amazed how much blood and sand coated her body. Leaves were stuck in the congealing blood. "Do... Do you have anything I could wear?"

"I don't think getting dressed should come first."

"What should come first?" asked Lizzie, her voice shaking.

"A long hot bath: wash all that crap off, lie there and relax; get your head straight, you seem like you might be a little bit in shock at the moment. After you've had a nice long bath, put Neosporin and bandages on them cuts, get one of my robes out of the bathroom closet, come back in the living room and we can talk then."

The old man took Lizzie's hand and started leading her down a hallway. "Young people don't got the proper appreciation for a hot bath. When you're an old retired guy like me one thing you appreciate is a long, hot bath. I keep adding hot water to keep it hot."

"I'm Lizzie. Do I remember right that you're Joey something?"

"Yeah, that's right. Here's the bathroom." Joey opened a door, reached in and turned on a light.

"I don't want to get you in trouble, Joey. I just killed a policeman, a sergeant."

Joey put his hands on Lizzie's shoulders, turned her toward him, and looked in her eyes. "That ain't good. I always told my boys; don't never kill no cops; it don't matter how they screw you up. It ain't worth it to kill a cop. It makes all the other cops mad like sick dogs."

"I couldn't help it," Lizzie cried.

"My dear sainted mother always made me promise not to get in no pissing contest with a dick. God rest her soul." Joey crossed himself. He sighed and shook his large head. "Anyway, what's done is done. Now the cops'll be seriously lookin' for you. I'm gonna turn the lights out in the living room and lock the front door. You can leave the light on in the bathroom. It don't show outside. Take your bath quietly. Don't sing or nothin'."

Joey gave Lizzie a gentle push into the bathroom and shut the door. She heard him walk off toward the living room. She wondered if he might be a little senile.

The bath water turned red as Lizzie lay soaking in the deep, old fashioned bathtub. She felt tainted by the water. Instead of the blood washing away, she soaked in it. Lizzie reached forward, opened the drain and let out the water. She had to scoop leaves and dirt off the drain to keep the water flowing. She shivered, feeling cold and naked in the empty tub. Lizzie wanted to cry but didn't.

Lizzie refilled the tub with hot water, almost scalding, and sat thinking: How had she gotten herself in such a desperate fix? Who was this old man? Is there any way he could help her? Or was he likely to turn her in? Was her life completely ruined, forever? Who had ordered Clete killed? She had no idea. Why was Aaron so undependable and jealous? Should she just turn herself in to the police and hope things would work themselves out?

Lizzie shook her head and felt new determination. No, she must find a way out on her own. After all, even though she had killed a man, she was innocent of evil intention. It was self defense. But she would have to prove it; the police certainly wouldn't since it was one of their own she had killed. Yes, it was all up to her.

Nodding her head emphatically, Lizzie scrubbed hard a second time and re-washed her hair. The water did not become red this time.

Lizzie stood decisively and toweled off. She stepped from the tub and walked to the wash basin, where there was a mirror. Lizzie's shattered inner feelings were reflected in her eyes.

Her hair needed attention. It was even worse than the usual mess it had been since she started working in the environment. Saving the planet was splitting her ends and drying her natural oils. She picked some white hairs from a brush beside the wash basin and brushed her hair.

For a moment she stared at the streak of white in her hair. That white streak had developed after her parents were killed. It marked the sadness in her life.

Lizzie put on one of the old man's cotton terry cloth robes. It engulfed her. She took a deep breath to center her chakras and settle her racing heart. Then she opened the bathroom door. The rest of the house was dark. She reached back and turned off the bathroom light. Now she was engulfed in total darkness. She made her way to the living room by following a wall with one hand while she held up the overly large robe with the other to keep from tripping.

"Hello?" Lizzie whispered when she reached the living room. It was pitch black and apparently empty. She wished she could see something. Being alone was frightening in this strange place.

"I made some tea." Lizzie jumped as Joey's voice came from the darkness adjacent to her. "Make yourself comfortable, the sofa's about two feet in front of you."

Lizzie slowly edged her feet forward until she encountered the sofa. She sat. Joey was silent. She thought she heard him breathing. Suddenly images of her encounter with Sgt. Malflic flashed through her mind. She pictured him large and hovering over her. She could not picture the bloody ragged holes she had blown in him. That image was vague, like her brain was editing out the worst parts.

"Here's your tea." Joey's voice was suddenly beside her, making Lizzie jump again. "Watch out, the cup is hot."

Lizzie reached over, found his hand, and took the cup. Her hand shook slightly.

A match flared as Joey lit a candle stuck in a wine bottle on a small table beside the sofa. Joey moved over to a chair on the other side of that table. Lizzie noticed spots of blood, sand, and a couple of leaves on his pajamas where she had grabbed him earlier to cry onto his chest.

"Well, here we are all comfy," exclaimed Joey, smiling at Lizzie like a benevolent elderly uncle. "'scuse me while I listen to the police radio for a couple minutes."

Joey picked up some earphones from on top the unusual radio sitting just behind the candle. He put the earphones on and then flicked a switch on the radio, which had a lot of numbered buttons on it and a little red screen. It had the words Uniden Bearcat on the front. The red screen reminded Lizzie of blood.

Joey sipped tea as he sat listening.

Lizzie felt she would burst from the oppressive silence filling the candle-lit room. The candle projected shadows of Lizzie and Joey which danced on the dark walls. Her tea warmed Lizzie's throat but burnt her lips slightly. She wondered what Joey was hearing. His craggy face was studious, betraying nothing.

Finally, the old man took off the earphones and spoke. "They found his empty patrol car in Bowman's parking lot. He ain't answering his radio so they're out lookin' for him. But they ain't found him yet. They're also looking for you: you were last seen near Bowman's Beach and a warrant is out for you for the murder of that guy Grimes. Wasn't he that jerk with the gun who chased you up from the beach?"

"Yes, but I didn't kill Clete."

"Well, sweet face, whether you killed him or not, the body count around you's multiplying up." Joey smiled at Lizzie. He had a fatherly smile. "We can discuss the jerk's death later. But while we're comfy here together without much else to do, why don't you tell Uncle Joey about killin' the policeman."

CHAPTER SIXTEEN

Crime: A Good Thing

Lizzie, leaning forward on the sofa, explained to Joey that Sergeant Malflic had confessed he killed Clete Grimes. "So I know who did it. I can't be arrested for ..."

Joey interrupted with a grunt: "Hold on a minute, back up there, sweet face. If I'm gonna understand this you gotta start at the beginning, from seeing that jerk Clete on the beach."

"Okay, but it's getting hot in here."

"Yeah, I hadda turn off the air conditionin'. Police would wonder why an empty house had air conditionin'."

A vehicle roared by outside as Lizzie described Clete's sudden appearance in her apartment.

Joey blew out the candle and whispered, "Shush, don't even whisper."

The darkness was absolute. Lizzie could hold her hand an inch from her face without seeing it.

Several more vehicles went by. Then silence reigned for a long time. After what seemed like an eternity, Joey whispered, "I been listenin' to the police band again. They found his body. They got everybody and his cousin from three counties out lookin' for you. They also found your car."

A vehicle's door slammed somewhere near the house. Something thunked. Creaking noises came from the stairs leading up to the front door. Lizzie felt a sudden chill. She shivered. The locked door rattled. Somebody knocked. Voices spoke to each other just outside. Lizzie couldn't tell what they were saying. She was amazed they couldn't hear her heart pounding and pounding. It seemed terribly loud to her.

Footsteps descended the stairs.

"They're going away," Lizzie whispered.

"Shush, quiet. They might come back and I only heard one set of footsteps."

"I'm scared. Could you sit beside me?" Lizzie pleaded in a voice thin as air.

"Okay, but I can't see a damn thing," Joey whispered back. "I'll hafta feel my way over there."

Lizzie jumped when Joey's hand touched her.

"Whoops, sorry," Joey whispered. "What happened to your robe?"

"It's hot in here."

The knock sounded again at the door.

"I thought they went away," Lizzie murmured under her breath.

"Shhh dammit."

"Let me hold your hand. I'm scared." Lizzie reached over and touched Joey's shoulder.

"Okay, just quit talking. And don't get no ideas. I'm an old man."

"Don't worry, Joey." Lizzie patted his hand then left her hand laying on top. "I'm already starting to think of you as a substitute father. Mine died."

"Yeah, okay, fine, just shut up, for God's sake."

The stairs creaked outside as someone descended.

"I think the other one's going," Joey whispered. "I hope no blood dripped off you onto my steps."

Lizzie squeezed Joey's hand. "If it did I'll clean it up in the morning."

"I ain't worried about nothin' gettin' dirty." Joey's hand turned over as though to hold Lizzie's hand but then quickly turned again. "I'm worried about them followin' the blood, figurin' out you're in here. They figure that out, they'll break in and arrest you. Hell, arrest us. Gettin' arrested ain't on my schedule. I'm retired."

Lizzie leaned closer to the old man. "Retired from what? What kind of consultant were you, Joey?"

"Security."

"But you don't usually lock anything, she whispered, "and you don't seem to have an alarm system."

"Not exactly that kind of security." Joey was silent for a moment. Lizzie could hear him breathing. Suddenly he spoke, startling her. "Lemme ask you, Lizzie: you really don't recognize my name: Joey Caunteloupo?"

"No, sorry, I don't think I've ever heard of you before."

Joey again turned over his hand. This time he lightly gripped Lizzie's hand. "You never heard of the New York Caunteloupo family, the Cosa Nostra?"

Lizzie pulled her hand away. "You mean the Mafia? You're in the Mafia? Oh, Joey, I don't believe this. What did you do for them?"

"I was the top guy." He sounded proud.

"You're a crime boss?" Lizzie's voice rose.

"I'm retired," Joey whispered.

"Oh no, Joey, you're a crook." Lizzie felt a shiver of fear go through her. She slid along the sofa a couple inches away from him. Her sliding made the robe, which she was sitting on, bunch up uncomfortably. She decided to put it back on.

I've gone from the frying pan into the fire.

"Hey, get off your high horse," Joey was no longer whispering. "You're charged with murder and cutting off a guy's dick. I ain't never been charged with cutting off nobody's dick."

All I did was see illegal aliens on the beach, now I'm wanted for murder, I've killed a policeman, and I've fallen into the clutches of the Mafia. But, wait a minute, the Mafia? This is Florida, not New York.

"If you're a New York crime boss, Joey, why aren't you in New York?" she asked sternly.

"I told you: I'm retired." Joey coughed. "But in addition to that, a friend of mine's trial's comin' up. I ain't no stoolie. So I disappeared for awhile; so they can't send me no subpoena."

Lizzie pulled at the robe, trying to make it more comfortable. "You're in hiding?"

"Sorta."

"But Joey I still can't believe you were a criminal. How could a nice guy like you do terrible illegal things?" Lizzie's robe seemed a little itchy.

"It crept up on me. At first I was just a traditional godfather; a normal Italian thing; attend baby christenings, stuff like that. I had respect." It seemed to Lizzie like Joey's voice was getting too loud. "People would ask for favors and I'd help 'em. Then more people needed help and the whole thing just kinda snowballed."

Lizzie tried standing, shaking the robe down, then sitting again. It seemed better. "But you must have done horrible things."

"I never done nothin' horrible. I never hurt nobody that didn't need hurtin'." Joey voice was becoming much louder, more emphatic. Lizzie worried somebody outside might hear it. "The bad stuff now is the drugs; hard drugs mess people up. But I didn't never get involved in that. No, it's the drugs that's given crime a bad name. I was old fashioned. I ran a traditional, family organization. We was like a social welfare agency. In fact, governments took over most of our functions and are messin' 'em up, cheatin' people. We was more honest."

Something else on the sofa was suddenly poking at Lizzie. "But you're really retired?"

"Yeah, these are strange times. It's difficult for a guy to make an honest living from crime these days; too much competition from the government."

Lizzie moved over another couple inches until she was more comfortable. "I don't understand what you mean."

"Lemme explain." Lizzie could hear Joey slide over next to her. "First there was the numbers racket. That was good business. But now the government does it, 'ceptin' they call it the lottery or lotto or super somethingerother ball or whatever. But still it's just the old numbers racket. Ceptin' now the payouts ain't as good. Today's political leaders ain't as honest as The Family usta be."

"I sometimes play the lotto."

"Everybody does. Lemme go on." Joey put a hand on Lizzie's shoulder. "Ah, good, you put the robe back on. We had the bookie shops. Again, the government took over. We had rooms with nice comfortable chairs where you could sit and listen to the races on the radio. Now they got televised races from all the tracks at the other tracks and the Jai Alai frontons and wherever. They got off track betting, which ain't nothin' but the old bookie joint ceptin' now it's run by the government.

"Then there's what the do-gooders call the protection racket. Hell, it was a bona fide service. We'd guarantee some small business it wouldn't get robbed. Supposedly the police and courts guarantee the same thing. Difference is our guarantee worked. Somebody robbed a business not protected by us, even if the cops caught the guy, which wasn't very likely, it'd take years to try him. If the business was protected by us; they'd find the jerk floating in the East River." Joey's hand left Lizzie's shoulder.

Lizzie loosened her robe. She was getting hot. "What about other things? What about prostitution, for example? You're not going to defend that: using women like commodities."

"Those girls were on the street, lost, and desperate. Men used them for the worst stuff imaginable and then beat them up. It was terrible, make you wanta kill somebody or somethin'. We'd take the poor creatures in; provide a roof over their heads, medical care, and a nice matronly madam to make sure nobody abused the young ladies." Joey's hand again touched Lizzie's shoulder; but the robe was now off that shoulder. "Oh, excuse me." The hand retreated again. "Hell, we was the best thing ever happened to those broads. And all we expected in return was for them to provide a little pleasure to the most respected men in the community."

"You're not going to tell me the government took over prostitution?" Lizzie pulled her robe back up. Lizzie was getting tired of making adjustments.

"Hell no, politicians don't need to. They're already prostitutes. I usta own a few of 'em myself." Joey was silent for a moment then suddenly spoke loudly. "And one more thing. And this really frosts me. We started gettin' in legitimate businesses and all the career anti-crime people and the news media and the low-life politicians started screamin' and moanin' that organized crime was gettin' into legitimate businesses. Well, hell and damnation, they complained when we did illegal stuff, but then when we did legal stuff they also complained. And all we really wanted was to serve our community, help our families, and follow the teachings of our church about doin' unto others." Joey's deep voice had risen even louder toward the end. He paused. When he resumed speaking he was less emotional. "I kinda got way off there. You need to finish tellin' me what happened to you the last couple days."

"Wait a minute," Lizzie exclaimed. "I just realized something. They called Finch a mob attorney from Miami. You must have hired him to represent me."

Joey laughed quietly. "Guilty as charged."

Lizzie hesitated a moment thinking, then asked, "but how did you know I needed an attorney? He called before anybody knew. The police were still questioning me."

"I was listenin' to the police scanner. It's a hobby of mine. But it's not usually very interestin' here, not like New York where there's all kinds o' excitement. Here people call the police if they find a frog in their toilet." Joey chuckled.

Lizzie leaned toward Joey's voice. "But why would you hire an attorney for me? You hardly knew me."

"Hey, I liked you, sweet face. Remember I said no friend of Joey C's gets hurt." Joey's hand found Lizzie's knee and lightly patted it. "So you get in trouble, I'm gonna help you. I told you we're like a social welfare agency."

"But you also told me you're retired."

"Sorta retired." Joey removed his hand from Lizzie's knee. "You know it's kinda hard to walk away when you're doin' somethin' you love. It's like you and them turtles; how could you stop doin' that?"

Lizzie laughed. She reached out her hand, found Joey's hand, and squeezed it. "Okay, Mr. Crime Lord."

Joey squeezed back. "Oh, no, don't call me no crime lord. That term came in later. It's too grand for a guy like me. Now they call these people this kinda lord and that kinda lord: crime lord, drug lord, whatever. It's ridiculous. I know these guys and, lemme tell you, ain't none of 'em about to be knighted a lord by no queen, not even by Queen Latifah. Now get back to tellin' me what happened."

"I forgot where I was."

"You was naked in your apartment when this guy Clete jumped out at you."

Lizzie told Joey about the tickling incident.

Laughing, Joey asked, "You're really that ticklish?"

Lizzie replied in a quiet voice. "Really."

"Hmmm… er, no, I better not… Go on."

CHAPTER SEVENTEEN

The Bad News Is…

It took some time for Lizzie to bring Joey up to date. During her long outline of events, the sounds of vehicles passing outside lessened then ceased.

"They've given up for the night," Joey said. "Let me think about everything you said."

A faint ticking noise marked the passage of time. Lizzie got bored. She was starting a mental meditation chant when Joey suddenly asked her, "What happened to Sergeant Malflic's gun?"

"I threw it away in the bushes."

Joey grunted, "That's too bad. Your prints'll be on it. Without that gun they couldn't prove you was the one who shot Malflic. Could'a been somebody else on that beach."

"Who?"

"The tooth fairy. What the hell difference does it make?" Joey's voice was rising again. "You got any brains you ain't gonna tell 'em you did it. Malflic sure as shit ain't gonna testify. They can't prove nobody else wasn't there."

Lizzie shifted slightly on the sofa. "Maybe I should go back and get the gun."

"Too late, they would've found it by now."

"Well, one good thing," Lizzy exclaimed, "at least now I know Malflic killed Clete Grimes."

Joey snorted. "What God-damn good does that do you?"

"That mystery is solved." Lizzie shrugged. "I'm innocent. I don't have to worry about that any more."

"Let me tell you, Lizzie girl, you got more worries now than you ever had.

You're way up shit's creek." Joey's deep voice almost seemed to be growling at her out of the darkness.

Lizzie turned toward that voice. She wished he'd switch the lights back on. "I don't understand, I was about to be charged with a gruesome murder and castration. Well, that is if they can charge you with castration as a specific offense. Now Malflic has confessed that he was the murderer and the mutilator."

"Yeah, he confessed to you alone on a beach and then you killed him. Before that your murder arrest would have been based on circumstantial evidence." Joey took Lizzie's hand. "You had a brilliant attorney. You'da been in jail a few hours, then bailed out, and then been free for a couple years while Finch delayed trial dates. When it finally came to trial, Finch woulda got you off. I can tell you from personal experience; he's good at getting' people off even when they're guilty. It woulda been a cinch for him to get an innocent person off. And, by the way, maybe I shoulda said somethin' earlier but castration is cutting off the balls, not the dick."

"I don't see what difference it makes, they're right next to each other."

Joey grunted loudly, was silent for a long moment, chuckled, and then squeezed her hand. "Distinctions are very important to attorneys. Little legal distinctions kept me outa jail a lotta times. Even if you're not guilty, you gotta know what you're not guilty of."

"Couldn't I just turn myself in," Lizzie pleaded, "and tell them Malflic killed Clete?"

Joey chuckled, "I can picture it now: you sashay in there, bat your pretty eyelashes at the cops, and tell 'em Malflic confessed to you he did it. So you killed him. They ask what evidence you got and you say: 'He told me he did it.' 'Anything else?' they ask. 'No,' you reply and, of course, they'll say, 'We believe you, yer free to go.'"

"I guess I might have trouble convincing them." Lizzie slumped back against the soft cushions on the sofa. Something prodded into her lower back. She shifted away from it.

Joey released Lizzie's hand as she moved away. "You gotta face the facts, little miss, not only are you up shit's creek but that creek's got diarrhea. You were being hunted for one murder. Then you killed the first policeman who found you after the warrant was issued. So now they're lookin' for you for two murders; one a policeman. At least you didn't cut off his dick."

"Oh no," Lizzie groaned.

"What is it?" Joey spoke slowly and deliberately. "Why did you say 'Oh no'?"

Lizzie replied in a very quiet, little girl voice. "When he was coming at me he might have still had an erection. It was amazing. I don't think most men would have an erection under those circumstances. Harry used to have a problem in that area. I used to have to keep whispering to Harry that he was a big success to get him to have an erection."

"Who's Harry?"

"My husband."

"Oh."

Lizzie shook her head at her memories. "I always had to say 'big success' over and over in his ear with the emphasis on the 'big.' It was like the stroking they do at a Chamber of Commerce banquet before they finally get the speaker to rise to the podium."

"I wouldn't know." Joey cleared his throat. "I had the biggest family run business in my borough but never got an invite from the Chamber of Commerce." He paused for a long moment. "What happened with Malflic?"

"My first shot was low."

"How low?"

Lizzie gulped then blurted out: "It blew off his penis. It was strange watching it fly through the air away from him. He had a look on his face which would be difficult to describe."

"I'll bet."

Lizzie's voice rose. "It was an accident. I could never aim that good. You believe me, don't you?"

"Yeah I believe you." Joey was chuckling. "But I still might put a chair against my bedroom door."

"You don't believe me." Lizzie sobbed. "You think I'm some kind of maniac."

"Hell no, Lizzie, I ain't scared of you."

"Then you're going to let me stay here?"

Joey grunted, and then murmured something to himself. Finally he said loud enough for Lizzie to hear, "Yeah babe, you can stay in the spare bedroom."

"Thanks, Joey," Lizzie moved over to kiss Joey on the cheek. But something hard stuck into her back from under the sofa's cushions. "Ouch, what's that?"

"Oh, you're probably sitting on a gun. I shoulda warned you. I got a few dozen guns stuck around here various places. Be careful; they're all loaded with their safeties off. So when you go to bed tonight you might wanta check to make sure you're not gonna set something off."

"How will I sleep from all the worrying I'll be doing?" Lizzie sobbed. "I feel like my life has ended."

Joey patted her on the shoulder. "Nonsense. There ain't nothin' can't be overcome if you're tough enough."

"It took all the courage I had to leave my husband and head off into the unknown." Lizzie sniffled. "I don't know if I have any courage left."

"Shit, we all got more courage then we think we got. You'll get through this, babe."

"But how?" Lizzie cried. "What am I going to do?"

"You mean what're we gonna do." Joey suddenly sounded more confident, more committed. "The first thing we do is we get you clothes and other stuff to change your appearance. You need to decide if you wanna have red, black, or brown hair. The second thing is we prove you didn't kill that Clete Grimes."

"How are we going to do that?"

"We find your husband's private detective and convince him to give us the time stamped pictures."

Lizzie gulped and tried to stop crying. "How will I convince him to do that?"

"Easy: take me with you to his office. I can convince anybody to do anything."

Lizzie thought over what that implied. It might be something dangerous or violent or illegal. But her situation was desperate. "Thank you, Joey. With your help we'll prove I didn't kill Clete. Then I'll get the charges dropped and be out of this nightmare."

Joey made a strange guttural noise. "Not quite so fast, sweet face. You'll still have to prove it was Sergeant Malflic who killed Clete. They ain't gonna excuse you for murderin' a cop just 'cause you was innocent of the charges he was arrestin' you for. You gotta prove he killed Clete and you was in fear he was about to kill you."

"But if I can prove he murdered Clete, then I'll be all right, won't I?"

"You're forgetting somethin' else." Joey's voice sounded rough to Lizzie.

"What?"

"Some unknown person ordered Malflic to kill Clete. That mystery person probably wants you dead for the same reasons he wanted Clete dead. So, even if you clear yourself of every murder and maiming charge, somebody's still out there who wants you killed. But don't give up hope. As they said in that movie, 'tomorrow's another day.'"

"Yes," Lizzie gasped, "but I'm Lizzie, not Scarlett."

CHAPTER EIGHTEEN

Camouflage

Lizzie jumped aside to avoid the bacon's splattering grease. She almost bumped into Joey who had silently entered the kitchen.

"That looks dangerous," Joey commented.

Lizzie gasped, sat her spatula aside, and closed the front of her robe. "You startled me. I thought I'd surprise you and make breakfast."

Joey opened the refrigerator and looked in. "Don't you worry grease might burn a hole in you?"

Lizzie blushed. "This robe is hot. I need real clothes."

"Getting you clothes is item number one." Joey, a carton of orange juice in one hand, pointed at Lizzie's head with the other. "What about hair color?"

"What?" Lizzie was flipping the bacon.

"Red, black, or brown? They're lookin' for a blonde."

"Oh, yes, of course… Do you like your bacon dry?"

"No, don't burn off the fat."

Lizzie removed the pan from the burner and began spatulaing the bacon onto paper towels. "I guess maybe a redhead; but not bright red; dark red, a serious color, dignified."

"Yeah, I always liked serious, dignified women." Joey laughed and shook his head. He sipped orange juice from the carton as he turned and opened the kitchen door, "I'll make notes on your sizes and tastes while we eat."

"Lock it. I'll be back in a few hours," said Joey as Lizzie followed him to the front door.

Lizzie touched Joey on the arm. "Thanks for all you're doing for me."

"You're risking being charged with harboring a fugitive."

"What the hell else I got to do?"

"How will you get into town?" Lizzie gestured toward the outside. "You haven't got a car."

"I rent a garage from snowbirds at those condos opposite the park entrance." Joey pointed down the dirt road. "I walk over on the beach so people'll think I'm a shell collector; won't tie me to this house."

Joey wore shorts, tennis shoes, white socks, and a t-shirt with the words *You Don't Know Me* printed above an official looking government seal and, below that, in smaller print, the words *Federal Witness Protection Program*.

Lizzie patted Joey's arm. "Be careful, Joey."

"While I'm passin' by I'll check what the cops are doin' up the beach." Joey started out the door but turned back. "Oh, don't cook nothin' else that smells. We was lucky the cops didn't sniff out that bacon. Definitely don't make no donuts."

As Joey started down the stairs, Lizzie locked the door behind him. She walked across the shadowy living room and plopped down on the white sofa.

"Ouch." She reached behind her, pulled out a gun, looked at it, and began crying. Lizzie carefully sat the gun on the table in front of her, fell over onto the sofa, put her arm over her eyes, and sobbed.

Several hours later, the front door banged open. Lizzie gasped. It was Joey. Lizzie let out her breath as Joey slammed the door shut. She stood to greet him. Vehicles had roared past earlier and, once, people talked for several minutes outside. She was not sure they'd gone away.

"You're famous," Joey exclaimed as he slipped a large backpack off his shoulders. He unzipped a pocket, pulled out a newspaper, and handed it to Lizzie.

She looked down at a photo of herself on the front page of the Fort Myers News-Press. It was taken six months ago for her employment file at the Sanibel Island Environmental Conservancy. Above the picture was a headline: Police Seek Murdering Sexual Mutilator.

The first subhead read: Second Murder on Sanibel Island.

The article itself began: Sanibel Police Sergeant Jack Malflic's dead, sexually mutilated body was found last night on an isolated Sanibel Island beach used in the past by nudists.

Police are looking for Sanibel Island Conservancy employee Elizabeth Shuttleford Grant for questioning in the murder of Malflic. The blonde, bikini clad Grant, 32, was already being sought in connection with the murder of Clete Grimes, whose dead, naked body was found nude and sexually mutilated in Ms. Grant's bed in her Sanibel apartment.

"This is terrible," exclaimed Lizzie, waving the paper in front of her, "They make me sound like a murdering monster and they even published my age."

"Read on," said Joey as he walked over and sat in his overstuffed chair. "I'm tired. I'm really gettin' old." He propped his feet up on the matching ottoman.

Lizzie sat on the sofa and read: Fort Myers psychiatrist Pasqual Crumpfast told the News-Press that many people often seem normal for years while beneath the surface torment rages from childhood abuse. "When these repressed feelings burst out," Crumpfast told a reporter, "The result can be a spree of murder and mutilation. This is true of a large percentage of serial killers. Ms. Grant was probably abused by a close relative when she was a child."

"My God," exclaimed Lizzie, "They not only have me tried and convicted; they're portraying my parents as sexual child abusers."

"Now you know the media," said Joey, shaking his head. "You wouldn't believe what they used to say about me. Some of it wasn't even true."

"Lemme show you what I got." Joey zipped open a second pocket in his backpack, which was on the table in front of the candle-lit sofa. Joey pulled three small boxes out of the backpack. He handed one to Lizzie. It was L'Oreal light copper golden hair coloring.

"It's multi-tonal," Lizzie noted.

"A woman at the store told me that's the style, to make it look like the sun did it."

Lizzie ran her hand through her hair. "Mine's already naturally blonder from the sun."

"But you ain't streaked. We gotta give you fake natural streaking so you'll look different than in the newspaper. This other stuff will really help." Joey handed the other two boxes to Lizzie.

"A curling iron? And mousse?"

"Yeah, I hope you know what to do with that stuff. Your hair needs something'. Every time I seen you your hair's always been short and messy, like you just came from a disaster or a crime scene."

A distraught expression appeared on Lizzie's face.

"Or like you just came from the beach," Joey added before Lizzie could start crying again.

"I usually just did." She paused a moment. "Come from the beach I mean. Mentioning which, did you buy me a bathing suit?"

Joey smiled. "Yeah." He fished in his backpack and dug out two small red pieces of cloth. He handed them to Lizzie.

She held them up in front of her. "I certainly won't sweat to death in these. The back of this bottom is little more than a thread. I thought you were embarrassed when I wasn't covered up like a nun."

"I'm tryin' to be a polite host. Besides, I like rear ends."

Lizzie blushed. "Men! Now I'll be self conscious."

"I'm too old for you to worry about. Except maybe…" Joey raised his thick eyebrows and smiled at Lizzie. "Anyway, the dye and the other stuff will make you look like you just came from an office, or a high class social event, or a fashion show. Whatever is the opposite of looking like you just came from the beach. Can you fix your hair, dye it and whatever without my help?"

"Of course."

"Okay, the bathroom's yours. I'll be in my bedroom. I got computer work to do."

Lizzie felt transformed as she looked at herself in the bathroom mirror. She had done some snipping and produced an asymmetrical bob resembling Victoria Beckham's. The coloring startled her. She had never been anything other than a natural dirty blonde. Now she looked more elegant. But hair hanging partly over her right eye would take some getting used to.

The white streak had disappeared. It had marked the memory of the death of her parents. But it was only covered up not obliterated. It was still there even if nobody could see it.

Joey let out a wolf whistle when Lizzie walked into the living room.

"You're a dirty old man," Lizzie stated as she adjusted the top of her tiny bathing suit.

"Guilty as charged." He smiled. "Sit down. Lemme show you the rest of what I got."

Lizzie sat beside Joey on the leather sofa. "Is everything you bought in there?" Lizzie asked, gesturing toward Joey's backpack.

"No, just a couple outfits. The rest is still in the car."

Joey rummaged in his backpack and brought out two dresses, which he handed to Lizzie.

She stood and held out the first one. It was a blue, sleeveless V-neck short Jersey.

"It's short at one end and plunging at the other," exclaimed Lizzie.

"We don't want people lookin' at your face."

Lizzie sat the Jersey on the table and held up the other dress. It was a bright yellow babydoll halter top dress.

"This one is short also," Lizzie commented.

"Hey, you got nice legs."

Lizzie's face turned bright red.

Joey smiled at Lizzie's legs. "I got one more thing," he said, pulling out a black wig.

Lizzie took the wig and curled her upper lip in distaste. "What did you do, run over a witch's cat?"

Joey's hands made a waving motion. "Fluff it out."

Lizzie shook the wig. The black hair fell long and straight.

"Put it on," Joey urged.

Lizzie pulled back her own hair and slipped on the wig.

Joey smiled. "You look like Cher when she had that TV show."

Lizzie pulled a strand of the wig around to examine it. "If I'm going to wear this, why did you have me dye my own hair?"

Joey stood and faced Lizzie, looking down at her. "A double deception; you'll wear this wig today, then tonight we'll deep six it. If anybody reports seeing you today, the police will think you got black hair. But, starting tomorrow, your hair will actually be a golden color."

Lizzie stood. "Who's going to see me?"

Joey placed his hands on Lizzie's bare shoulders. "That detective your husband hired. I did some internet research; his name's Milos Anila. He's got an office in downtown Fort Myers."

Lizzie blinked and looked distressed. "He'll recognize me. He was taking pictures of me."

Joey smiled and nodded. "Yeah, that's why the double deception. I'll try to convince him not to tell no one he seen you. But some jerks don't learn to keep their traps shut."

"What are you going to do to him?"

"Just talk. First a little field research then we'll go to his office and surprise him."

Lizzie reached down and picked up the yellow babydoll dress. She walked past Joey toward the hallway leading to the bedrooms but then hesitated and pointed toward the backpack. "What about underwear?"

"You don't think I'm gonna go into a store and buy women's underwear?" Joey's voice became louder and more emphatic. "That's not something Joey Caunteloupo's gonna do. People'd think I'm some kinda pervert."

Lizzie shook her head in exasperation. "I hope its not windy today in Fort Myers."

"A little wind would be nice." Joey smiled. "It'd keep people's eyes off your face."

Lizzie blushed again as she looked appraisingly at Joey. "Do you really think you can get that private eye to give you those pictures?"

"I know I can."

CHAPTER NINETEEN

Convincing Milos

"LOOK like a shell collector," Joey mumbled as he and Lizzie examined a mound of shells on Bowman's Beach. Joey made a show of looking at one he'd picked up.

Lizzie hesitantly glanced up at the Sanibel Island Police and Lee County Sheriff's deputies combing through the grass and low bushes edging the beach. One of the deputies stared at Lizzie and Joey.

Lizzie put her hand on Joey's arm, "They've seen us."

"Of course they seen us. We're right out here on the beach. They'd be blind not to see us."

"But…"

"No buts, calm down. They're lookin' for a naked blonde not two dark haired people wearin' clothes."

Lizzie looked over at Joey's snow white hair but said nothing.

"Police ain't loaded with smarts," Joey continued. "They can only concentrate on one thing at a time and right now they're spread out lookin' through the grass and bushes for somethin'."

"My car keys are up there somewhere. So is my bathing suit. But it's ripped to shreds. And my bag." Lizzie squeezed Joey's arm. "The gun; maybe they never found the gun. Maybe they're still looking for it. Maybe they won't find it. Maybe my prints will have washed off by the time they find it. Damn, that one deputy is still looking at me."

"Maybe, maybe, maybe. Quit worrying and pick up a shell."

"But he's still looking at me."

"Of course he is; you got great legs. Pick up a shell."

83

"These are all just common varieties. Most are broken."

"That don't matter; pick up anything. Look like a shell collector. Look like you just found a juniper."

Lizzie gave Joey a confused look, her brows furrowed. Then she laughed, "You mean a junonia, that's the rare one."

"I don't care if you call it a mint julep." Joey made a quick series of New York Italian gestures toward Lizzie. "Look like you found one; play shell collector."

Lizzie gasped. She ran a couple feet ahead, reached down excitedly and picked up a shell. "Joey look at this; look what I found." She waited, turning over the shell in her hand, while Joey walked up to her.

Joey whispered, "Don't overact. You're pretending you found a shell, not the lost mines of El Dorado."

"But Joey, I really did find a junonia." She held the shell up for him to see. "Some people look all their lives for one of these."

Joey took the shell from Lizzie and examined it. "It's just a shell."

"Give it back." Lizzie snatched the shell from Joey. "It'll be my good luck shell."

"Any kinda luck would be an improvement."

"Look up the beach," Lizzie exclaimed. "The police are going the other way. My luck's already improved."

"I'll wait to see how things go with Milos."

"I thought you were sure about getting the pictures?"

"I'm getting' a little old for strong arm stuff."

Lizzie stopped dead and stared at Joey. "Strong arm stuff?"

"Forget I said that."

Joey drove his Buick Le Sabre down a residential street off McGregor Boulevard in Fort Myers.

"I'd pictured you driving something snappy and foreign," said Lizzie, looking around at the old houses in one of the city's original neighborhoods.

"Look for 1590." Joey patted his steering wheel. "I've had this car a long time. It's old, like me."

"There it is," said Lizzie, pointing to a frame house with a wraparound porch.

"There's a golf course on the other side, good way to sneak up," Joey murmured, as he slowly drove past the house. "Lotta wood, make one hell of a fire. You didn't notice any fire hydrants since that one two blocks ago, did you?"

"I'm backin' in so you can drive out quick with no problems." Joey maneuvered his Buick up a wide alley in downtown Fort Myers. A couple of shops and a restaurant had alley entrances. Colorful planters containing small trees sat beside doorways.

"Me? Drive?"

"Yeah, you're my getaway driver." Joey pulled on the emergency brake and climbed out of the car, leaving the engine running. He leaned back in through the open door. "Slide over behind the wheel."

"Getaway driver? What are you talking about? What are you going to do?" Lizzie slid behind the wheel, being careful to keep her short dress from sliding up.

"If everything goes right, this Milos character will be joining me in the back seat in a few minutes. When we get in, drive off slowly. Be careful of the traffic laws, we don't wanna be stopped by no cops. I'll be back in a minute."

Joey disappeared behind the building he had parked beside. Lizzie leaned down to look at the building's alley side doorway, which was flanked by skinny potted trees, like the decorative plants from Home Depot. The doorway was adjacent to the Buick's back seat. A metal plaque on the brick wall beside the door read: Milos Anila, Private Investigator, Divorce Specialist, Background Checks.

A young couple walking through the alley looked quizzically at the Buick. Lizzie was getting nervous. She thought of blowing the horn but decided that might upset Joey.

Joey stepped from behind the building. He was looking around and rubbing his hands together. He looked down the alley at the people walking away. Joey leaned down and indicated with a hand motion for Lizzie to roll the passenger side window down. She fumbled with the switches and put the driver's side window down first. Finally she got the right switch. She cursed her nervousness.

Joey leaned in the open window. "He should be down any minute."

"How do you know?" Lizzie gripped the steering wheel hard.

"I shut off the building's electricity. People always come out to see if it's just them or if the whole neighborhood's out." Joey lurched away and stood up.

"Maybe he'll call somebody."

"Hey, be an optimist." Joey spoke back over his shoulder. "We can go in if we gotta but I'd rather have him on our territory."

"You're going to kidnap him?" Lizzie was gripping the steering wheel so hard her hands were turning white.

Joey chuckled. "Nah, just a little ride in the country for some uninterrupted conversation."

The door beside Joey opened and a man stepped out. Lizzie recognized him immediately, even though she'd only gotten a quick glimpse of Milos when he was photographing her. She pointed to him and shook her head up and down. Her heart was pulsating. She was too scared to speak.

Joey opened the Buick's rear passenger-side door and pulled something from his pocket as he darted over behind Milos. Lizzie was amazed how quick the old man moved. Joey stuck a pointed object into Milos's back and growled, "Get in the car."

"Wha…?" Milos's right hand reached toward his sports jacket.

"I wouldn't," said Joey, tripping Milos as he knocked Milos's arm aside, pushed him into the car, and stripped a gun from Milos's jacket.

"Drive," yelled Joey, as he jumped in beside Milos, who was sprawled face down on the back seat. Joey pushed Milos over to make room for himself.

Lizzie sat with her mouth open staring in the rear view mirror at the two men in the back seat.

"Drive," Joey yelled again, louder this time.

My God he can move fast for an old man, Lizzie thought as she jammed down the accelerator and spurted down the alley. *It's like watching a criminal ballet.*

She screeched to a stop at the end of the alley and asked, "Which way?"

"Considerin' it's a one way street, I'd go the way the other cars are goin'" Joey suggested.

"Yeah, right." She turned out into the street.

Milos sat up and looked around. "You won't get away with this."

"With what?" asked Joey. "We're just goin' for a friendly drive." As he spoke, Joey was patting Milos down. He held a small gun pointed at the middle aged, overweight private detective.

A couple of pistols landed on the front seat beside Lizzie.

This is like being in a 1930's gangster movie.

"Where should I go?" Lizzie asked, her voice trembling.

"It don't matter; somewhere scenic." Joey responded.

"What do you people want?" blurted Milos.

"You took pictures of Lizzie Grant for her husband, whatsisname, limp dick."

Joey's voice came from right behind Lizzie, almost in her ear. She thought he sounded a little like Marlon Brando in The Godfather.

"Harry," interjected Lizzie.

"Yeah, Harry."

"I can't talk about my private dealings with a client; professional ethics," sniffed Milos.

Joey's voice was suddenly rougher, more gangsterish. "I ain't askin', I'm tellin'. You took those pictures with time stamps that prove Mrs. Grant couldn't have murdered that guy. I'd strongly suggest you give those pictures to the police so they'll know she didn't kill him."

"They aren't my property. They're the property of my client, Mr. Grant."

"Should I go up onto the bridge?" asked Lizzie. The Buick was approaching the on ramp for the U.S. 41 bridge over the Caloosahatchee River.

"Yeah, cross the bridge," responded Joey in a normal, conversational tone.

Lizzie risked a glance in the rear view mirror. Milos's eyes were darting around and he was leaning forward in his seat. "Where are you taking me?"

Joey shoved him back. "That depends on your answers. First I gotta find out what kinda human bein' you are. You got in your possession proof Lizzie Grant didn't do that murder." Milos tried to sit up but Joey shoved him back down and continued talking. "You'd let an innocent person be executed because of some bullshit client relationship malarkey. Right?"

Milos was silent.

Joey pushed his left hand into Milos's chest while the gun in his right hand was pointed close to Milos' face. "Am I right?"

"What does it matter? She's wanted for another murder anyway."

"I ain't discussin' that. What I'm doin' is comin' to the conclusion you're the type of worm who'd let somebody be executed when you got the evidence to clear them."

"I have professional responsibilities." Milos's voice was edged with pride.

"Professional? You're a paid Peepin' Tom, for Christ sake." Joey looked at Milos and shook his head. "Shit, you don't deserve to live and I don't got time for this." He pressed the barrel of his small gun to Milos' forehead and pulled the trigger.

"No," screamed Milos.

He yelled so loud Lizzie almost lost control of the Buick. She swerved into the adjacent lane just missing a car which blew its horn as it braked to avoid her.

"Whoops," said Joey, "I forgot the safety." He clicked the safety mechanism. "Now it'll work. What's that smell? Damn Milos, I think you done somethin' in your pants."

"You're crazy. You can't do this in the middle of a city in broad daylight."

"I'm just tryin' to convince you to do what's ethical, Milos. Don't get confused. You're the bad guy here. You're the one withholding evidence that would clear an innocent person of murder."

"Should I go out Pondella Road?" asked Lizzie.

"Yeah, that's a nice ride. Oh, hey, mentionin' nice ride, Milos, earlier we drove by your house on Olmeda Way. 1590: nice old house. But it's frame. Man, all that wood, a little fire the whole place would be gone in seconds. Could be fatal if the fire starts in the middle of the night when you're asleep."

"Don't threaten me," whimpered Milos.

"Me, threaten? Never. I either do something or I don't do it. I don't threaten. How's your wife?"

"What? What about my wife?"

"I read in an old News-Press online that she was crippled in an accident a couple years ago. She'd have trouble getting' outa a house on fire."

"You son of a bitch," Milos growled.

"Not me, Milos. I'm not the one thoughtlessly havin' a crippled person live in an old firetrap of a house. I'm just thinkin' what could happen, sorta like an insurance company…"

Milos was crying. "You goddamn son of a bitch."

"Take Old 41 back to town," Joey told Lizzie. "I'm almost finished." He turned back to Milos. "Does your pretty young daughter wait for the school bus at the end of your street?"

Milos was shaking. He didn't answer.

"It worries me, them kids standing by the road early in the mornin' when people are half awake. An out-of-control car could plow into them."

Milos sobbed loudly.

"Hey, all I want is a copy of some photos. Do I get 'em?" Joey spoke in his most reasonable tone of voice.

"Yes, you goddamn son of a bitch."

"Good, we're only a few minutes from your office." Joey called up to Lizzie, "Take the second right after we get off the bridge. Then the alley'll be about four blocks down."

"I don't have copies now," murmured Milos.

"You got 'em on a computer, don't you?"

"Yeah."

"Copy 'em onto this disc."

Joey pulled a computer CD disc from the pocket behind the Buick's passenger seat and tossed it to Milos.

"Pick them guns off the seat and watch him for a minute," Joey told Lizzie as he opened the rear door and jumped from the Buick.

Lizzie picked up the guns, holding one in each hand. She twisted halfway around so she was facing Milos in the back seat. "Don't move," she said, trying to keep her voice from shaking.

"You look familiar," Milos said.

"People think I look like Cher used to look when she had that TV show."

"No, I've seen you somewhere."

Joey ran back out from behind the building and up to the car. He was out of breath. "Somebody already turned the electricity back on."

"Probably my secretary," said Milos.

"Anybody else in there?" asked Joey.

"Not unless she called the police to report me missing."

"We gotta chance it," said Joey. He looked up and down the alley; nobody in sight. "Okay, me and Milos will go in first. Follow us. Bring the guns. Don't want nobody to see 'em lyin' on the seat. Leave the car running.'

A gun in his right hand as his left gripped Milos' elbow, Joey urged Milos out of the Buick, ordered him to open his office door, and then shoved him through it.

Lizzie, holding an automatic in each hand, followed. She felt like Bonnie Parker. Just inside the office door was a flight of stairs and a small elevator. Joey and Milos were halfway up the stairs. They disappeared through a doorway at the top.

Lizzie followed, finding herself in a small reception area just beyond that door. The black girl behind the reception desk scolded Milos, "Where have you been? I had to turn the electricity back on myself. Must be kids playing pranks again. I don't like going down there, could be snakes in those bushes. Your three-o-clock is here."

Lizzie hid the two guns behind her back.

Joey smiled at the secretary and nodded toward Milos. "He'll only be a minute." Joey's right hand was stuck in his bulging right front pants pocket. His left hand still held Milos' arm.

"Where's the computer?" Joey asked Milos.

"In my office." Milos's voice was subdued, shaky. He made a button pressing hand gesture toward the receptionist.

"Lizzie," shouted a man sitting in the reception area reading a People magazine. It was Harry. He dropped the magazine and stood up.

Lizzie's hands sprang out from behind her back. She pointed both guns in the general direction of her husband. "Harry, what a surprise."

Harry walked toward Lizzie but Milos and Joey were in between blocking the way.

"Oh, the husband," Joey exclaimed. He released Milos' arm and shook Harry's hand. "Lizzie tells me you're a great success."

"I've done okay," responded Harry, giving Joey a who-the-hell-are-you look.

"Sorry I can't stay to chat," exclaimed Joey, releasing Harry's hand and grabbing Milos again. "We got business." He pushed the private eye toward the office door marked: "Milos Anila, Private."

"Keep 'em covered," Joey told Lizzie.

Harry looked stunned. He watched as Joey led Milos into the private office slamming the door behind them. Then Harry turned back to Lizzie and took a step in her direction.

Lizzie brought both guns up pointed directly at Harry's face. "Don't tempt me. Considering all the charges already against me, shooting you would be easier, cheaper, and have far fewer consequences than divorcing you."

The receptionist, who wore a conservative pants suit but sported dreadlocks, had stood and was backing away from her desk. Her shaking hands were raised high above her head.

Lizzie glanced at her.

"No problem here," blurted the young woman, whose slender body was visibly trembling.

"Lizzie, have you gone completely out of your mind?" asked Harry, his eyes wide.

Lizzie turned her gaze back toward her husband. "I'm ticked off at you, Harry. If you'd told the police right away about those time stamped photos, that policeman would still be alive and I wouldn't be in this mess."

"I don't understand what you're doing here." Harry gestured toward Milos' office. "Who is that old man?"

Lizzie glanced toward the closed door, "My godfather."

"Your godfather?" Harry took a step toward Lizzie. "What are you talking about? You're not Italian."

Lizzie raised one automatic so it was pointed directly at her husband's face. "Neither was Meyer Lansky."

"I'm all confused," grumbled Harry, scratching his thinning hair and backing away.

"Hey," exclaimed the receptionist, "I just realized; you're Elizabeth Shuttleford Grant, the woman on the front page of the News-Press. You don't look at all like your picture."

"Yes," said Harry, "you've done something with your hair."

Lizzie reached up and touched the black wig. "I'm surprised you noticed."

The receptionist cautiously lowered her hands. "Would you mind if I asked you something?"

"What?" responded Lizzie, pointing a gun back at the receptionist.

The receptionist quickly raised her hands in front of her, at shoulder height. "Could I get your autograph?"

Lizzie cocked an eyebrow. "My autograph?"

"Yes, I collect autographs and the autograph of a murderess gotten while she is on the run would be priceless." The secretary continued eagerly, "It would be the best one in my collection."

Lizzie looked bemused. "I've never signed an autograph before. You're the first person to ever ask me."

"You also never killed anybody before," interjected Harry.

"Shut up." Lizzie waved the gun pointed at Harry toward the battered chairs on the far side of the small room. "Go sit over there."

Lizzie watched as Harry obediently went and sat, and then she turned her attention back to the receptionist. "What do you want me to sign?"

"The front page of my newspaper, next to your picture. It's there on my desk." The woman stepped back toward her standard wooden, deceptively ornate reception desk.

"Hold it," ordered Lizzie. "Is there an alarm button on that desk?"

"Sure," responded the receptionist, "but if I were going to press it I would have pressed it when you first came in, when Frogface, I mean Mr. Milos, was signaling me to push it."

"But you didn't?" asked Lizzie, keeping the guns aimed at Harry and the woman, but looking down at her front page picture.

"Hell no. Listen sister, I know how that works. I press the alarm and the Fort Myers Police and the Lee County Sheriffs and the Highway Patrol and the Florida Division of Law Enforcement all come charging in shooting at you. Meanwhile, you and that old man are shooting away at them. The only person actually hit by all those bullets is the innocent bystanders. And, by my count, I'm the only innocent bystander in this room. Me press an alarm? No way, Jose. My mother didn't raise a dumb ass." The secretary paused giving Lizzie an appraising look. "You going to give me that autograph?"

"Sure." Lizzie sat one of her guns on the desk and picked up a blue pen lying there. "Who do I make it out to?"

"Nadira Johnson. That's N-A-D-I-R-A. It's African for 'rare.' When my momma named me she didn't know she was going to have six more kids." The girl smiled shyly.

"What do you want me to say?"

A serious look came onto Nadira's face. "Wish me luck in my career in law enforcement."

"What?" Lizzie dropped the pen and grabbed the gun from the desk.

Nadira shook her head and raised her hands slightly. "I'm studying forensics at night. I want to join a CSI unit. It looks interesting on TV."

Lizzie sat the gun back down, close by, on the opposite side of the table from Nadira. She picked the pen back up and wrote, "Dear Nadira: Sorry we couldn't meet under better circumstances. Good luck in your law enforcement career. Your friend, Lizzie Grant. PS: I'm innocent."

"Could you date it?" Nadira asked.

"Sure." As Lizzie dated it, she commented, "For someone interested in law enforcement, you don't seem to be working very hard to catch me."

Nadira emitted a less-than-ladylike snort. "Nobody's paying me to catch you."

Joey emerged from Milos's office. There was no sign of Milos. Joey held up the CD for Lizzie to see. Its plastic cover was smeared with a dark red stain. Joey smiled and winked. "Got the photos. How's it been out here?"

"Fine," said Lizzie. "I was just giving Nadira my autograph."

"Really?" Joey looked surprised. His thick eyebrows rose. Then he chuckled and gestured toward Harry. "How's everything with the big man?"

"He's unusually quiet."

"I'm stunned by the changes in you, Lizzie." Harry started to stand but sat back down when Lizzie picked up the second gun off the desk and pointed it at him. "You have more spirit. If you could get clear of these charges and if we could get back together again you'd be invited everywhere, just like Patty Hearst. You'd be in demand at all the most prestigious social events."

Lizzie allowed herself a slight smile. "Your approval comes a little late."

"But, Lizzie, I still have hopes for us," Harry pleaded. "I'm looking for a house in Naples and, if you ever get out of this mess you've gotten yourself into, I'd still consider taking you back."

"That's nice of you, Harry. So I guess I won't shoot you today." Lizzie turned toward the stairs.

"Goodbye, it was nice meeting you," Nadira called after her.

"You too, Nadira." Lizzie, smiling, waved goodbye with one of her automatics.

"Sorry, I didn't get a chance to give you my autograph." Joey winked at Nadira as he strode through the door.

Joey pushed past Lizzie on the stairs. "Let me go first."

A Fort Myers city policeman was leaning down looking into their idling Buick as Joey and Lizzie emerged from Milos' office building.

"Can I help you, officer?" Joey asked, his left hand stuck in his bulging pants pocket.

"You can't park here," stated the policeman.

Lizzie, holding the two guns behind her, backed on wobbly legs to the planter on the far side of the door. She dropped the two automatics into it. They made a clunking noise.

The policeman didn't seem to notice.

"We just stopped in for a moment to pick up something." Joey held up the CD in his right hand. "We're leaving immediately, right now in fact."

The policeman scratched his belly and gave Joey an evaluating, tough cop look.

Joey bent slightly, making himself look older and feebler.

"Okay, old timer." The policeman smiled at Joey. "But don't do it again or I'll be forced to give you a ticket."

"Yes, officer, thank you, we're leaving right now." Joey spoke quickly. "Uh, get in, daughter, I'll drive."

Lizzie jumped in the passenger side as Joey got behind the wheel. She watched the policeman in the side mirror. The officer stared at the Buick as Joey and Lizzie drove off. Then he spat on the pavement, turned and walked away.

Nobody came out of Milos' office.

"Whew," exclaimed Joey.

"Daughter?" asked Lizzie.

"I hadda call you somethin'. Best I could think of on the spur of the moment."

Lizzie suddenly smiled. "This was fun. I'm beginning to understand why you enjoyed being a criminal."

Joey gave Lizzie a surprised look; raised eyebrows and a slight smile. "You got more to you than just looks; you got some spirit in there." He pointed toward her partially covered chest.

Lizzie glanced down at where Joey had pointed, at her brief outfit. "Whatever I've got what I need is some decent clothes and some underwear. I'm tired of looking like a hooker."

"We gotta be careful about the cops." Joey's voice was stern.

"The police won't be looking for murder suspects in the dress department at Saks."

Joey shrugged and turned the Buick south, toward the shopping malls. "I guess we got time for some shopping. Anyway, we can't do the next thing I got planned until later tonight."

"What are you planning?" Lizzie asked, smiling over at the old man.

"Just a little breaking and entering."

Lizzie's smile vanished.

CHAPTER TWENTY

B & E

"It's good his apartment's on the other side," whispered Joey. "Ain't nobody gonna see us from the road."

"It's not much of a road," observed Lizzie, looking down the moonlit dirt path winding between apartment buildings in the small complex near the southern end of Sanibel Island. "It's quiet back here."

"Not many people around in the summer." Joey motioned for Lizzie to follow him. "Here we go."

With Joey in the lead, the two black-outfitted figures crept from behind an island of cabbage palms and decorative, flowery bushes. They dashed across the gravel driveway into the shadows beneath the apartment building at 167 Ferry Road.

Only two cars were parked at the sixteen unit complex.

Joey and Lizzie edged through the shadows beside maintenance, exercise, and utility rooms beneath the building. They paused, looking around. All was silent. They dashed over to the rear stairwell and looked up - nothing.

"Gloves," Joey said, handing Lizzie a pair of vinyl health care worker gloves.

Lizzie looked down at the gloves in her hand. "Oh, for fingerprints," gasped Lizzie, fumbling on the gloves.

Crickets began chirping in bushes beside the building. At least one was beneath the building, just beyond the parked cars.

Joey led the way up the stairs. Lizzie followed, wishing she was invisible or somewhere else.

They both looked at the numbers on doors as they tiptoed along the open corridor lit by pale yellow lighting. First came 101 then 103.

"It'll be the end one," Joey said.

When they got to 107, Joey stopped in front of the door, listening.

"Sounds empty," he said.

"Are you sure Sergeant Malflic lived alone?" Lizzie asked.

"No, not certain," responded Joey. "But his was the only name linked to this apartment on the internet and he sure ain't gonna be home now."

Lizzy gasped down a hiccup. "I'm nervous."

"I hope my lock-picking skills ain't got too rusty. It's been a few years." Joey pulled a small cloth-wrapped set of tools from his pocket and began fiddling with the door lock.

"What if we don't find anything?" Lizzie was trembling as she looked around, expecting somebody to spring out of the shadows at any moment. She jumped at a slight scraping noise from the other end of the corridor.

"We sure as shit ain't gonna find nothin' if we don't try." Joey held one of his tools up to the dim light cast by a filthy forty watt bulb. "Hell, I don't expect to find no confession. But we might find something linking Malflic to Clete's murder or to the illegal immigrants. Anything that gives the police another lead so you're not the only suspect. Be optimistic."

Joey jiggled a tool in the tiny slot in the lock. Then he gave it a twist. A click sounded. "Ah, the master hasn't lost his touch."

"Open it. Open it," Lizzie hissed.

"Calm down."

Lizzie placed a cautioning hand on Joey's back. "Somebody could come from one of these apartments and catch us out here."

Joey glanced over his shoulder at her. "Relax, I got my gun."

"That makes it worse," hissed Lizzie.

Joey pushed the door open. Lizzie dashed around him and inside. Joey ambled in, calmly shut the door, and snapped on the light switch beside it.

"What are you doing?" Lizzie was trembling. "People will see the light."

Joey put his hands on Lizzie's shoulders. "Relax. We can't see nothin' in the dark. People'd be more suspicious watching flashlight beams moving around in here. Lights bein' on in an apartment is normal."

Joey turned away from Lizzie then quickly tottered around inspecting each room. "We're alone," he announced as he returned to Lizzie, who still stood trembling by the door.

"You take the bedroom and kitchen," directed Joey. "I'll take the living room and bathroom."

Lizzie felt completely terrified. "How will I know what to look for?"

Joey patted Lizzie's shoulder. "Anything that connects Malflic to Clete or to illegal immigrants or smuggling."

Lizzie found nothing suspicious in the kitchen. Sergeant Malflic had apparently lived primarily on frozen dinners, canned soup, and restaurant take-out.

Nothing unusual was around the sergeant's bed. Stains on his sheets did not appear to be blood. Lizzie lifted all four sides of the mattress one after the other then looked under the bed. She glanced behind pictures on the wall. All she found was dust.

Next she turned to a desk across from the bed. The portable telephone on the desktop displayed a long list of recent numbers when Lizzie pressed the caller ID button. She slipped the phone in her jeans pocket.

Lizzie was stunned by the item she found amid the mess in the cluttered top desk drawer. It was a digital video cassette. On the side of the cassette was written, in Lizzie's own handwriting, the words "loggerhead laying eggs, Bowman's" and the date when she had seen Clete off-loading the black people onto the beach.

It was the tape Lizzie had shot that night. She had left it at the Conservancy Office. She wondered how it had gotten from there to Malflic's apartment. She stuck the cassette into her left front jeans pocket and started toward the bedroom door but then paused. She realized she hadn't checked the closet.

On a high shelf in the closet was a metal box. In the box, Lizzie found a pile of envelopes. She opened the top envelope. It contained hundred dollar bills. The second enveloped contained a mixture of fifties and hundreds. She counted fifteen envelopes.

Lizzie rushed into the living room. "Look what I found," she exclaimed, handing Joey the metal box full of money.

Joey peeked into a couple of envelopes. "He's guilty of somethin'. This ain't the way an innocent cop does his banking." He handed the money box back.

"What did you find?" Lizzie asked eagerly.

"Nothin', except the guy didn't like to clean his bathroom." Joey glanced around. "We probably oughta be goin'."

Lizzie turned back toward the bedroom. "Shouldn't we straighten up?"

Joey grabbed her arm. "No. Our problem is the cops aren't suspicious enough of Sergeant Malflic. They see somebody's tossed his apartment they might wonder what somebody thought they'd find."

The sound of a television blasted through the wall from the adjacent apartment.

Lizzie jumped toward Joey then laughed nervously. "I found a couple of other things in addition to the money."

Joey held up a cautionary hand. "Show me later. I didn't realize how thin these walls are; cheap construction. If we can hear their television, they can hear us."

Joey snapped off the light switch by the door. The bedroom light was still on.

"I better turn that light off," said Lizzie.

Joey still held her arm. "That don't matter. Let's go."

They hurried out the door and started down the corridor.

"Aren't you going to lock the door?" asked Lizzie.

"No reason to," whispered Joey. "Hurry, my old sixth sense is acting up. I got a bad feelin'."

CHAPTER TWENTY ONE

Eat Dirt

Joey and Lizzie hurried down the apartment complex's concrete stairs. Joey held a hand out to stop Lizzie. "It's too quiet."

"We did it," exclaimed Lizzie, jumping up and down and patting Joey on the shoulder. "We got in. We got evidence to clear me. We got away. We did it."

Joey, serious, shook his head. "We ain't got away yet."

"I thought I was the Nervous Nelly." Lizzie prodded Joey playfully. "Now that we've done it, you're suddenly the nervous one."

"Somethin' ain't right," Joey whispered.

Joey crept forward looking around. He pulled the gun from his pocket. Lizzie followed close behind him, her hand still on his shoulder as they slipped into the darkness under the building.

A large shadow sprang from the blackness beside the utility room, knocked the gun from Joey's hand, and kicked Joey's feet out from under him. Joey fell backward knocking Lizzie over onto the rough gravel of the parking area.

"Oh, goddamn," screamed Joey.

"Hands up, both of you," ordered a man's voice. Lizzie lay on her back with Joey sprawled across her. All she could see were shadows above her.

"Get your hands higher, get off each other, roll over, face down," yelled the man, who seemed to be behind her.

A painful kick struck Lizzie's side.

"Shit," Joey screamed as he rolled off Lizzie. "Quit kicking, I'm old."

"Hands higher, face in the dirt," the man ordered.

Lizzie stretched her hands as high as they could reach.

"What we got here?" The man ripped the money box from Lizzie's hand.

"When I was younger you'da been dead," Joey growled.

"You find this money in Malflic's apartment?" asked the man standing over them.

Lizzie whimpered.

"Answer me." The man kicked Lizzie in the ribs again.

Lizzie screamed.

"You asshole," Joey yelled, starting to stand.

From the corner of her eye, Lizzie saw a reflection off a gun barrel as it was pressed against the back of Joey's head.

"Get back down, old man. A dead hero won't help her any."

"You fucking asshole," Joey growled. He still was halfway up.

"Yes," yelled Lizzie, "the money was from Malflic's apartment... Joey, relax, I'm okay."

"Listen to the lady, granddad."

Joey slumped back down into the gravel.

"You find anything else?" asked the man.

Both Joey and Lizzie were silent.

The man placed a foot onto the middle of Lizzie's back. A hand patted the empty back pockets of Lizzie's black Versace jeans. Then the hand was stuck under her and reached into a front pocket.

Lizzie started to cry.

The man pulled the video cassette from Lizzie's pocket.

"That's mine," sobbed Lizzie.

"Yeah, sure, you go around with no ID on you but with a video cassette in your pocket as you burgle an apartment."

"That's my handwriting on it."

"Unfortunately, I don't have time to do a comparison."

The man tossed the cassette over beside where he'd put the money box. His foot was still pressing down on Lizzie's spine.

He rammed a hand into her other front pocket and pulled out the phone.

"That's my cell phone," Lizzie sobbed.

"This isn't a cell. It's a portable home phone. You think I'm stupid or something?'

The phone was tossed over onto the money box.

A hand patted up and down Lizzie's legs then slid up her waist and onto her left breast.

"Nooo," sobbed Lizzie. "Please don't, please."

"Sorry, thought you might have something in a shirt pocket. Stay still while I check grandpa."

The foot left her back.

Lizzie heard Joey blow out a long breath then say, "All I got is some tools in my left front pocket and some car keys in my right."

"Then you don't have anything to worry about if you just lay still."

All Lizzie heard for several minutes was the two men breathing and her own crying.

A clinking metallic noise sounded in front of Joey.

"There are your keys," said the man's voice. "Don't bother looking for your gun."

The shadowy man bent over and picked up the money box, phone, and video cassette. Then he walked away behind Lizzie's feet, where she couldn't see him.

"You two lay still a few minutes. Don't look around." His footsteps crunched away on the gravel. Then they stopped. "Oh, and thanks for your cooperation." The man laughed. Gravel crunching faded down the dirt road. Everything was silent for a couple minutes then the crickets began chirping again.

"Damn," mumbled Joey, "that's why I thought I had a sixth sense; the crickets had stopped making noise."

"He also turned off the lights in the parking area," Lizzie gasped between sobs.

"I never even noticed. I am getting old."

Lizzie sat up. "I'm just glad to be alive. I thought we were dead for sure."

Joey also sat up, but unsteadily. "You shouldn't have worried, Lizzie girl. Don't you remember I said, 'nothin' bad happens to Joey C's friends?'"

Lizzie started laughing. "Sure Joey, my life's been perfect since I met you."

Joey grunted. "We better get up and go home. This ain't funny." After a moment of silence from Joey while Lizzie continued laughing, Joey started chuckling. "We can't stay here all night."

"Why not?" Lizzie was laughing so hard she started to hiccup. "You think we look suspicious sitting on the ground under an apartment building after midnight, wearing plastic gloves, and laughing hysterically?"

"Nope, that's normal for me. Oh my aching back. Lemme help you up." Joey tried to get to his feet but fell back onto the ground. "Humph, wind's been knocked outa me."

Lizzie jumped to her feet and then helped Joey up. She wondered how she could possibly sleep tonight and what in the world tomorrow would bring.

CHAPTER TWENTY TWO

Interlude

Later that night, after Joey had gone to bed, Lizzie crept from the house, unable to sleep. She paused on the steps making certain everything was quiet, and then dashed the rest of the way down the stairs, across the road, and through the bushes on the other side. A narrow trail led to the edge of the beach.

Lizzie's bare feet were tickled by the Australian pine nutlets which littered the ground. Her filmy black translucent nightgown swirled about her, caught by the Gulf breezes. She stopped at the edge of the beach. She dared not walk out onto the broad expanse of sand and shells. Anyone for miles would be able to see her. So she sat at the beach's edge to reduce her silhouette and watched the dark moonlit waters. Waves stirred up eerie spots of phosphorescent light just beneath the rippling surface.

Lizzie remembered times she and Aaron had walked the beach together. She remembered his smile and his gentle hands. She missed him. Was he thinking of her now? Would he even miss her? He had been so jealous and angry. And he seemed to believe she was a murderess. Months of loving had ended in suspicion, jealousy, and despair.

The rhythmic sound of the waves lapping the sand put Lizzie into a mild trance. She saw again the boat with the refugees, Clete surprising her in her apartment, his body on the bed with all the blood, the interrogation by the police; an unending nightmare. Then she was handcuffed to the palm tree and the policeman was going to kill her. She saw his body blown apart. Then she couldn't see anything.

Lizzie lay on the sand and cried...

Someone's arms were around her, under her shoulders and legs. She was being carried. Lizzie surged awake and tried to push against the man holding her.

"Hey, stop," yelled Joey.

Lizzie opened her eyes. Joey was carrying her up the narrow trail toward the house. He sat her on her feet.

"You must have been sleep walkin' or somethin'. I found you down by the beach out like a light." Joey held her steady, his hand on her back.

Lizzie shook her head awake. "I was restless."

"You looked like you'd been crying. Your eyes're all red."

Lizzie wiped at her eyes. "I was just remembering."

"Sometimes rememberin's dangerous."

Lizzie drew herself up, feeling a sharp pain in her side. She concealed the pain. "Don't worry, Joey. I'm solid inside; only the outside leaks. Your help is really great. I'm sure the next thing we try will work perfectly."

"Yeah, right, good girl." He patted her on the back.

Lizzie looked over into Joey's eyes. Her heart sank. He didn't look like he had a next thing.

CHAPTER TWENTY THREE

Bang, Bang

The next morning at breakfast, Lizzie, wearing a pants suit from Saks, sipped her steaming coffee and appraised Joey as he eagerly devoured her eggs and prosciutto. In addition to being old, Joey was wrinkled and worn looking. But Lizzie appreciated the strength hidden beneath those wrinkles.

The constant police patrols had ceased; authorities apparently concluding Lizzie escaped Sanibel. So Joey had turned on both the lights and the air conditioning.

Lizzie was still upset the man who accosted them last night had taken the evidence from Sergeant Malflic's apartment. It might have cleared her. She couldn't figure out who the man was. If he'd been with the police, he'd have arrested her. If he'd been one of the traffickers, he'd have killed her.

As Joey finished his meal, Lizzie spoke up, "Joey, I never got to tell you what I found; what that man took from me."

Joey licked his lips. "I figured you'd get around to it." He nodded toward her. "How's your side, where that bastard kicked you?"

Lizzie put her hand down gently against her lower ribs. "It hurts but I don't think anything's broken."

"You probably got bruised ribs," Joey said. "I've had that a few times. It'll get better."

Joey took a sip from his iced tea. He looked a little depressed.

"I wanted to thank you again," Lizzie spoke quickly. "You've saved my life and given me hope. I don't really understand why you're helping me. You're risking jail letting me hide here; why?"

Joey smiled and nodded toward his cleaned-off plate. "I get some great meals. If you could only do pasta like my momma, everything'd be perfect."

"Seriously," Lizzie said. "How can I repay you?"

"I don't need nothin'. I'm enjoyin' this." A serious look came over Joey's wrinkled face. "Before you showed up I was sitting here staring at the four walls bored silly. Back when I could show my kisser on the island, I was snubbed by all the stuck-up assholes because of my past. Then, when them subpoenas was issued, I hadda go into hiding and couldn't even go to the golf club to watch the eyes avert and the noses go up. Hell, you've brought companionship and entertainment. I'm havin' a ball."

Lizzie smiled.

Joey smiled back then looked serious again. "Okay, enough of the hearts, flowers, and violins. Back to business. What did you find last night?"

"Well, you already know about the money."

Joey nodded. "Yeah, that sure points to him doin' somethin' not in police academy trainin'."

"I also took his telephone." Lizzie sipped her coffee.

"His phone? why?"

"He had caller ID. We could have checked back over the calls he made and the people who called him."

"Good thinkin' girl." Joey reached over and patted Lizzie's hand.

"Thanks." Lizzie smiled shyly then shook her head. "It's a shame it didn't work. Those phone records might have led us to the smugglers."

Joey shrugged. "Every step we take can't be forward."

"It would be nice if every step I take wasn't off a cliff." Lizzie sniffed back a tear.

"Did you find anything else?" Joey quickly asked.

"Oh yes, I haven't mentioned the strangest thing." Lizzie wiped under her right eye with a napkin. "I found the video cartridge I shot that night on the beach, when Clete chased me with the gun." Lizzie stood and picked up the dirty dishes from the table.

Joey looked thoughtful for a moment, and then asked, "How'd the video get in that cop's apartment?"

"I don't know." Lizzie paused, a plate in each hand. "I last saw that cassette when I handed it in at the Conservancy."

"Maybe somebody there..."

"I didn't give it to just anybody. I handed it personally to Augie." Lizzie turned toward the kitchen.

"Who?"

Lizzie stopped at the kitchen doorway and looked back. "August Winters, the director of the Conservancy; I gave it to him personally."

"Maybe this Augie guy…"

"No, that's impossible. He treats me like a member of his family." Lizzie vanished into the kitchen.

When Lizzie returned to the living room, Joey was writing something on a manila envelope. He looked up at Lizzie. "Do you remember the name of the detective handlin' your case?"

"Hunter, uh, let me think – Brian Hunter, chief detective with the Sanibel Police. He didn't believe a word I said. What are you doing?" Lizzie looked down at the envelope. It had the Sanibel police department's address on it.

"I'm sending the cops copies of the pictures. I printed them out last night after we got home. Then I got to thinkin' while I was asleep and got up to make a second copy. That's when I found you missing and went out to look for you and found you sleep walking."

"Why did you make a second copy?

"To send to Finch. Your lawyer should have a copy."

Lizzie put a hand on Joey's shoulder. "Can I see them?"

"Sure." Joey opened the envelope, which had not yet been sealed, and took out the pictures. "Here."

Lizzie sat down on the sofa and looked through the pictures, examining each time stamp and noticing only seconds passed between her going into her apartment and coming back out. "Hey, you're sending everybody a picture with me naked."

Joey shrugged. "Of course. Do you want to be considered modest or do you want to be considered innocent. It's one or the other."

Lizzie sighed deeply, blushed, and handed the pictures back to Joey. "Innocent."

"Good girl." Joey looked at the naked picture and wiggled his bushy eyebrows Groucho Marx style. Then he stuffed the pictures back in the envelope and sealed it. He picked up a second envelope and sealed that one. "Okay, I'm off." Joey stood up.

"Where are you going?" Lizzie stood also.

Joey turned toward the door. "Into Fort Myers to mail these. We don't want them to have a Sanibel postmark."

Lizzie followed Joey. "Can I come?"

Joey held up a hand. "No, the less you're seen the better, even with your new hair style, which, by the way, I like."

Lizzie fingered a light copper golden strand of hair out from in front of her eyes and smiled. "Thanks."

Joey smiled. "Okay, hang in there. I shouldn't be too long."

A concerned look crossed Lizzie's features. "What'll I do if somebody comes around?"

Joey turned back toward her, his hand on the doorknob. "Stay in the house, be quiet, and, most important, don't shoot them. You already done enough of that."

Lizzie sniffled. She looked like she might cry. Joey hurried out the door.

Lizzie decided to research Haitians and the smuggling of illegal immigrants while Joey was away. Joey hadn't authorized her to use his computer but he also hadn't said she couldn't. She entered his bedroom with some hesitation.

The Uzi machine gun leaned against the headboard of Joey's bed. The desk with the HP computer was on the opposite side of the room. The computer was already on and Lizzie had no trouble accessing the Internet. Apparently Joey didn't use security codes.

Lizzie was soon lost in her research; discovering that Haiti, which occupies the western part of the island of Hispaniola, is the poorest country in the Western Hemisphere: half the population is illiterate, 80 percent live in poverty, and 66 percent work in agriculture. The recent earthquake made things worse.

Lizzie was reading a 2002 news article about 200 Haitian illegal aliens jumping off a freighter in Biscayne Bay and wading ashore on Miami's Rickenbacker Causeway when her concentration was interrupted by somebody pounding on the front door.

BANG, BANG, BANG

Lizzie jumped up, her heart thumping.

BANG, BANG. Somebody pounded again.

Lizzie looked over at the machine gun beside the unmade bed.

No, not a good idea. I don't even know how to work it.

She crept into the living room.

"Joey, you home?" The voice came from beyond the front door, from just beyond the front door. Somebody was at the door.

Lizzie tiptoed on her bare feet over to the door.

BANG, BANG.

She almost fell backwards at the loudness of the pounding immediately in front of her. Lizzie took a deep breath and moved up to peek through the security view thing.

A blond-haired man stood at the door. He seemed impatient: glancing around quickly. He looked, large, muscular, and tough, in a handsome sort of way.

"I'm sorry I missed you. I'm only passing through today," the man yelled. "I'll be back in a week. I hope you'll be home then. Maybe somebody will tell you Val dropped by." The man turned and stepped away from the door giving Lizzie a wider view through the fisheye lens. She watched his retreating rear end as the man disappeared down the stairs.

My God my heart's going to pound out of my chest. I didn't expect anybody, particularly not anybody so sudden and so noisy. It was like he was talking to himself. But when he said he must have missed Joey he kept talking like he knew somebody was listening, like he knew I was listening. My God, I'm babbling to myself inside my head. Could he have known I was here? No… Or maybe… Oh my God, maybe he knew I was here. How would he know that? How? And he said he'd be back. And who was he? For God's sake, who was he?

Lizzie's was still distraught when Joey returned. She met him at the door. "Somebody was here. Somebody knocked on the door." Lizzie was trembling.

"Calm down." Joey placed his hands on her shoulders. "Did they see you?"

"No"

"Did you shoot them?"

"No."

"Good. Let me come in and sit down. I'm tired." Joey moved Lizzie aside and went to the blue overstuffed chair. He sat and let out a long sigh. "The pictures are mailed. You know walking in loose sand is like walking three or four times further than walking on solid pavement."

"Don't you want to know about the man who was here?" Lizzie stood directly in front of Joey.

He looked up at her and smiled, "Sure, now that I'm sitting."

"He was very blond and… and very masculine… and he knew you."

Joey's brow furrowed, increasing the number of his wrinkles. "How do you know all this?"

Lizzie blushed. "I peeped at him through the thing in the door."

Joey chuckled. "And he had a sign on him sayin' 'I know Joey.'"

Lizzie shook her head in exasperation. "No, of course not. He called out something like 'Joey, are you there?'"

Joey shrugged. "Doesn't mean he knows me; might just know a Joey owns this house."

"He said his name was Val."

Joey, who had been leaning back looking exhausted, sat forward suddenly and smiled. "Val, really? Val was here? Now that's interesting. Yes, that's very interesting."

"Who is Val?"

Joey was silent a moment looking up at Lizzie. His eyes lit up. "So you thought Val was good looking?"

Lizzie tilted her head slightly. "He was okay. Who is he?"

"Somebody who could be very helpful. But he also could be very dangerous. I'm gonna hafta think about this." Joey waved Lizzie away. "Ask me who he is later."

Lizzie stood her ground. "Why not now?"

"Cause I gotta think." Joey shook his head. "There'd be some risks. Did he say where he's stayin'?"

"No, but he said he'd be back in a week."

"A week? That oughta be enough time for me to think."

"A week?" Lizzie's voice rose. "While I'm sitting scared to death the police will show up any minute. A whole week? Can't you think faster? What'll I do while you're thinking?"

Joey gestured toward the kitchen. "Learn to cook pasta. My mother's recipes are around here somewhere."

Lizzie glared at Joey as she placed her hands firmly on her hips. "Learn to cook," she exclaimed. "Did you say I need to learn to cook? Well, mister gangster-Mafia-big-shot-women-stay-in-the-kitchen-full-of-yourself-son-of-a-bitch, the hell with that. I'm going into your bedroom…"

Joey raised his eyebrows.

Lizzie stamped her foot. "Get your mind out of the gutter. I'm going into your bedroom to use your computer to do research to clear my name and if you don't like me using your computer then I don't give a damn."

Lizzie turned away from Joey and stomped off into his bedroom.

Joey sat in his blue overstuffed chair staring after her. He shrugged an exaggerated shrug. "Whatsa matter with you?" he called. "Did I say somethin' wrong?"

His bedroom door slammed shut.

About an hour later, Lizzie looked up from Joey's computer when she heard a light tap on the bedroom door. She had been examining a picture of a smuggling boat seized by the Drug Enforcement Administration. The boat looked exactly like the one that dropped the Haitians off onto Bowman's Beach. But the boat she was looking at had been seized prior to the Bowman's Beach incident.

"Yes, what is it?" Lizzie was annoyed by the interruption. She felt she was making progress, not much progress but some.

"Can I get a book from beside my bed?" Joey's tone was unusually mild for him.

"Come in."

Joey opened the door, went over to a small table beside his bed, and picked up a paperback. He turned to Lizzie. "I'm sorry I upset you. I can handle men; they learn who's boss. But women… women… well."

"That's okay," Lizzie responded. "I've been a little tense lately."

"Why would you be tense?"

Lizzie jumped up and shouted, "Why would I be tense? My life's fallen apart. My God, why would I be tense?" Lizzie paused. She noticed a smile tugging at the edges of Joey's lips. Lizzie shook her head and laughed. "You're trying to rattle me."

"Rattlin' you ain't hard. Listen, babe, you're welcome to use my computer any time and good luck. I'll be in the bathtub reading. Take your time."

Joey sauntered out.

CHAPTER TWENTY FOUR

Snake

"I'm going cross-eyed looking at your computer screen." Lizzie stood before Joey in the living room. "What is the plan, Joey? What do we do next?"

Joey eyed her. "Sometimes it's best just to wait."

Lizzie sighed. "You don't have a plan."

Joey gestured toward the sofa. "Sit down."

Lizzie sat.

"Listen, girl, we got copies of them pictures from that private eye jerk and we sent 'em off to the cops." Joey leaned back, shrugged, and spread out his arms. "Now all we gotta do is wait and see what effect the pictures have on the police."

Lizzie shook her head. "They'll probably pass the one of me naked around to every policeman on Earth."

"I don't give a shit about that."

Lizzie leaned forward suddenly raising her voice. "Of course you don't, the picture isn't of you."

Joey chuckled. "They wouldn't pass one of me around."

Lizzie glared at Joey.

"Our concern..." Joey paused. "Our only concern is whether the pictures convince the cops you couldn'ta had time to kill that Clete guy."

Lizzie drew in a deep breath. "How will we know?"

"We give it about a week then have Finch call and discuss the photos with them."

"And then what?"

Joey shrugged. "That depends on their reaction."

Lizzie suddenly stood up. "But do you have a plan? Do you have something in mind?"

Joey gave Lizzie an appraising look. "Even if we can't convince them, over time the cops will forget all about you. I wouldn't mind if you just stayed here. You could be like my daughter. Look after me. Then, when I die of old age, you'd inherit my house and a shitload of money. Before all that, we'd get you a new identity. Hell girl, you'd be a rich, new person. You'd own the world."

Lizzie shook her head. "No, Joey, I'm sorry, I want to be me. I want to be cleared. I don't want to spend my life worried who might see me or who's at the door."

Joey nodded sadly. "I understand."

Lizzie placed a hand on his arm. "I'm sorry, Joey, I really appreciate the offer."

When Joey was out, Lizzie snuck looks at the cookbooks and hand-written recipes she found in a kitchen cabinet. She did not want to give Joey the satisfaction of catching her studying anything to do with cooking. The handwriting on the recipes was small and precise. Most was written in what looked like Italian. Fortunately, someone had written an English translation in larger script beside the Italian words.

"Hey, where'd you learn to cook lasagna like this?" Joey asked one night at dinner.

"It's an old family recipe." Lizzie responded.

"Whose family?"

Lizzie smiled and sipped her wine.

"How about our walk?" Joey asked one evening later that week. Over the previous few days he and Lizzie had walked old trails through the woods behind Bowman's Beach each afternoon or evening. They almost never saw other people. Only lovers seeking concealment left the open beach to explore the mazes of trails and vegetation. On one memorable occasion they came across a pair of copulating lovers in a thicket of small trees and bushes. But it seemed unlikely that frantically dressing, red faced couple would report seeing the Mafia don and the fugitive.

"Give me a minute." Lizzie was gluing her junonia onto matting. She adhered the decorative shell artistically off center inside a shellacked wood frame. Her original plan of making her lucky junonia into a necklace turned out to be unworkable.

Joey glanced at her creation.

"What do you think?" asked Lizzie.

"It's a nice shell, I guess. How about that walk?"

Lizzie smiled. "Sure."

They walked in silence for several moments. The drilling noises of a pileated woodpecker echoed through the woods almost drowning out the distant sound of surf.

"Isn't it about time we called Finch?" asked Lizzie, who wore short shorts and a plain t-shirt.

Joey stopped and looked around at Lizzie. "Tomorrow."

"Good, I'm going stir crazy."

You don't know nothin' 'bout stir crazy. You ain't been here near as long as me. Hell, you ain't even been in a real stir." Joey wore striped Bermuda shorts and a t-shirt which read, "Insured by the Mafia."

Lizzie resumed walking. "How can you stand not doing anything?"

Joey walked beside Lizzie on the narrow trail. "I've been doin' somethin'. I been eating your cookin'. My compliments to the chef."

Lizzie skirted around a fallen tree. She stopped suddenly at a rattling sound immediately in front of her. A snake rose up, its head drifting from side to side, its eyes fixed on Lizzie.

"Don't move," Joey whispered. "It's a rattler. I'll get somethin' to bash him."

"No don't." Lizzie slowly and carefully backed up, moving out of striking distance. "He has as much right to be here as we do." When she had gotten far enough away, she turned and walked quickly down another trail. "We'll just go around him."

Joey mumbled as he followed her. "He don't got no right to be here. Ain't supposed to be no rattlers on Sanibel. Besides, my motto's always been to wipe out any snake I come across."

Lizzie raised an eyebrow. "In New York City?"

Joey gestured around him. "Anywhere. In New York we had a lotta the two legged kind."

"Sometimes it's easier just to go around them."

Joey stopped suddenly. "That's not the way we done it in the old days."

Lizzie stopped also, turned to Joey, and smiled. "These aren't the old days."

"Yeah we've gone downhill." Joey shook his large head, looking sad.

Lizzie frowned. "Now instead of taking action, you spend a week thinking about it."

Joey looked hurt. He walked over to a log, started to sit down, paused, looked under and around the mottled wood, then sat down. "I'm old; I've learned caution."

Lizzie sat beside Joey. "And I guess you think I'm becoming less cautious because I want action. What about that guy Val? Have you finished thinking about him?"

"Yeah."

"And?"

"He could be useful. He knows somethin' about the law."

"Oh no, another gangster."

"Not exactly."

Lizzie stared at Joey. "What is he, exactly?"

Joey returned her gaze. He smiled. "I think Val is lonely. His wife died in a freak accident."

"Okay, I'm gonna call Finch." Joey dialed the cell phone he had pulled from his pocket after driving into south Fort Myers. Joey put up one finger then a second. Lizzie guessed he was counting rings.

Suddenly, Joey spoke, "Hey, Birdie, how's it hangin'?" Joey paused listening and then chuckled. "Great, hey listen, I got our friend here with me."

Joey looked over at Lizzie. "Yeah, the bikini babe. We was wonderin' what the cops' reaction to them pictures was."

Joey was silent a moment.

"Uh huh, yeah." Joey chuckled, "Aside from that." Nodding and smiling, Joey looked Lizzie up and down. "I imagine they did. She's quite a looker with or without."

Lizzie blushed.

Joey became serious. "But what about the time stamps? What did that defective say about them?"

Lizzie leaned toward Joey, trying to hear what was being said on the other end. She couldn't hear anything.

Joey drummed his fingers on the steering wheel "That's a shame. Didja try talking to him; make him see she couldn't do it?"

Joey bobbed around his large head, as though following tedious words on the other end of the phone connection.

"Yeah, well that's why we called 'em bulls in the old days, bull-headed assholes."

Joey looked over at Lizzie and shook his head negatively. He listened a little bit longer. "Yeah, well, keep at it, Birdie, our little lady's countin' on you.

And man you should taste her lasagna." Joey licked his lips. "Yeah, there are some blessings. Call you in a few days."

Joey clicked off the phone and turned to Lizzie. "You're still their candidate for murderess of the month."

CHAPTER TWENTY FIVE

Val

They had just finished eating a salmon dinner with Boursin cheese and white sauce when a knock sounded at Joey's front door. Both Lizzie and Joey froze.

"What's that?" asked Lizzie.

"Shhh," hissed Joey, "turn out the lights in here. Maybe they didn't see 'em. I'll get the others."

The knock sounded again as the two crept about turning off lights.

"Hey, Joey, I know you're in there. It's Val," shouted the man outside the front door.

Joey grabbed Lizzie's arm in the dark. She didn't know how he figured out where she was. "I'm gonna let him in. Go back to your bedroom. Don't come out unless I call you."

Joey turned a nearby floor lamp back on.

Lizzie was trembling. Joey patted her on the shoulder and said, "Don't worry, I told you before; Val's okay." Joey hesitated and then shrugged, "for a cop, that is."

"He's a cop?" Lizzie almost exploded.

Joey put a finger to Lizzie's lips. "Shhh, don't worry about it." Then he shouted toward the door, "Hold on a minute, Val. I'll be right there."

Lizzie turned toward the bedroom. Joey drew back his hand to give her an affectionate pat on the rump but then checked his arm in mid-swing as he remembered he was an old man and she was young enough to be his granddaughter.

Lizzie heard Joey greet Val and let him in.

"You sly old dog," exclaimed Val, "everybody looking for you and you're in your own house. Who else but Loupy Joey?"

"Hey, nobody calls me that no more. Have a seat, Val. You want something to drink?"

"You got Pepsi?"

"Sure, but don't you want no beer or wine?"

"No, thanks."

"You on duty?"

"Yeah, sorry Joey, this isn't really a social call."

"Should I worry?"

"Oh, no… No Joey, I'm only looking for information."

Lizzie heard the door to the kitchen open and close. She eased open her bedroom door and peeked through. Sitting on the long sofa in the living room was a darkly tanned, well-built, blond-haired man in his mid-thirties. He had broad shoulders and a rugged, finely chiseled profile. He looked to Lizzie like the Nordic version of a Greek god. A week ago, seeing him through the fisheye viewer in Joey's front door her view had been distorted. Now she saw him clearly and he was as handsome as a male model on a romance novel cover.

Lizzie hadn't realized she was staring until Joey returned and walked past Val, blocking her view for a second. Lizzie gasped and pulled her door shut.

"What was that?" asked Val.

"House settling," mumbled Joey. "Here's your Pepsi."

"Your house is certainly isolated."

"It's not isolated enough recently."

"Yeah, you've had some excitement. Thank you for the call about that boat."

"Hey, anything for an old friend."

"Did you know the captain was killed a few days later?"

"I heard somethin' about it."

"And the cop who intercepted the Haitians was killed a couple days after that."

"Yeah, I know. We were up to our kneecaps in cops 'round here."

"Make you a little nervous?"

"A little."

They both were silent for a moment. Lizzie heard ice clinking. She opened the bedroom door a tiny crack. The blond man, Val, was setting down his drink and turning away from her, toward Joey. He had a deep voice.

"I was wondering, Joey, if you might know anything more about the two murders."

"That depends." Joey spoke slowly.

"Depends on what?" asked Val.

"Depends on my understandin' your interest. Why would the fed's Immigration and Customs Enforcement service be interested in local murders, supposedly done by a crazed, bikini-clad, sexual mutilator?"

Lizzie was not pleased at Joey's description of her.

Val's voice became subdued, serious. "I need your assurance what I say won't get beyond this room."

"Ain't I known as 'Silent Joey'?"

"Not that I ever heard… 'Loupy Joey' Maybe 'Crazy Joey' but 'Silent' – I don't think so."

There was a long pause during which Lizzie heard her heart beating like a kettle drum. She was amazed the two men in the other room couldn't hear the thumps.

Val cleared his throat before speaking again. "Okay, Joey, here it is. Clete Grimes, the man who was murdered, was an I.C.E. undercover agent and that cop, Sergeant Malflic, was the primary suspect Clete was investigating. We're completely stymied. We have no idea why this Elizabeth Grant person would murder either of them. We never heard of her before the murders. We don't know how she fits into the smuggling ring or why she would kill either man. Then, if that's not confusing enough, I get a report you're burgling the dead police sergeant's apartment. Breaking and entering's a little beneath you, isn't it Joey?"

"A guy likes to stay busy. But you're not here to talk about me… At least I hope not." Joey shifted slightly in his seat and cleared his throat. "So down to brass tacks; what did your investigation actually find?"

"A big fat zero; our investigation fell apart when Clete was murdered. He was a good man. His loss sent us back to square one. But, God damn it to hell, it's not in my nature to give up. All this stuff; the smuggling, the murders, your B&E, must somehow fit together. I need to find the common thread. I need information and I need it quick before more people die."

"So you want to arrest Lizzie Grant?"

"Not necessarily… Her arrest is what the local authorities want. My primary interest is reviving an investigation that's gone seriously south, an investigation into a group that not only smuggles illegal aliens but, we suspect, works them to death. We were about to blow the smuggling ring wide open. We'd finally gotten a man on the inside. Then up pops this woman we never heard of, our guy is dead, our suspect is dead, and she vanishes. What's her name again?"

"Lizzie Grant."

Val chuckled and shook his head. "I called her Elizabeth but you called her Lizzie." He raised an eyebrow and looked speculatively at the old man. "So, Joey, maybe you know her; maybe you even know her whereabouts."

Joey leaned forward toward Val. "If she knows somethin' to help you stop this smuggling ring, would you protect her as a witness like you done for me a couple times?"

Val took a sip of Pepsi and looked thoughtful. "That would be sticking my nose out."

"If I can prove she didn't kill your man Clete, will you protect her?"

Val shrugged. "If she knows anything that would be of help and if she's not guilty of those murders, I might be able to protect her. But I can't do anything for her until I find her. She's disappeared without a trace."

"What if the cop killed your guy, Clete, and she killed the cop in self defense when he was trying to kill her?"

"That's not what the locals are saying. That's pretty far fetched, Joey."

Joey raised his voice slightly. "You already knew the cop was bad. You were investigating him."

Val spoke slowly. "Well, maybe…"

"If I give you my word? If I promise to work with you on this?"

Val nodded. "Okay, I may regret this but okay. Any help finding her would be appreciated. So, Joey, down to the nitty gritty, do you know where we can look for this Elizabeth Grant?"

Joey chuckled and gestured toward Lizzie, who slammed her door shut. "Sure, look for her in my back bedroom."

"That's what I figured."

Lizzie could hear Val even through the closed door.

"You knew all along she was here?"

"Sure, who else would have helped you break into Mulhaney's apartment?"

"Damn." Joey's voice rose. "Hey, Lizzie, you might as well come on out."

After Joey called a second time and Lizzie still didn't appear, he walked back to her bedroom and opened the door.

Lizzie stood in the middle of the room crying. "You turned me in. You betrayed me."

Joey shook his head. "No I didn't. I'm helping you. We need Val's help on this. He knows a lot about illegal aliens."

"I'm scared," Lizzie exclaimed as she threw herself into Joey's arms.

"Oh, so that's how it is," said Val, who had followed Joey down the hallway.

"No, it ain't," said Joey. "She's scared; give her a minute."

Without added comment, Val returned to the living room. Joey took hold of Lizzie's trembling shoulders and held her out away from him. "Compose yourself. I'll be waiting for you with Val. That man could hold the rest of your life in his hands."

A trembling Lizzie smiled as she walked into the living room. Val stood. She approached him slowly. Lizzie had changed into her bright yellow, very short babydoll dress.

Her eyes shyly not quite meeting his, Lizzie shook Val's hand. "I'm Lizzie Grant, pleased to meet you. I believe you've been given some misleading information about me." Lizzie noticed Val stood very erect, like a soldier. She looked down and saw his hand still held hers firmly, very firmly. She felt suddenly numb. Her toes curled. She pulled her hand from his grasp.

Val gave her a thin smile. "Pleased to meet you, Lizzie, I'm Val Knutsen."

Lizzie paused, not sure what to say next. She looked up along his muscular body, the chiseled features of his face, to the curly mess on top his head. "You're a blond like me."

Val eyed Lizzie. "Your hair isn't blond."

"Oh, this," Lizzie brushed her hand through her hair, "Joey had me dye it to help hide me from the police."

"Hey, I'm not colluding in nothin'," Joey loudly interjected. "My suggestion was purely for aesthetical considerations."

"My real hair color is exactly the same as yours," stated Lizzie.

"Maybe we're related."

Lizzie stepped back. "I hope not."

"Would you object to being related to someone in law enforcement?"

Lizzie blushed. "That's not what I meant."

The air in the room suddenly seemed heavy. Smiling, Joey nervously broke the silence, "Don't worry none about her reputation as a castrationist, she's been here a couple weeks and I'm still intact."

Both Lizzie and Val stared at Joey. Lizzie felt the Earth might swallow her up. Val shook his head, obviously holding back a smile.

Joey shrugged and stood slowly. "I'm gonna go look for shells. I'll be back in a half hour or so." Joey tottered across the room. He turned back to Lizzie when he reached the front door. "Tell him everything from the beginning."

CHAPTER TWENTY SIX

Lizzie and Val

Lizzie's self control broke while describing her encounters with Clete. She choked up, gasped, and began crying.

"You need something to drink," Val said. "Water? Coffee?"

"No, no," Lizzie sobbed, "I'll get it."

But she didn't stand up.

Val slid over beside Lizzie and put his hand firmly on her shoulder. "Take as long as you need. Ouch, what's that?"

"You probably sat on one of Joey's guns." Lizzie used her fingers to wipe below her eyes. "He's got them all over the place." Lizzie stood up. "Do you want anything?"

Val looked up along Lizzie's slim body. He hesitated before saying, "No thanks, I'm still working on my Pepsi." He reached behind his back and pulled a gun from between the sofa cushions. He looked at it, shook his head, and placed it on the table beside his Pepsi.

Val gave Lizzie a puzzled look.

Lizzie suddenly realized she was staring. "Be back in a minute." She turned and walked toward the kitchen. At the doorway she glanced back. He was watching her.

When she returned, Lizzie placed her glass of ice and her soda on the table next to Val's, sat, and turned toward him. Her knee rubbed up against his knee.

"Oh, sorry."

"That's no problem," said Val, his voice low and dry. "Relax, take your time." Val gave her an encouraging smile.

Lizzie took a sip from her drink then described her return to Sanibel after the Immokalee trip. She choked up as she told about finding Clete's body. Her breathing came in short gasps. "I've told everybody the truth about the way I found him," she sobbed. "But nobody believed me, except Joey. He helped me get proof that I couldn't have done it. We got copies of the pictures taken by my husband's detective."

"You have a husband?"

"He doesn't count."

Val looked at her strangely. "Okay, if you say so…Why are the pictures important?"

"They're time stamped. The time sequence proves I didn't have time to murder Clete. I'll show you."

Lizzie stood, went to her room, and came back a moment later with the photos. She handed them one at a time to Val, who seemed startled at Agnes standing beside Lizzie and Aaron in one of the first photos.

"Is that a panther?"

"That's just Agnes," responded Lizzie. "We haven't come to the important pictures yet; the ones where I go into my apartment."

"You have a pet panther?"

"Agnes isn't a pet. Now this next picture shows where Aaron goes toward his apartment and I go toward mine."

"So you weren't sleeping with him?"

"We'd had an argument that night."

"Then you'd been intimate with him before?"

"He was my boyfriend."

"But he isn't your boyfriend any more?"

"I'm not sure. I just don't know what our relationship is now. Is that important?"

"It might be."

Lizzie paused momentarily then nervously pointed to the pictures. "Notice the time stamp on this one showing me going into my apartment. Now look at the time stamp on the next one, which shows me rushing out of my apartment just after I found Clete's body. It was only a couple minutes. I didn't have time to kill him."

Val held the picture up, looking closely at it. He looked at Lizzie then looked back at the picture. "You were naked."

"I undressed for bed. I thought I was alone. When you figure in the time it took me to get undressed, I really didn't have time to do anything else, especially kill somebody I'd met only a couple days before. Look at the time stamp down in the corner, not at me." Lizzie took the picture from him. "Here's the next one, showing me running over to Aaron's apartment."

"You put your clothes on."

"Of course."

"Let me see the other picture again."

"Why."

"I want to check the time stamp."

Lizzie handed the other picture to Val, who commented, "Very nice." She snatched it back from him and blushed scarlet as he laughed.

"You're naughty," she complained. Then she sighed. "My life has been difficult lately."

Val put his hand on her shoulder. "I'm sorry. I am taking this seriously. The time stamps are convincing; go on."

Lizzie was calmer as she described the questioning by the Sanibel police, her meeting with her attorney, and the surprise visit from her husband. "After that I talked to Augie then returned to the hotel. Later Aaron dropped by."

"Go back," said Val, "what did August Winters say to you?"

"I was afraid he'd fire me but he didn't. Next I went back to my hotel room, Aaron came by, we argued. He got mad and left."

"What did you argue over?"

"That's private: it has nothing to do with this, with refugees or murder or any of this."

"At this point anything could be relevant."

Lizzie shrugged. "He thought too many men are attracted to me."

"So," said Val, "in addition to breaking up with your husband, you've broken up with a very jealous boyfriend?"

"Yes," gasped Lizzie as she leaned forward, put her face in her hands, and sobbed.

Val hesitated then gently rubbed her shoulders. "Relax; things will get better."

"No, they got worse," cried Lizzie. "They got worse and worse." She suddenly sat up straight and turned toward Val. She put her hands on his arms. "I'm sorry I keep breaking down. I'm a lot more solid inside. I'm going on to tell you what happened next. Don't interrupt or I'll never get through it."

Lizzie began relatively calmly but spoke more and more rapidly while describing Sergeant Malflic's plan to kill her. She told how she kicked Malflic in the crotch, got his gun, and shot him. "I killed him. I'd never hurt a flea but I killed him," she sobbed.

Val took a napkin from the table and was wiping tears from Lizzie's eyes when Joey came in through the front door.

"Oh," exclaimed Joey, "I guess I'm back too soon. Hope you got lots of tissues. I'll go find one of them junonia things." He disappeared back out the door.

Lizzie tried to catch her breath and stop crying. "Oh, God, I'm hopeless; wanted by the police for two murders and, even if I get cleared of those murders, somebody is still out there who wants to kill me."

"Who?" asked Val.

"I don't know. But Joey figures if somebody wanted Clete dead because he was talking; they'd want me dead because I know even more; I know somebody ordered Sergeant Malflic to kill Clete."

"But you don't know who?"

"It had to be Malflic's boss in the Haitian smuggling operation." Lizzie placed her hand back on Val's arm. "You're in charge of the investigation Clete was working on. Who was Malflic's boss? Who would want to set me up for a murder? Who would want me dead?"

Val shook his head slowly. "We're not absolutely certain; but your August Winters is our prime suspect."

Lizzie stared at Val in disbelief. "Augie? That's impossible; he's a conservationist. He treats Aaron like part of his family, giving him land for an animal refuge, and he's praised my work for the foundation. I think of Augie as a replacement father. Now you say he wants me dead. That's ridiculous. What would make you suspect Augie?"

"Do you know anything about his Immokalee farm?"

"Just that it's so big he could offer the land on one side to Aaron."

"His farm is one of the largest in Florida. He has a section devoted to tomatoes and several sections of orange trees; plus other crops. But he never hires the migrant farm workers used by other Immokalee farms."

"He probably has permanent workers he treats well. He has been very kind to Aaron and me."

"Nobody knows who he employs. He refuses to let anybody onto his farm to find out."

"Aren't you the government? Can't you insist on inspecting for cleanliness or decent living conditions or something?"

"He's very well connected politically. He's a major donor to influential people in both parties. If we went in without proof of something serious, he'd have our jobs."

"I can't believe we're talking about the same person. He's so well liked on Sanibel."

"He's also popular with local law enforcement and government officials. He's a big contributor to their projects, campaign funds, and benefits. But he definitely has another side. That foreman of his has driven farm worker organizers off at gunpoint. And rumors circulate that the people on his farm work in slave-like conditions. Those workers never seem to go anywhere. They aren't seen at the local convenience stores or even in the bars."

Lizzie stared at Val for a moment then shook her head. "No, I'd never believe what you're saying, not of Augie."

The front door slammed open. Joey rushed in. "I need one of my guns. Somebody's sneaking around in the woods."

Joey grabbed the gun Val had placed on the table, turned, and rushed back out the door.

Val and Lizzie stared at each other for a second. Then Val stood, snapped a gun from a belt holster at the small of his back, and rushed out after Joey.

CHAPTER TWENTY SEVEN

Arrest

"He got away." Joey was out of breath as he rushed back in and returned his handgun to the table.

"I didn't see anybody. What did he look like?" Val was just behind Joey. He was much calmer.

"I didn't get no good look at him, just bushes moving like somebody was there." Joey sat down hard. "I ain't as young as I usta be."

"Maybe it was an animal," suggested Lizzie. She had stood in nervous alarm when the two men ran out and was still standing when they returned.

Joey shook his head. "No, ain't no animals that big around here. It was definitely somebody spying on me. It ain't good, somebody sneaking around outside my house."

"The police?" asked Lizzie.

"No," responded Val. "They're convinced you've left the island."

Lizzie turned to Val and placed a hand on his arm. "You came looking for me."

"I came looking for information." Val winked at Lizzie. "But you never know what to expect with Joey."

"So where do we go from here?" asked Lizzie, dropping her hand to her side.

Val looked down at the gun in his hand. "First I should officially state that you, Elizabeth Grant, are in my custody until you can be turned over to the local authorities."

"What?" exclaimed Joey, springing up.

Lizzie took a step back away from Val. "I don't understand," she gasped.

"You are wanted for two murders. As a law enforcement official I can't allow you to run around loose." Joey had stepped between Val and Lizzie. Val looked past the old man at Lizzie. "But I have no reason to rush you to jail. You aren't a threat to anyone now." Val snapped his gun back into its holster and smiled. "Relax; it may take me a while to transport you."

"So what do you think you're gonna do?" asked Joey, tilting his jaw and eyeing Val with hostility.

Val raised his hands in a placating gesture. "I'll stay here a couple days, keeping watch on Lizzie while trying to break open August Winters' slavery ring."

"Slavery?" exclaimed Lizzie.

"If he is bringing in illegal aliens to work without pay on his farm, that is slavery, pure and simple."

"You don't know Augie," asserted Lizzie. "If you knew him you'd realize that's ridiculous."

"How can you stay here?" asked Joey. "I only got two bedrooms."

"He could sleep in my bedroom," suggested Lizzie.

"What?" exclaimed Joey.

Val smiled. "Is that an offer I'm not supposed to be able to refuse?"

Lizzie blushed. "I'd sleep on the sofa in here."

Val shook his head. "No, I appreciate the offer but I'm the one who will sleep on the sofa. I'm used to roughing it."

Joey cracked a wrinkled smile. "I guess that'll be okay."

"You'll have to dig the guns out from between the cushions so you don't have an accident," commented Lizzie.

"Yeah, we wouldn't want any unexpected discharges in the middle of the night," laughed Joey as he plopped himself down in his blue overstuffed chair.

Both Val and Lizzie gave Joey disapproving looks.

Silence hung in the room for a moment. Finally, Joey cleared his throat. "How you gonna explain your absence to your office?"

"I'll tell them the truth: I'm going to patrol the beach for several nights; hopefully another boatload of Haitians will come in."

"You expect the slavery ring to bring more illegal immigrants in here?" asked Lizzie.

"They lost their last shipment when you happened to be on the beach. Those particular Haitians are back in Haiti."

"So you think they'll try again?" asked Joey.

"I suspect they need an ongoing supply of new workers," said Val. "Winters must work his slave laborers to death, none ever leave his farm."

"No not Augie," cried Lizzie, taking a step toward Val. "You don't know him."

"I know people," stated Val.

That night the three of them enjoyed a leisurely dinner prepared by Lizzie.

"Good lasagna, Lizzie," said Val

"Thanks, I…"

"Old family recipe," interjected Joey.

"I miss family dinners," commented Val.

Lizzie smiled nervously and blushed slightly.

"Well," Val said as he slowly stood up, "about time I began my first beach patrol. I think I'll enjoy walking the beach at night."

"I'll walk with you." Lizzie also stood.

"I was counting on that." Val looked intently at Lizzie. "With you in my custody, I've got to keep a close watch on you."

"This is a beautiful beach, very quiet," said Val as he walked barefoot through short, choppy waves. The moon was full and low on the horizon. Crickets chirped in the woods behind the beach.

"I've loved it since the first day I saw it." Lizzie walked beside Val, her flip-flops slapping the water washing onto the beach.

"Ouch," muttered Val.

"I warned you, some shells can be sharp."

Lizzie let Val lean on her as he checked his foot.

"No blood," he said, gingerly placing his foot back on the sand.

"You need to be careful on the beach at night," said Lizzie. She still held onto his hand although he no longer needed her for balance.

Lizzie was trembling.

"Are you chilly?"

"No, it's just the last few days…"

"Just relax," said Val, running a hand through her hair.

Lizzie pulled back away from him. "I'll be okay. Let's continue walking."

"Okay."

They continued along the shore, their hands almost touching.

CHAPTER TWENTY EIGHT

Planning

The next morning Val and Joey conferred together before calling Lizzie into the living room.

"Here's our plan to clear your name," said Val, shifting around to face Lizzie as she sat down. "I'll order the ICE office in Fort Myers to reemphasize the need to watch the Winters' farm."

"That's a waste of time," Lizzie grunted.

"I don't think so. I see Winters differently than you. Both his office and his farm phones were on that policeman Malflic's phone."

Lizzie's eyes widened. "How do you know what was on his phone?"

Val held up his hand as though directing traffic to stop. "That's not important right now. I'll also intensify the effort to trace the bus the smugglers planned to use to take the Haitians from the beach."

"Meanwhile," interjected Joey, "I'm gonna use a pay phone to get in touch with the boys in Miami. I don't want my cell phone registered on the traces the government has on their phones. You know it's harder and harder these days to find a pay phone."

"What are your, er, Miami boys going to do?" asked Lizzie.

"Val thinks it might be helpful to find out if either Winters or Sergeant Malflic had any ties with the Florida organization."

"You can find that out?" Lizzie asked.

"Sure. We ain't amateurs. Everybody knows what everybody else is doin', whose territory is whose, who's a made guy and who ain't. That way it all works smoothly."

"That's good to know." Val chuckled "It certainly contradicts everybody always testifying they don't know anything about anything."

"Hey, it's you don't know nothin'. Ain't nothin' writ down."

Val smiled at Lizzie and continued, "I'm also going to talk to the local police; see if those pictures had any effect."

"I'm not sure I like stoppin' at cop's shops," Joey complained.

"You'll have to; you're driving."

"Yeah, but I sure as shit ain't goin' in."

"I'll also let the Sanibel police know Clete was an undercover immigration agent investigating Sergeant Malflic; together with the pictures that should cast doubt on your guilt."

Lizzie stared fixedly at the Federal officer. "But it won't clear me?"

"It'll be a start."

Joey stood. "We'll be out for awhile doin' all this stuff."

Lizzie stood also. "What will I do while you're gone?"

Joey pointed at the floor. "Stay here, lay low. If the cops find you nothin' we do will be worth a cockroach's patooty.'"

That afternoon, with both men gone, Lizzie got restless. Planning a short walk, she stepped out the door onto the steps. But she hesitated when she noticed bushes moving unnaturally on the other side of the road.

Lizzie's breath caught as a tennis shoe and blue-jeaned leg emerged from the bushes.

Lizzie didn't wait to see who they belonged to. She turned and ran back into the house, slamming the door behind her. After locking the door she grabbed a pistol from the table beside the sofa.

Footsteps creaked the stairs. Somebody knocked on the door.

"Go away," yelled Lizzie.

The knock sounded again. A man's voice called out "I only…"

"Please go away," yelled Lizzie. "I have a gun."

Suddenly the person outside pounded on the door. The doorknob rattled. Then a crashing sound resounded through the house as the door shook on its hinges.

Lizzie unsteadily took aim and fired the gun, shattering the upper right corner of the door.

Footsteps ran down the stairs, followed by silence.

Gun in hand, Lizzie carefully opened the door and looked out. No blood was on the steps. She was relieved.

"What happened to the door?" asked Joey when he and Val returned.

"Somebody knocked," Lizzie responded.

Val examined the damage to the door. "I'm glad Joey gave me an extra key."

Several days later, on their nightly beach walk, Val and Lizzie came to a two foot high ridge of sand and shells cut by a previous high tide. Val swept rough shells from the ridge then gestured for Lizzie to sit.

Val and Lizzie looked out over the gulf waters in silence for several moments. Val scratched his leg where mosquitoes had bitten him.

Lizzie, looking around, noticed the taped area a short distance down the beach where what seemed like ages ago she'd put up signs announcing a protected turtle nest. "This is about where that boat came in."

Both Lizzie and Val glanced up and down the silent, shadowy beach and then looked at the gently rolling waters of the Gulf of Mexico. Out toward the horizon a rumbling boat engine noise gradually grew louder.

"Something's out there now," Val said, standing and staring over the dark, moonless waters. Low clouds left only scattered stars visible.

"Yes," said Lizzie, also standing. "It sounds just like that other boat."

"He's running without lights," murmured Val.

Lizzie placed a hand on Val's arm. "Maybe they're coming back, trying again tonight. What'll we do?"

Val drew his pistol from the holster clipped to the back of his bathing suit. "If he comes in, I'm ready."

"Shouldn't we go up behind the bushes?"

Val was silent for a moment, listening.

The boat engine's throbbing roar reached a peak then decreased toward the south.

"No, I don't think we need to worry this time." Val holstered his pistol. "He's far out and heading south."

"So it might be nothing at all?"

"Either that or a practice run."

"It wasn't a practice run that night I was here." Lizzie sat back down.

"That operation sure fell apart," murmured Val, sitting beside her. "And we lost a good man in the bargain."

"Was it my fault?"

"You couldn't help being here." He placed his hand on the sand beside her.

"What was the object of your operation?" Lizzie reached down and squeezed Val's hand as she looked over at his handsome profile.

Val turned slightly toward Lizzie. "We knew Haitians were being brought in by boat somewhere in this area but we didn't know where or when. We kept missing them. It took some doing but we finally got a man on the inside."

"Clete?"

He nodded. "Yes, Clete. As the captain of the boat bringing the Haitians in, he could radio us the where and when."

Lizzie looked intently into Val's eyes. "Then what?"

"The plan was to let them load up the Haitians on a truck or bus. Then, when they drove off over the island's only bridge, we'd follow and have proof where the Haitians where taken." Val shook his head and shrugged. "It all fell apart when the Coast Guard helicopter came in. They were only supposed to do that if something went wrong."

Lizzie removed her hand. "And my showing up was the something that went wrong?"

"We're not sure what happened. Joey called me reporting the boat and then right after that called again to say a young woman was also on the beach, I called the Coast Guard to let them know a civilian was involved."

"So you sent them in to save me?" Lizzie slid over against him.

"No, I told them to continue standing by. They must have misunderstood."

"Maybe you didn't realize you were saving me." Lizzie placed her hand on his chest. "Sergeant Malflic would have killed me if that helicopter hadn't come along. I was a witness he couldn't afford."

"I didn't know who you were or that your life was in danger." Val stood.

A short time later, as they were walking back toward Joey's house, Lizzie reached out and touched Val's arm. "I have an idea."

Val stopped and turned to Lizzie. "What?"

"Your problem is you think Augie's farm is some sort of slave camp. But you can't prove it because you haven't been able to get anybody on the inside. Right?"

"That's about it."

"Here's what I was thinking: I call Augie and beg him to hide me. He'd have to take me to that farm. He certainly couldn't hide me at his Sanibel home because of his wife."

Val shook his head. "He'd probably turn you over to the police."

"Not Augie, he believes in me. You don't understand Augie. You're wrong about him. He's a good man."

Val sighed. "What does this achieve?"

"He hides me on his farm." Lizzie spread out her arms. "I see everything there is okay. So you drop him as a suspect and move on with your investigation.

And I've gained an additional place to hide, taking some of the burden off Joey."

"What if I'm right and you find yourself in the middle of a slave labor camp?"

Lizzie dropped her arms to her side. "I can't believe that. But if I am wrong and it's a hellhole then I call you on a hidden phone, you come in like the cavalry, arrest the slavers, save me, and free the slaves."

Val chuckled. "I'd be Abraham Lincoln and you'd be cleared of the two murders by uncovering the reasons for the murders."

"Yes, it's perfect." Lizzie smiled.

Val shook his head. "I could never allow it."

"Why not?"

"It would be too dangerous."

"But I'm volunteering."

"And I'm refusing your offer. I can't afford to risk you."

"You risked Clete's life. You send men out on dangerous missions all the time."

"They're professionals."

Silently Val and Lizzie walked through a break in the intermeshed bushes at the upper edge of the beach. They both stopped walking when they reached the dirt road which wound through the woods behind the beach. They turned toward each other.

"Am I really so important you wouldn't risk me. Am I that important to you?" asked Lizzie.

Val said nothing. He threw his arm around Lizzie's waist and pulled her close against his chest, kissing her hard on the lips.

Lizzie responded, her soft lips opening as his tongue probed. She moaned as he held her tighter. He kissed her cheek then her neck. He reached up and stroked his fingers through her hair.

"No." Lizzie pushed back out of Val's embrace. "No, no, I'm sorry. If...if I... I... I'm not ready." She backed further away and shook her head, crying. "I don't even know if I still have a relationship with Aaron. And the murders. And I'm wanted by the police. And I'm still married. I just don't know where I stand."

She turned and ran up the road toward Joey's house.

Val stood watching as Lizzie disappeared around the curve in the road.

"The waterworks is in her room." Joey mockingly wiped at his eyes. Val didn't respond. He looked grim as he closed the front door behind him. He'd walked back slowly; thinking as he distractedly swatted mosquitoes. Now he tossed himself onto the overstuffed chair muttering, "I don't know. I just don't know."

"What's the matter?"

"She's so frustrating. I lost it. I behaved unprofessionally."

Joey chuckled as he sat on the sofa across from Val. "Hell, if I wasn't so damn old, I'd be after her myself."

"Damn it all, I've been through just about everything. I don't listen to a sob story easy. I'm a cop, for Christ sake. But here's a woman wanted for two murders; instead of cuffing her and turning her in, I make a play for her."

"That's love."

"Then when I put my arms around her, she turns and runs away."

"Give her time."

"Time's something I don't have. I need to get back to Atlanta." Val pounded his knee. "Nothing makes sense. I can't stay here. I certainly can't take her back to Atlanta with me, a suspected murderer, with a husband and a boyfriend. This is crazy, she..."

The door to Lizzie's bedroom creaked. Her footsteps sounded in the hall. Both men fell silent. Lizzie was smiling as she entered the living room. "Hi, you two; what are you talking about?"

"Er, well, I..." mumbled Val.

"We was discussin' when I first met him," Joey interjected.

"I've been curious about that," said Lizzie, as she sat in a hardback chair brought in earlier from the kitchen. "Tell me about it."

"It's kinda complicated," mumbled Joey.

"He violated his vow of silence."

"I did not. Those guys don't count. They weren't family."

"What guys?" Lizzie adjusted the kitchen chair to better face the two men.

"Low-life's bringing in women from Eastern Europe," said Val.

"They had nothing to do with none of the families."

Val laughed. "Joey developed a conscience and he's embarrassed by it."

"What exactly did he do?" asked Lizzie.

"Turned in a gang of sex slavers."

"I don't understand." Lizzie blushed. "What do you mean by 'sex slaves'?"

Joey loudly grunted, "Those assholes were importing innocent farm girls from Eastern Europe, mostly Czechs and Rumanians, and turning them into prostitutes. So I ratted out the scum."

"But you ran whore houses. What's the difference?"

"I got my girls from the streets. They was already at rock bottom. Going into my houses was a step up. Also I had some housewives in from the suburbs for a little extra dough; one from Park Avenue. My girls could leave when they wanted. Those girls couldn't leave. Their 'sponsors' held their passports. Some of them girls committed suicide."

"I told you," Val interjected. "Loupy Joey developed a conscience. Fortunately his people didn't see it as going soft but as eliminating competition. So they forgave him."

"They didn't exactly forgive me. They just didn't put out a contract on me. I hadda leave New York, retire. But don't get me wrong, I still got influence."

Lizzie looked quizzically at Val. "I thought you worked in Atlanta."

"That was before Atlanta. I was in the New York Immigration and Customs Enforcement office then. Joey contacted me with a ton of information about how those men were enticing women with stories of finding a rich American husband and living in luxury."

"How did they get the women through immigration?" Lizzie asked.

"Sponsored work visas, as waitresses. Anyway, Joey's information enabled us to arrest the men and free the women."

"They was deported back to Eastern Europe," added Joey.

"And Joey ended up down here, deported by his own people out of New York," added Val.

"Yeah, and now that idiot New York Attorney General is trying to force me to testify before that stupid grand jury."

"And Joey doesn't want to testify."

"I set foot in New York, I'm a dead man."

Val disappeared early the next morning and didn't return until after noon. He looked glum as he joined Lizzie and Joey for lunch, chicken saltimbocca.

"Why the long face?" Joey asked.

"I dropped in to see that Sanibel Detective Brian Hunter."

"The one leading the search for me?" Lizzie sat her fork down and fixed her attention on Val.

"Yes. I wanted to find out if Clete being an ICE undercover agent and the time stamped photos made any difference now that they'd had time to examine them."

"Did they?" Lizzie asked eagerly.

Val took her hand in his. "Not at all. You're still their only suspect."

"Most cops don't got no brains at all," stated Joey, "present company excepted."

"Thanks."

"Didn't they see by the time stamps that I couldn't have murdered anybody, that I wouldn't have had time?"

"They see what they want to see."

"I thought we would be able to convince them I was innocent. I thought I'd be free to go back to my job at the Conservancy." Lizzie's voice trembled.

"Unfortunately, it's not going to be that easy," Val said.

"Sometimes I feel as though I've been alone all my life," Lizzie said later that afternoon. She sat beside Val on the dirt bank of an inlet cut by tidal washes into the woods a little over a mile from Joey's house. As she spoke she glanced out over the narrow body of water at some white egrets wading on the other side.

"I'm sorry to hear that. Things were always bad?" Val asked.

"Actually I had a happy childhood, growing up in Pennsylvania and then in the Maryland suburbs when dad got a job with the Commerce Department in D.C." She smiled at some distant memory. Then she coughed and shook her head. "Both were killed in a terrible carnival bumper car accident. I hadn't gone with them. I've felt alone ever since."

Val squeezed Lizzie's hand.

"So I rushed into marriage with Harry. I guess I wanted somebody to take the place of my parents."

"You needed to be in control of your life." Val reached up and brushed back a strand of Lizzie's hair.

She looked pleadingly at Val and spoke in a rush of words. "All Harry wanted was social advancement. He came from an old family that drilled into him an obligation to carry forward the family name and social position. He didn't love me. I was his trophy wife. I had the family background he needed in a wife and people thought I was cute."

"You are cute, in a deadly sort of way."

"No I'm not. I'm just me... Anyway, about six months ago I finally built up the courage to leave Harry. I ran away to Florida. My life blossomed. I'd always loved animals so I looked for a job at the Conservancy. I was amazed they hired me. I really didn't have any background except some volunteer work. It was like a miracle. Augie hired me on the spot. It was like he wanted to hire me as soon as he saw me walk into his office."

"Some walk."

Lizzie blushed. "No, Augie's not like that."

Val's eyebrows rose. "Is he gay or half dead?"

"No, I think he saw how dedicated I would be, how hard I would work. The job was something I could do that was useful, that was of benefit to others. I'd always wanted to be useful. And the job came with housing, which was great because I'd left Maryland with little more than the clothes on my back. So I ended up with both a worthwhile job and a place to live."

"And a boyfriend," interjected Val.

Lizzie nodded. "Yes; Aaron. We did get together awfully fast." She sighed. "I was in a new place. I'd felt alone married to Harry. I always felt like I was different from the people around me, from his so-called friends. But without him I was desperately lonely. And Aaron loved wildlife also."

"How do you stand with him now?"

Lizzie shook her head. "I don't know. I just don't know. Aaron gets so jealous and he seemed to think I murdered Clete. I really don't know." She gripped Val's hand hard.

"What about children?" Val asked. "Children can fill a void in a woman's life."

Lizzie's eyes opened wide. She stared at Val for a moment. "No children," she blurted. Then she shivered and jumped up. "I'm getting cold. Let's go back to the house." She darted off in that direction, almost tripping over a fallen tree limb.

Val stood slowly and followed her, mystified. It was summer in Florida; the temperature was in the high 80's

CHAPTER TWENTY NINE

Night Encounter

Lizzie avoided Val for the rest of the afternoon; not easy to do in Joey's small house. She stayed in the kitchen cooking, shooing the men out, saying they were in the way. Cooking helped her think.

Later that night, after a fattening six course dinner, she asked Val, "How about a walk down by the water?"

"Okay." Val felt like he had been holding his breath since Lizzie suddenly stood and darted away from him.

"Great, let me get my bathing suit; we can go for a swim." Lizzie stood and hurried back to her room.

"I guess I'm stuck doing the dishes," grumbled Joey.

"Thanks, old buddy." Val patted Joey on the shoulder. "I need time alone with her to get some things resolved."

"Good luck."

Lizzie paused at the water's edge, looking hesitantly at Val, her eyes narrowed. A smile tugged at the edge of her mouth as she glanced quickly up and down the deserted beach. "I always used to be alone here at night."

"It's very peaceful. I can see why you liked it at night."

Lizzie suddenly blurted out, "What I didn't like was having a soggy suit and nobody was around, so I skinny-dipped."

Val smiled. "Sorry I wasn't here then."

"Would you mind?" Lizzie asked as she quickly reached behind her back, hands on each side of her bra straps. "It wouldn't violate the terms of my custody?"

"Feel free." Val gestured toward the water.

Lizzie stripped off her two piece suit, first the bra, and then the panties, threw them up onto the beach, ran out, and dove into the Gulf.

Val watched until she hit the water. He looked around and then said, "Oh, what the hell," out loud to the empty beach. He stripped off his bathing suit and tossed it, with his holstered gun, up beside Lizzie's suit. He waded out, dove in, and swam to where Lizzie was splashing around.

"The water's almost too warm this time of year." Lizzie's voice trembled.

"Like a bathtub," agreed Val.

A boat engine roared far to the south.

"Uh oh," Lizzie exclaimed.

"Don't worry, chances are a million to one those smugglers come ashore here again."

"Maybe we should get out."

"We just got in."

The boat engine grew louder.

"It sounds like the other day, the practice run, and that time before." Lizzie started toward shore.

Val looked off to the south. "No running lights." He hurried to catch up with Lizzie who was pushing her way through the waist deep water, moving as fast as she could, a small wake splashing behind her. Lizzie suddenly stopped when the water was a little above her knees.

"What's the matter?" asked Val, whose attention had been riveted on Lizzie's back.

"Somebody's on the beach," Lizzie gasped.

A man stood on the sand where Val and Lizzie had thrown their clothes. He was shaved bald, young, heavy set and wore work clothes. Moonlight glinted on the gun in his left hand.

Val came up beside Lizzie and put his hand on her trembling shoulder. "It'll be all right. Let me handle this."

"Stay right there," barked the man.

Lizzie used hands and arms to cover herself as best she could.

"Can we get our clothes?" asked Val.

"Sure, you can also get your gun." The man laughed and took a step forward. "I ain't stupid, man."

The boat engine grew louder, coming in directly behind Val and Lizzie.

The man on the beach tilted his head to the side. He looked Hispanic. "I've seen you before, babe. On the news. You're the bitch killed Clete and Jack. Ain't no way you mess up another our operations."

Val stepped in front of Lizzie. "To get to her you'll have to come through me."

"Listen, Sir Galahad," sneered the man. "I don't got to come through nobody. Gut shots'll take care of both of you."

"Back up," whispered Val.

"But the boat's behind us," Lizzie cried.

The large boat was about fifteen feet away.

"Don't 'spect no help from them; my people, not yours." The man theatrically raised his gun up high, visibly enjoying the terror in Lizzie's and Val's eyes. "Why don't you two try to run? Make it interesting."

As he started to bring the gun down, the man's head and body exploded into red pulp. The rattling of machine gun fire echoed up and down the beach. The unfired pistol flew from the man's hand. His shattered remains splattered onto the sand.

Joey ambled out from behind a clump of bushes a hundred feet up the beach. He raised his smoking Uzi, aiming it at the boat hovering off shore. With a sudden roar of engines that boat tore off toward the south, leaving behind a rooster tail of spray.

"Joey," exclaimed Lizzie, "you've killed him."

"What did'ja think I shoulda done, reformed him?"

"No…No, thank God you came along." Lizzie started to run up toward Joey but then stopped. She looked around for her clothes. They were under the dismembered body. She stood immobile staring at a strap from her top sticking out from under the dead man's right leg.

"I thought I'd see how you two were doin'" Joey's eyes roved up and down Lizzie's naked body. "Looks like you was doin' okay…" He gestured toward the man's bloody remains with his machine gun. "… 'til this fool came along."

"We were only swimming," Lizzie gasped.

"How are we going to explain this?" asked Val, walking over to the body.

"We need to get dressed," murmured Lizzie. She started to reach down toward her bathing suit trapped under the body, stopped, and backed away. "But I…

"It don't make no sense for you to get dressed yet," interrupted Joey. "You need to push the body out to sea first, while you don't got no clothes to get wet or get no blood on or 'nothin'."

"We can't do that, that's tampering with evidence. This needs to be reported right away. Don't worry about any charges, Joey, it was self defense." Val looked down at the body.

"Think again," responded Joey. "You gonna report how you left your gun up on the beach while you was swimming naked with a woman wanted for murder. You gonna tell them a Mafia guy whose house you're stayin' at machine gunned some guy on the beach while you was cavorting out in the water? You submit that report your career is over."

Val stood immobile staring at the body, shaking his head and mumbling to himself. Finally he looked up at Joey. "You think if we push him out far enough the tide will take him away into the Gulf?"

"Yeah, probably."

"Damn it all to hell, everything has spun completely out of control," Val slapped his hand against his hip. "How did I ever get involved in this...? Damn, damn, damn..."

Joey looked askance at Val. "Hang in there, 'ol buddy."

Val inhaled deeply. "Okay then, let's get busy."

Joey raised a hand. "Hey, don't look at me. You don't think I'm getting' my clothes wet, do you? I'll let you two kids resume your private naked business." Joey turned, propped the machine gun up onto his shoulder, and, whistling, walked up into the woods behind the beach.

"I think I'm going to throw up," Lizzie exclaimed.

"I'll drag him out; somebody has to." Val grabbed one of the man's feet and started to pull the body down the beach into the rippling surf. "This amount of damage, Joey must have used hollow points."

Lizzie stared down at a disconnected arm lying bleeding onto the sand. She turned and threw up pieces of orzo, tomato and Italian sausage into the Gulf.

CHAPTER THIRTY

Goodbye

AS Val shoved the man's shattered body out into the Gulf, Lizzie washed her bathing suit in the shallow water a safe distance up the beach. She was in a daze, moving in slow motion. She felt guilty about not helping Val; but she couldn't.

His mood had also turned bad. "This just isn't right," Val growled. "Everything's all messed up. Things have taken on a life of their own."

"Welcome to my life." Lizzie pulled on her bikini bottom.

Val came to her, looking hard into her eyes.

They both spoke at once. "We need to talk."

"You first," murmured Lizzie, as they stepped out of the water onto the beach.

Val took Lizzie's hand and looked down at it. "I must get back to Atlanta."

"What about me?"

"You'll... well; I guess you'll just stay here with Joey."

"But... But I've enjoyed being...being in your custody." She put her arms around his waist. She still held her bikini top in her hand.

"I've been thinking and you're right about what you said before." Val reached up and gently stroked her cheek. "It's hard to see a future the way things are. We still must prove your innocence. I can't do it here. At my office I'll have more resources to pursue information on the smuggling ring. I'll have control of what's happening around me."

Lizzie placed her hand lightly over his hand. "You will come back?"

"As soon as I can." Val withdrew his hand.

"When are you leaving?"

"Tomorrow, first thing." Val suddenly pulled her to him. They kissed, her naked breasts pressing against his chest. When their lips finally parted, Lizzie was trembling.

"What was it you wanted to tell me?" asked Val.

Lizzie hesitated a moment, looking into Val's eyes, and then blurted out, "Val, I'm in love with you."

Val dropped his arms and stepped away from her. "Love is a serious word. All this is too much, Lizzie. What just happened. What Joey just did. The trouble you're in. Everything. It's just too much for me right now. I need to get back to Atlanta. I need time to think." Val turned from Lizzie and hurried to the house.

Just after daybreak the next morning, Joey and Lizzie stood on the dirt roadway in front of Joey's house watching Val walk away.

Lizzie pulled at a strand of her hair. "He can walk out of my life. I'm stuck in it." She hoped Val would turn and wave or smile or something, but he didn't. At the first curve in the rutted road, he seemed to hesitate a second; but then continued around that curve without looking back.

Joey and Lizzie went inside to finish breakfast.

"He seemed changed since last night," Joey commented. "Meeting the real world head on; violent death and guilt and all that psychological stuff. I remember the first time I killed somebody it bothered me some."

Lizzie held her fork poised over her plate. "Don't you have any feelings about what you did last night?"

"What did I do?" Joey raised his arms Italian style. "There was some dirt on the beach. I cleaned it up; kept my neighborhood clean."

Lizzie shook her head. "I don't think things will never be right again. I think it was what I told him that drove Val off." Lizzie pushed her eggs around with her fork.

"Which was?"

"I said the word 'love.'"

"The most dangerous word I know." Joey reached across and patted the back of Lizzie's hand. "Give Val time. He told me he wanted you. Eventually things will work out."

"He said he wanted me?" Lizzie looked up from her food. Her eyes glistened.

"Yeah," Joey nodded, "he's turned to mush; not the Val I used to know."

"Maybe I've been foolish. Maybe I should have given into my urges and said the hell with the future."

"But you didn't"
"No, I didn't. I might have if that man hadn't come along."
"Then he deserved what he got," Joey grunted, "interfering with sex."
"Love."
"Whatever."

CHAPTER THIRTY ONE

Joey Down

Later that day, Lizzie and Joey took a walk in the woods to where a narrow inlet from the Gulf had been cut inland by an old storm. The dead trunks of ravaged trees stuck up from the water. The old man and the young fugitive sat on a short treeless stretch of sandy bank. Their feet hung down almost touching the placid, musty smelling water.

"You should call Val tomorrow to talk everything over," said Joey.

"How will I reach him?" Lizzie kicked her feet back against the bank below her, knocking loose some shells.

"Here," Joey reached into the pocket of his walking shorts and pulled out a cell phone. "Take my phone; his private number is on the whatchamacallit, the index or speed dial. Call him tomorrow after he gets back to work."

"What will I say?"

"Tell him you'll continue to love him no matter what. Place your future in his hands. Make him feel responsible for you."

"What if somebody else answers, his secretary or somebody?"

"Nobody else'll answer. He only uses that line for people he ain't supposed to know. If he's not in, leave a message. He's the only one who'll get it."

Lizzie took the cell phone. "Okay, I'll do it, I'll call him. Thank you, Joey." She reached over and patted the wrinkled hand resting on the warm sand beside her. She looked down at the phone. "Are you sure you won't need this?"

"Nope." Joey shook his head sadly. "Since I retired the only people ever call me are fools wanting donations or assholes asking me to vote for some jerk."

After a few more minutes looking out over the water watching fish jump, Lizzie and Joey stood. Lizzie clipped the cell phone to the right front pocket of her short shorts.

Joey looked down at Lizzie's legs and sighed.

She turned and walked ahead of him back through the woods.

Joey looked her up and down as her body swayed with her movement along the winding trail between the tall pine trees. Joey sometimes felt young himself but was jolted back to the reality of his age by a mirror or an ache.

At the edge of the woods, just before reaching Joey's house, Lizzie stopped and turned to face Joey. She patted the phone. "Thanks again for the phone, for thinking of me, for your advice."

"Oh, it ain't nothin'. I got so I think of you as like the daughter I ain't never had."

Lizzie stared at Joey for a moment then, crying, turned, and ran toward the house.

"Of course, if she'd been my daughter, I'd have cured her of this cryin' crap," Joey mumbled. He thought maybe Lizzie would really want him as a father. Joey wiped a tear from his own eye.

The next morning at breakfast Joey asked, "When you gonna call Val?"

"I thought I'd wait until this afternoon."

"Nervous?"

"A little; but for the first time in weeks I'm hopeful."

"Good," said Joey, taking a bite of his peanut butter and banana French toast sandwich. "I wouldn't want no daughter of mine going around without hope."

Early that afternoon, Lizzie was at the front door. She wore blue jeans and a green "Life is Good" t-shirt.

"Where you goin'?" asked Joey.

"Outside, for privacy, for my talk with Val." She held up the cell phone.

Lizzie opened the door. As she descended the steps, Joey stepped onto the wide top step behind her. "Remember: love conquers all," he called down to her.

Lizzie half turned, looking back, smiling at Joey.

A man's voice yelled from across the road, "Shame, Lizzie"

Joey's eyes opened wide. He started to crouch. "Look out," Joey warned Lizzie as he pulled a gun from the waistband of his walking shorts.

Before Joey could raise the gun a shot cracked from the bushes across the roadway. The center of Joey's chest burst red as the sound of the shot echoed off the side of his house and among the trees in the surrounding woods. He crumpled; falling head first down the stairs.

Lizzie jumped aside as Joey's body slid past her. His large balding head pounded each step. Blood spurted from a gash above his left ear. Joey's right foot caught on a banister leaving his body sprawled half on the last three stairs and half on the ground.

Lizzie followed Joey's body to the base of the stairs. She climbed over his legs, knelt down beside the old man, grabbed the gun from Joey's hand, ducked behind the stairs, and began firing toward the clumps of bushes and woods, shot after shot after shot. She didn't see anybody. She fired anyway until the gun was empty. Then she threw the gun away.

Lizzie rolled Joey over hoping to do artificial respiration. But when she saw the blood coming from his chest she concluded Joey must be dead. She saw no use checking his pulse for verification.

CHAPTER THIRTY TWO

Phone Calls

The sound of approaching sirens jolted Lizzie. She had turned numb staring at Joey's body. She felt like she was in shock. Jail would just make everything worse. Lizzie dashed into the woods, away from the sirens.

Hiding behind a clump of bushes and the rotting trunk of an old tree, Lizzie watched a Sanibel Island police cruiser arrive. Two policemen, weapons drawn, jumped out and ran over to Joey's body. One checked his pulse while the other hurried back to the squad car. Lizzie slumped down on her stomach and peeked around a bush. A fan shaped clump of ferns brushed against Lizzie's right cheek.

The second policeman's gaze caught on something. He walked over and picked up the gun Lizzie had used to wildly shoot into the bushes. He called to the policeman in the squad car, "I found the weapon."

Lizzie realized her prints would be on that gun. The police would think she shot Joey. She backed away, crawling on all fours through scattered ground vegetation and accumulated leaf debris. When she got far enough that the policemen couldn't see her, she rose and ran toward the north end of the island, away from the dirt road the police used for access behind the beach, away from everything.

Eventually finding herself deep in the woods, far from both the road and the water, Lizzie sat down, leaned her back against a tree and thought about what she should do.

Even though she saw no familiar landmarks, Lizzie knew roughly where she was. The narrowness of Sanibel made it impossible to get completely lost.

If she went in any direction long enough she would end up at either the Gulf of Mexico or the back bay. But she couldn't stay on Sanibel Island, not after this latest shooting. They were bound to find her clothes in Joey's house. They were certain to figure out she had been there. Lizzie had to get away. Augie's farm was her only alternative. Lizzie took out the cell phone Joey had given her and dialed Augie's private office number from memory.

"Hello, August Winters here."

"Augie, oh Augie, I need your help," Lizzie cried.

For a moment the silence on the other end of the phone matched the silence of the woods around her. Then Augie spoke: "Lizzie? Is that you, Lizzie?"

"Yes Augie."

"Where are you?"

"In the woods near the north end of the island."

"You're still on Sanibel?"

Several sirens sounded in the distance.

"Yes."

"The police combed the island looking for you."

"I know. Augie, I'm innocent."

"I've always thought you were, Lizzie. What do you need me to do?"

"I need a place to hide."

The sirens seemed to be getting closer, coming from different directions. Lizzie knew the police cars could not get to her where she was now; far beyond roads deep in the woods. But a patrolman on foot or on a motorcycle could reach her.

Augie's voice interrupted her fearful thoughts. "The only place I could hide you would be my Immokalee farm. Would you be willing to be taken there?"

"Yes, yes, please. I'd be eternally grateful. I'd offer you anything." Lizzie could feel her heart beating as the phone was briefly silent.

Augie's voice suddenly came back sounding decisive, almost eager: "Can you meet me at the convenience store at the north end of the island?"

"I'll be there in a half hour if I don't run into the police."

"Good. I'll drive up there in my BMW. You know the car?"

"Yes."

"Hide until you see me pull into the parking lot. If no police are around, jump in and we'll be off."

"Thank you, thank you, thank you. Your farm will be perfect for me, away from everything, perfect isolation. I just need to get away, to think."

"My farm is like a fortress. Nobody from outside will get to you there. It's God's last bastion for the American family farm. You'll find it interesting."

After completing her call to Augie, Lizzie used the speed dial to reach Val. He answered on the second ring.

Lizzie's emotions burst out as soon as she heard Val's voice. She sobbed into the phone, "Oh, Val, it's horrible. Joey's dead."

"What happened?"

"Somebody shot him."

"Who?"

"I don't know. They shot him from the bushes. I didn't see them. I tried to shoot back but didn't see anybody. Now the police have that gun and I'm sure they'll think I killed Joey. I can still hear the sirens."

"Slow down. I don't understand any of this. Everything was calm when I left."

Lizzie's breath caught in her throat. Val sounded like he suspected her of shooting Joey. "I...I... Oh Val, I'm scared."

"Where are you now?"

"In the woods; I'm hiding in the woods."

"Perhaps you should turn yourself in."

"No, Val, no, I won't do that."

"What do you plan to do?"

The sirens abruptly stopped.

"I've called Augie. He's agreed to hide me on his Immokalee farm."

"No." Val shouted so loudly Lizzie had to hold the phone away from her ear. "You'd be safer in a jail cell."

"Val, you're wrong about Augie. I know him. I've worked with him for months."

"I'm not wrong. That farm is a slavery death camp. If you go there, I may never see you again."

A creaking noise came from behind a palm tree clump about 20 feet away. Lizzie ducked down behind a flowering bush.

"It's my only chance," she whispered.

"No, Lizzie, you're making a terrible mistake."

"Goodbye, Val."

Lizzie snapped the phone shut, counted to ten, rose up slightly, and looked around. A raccoon dashed out from behind the tree that had creaked. The furry, masked creature ran behind another tree and vanished. Lizzie stood and began walking north, where she would meet Augie at the convenience store. She thought it was nice of Augie to take the risk of hiding a fugitive by taking her to his Immokalee farm.

CHAPTER THIRTY THREE

The Ride

Lizzie was hiding behind a large dumpster at Island Hopping Shopping when August Winters pulled his amethyst black BMW into the convenience store's parking lot. She peeked around the dumpster, which smelled like rotting meat. The lot was deserted except for the BMW. Lizzie dashed over as Augie leaned across to open the passenger side door. She slid in and scrunched down.

Augie sped off.

Lizzie raised herself to see where they were going.

"Stay down."

Lizzie mashed herself halfway to the floor; being short helped.

Augie glanced over at her. "I'm going to find some place deserted where nobody will see you get in the trunk."

Lizzie glanced sideways at him. He was more overweight than she remembered. His double chin was obvious from this angle. "The trunk? Why?"

"They're searching cars at the bridge to the mainland." Augie gripped the steering wheel with both hands, white knuckled.

"Won't they search the trunk?" Lizzie could feel herself trembling.

"Not of my car they won't. They wouldn't dare."

Lizzie couldn't see where they were going.

Augie drove mostly straight then made a sharp right turn. He brought the sedan to a sudden stop. "Nobody's around. Let's move, get out, quick."

They both jumped from the car. Augie popped open the trunk. The car was on a narrow dirt roadway between clumps of sea grapes.

Lizzie was terrified looking into the dark interior of the trunk. "What if I get stuck? What if I suffocate?"

"You'll be okay. Get in. It's only until we're over the bridge. Look, there's an interior trunk release." Augie pointed to a small lever. "But don't pull it."

Lizzie climbed into the trunk. She had to lie sideways in fetal position to fit. Augie slammed the trunk closed. The loud bang hurt her ears. She was smothered in darkness.

The car lurched forward, drove a short distance, turned, backed up, and then went forward again. There was a bounce, probably going from the side road back onto the main road. Something metallic rolled against Lizzie's left ear. Awkwardly, she pushed it away. She had almost no space for movement.

Eventually the car slowed to a crawl. Lizzie was finding it difficult to catch her breath. She could smell exhaust.

The slow, on and off forward movement of the BMW continued for some time. Lizzie assumed it was the roadblock at the bridge. Her mind was drifting. She saw images of Val running on the beach, sitting at breakfast smiling at her, walking with her at night, naked in the water. The darkness around her seemed darker.

The car stopped. Lizzie heard an authoritative voice. It startled her. "Hello, Mr. Winters. There's been a shooting on the island. We're asking people if they've seen anything suspicious."

"I haven't seen a thing, Murray." Augie's voice sounded like it was right beside her. "Everything's normal."

"Sorry to bother you."

"Not at all, Murray; keep up the good work: defend and protect."

"Yes, sir."

The car moved again, picking up speed. It drove what seemed like a long distance and then turned twice. Every time the car turned, Lizzie slid back and forth bumping into metal. She was losing track of time. She was losing track of everything as she was jarred by bumps. The BMW must have pulled off the road onto an uneven, rutted, or rocky surface. It turned sharply then screeched to a stop. She heard Augie get out and close the driver's side door. Everything was silent for a long time. She heard distant voices. Her head swam. The wait went on forever. She tried to move. Her head hit the trunk lid which seemed to be shrinking down onto her. She felt like screaming but couldn't make a sound.

The trunk suddenly popped open. Light blinded Lizzie.

"Get out quick," Augie ordered. "Before anybody else comes."

Lizzie tried to untangle herself but felt weak and dizzy, like she was drunk.

"Here, I'll help you," said Augie, putting his hands under her armpits and yanking her up. It seemed to Lizzie like his hands moved slowly across her breasts to reach under her arms. But she couldn't believe Augie would do that.

Augie virtually dragged her out of the trunk. The edge scratched at her. Then Augie held her up with one hand while he slammed the trunk shut with the other.

Lizzie stood unsteadily. She leaned against Augie.

A couple walking past stared at Lizzie and Augie.

"Too much partying," Augie commented.

The couple shook their heads as they moved on.

Looking around, Lizzie recognized the public parking lot of a little used beach on a side road off of Summerlin Road, the main road to Sanibel.

Augie half carried Lizzie to the passenger side of the BMW. He juggled her around as he opened the door. "Get in."

Lizzie stumbled slightly, catching herself by grabbing the side of the BMW.

Augie pulled her back away from the car. "Watch it, don't scratch the paint."

Lizzie shook her head. It seemed to help clear it. She plopped herself into the passenger seat as Augie got behind the wheel. He started the car, drove from the parking lot, then up the side road to the main road.

"Should I slump?" asked Lizzie.

"No need, we're off the island." He glanced over at Lizzie. "You look different."

"I dyed my hair." She patted her hair. It seemed messy, disarranged.

Augie studied her. "I think it's more than that. You look more determined, fierce almost, wilder."

"I do?"

"Yeah, I like it. What's this about a shooting today, some old guy out near Bowman's?"

Lizzie stared straight forward as the BMW devoured the highway. "That was Joey, a wonderful friend. Some coward shot him from behind a bush. I intend to track down the bastard and make him pay, slowly and painfully."

"You are fierce. You almost scare me." Augie chuckled then looked appraisingly at Lizzie. "Were you staying with this Joey?"

"Yes."

Augie said nothing. He drove in silence through south Fort Myers until they reached the road to Immokalee.

After driving through Immokalee, Augie turned onto a narrow road

Lizzie recognized as the one leading to Aaron's animal sanctuary land. Augie drove past that turnoff.

A moment later, a tall fence stretched out of sight along the left side of the road. Behind that fence were rows of orange trees heavy with fruit. The rows alternated making it difficult to see what was beyond them. However, through a gap left by a dead tree Lizzie caught sight of another high fence. That second fence was topped with razor wire.

Augie pulled his BMW onto the dirt shoulder of the road and brought it to a sudden stop. A light wind blew a dust cloud past them.

Lizzie looked around. "Why are we stopping?"

"I wanted to make sure you understand my farm before we get there."

"What do you mean?" Lizzie was nervous. Stopping to explain a farm seemed like a strange thing to do, particularly when police were combing the country for her.

Augie turned slightly in his seat and looked intently at Lizzie. "Do you realize that 70 years ago there were over seven million farmers in the United States? But now there are only about 50,000 and the average farmer is over 55 years old."

"I didn't know that."

Augie clenched his fists. "Most people don't. Most people are unaware what is happening in this country."

Lizzie had never seen Augie this worked up before. He was a little scary.

"Most of the farm products grown in the United States now are grown on farms owned by large multi-national corporations. But that's not even the worst of it. Look at the produce in your supermarket: 'grown in Chile' 'product of Spain' 'from Mexico'. The foreigners have control of our food supply. Can you see the danger to America in that?"

"What danger?"

Augie shook his head and leaned toward Lizzie. "We get in a major war or something and they can cut off our food. Americans will be starving like Chinese or Indians or Africans or other backward people."

"What does this have to do with your farm?"

"My farm is an effort to blaze a new trail, to show that an American family farm can work, can be profitable." Augie reached over and placed his hand on Lizzie's shoulder. "But I'm getting ahead of myself; I haven't finished listing the problems."

"You mean the general economy, the economic slump?"

"No, I mean foreigners coming here and taking American jobs and Americans getting so lazy and welfare-state-pampered they won't work farm jobs. In large parts of Miami they don't even speak English any more. Did you notice the Mexican grocery stores back there in Immokalee?"

"Not really."

"We passed a couple. The damn Mexicans can't even shop at Publix like everybody else. It's bad enough these foreigners are destroying American agriculture from their own countries. Now they're here taking over our American agriculture from inside with their farm worker's unions, and marches, and boycotts." Augie's grip on Lizzie's shoulder was becoming painful. "We need to find a way to stop them, a way to defend America, a way to save the American farmer. That's what I'm doing on my farm."

Augie released Lizzie's shoulder and transferred his hand back to the steering wheel. He held onto the wheel with his hands in the ten-o-clock, two-o-clock position. His knuckles were white. He stared ahead in silence for a few moments.

Lizzie rubbed her shoulder. She thought it safest not to say anything.

Suddenly, Augie proclaimed. "If you read your Bible, you'll learn that God endorses indentured servitude."

"What?" Lizzie was startled by Augie's messianic tone. Augie seemed very different from the Sanibel conservationist she had known. "What do you mean God endorses servitude?"

"Most people don't know that. I've memorized the Bible verses of First Timothy 6." Augie closed his eyes and began reciting with a voice that sounded like an imitation of a television evangelist: "'Let as many slaves as are under the yoke count their own masters worthy of all honor, that the name of God and his doctrine be not blasphemed.

"'And they that have believing masters, let them not despise them, because they are brethren; but rather do them service, because they are faithful and beloved, partakers of the benefit. These things teach and exhort.'"

"You see how far we've strayed from God," Augie stated. "It is God's will that the inferior people faithfully and willingly serve us. Anyone who opposes that, opposes God."

CHAPTER THIRTY FOUR

The Farm

After pulling back onto the highway, Augie drove a short distance, and then turned left into a dirt road at a large old worn wooden sign reading: "No admittance. Trespassers will be shot."

Augie pulled up to a gate in the long wire mesh fence dividing the highway from the orange groves and pressed a button on his BMW's sun visor. The gate creaked open. He drove through, looked back to watch the gate close behind him, and then drove slowly forward down a narrow dirt road winding between orange groves. The winding made it impossible to see very far into the farm.

They pulled up to a second fence, a solid sheet metal fence topped with razor wire. An attached sign read "DANGER – ELECTRICITY." Augie pushed another button on his visor and the gate whirred open. Augie drove through.

"It's like entering Sing Sing," thought Lizzie

A vast arc of fields spread out around them, hundreds of acres stretching to the horizon. In the distance off to the right Lizzie could see raggedy people bending over picking something; maybe tomatoes. A man stood nearby holding a rifle.

After the car bounced down a long straight stretch of rutted road between several fields and after a sharp turn to the right past more fields, the road wound around a wooded area, revealing a large old southern plantation-style house tucked back beside those woods. A tall fence surrounded the faux-antebellum structure.

Augie pushed a third button on the driver's side sun visor. The final fence's gate rolled open. Augie drove through then turned into a white, pebbled circular driveway and parked in front of wide steps which led to a verandah stretching around the front of the house.

Augie switched off the BMW's engine, looked over at Lizzie, and grinned devilishly. "Home sweet home."

Three black women ran down the house's front steps. One stopped at the base of the steps while the other two rushed to open the driver's and the passenger side doors. All three wore brief frilly skirts reaching mid-thigh.

Augie got out without a word and walked around the front of his car. Lizzie stepped hesitantly from the BMW and thanked the beautiful, exotic looking girl who held the door for her. That girl had light skin, even features, and slanted Oriental eyes.

A chicken pecked at the pebbles in the drive. Augie stopped to stare at the bird. "What's that pile of feathers and bird shit doing inside the fence?"

Nobody responded. The girls nervously looked from one to the other.

Augie turned on the three girls, shouting, "Don't just stand there like God-damned statues. Somebody kill that damn interloper."

One of the girls nodded rapidly." Yes, sir, Mr. Winters." She ran around Augie toward the chicken, which squawked, flapped its wings and tried to escape. The girl dove for it, grabbed it by the neck, and held it up.

"I don't want to inspect it," Augie shouted at the girl. "Kill the damn thing."

The girl slowly lowered the struggling bird until it was even with her eyes. Then, suddenly, she shoved the bird's body down under her arm with her hand gripping the base of its neck. With her other hand she gave a sudden twist to the screaming bird's neck. A crack sounded. The bird struggled for a moment, and then was still.

Augie smiled.

The girl, her shoulders slumped, held the chicken down beside her as she climbed the stairs, opened one of the pair of front doors, and disappeared into the house.

Augie yelled after the girl. "Fricassee the little son-of-a-bitch." He winked at Lizzie and stepped toward the house.

As Augie mounted the stairs a girl ran ahead of him her skirt flapping up revealing bare buttocks. She opened the other twin door. Augie strode through like an emperor returning from a conquest.

Lizzie climbed the steps slowly, nervously looking around. She was shaking slightly but felt hard inside. After what she had already faced she was determined to stand up to whatever was going to happen in this bizarre place. Wicker furniture and an old sofa swing decorated the porch. The third girl accompanied Lizzie, keeping a couple paces behind her. "Do you have luggage?" that girl asked.

"No," responded Lizzie, jumping slightly, startled at being suddenly asked a question.

Lizzie and the girl entered the house and crossed to an elaborately furnished front room adorned with paintings from the Colonial period of American art, possibly originals. A grand piano dominated the room.

The girl who had opened the door for Augie quickly vanished through a back doorway. The girl with Lizzie stood behind her facing Augie.

Augie stepped closer to them. "Celia, show Lizzie here to her room, the bedroom next to mine; the one with the connecting door."

Lizzie silently riveted a hard stare on Augie. How was he planning to use that connecting door?

Celia stepped forward, smiled shyly at Lizzie and gestured, "This way, miss."

"Call me Lizzie."

"I'm Celia."

Lizzie extended her hand. "Pleased to meet you."

Celia looked at Lizzie's hand but did not shake it. She backed away slightly.

"We are careful how we fraternize with the servants," Augie stated. "They know their place."

Augie looked Lizzie up and down.

"Celia, find an appropriately short dress for Lizzie."

"Yes, sir."

Lizzie and Celia started to turn away but were stopped by Augie saying, "Just a moment." He smiled, lumbered over, and took Lizzie's right hand in both of his huge hands. He gently rubbed the back of her hand as he spoke, "My home is now your home, Lizzie. Respect my rules and this paradise is yours, this land of milk and honey where I am rebuilding the world for America and for God."

He paused, his expression serious. "But beware of treasonous acts. I despise betrayal; you have nowhere else to go, no place where the cops aren't hunting you. This is your home now. If you behave agreeably it will be paradise. If not... well, let's just say you don't want to find that out."

CHAPTER THIRTY FIVE

Settling In

Celia ushered Lizzie into a large bedroom decorated with antiques; old intricately carved furniture, pottery decorated with hand painted naked nymphs, and a hanging tapestry depicting a hunting scene.

Lizzie was still stunned by the slave-like conditions on the farm and Augie's Jekyll and Hyde transformation. She forced a smile. "What a beautiful four-poster bed."

"It not as big as the one in Mr. Winters' room." Celia gestured toward a doorway beside the bed.

Lizzie walked over to try the knob. "It doesn't open."

"You can't open it from this side when locked on other side."

Lizzie turned toward Celia. "So he can get to me but I can't get to him."

She nodded. "Yes, miss."

"You have an accent."

Celia pointed to herself. "I am Haitian."

Lizzie approached Celia. "Are you a farm worker?"

Celia glared at Lizzie. "I am house servant. I never farm worker again. I die first. Give me your clothes."

Lizzie stepped back. "What?"

"You must take bath. I help." Celia reached toward Lizzie's waist.

Lizzie backed away. "I can take off my own clothes. Why must I take a bath?"

"Woman cleanliness important Mr. Winters."

Lizzie was about to protest it was none of his business but then realized how filthy she was from hiding in the woods. Some of Joey's blood was still on her clothes. Her t-shirt was torn and oily. She unbuckled her belt and undid the button on the waistband of her jeans. She unzipped them but then hesitated. "Augie seems very different from on Sanibel."

"I not know him there. I know him here." She crossed herself.

Lizzie looked away from Celia. "I'm going into the bathroom to undress."

"It there." The black girl pointed to a doorway on the opposite side of the bedroom. "You lose shyness after you here long time."

Lizzie entered the bathroom, undressed, handed out her clothes, and then took a long, hot bath. She remembered what Joey told her about hot baths. She missed Joey.

As Lizzie rubbed herself down with a towel, she called out, "I need something to wear."

Celia responded immediately, as though she'd been waiting outside the bathroom door. "I have dress for you. You come put on. Very important I talk you now."

Lizzie wrapped the towel around herself and went into the bedroom.

Celia looked upset. She glared at Lizzie, who could not understand what the problem was. "What's the matter?"

Celia held up the cell phone Joey had given Lizzie. "I find this in jeans,"

Lizzie glanced at it. "Yes, it's a cell phone."

"Mr. Winters get very upset, very dangerous if he find you have way communicate with outside. This very dangerous." Celia looked at the cell phone like it might bite her.

Lizzie reached out. "I'll hide it."

Celia shoved the cell phone into Lizzie's hand. "I never saw it. I not know it exist."

"I'll hide it under the mattress."

Celia shook her head. "They look there."

Lizzie's brow furrowed. "Do you think they'll search my room?"

Celia nodded. "Yes, they search your room."

Lizzie looked around. "Where can I hide it?"

Celia walked past Lizzie into the bathroom, opened a bathroom cabinet and got out a box of Kotex. "Put in here."

"In the Kotex box?" Lizzie took the box.

"Men won't touch."

Lizzie slid the cell phone down between the Kotex pads. She noticed the cabinet also contained an assortment of creams, powders, and medicines.

"Looks like he's thought of everything," Lizzie observed.

"That not all." Celia opened a drawer under the sink. It contained a sewing kit, nail scissors, an assortment of lipsticks, and a variety of nail polish bottles. "Mr. Winters like women look perfect. He mad if don't."

Back in the bedroom, Celia held up a short red dress. "This for you."

Lizzie hesitated a second then took the dress. She looked at Celia's now empty hands. "Is that it? What about underwear?"

Celia shook her head. "Mr. Winters not allow women wear underwear."

Lizzie's eyebrows rose. "He doesn't allow it?"

"No, he say it get in way."

Lizzie stepped toward Celia. "But… but I'm a guest, not a servant."

Celia shook her head. "When Mr. Winters tell me get you dress, I know what you are."

Lizzie spread her arms wide. "But he can't order me to wear a short dress and no underwear."

"He can do anything he want. He can rape you. He can kill you. He only law here. He do what he want do and proclaim it the American way and God's will." Celia crossed herself again.

As Celia left the bedroom she told Lizzie, "Dinner at seven-o-clock downstairs in dining room, behind front room. Be on time. Late make Mr. Winters angry." She stepped out the door but then leaned back in. "It best you stay in room until dinner."

"Am I a prisoner?"

"No, but safest you stay in room."

After Celia left, Lizzie rushed into the bathroom and recovered her cell phone from the Kotex box. She used the speed dial to call Val. His answering machine said he was out; leave a message.

"Val, you were right, it is a slave labor camp. Please come and get me. Please save me."

Lizzie snapped the phone shut and returned it to the box. She walked back into the bedroom and looked around at her unfamiliar surroundings. She felt the urge to cry but repressed it. Her crying days were finished. Lizzie intended to gather up every ounce of strength inside her to fight the bastard.

A short time later Lizzie looked out the window of her room. Bars on the window partially blocked her view; but from the second story room she could see over the fence surrounding the house. Off in the fields beyond the fence was a work crew. Men and women in gray, ragged clothing, appeared to be picking tomatoes, working their way methodically along rows of plants. An armed white guard stood a short distance away.

As Lizzie watched, a picker fell over. She lay on the ground unmoving.

The guard sauntered over and stood above the woman. He kicked at her legs. She didn't move.

A man hesitantly separated himself from the other pickers, who had all stopped work. The man slowly walked forward, crouching down with his hands up making placating gestures. He said something to the guard and tried to get to the woman on the ground.

The guard raised his rifle butt in a threatening manner. The man backed off. The guard then kicked the woman on the ground in the stomach.

The man screamed and rushed toward the guard, who smashed his rifle butt into the man's head. He fell to the ground. The woman, now on her knees, was vomiting.

Lizzie turned away from the window and clenched her fists. She wanted to do something but there was nothing she could do.

CHAPTER THIRTY SIX

Encounter

At about 6:45 p.m., Lizzie left her bedroom, wearing the short red dress. She had tried stretching it down in front for modesty but that only made it rise up in back. She had no choice but to refuse to leave her bedroom or to soldier through. As she walked down the hallway toward the stairs to the ground floor, Lizzie heard heavy footsteps clomping up those stairs.

She hesitated a few feet from the stairs.

Boss Pigott ascended the stairs. His eyes locked on her legs as his puffy face reached floor level. Lizzie pushed her dress down in front. Pigott stomped onto the second floor, stopping inches in front of Lizzie. Towering over her, he blocked her access to the stairs. He held a riding crop in his left hand.

Pigott smiled down at Lizzie. "Well, well, well, the pretty little thing is in the main house. And she got on a red dress. Don't you look pretty, little sexy thing. I bet you don't got no underwear on at all."

The farm foreman reached out with his riding crop and began to lift the front of Lizzie's dress. She slapped the riding crop away with one hand while continuing to hold down the front of her dress with the other.

Pigott rushed in and grabbed Lizzie's neck with his right hand. He drove her backwards and around until her spine slammed into a wall. She was choking. Pigott tossed aside his riding crop and placed his left hand under her right arm. He removed his other hand from her neck and placed it under her other arm pit. He then lifted her until her face was even with his. He was holding her mashed against the wall. A picture was knocked from that wall and clattered to the floor, its glass shattering. Lizzie struggled but couldn't move. Terror and desperation surged through her.

Glaring at Lizzie, Pigott snarled, "You best learn the rules 'round here real quick. You don't knock away my stick."

His foul breath almost made Lizzie gag. His scarred face with its mashed nose was so close it blotted out everything else. "Mr. Winters may be in charge while he here. But get this straight right now, little sexy thing; he not here most of the time. He over to Sanibel playing conservationist. And when Winters ain't here, you gotta believe Boss Pigott, he in charge."

Pigott continued to hold Lizzie up against the wall. Out of the corner of her eye she saw one of the house servants emerge from a doorway, gasp, and then hurry back through that doorway.

Pigott ground Lizzie's back into the wall. His tight grip was certain to leave bruises. "Mr. Winters is a gentleman. He'll want to feed you before he fucks you. He might even want to save you as a gift for that useless, ugly son of his. But I ain't that way, no sir. When I'm in charge I'll just throw you on the bed or the floor or wherever I like, pull it out, and stick it in you. So you best not make me mad."

Pigott glared into Lizzie's eyes for a moment and then suddenly released his grip. Lizzie's feet dropped to the floor. She just managed to hold herself up against the wall. She certainly didn't want to fall against Pigott. Dizzy, her heart thumping, Lizzie fought to catch her breath.

Pigott backed away and picked up his riding crop. He looked Lizzie up and down. "You are a sexy little thing." Pigott smirked, gestured toward the stairs with the riding crop, and bowed slightly. "You best not be late for dinner, miss."

CHAPTER THIRTY SEVEN

Dinner

Augie rose from his seat at the head of a long table and gestured toward the seat beside him on his left. He smiled his politician's smile. "You look quite beautiful tonight, Lizzie."

She hesitated at the entrance to the dining room, still shaking from her encounter with Pigott. A chandelier hung above the center of the inlaid wooden table. The chandelier's small candle-shaped lights reflected in hundreds of tiny glass pendants.

Lizzie walked slowly, silently across the room and then smoothed down her dress as she sat. She shuddered as the wooden seat contacted her skin.

Three place settings adorned their end of the long table but only Lizzie and Augie were in the room. The silverware was immaculately shiny. The china had a restrained hand-painted Oriental pattern, a dragon design.

"Is the third setting for your son?" Lizzie asked.

Augie gave Lizzie a questioning look; eyebrows raised and head tilted slightly. "No, he's away on business. Boss Pigott is joining us. We got some farm business to discuss. He should be along in a minute."

Augie picked up a small bell from beside his place setting. He shook the bell, producing a high tinkling sound.

One of the girls who had greeted them at the car rushed in through a side door.

"Serve the soup, Lydia, we won't wait for Pigott."

As Lydia was dispensing mushroom barley soup into bowls, Pigott arrived and quickly sat down. "I apologize for being late, Mr. Winters. I had some business with one of the maids." Pigott winked at Lizzie and licked his lips.

Augie poured wine into three glasses. "Now that we're all here, let us pray," Augie intoned.

Immediately both Augie and Pigott nodded their heads and folded their hands as Augie began the prayer. "We thank you, oh great and merciful Lord, for this abundant fare we are about to consume. It is you who have led our hands and our hearts to this productive and enriching bountifulness."

Augie looked up suddenly at Lizzie, who had not bowed her head or folded her hands. He glared at her. "We pray around here."

"Sorry," Lizzie mumbled, resisting an urge to ask if it was spelled P-R-E-Y. She wished she had paid more attention on Sanibel when Augie had talked about the importance of saving family farming. She might have gotten a clue what a nutcase he really was. Now he was going on and on about the importance of prayer.

"...Don't forget again..." Augie paused as he pasted a congenial smile on his face. "Amen... I'm surprised you know about my son." He handed Lizzie a glass of wine. "But I'm glad you do; it will make it easier for me to give you to him."

"Give?" Lizzie exclaimed as she slammed the wine glass down beside her plate spilling some of the dark liquid. "I'm a person, a human being, not an object to be passed around like a commodity."

"You are a woman, made to do what men command," proclaimed Augie. "It says so in the Bible." He chuckled. "You also have no choice. Do what I say, and I mean whatever I say, or I'll turn you over to the cops, which will begin your road to Raiford prison and a lethal injection." He paused and wiggled his eyebrows. "What my son will inject into you won't be quite as lethal."

Both Augie and Pigott laughed.

Lizzie felt alone and vulnerable with no one to turn to for help. So for now she would have to go along with these crazy people. Even if they didn't turn her in to police, who knows what else they might do to her. She tasted her soup. It was too salty. She smiled, determined not to upset Augie until she found a way to escape.

Augie slurped a couple spoonfuls of soup and then sipped his wine. He looked Lizzie up and down. "Ummm, ummm, ummm, I sure could be talked into exercising *Droit de Seigneur.*"

"What's that?" Lizzie's voice trembled.

"It's from the Middle Ages when the lord of the manor exercised the right to deflower virgin brides on their wedding night before they were bedded by their new husbands."

"I'm not a virgin."

"I'm not a stickler for detail," laughed Augie as he clinked wine glasses with Boss Pigott, who again joined in Augie's laughter.

As Lydia served the main course of chicken piccata, okra and tomatoes, and string beans, Augie told Lizzie the food was grown on his farm. "Wait until you taste this. Even the freshest produce in stores has lost its taste and nutritional value because it's several days old. These vegetables were picked earlier today and the chicken was killed only a couple hours ago. It's the best tasting food you've ever had."

The three of them ate for several moments in silence; Augie and Boss Pigott pigishly, Lizzie mechanically. She realized the chicken was probably the one in the driveway that had been in the wrong place at the wrong time. She felt she was in the same situation.

Augie took another sip of wine, pointing at the food with his fork, and proclaimed as he chewed, "Good food like this is threatened by the loss of the family farm, the basis of America's strength." Augie suddenly turned to Boss Pigott. "Why haven't your workers started picking the oranges?"

"They're still picking tomatoes."

Augie poked at the air with his fork. "Work them harder; we can't have any part of the crop go bad."

Pigott put down his fork. "I'm already half killing them. They're falling over from exhaustion. They're working twelve hours a day, seven days a week."

Augie shrugged. "You're going soft. Work them fourteen."

"That'd kill them. They cain't work too good dead." Pigott leaned forward glaring at his employer. "And don't be calling me soft. I ain't not never been soft. But I do got enough smarts to know which side of our bread is buttered. We can't afford to lose no more workers. We really needed that last shipment what got intercepted."

"Courtesy of Lizzie here." Augie shook his head. "I knew she'd be on the beach that night but I didn't think she'd screw up our operation. Damn women, you never know what to expect."

"The question is when we can get more workers," insisted Pigott. "We need replacements."

"I know that." Augie slammed down his fork. "Don't get above yourself. Remember we lost both the police officer directing the operation and the boat captain."

"Yeah, you sure picked 'em; an undercover investigator and a pervert."

Augie glared at Pigott. "Bad luck."

"If that's what you want to call it, but don't beef about the workers we got 'til you provide more," Pigott growled. "Or tone down the punishments. It don't help none maiming and killing workers 'cause you gotta have biblical punishments."

"You better damn well remember which of us is in charge here," Augie snarled back as he recovered his fork and stabbed it into a piece of chicken.

Lizzie silently continued to eat. The food really was good and she needed to build up strength for whatever horrors lay ahead. Maybe these two lunatics would kill each other. But that was too much to hope for.

CHAPTER THIRTY EIGHT

Night Wandering

After dinner, the two men grunted "good night" to Lizzie and hurried to the front room for drinks and more discussion of farm business.

Lizzie climbed the stairs to the second floor, where Celia was emerging from Lizzie's bedroom.

"Is everything okay?" Lizzie asked.

Celia gestured back toward the room. "I drop off dresses, many colors."

"All short?"

Celia shrugged. "Yes, Miss Lizzie."

Lizzie shook her head. "This seems demented."

Celia nodded. "Yes, I think so."

Lizzie gestured toward downstairs. "Augie has complete control here. If he wants to see you naked why doesn't he just order you to take off your clothes?"

"He like peek. He like game. He like see something by accident; not happy if it just out there."

Lizzie spun a finger in a circle beside her forehead. "He's crazy. He wasn't this way on Sanibel. He's like Dr. Jekyl and Mr. Hyde."

"He want political power on rich people island. Here he already in charge. Here he do what he want. Nobody stop him." She crossed herself.

"Can I talk to you?" Lizzie gestured toward her room.

"Sure." Celia turned and walked back into Lizzie's room.

Lizzie followed Celia. "How can you put up with this barbaric treatment?'

Celia sat on the edge of Lizzie's bed. Lizzie sat beside her. Celia looked at her hands resting in her lap and spoke quietly. "I know it shameful. But you not here long enough know how horrible it is for farm worker: work until drop, sleep in filth, itch from bed bug, dig trench in ground for toilet, terrible rotten food." Celia laughed ruefully. "Picking beautiful food and eat crap food. If worker eat what he pick, he beaten."

Lizzie leaned closer to the girl. "But aren't you ashamed of the way you're treated?"

"Real shame on those use me." She gestured with her head toward Augie's room. "Shame not on victim. I have own room and good food. I sad my husband and son still forced do farm work. I sad I separated from them."

Lizzie took Celia's hand. "You have a husband and son?"

"Yes, eight year old. He beautiful before we trapped here. Now he sick, very thin." A tear slipped from Celia's right eye onto her cheek.

"Do you get to see them?"

"Yes, I sneak out at night to visit. It dangerous and often they too exhausted to do more than say hello. Often not even that. Often they asleep." Celia wiped away the tear. "I look at them but not wake them. They need sleep."

"How do you get through the fence that surrounds the house?"

Celia looked at Lizzie with wide eyes. She looked afraid. "I talk too much. I miss husband and son too much. It feel good talk somebody." Celia jumped up and ran from the room.

Lizzie stared after her, determined to discover how Celia penetrates the fence.

Lizzie quickly changed into a black dress, went downstairs, and walked toward the front door. The two men in the front room were still deeply engrossed in discussion, their expressions serious. They looked up as Lizzie passed.

"I'm getting some air; that okay?"

They nodded and returned to their loud interaction.

Lizzie opened the heavy front door and walked onto the porch. Light streaming from the windows lit the yard. Lights were also strung along the fence. Lizzie realized Celia couldn't go through here. Anyone looking out a window would see her.

Lizzie tried to look casual as she walked down the steps from the porch onto the driveway. She strolled toward the south side of the house, the side her bedroom window faced. As she walked along that side, she glanced at a large dilapidated barracks building and several old metal trailers beyond the wire mesh fence. A barren area of short scruffy plants and bare dirt stretched between the fence and the barracks.

This section seemed unlikely to Lizzie. Lots of people must be housed in those barracks. Guards must patrol regularly. Celia couldn't get through this section of fence with so many people nearby and with the possibility of people looking out from the bedrooms in the house.

It was darker behind the house. The fence stretched in an unbroken line. Beyond it were woods. Animal noises, a rumbling sound followed by a screech, came from the woods. Wind ruffled the leaves. Lizzie thought this was more likely. It was darker here and people usually stayed in front of the house. Nobody would be in those woods. But the fence looked solid.

Lizzie continued around the corner to the fourth side of the house. Beyond that section of fence stood several neatly maintained trailers which she assumed were for the guards. So Celia obviously couldn't go through that side, not with the guards' quarters there. She must go through behind the house. Celia must do it before the workers go to sleep in order to see her husband and son while still awake. So it should be soon. All Lizzie had to do was wait and watch.

Lizzie found a dark area against the house. She sat on the ground between a bush and a bottled gas tank and waited.

Insects crawled on Lizzie's exposed bottom. A couple bit her. She was trying to brush the creepy little creatures off when she saw movement. A shadow detached itself from the rear of the house near the back stairs.

Celia looked around then dashed across the yard to the fence. Quickly she gripped the fence near a post and worked her way down it from shortly below eye level to knee level. She seemed to be undoing it in some way. After spreading open a gap in the fence, Celia stepped through, and then quickly reconnected the wire fence to the post. She disappeared into the shadows of the woods. The whole process took only seconds.

Lizzie stood up and dusted the insects off. She hurried to the fence. Where the interlaced diamond patterns of the wire fence were connected to the post, the wire had been cut in about eight places. The fence was severed in such a way that the wire had been turned into hooks which connected to the metal loops along the post.

Lizzie pushed one hook-loop set together. It became unhooked easily so that it could be spread apart. She hooked it back up; also easily. Lizzie took several steps back. The fence looked solid from even a short distance away.

Now she knew how to get through the inner fence. But she still needed to figure out how to tackle the other two fences.

As Lizzie climbed the steps onto the front porch and approached the front door, she heard piano playing; classical music; very stormy and dramatic.

She wondered who could play like that.

Lizzie entered quietly. Her bare feet didn't make a sound as she looked into the front room. Seated at the grand piano, thoroughly absorbed in his intense playing, was Boss Pigott. Bent over, his hands attacking the keys, his face grimacing, Pigott seemed not to notice Lizzie.

The music throbbed through the room. Lizzie had been to many concerts, dragged to them by her social-climbing husband. This passion-filled music seemed equal to the best. She was afraid to be near Pigott, but she was mesmerized.

A crescendo of sound was followed by dead silence as Pigott completed the musical piece. He sat hunched over the keys, sweating. He looked up and noticed Lizzie. "Damn, little sexy thing, you still wandering around?"

"I'm amazed," said Lizzie. "You play brilliantly, a side of you I would never have expected."

Pigott glared at Lizzie and raised a clenched fist. "There's some assholes I can't crush." He nodded toward the stairs. "So I take my shit out on the goddamned piano." Pigott smiled broadly, revealing a couple gold teeth, and made a grasping motion with his fist. "I'd rather crush people, see them squirm, see them suffer."

Lizzie took a step back away from Pigott. "But you're an amazing pianist."

"My mother wanted me to be a musician. I went down another path. She never forgave me. Mothers are supposed to forgive, aren't they?" Pigott's eyes were intense. "Want to hear Rachmaninoff's Prelude in C-Sharp Minor? It's got a lot of pounding; I feel like pounding."

"Yes, I'd enjoy that."

"Rachmaninoff really stirs me up. Lock yourself in your room tonight. I'll wanna pound something else when I finish the piano."

"The door to my room doesn't lock."

"I know."

CHAPTER THIRTY NINE

—⦿⦿⦿—

Crucifixion

Lizzie was restless with fear after going up to her room. Eventually she fell into a nightmare-tossed sleep involving Pigott sporting an enormous penis. She shot him but the bullets went right through him without any obvious damage. His penis got bigger each time she shot him until it was about four feet long. He was hitting her with it. She was being shaken. Lizzie screamed and tried to fight off her molester. "It me," shouted Celia, pushing back at Lizzie. "It's morning. I here to help you dress."

"I don't need help," Lizzie grumbled, relaxing and rubbing the sleep from her eyes.

"Mr. Winters angry if I not guarantee you clean."

Lizzie sat up abruptly, jumped from her bed, and rushed to the bathroom. She felt nauseous, probably from tension. She wondered why nobody had bothered her during the night. Was she being saved for Augie's mysterious, "ugly" son?

Lizzie shut the bathroom door behind her. She wished she could lock it to keep Celia from insisting on helping. However, the door had no lock. Lizzie leaned over the toilet, expecting to throw up. But the nausea passed. So she did her normal morning bathroom routine.

As Lizzie finished, she heard Celia gasp, "Oh no."

"What is it?" asked Lizzie as she emerged from the bathroom.

Celia was looking out the bedroom window. "Gaston must have tried to escape."

Lizzie went over beside Celia and peered out the partially open window. One of the guards was dragging a young man to the side of the dilapidated barracks building. Other guards herded a group of about thirty farm workers so they faced the barracks. From their second story window, Lizzie and Celia could see just above the fence and over the heads of the farm workers.

The guard threw Gaston up against the building.

Boss Pigott strode around the end of the barracks off to Lizzie's right.

"Oh no, this bad," Celia said.

"Why do you say that?"

"If Boss Pigott himself administer punishment, it bad."

Gaston stood defiantly facing the guard. He spat at the guard's feet.

The guard drew back his fist.

"Push him against the wall." Pigott yelled. Pigott's voice echoed off the side of the barracks as the guard punched Gaston in the stomach then shoved him backwards. As Gaston was pushed against the wall, Pigott turned toward the house. He looked up at the west end immediately beside Lizzie's room. Lizzie at first thought he was looking at her. She stepped away from the window.

Celia gestured toward the next room. "He getting Mr. Winters approval. Mr. Winters watch from his bedroom."

Lizzie hesitantly returned to the window. She was afraid of what she might see but was fascinated by the barbaric spectacle and ashamed of her cowardice in looking away. She no longer wanted to be a cowardly person.

Pigott held up several metal spikes and a large hammer. After a few seconds he smiled and nodded as though he had gotten a signal, like the thumbs up or down signal from a Roman emperor. He looked away from the house and toward the workers being forced to watch. He addressed them: "This is what we do to people who try to leave the farm without paying their debts. We provided you transportation to this country, food, and housing. You owe us."

As he spoke, Pigott looked from one worker to the next. He turned suddenly and shouted at the guard, "Hold him tight."

The guard pulled Gaston's right arm out as far as it would go. Pigott used the hammer and spike to nail brackets onto Gaston's arm affixing his wrist to the building. The ringing impact of the metal hammer hitting the metal spike echoed back and forth between the barracks and the house.

Lizzie's stomach turned.

The guard and Pigott moved to Gaston's other arm. Pigott attached that arm to the building and stepped back. Gaston's feet were just above the ground. His arms were stretched out forming a cross with his body. His head was up. His eyes glared at Pigott and the guards.

"That's barbaric," exclaimed Lizzie.

"He lucky he valuable worker," whispered Celia.

"Why?"

"If he old or sick they nail spike through hand and leave him to die." Celia's eyes were slits of hatred. "He lucky they need his hands to pick things."

"Okay, everybody back to work," Pigott ordered. "This boy'll be here awhile. He sure as shit ain't goin' nowhere."

Pigott laughed and turned away from Gaston. The guards ordered the workers to move quickly back to the fields. They turned away slowly, glancing at each other and back at Gaston as they slumped off. Pigott followed behind the workers as the guards marched them out of sight.

Gaston was left alone, crucified to the old wooden building with its peeling green paint and newer splashes of red.

As Lizzie continued to stare at the man crucified to the building, a breeze blew ruffling the leaves and smaller branches on the trees in the wooded area to the left of the barracks building. A small scarlet bird flew from the woods, passed close by Lizzie's window, then soared out of sight. Normal country sounds returned, the chirpings and the breezes. Lizzie wasn't sure whether they had stopped for the crucifixion or whether she had just stopped hearing them.

Lizzie turned away from the window. "How can you just stand there and do nothing? How can all the workers take that treatment day after day?"

Celia put her hand on Lizzie's arm. "We have no choice." She gestured toward the window. "See what happen to someone who resist."

"What's this about owing money for transportation here?"

Celia shook her head. "That joke. We pay lot money be brought to states. When we say we already pay, Boss Pigott ask 'where your receipt?' then laugh and beat us."

"Boss Pigott is a monster," Lizzie spat.

"Real monster Mr. Winters. Pigott follow orders."

Lizzie's eyes widened. "It just hit me; it must have been Augie who ordered the policeman to kill Clete."

"Huh?" Celia looked confused.

"Do you know I'm wanted for murder?" Lizzie asked.

Celia blinked and took a step away from Lizzie. "No, Mr. Winters not tell about you."

Lizzie followed after her. "Don't you get news here?"

Celia held her hand up in a resisting motion and shook her head. "Mr. Winters not let us listen to anything from outside the farm."

Lizzie took Celia's hand. "Come sit beside me on the bed. I'll tell you what I've been through."

It took some time for Lizzie to complete the history of everything that had happened to her. "So you see," Lizzie concluded, "Augie was the most likely person to order Clete killed. He was the one bringing in you Haitians. If he found out Clete was a government agent, the logical thing would be to have him killed."

"He capable of murder," Celia interjected. "But I not believe Mr. Winters or Boss Pigott sneak in bushes to shoot your friend Joey. It not like them."

"Maybe Augie wanted to force me to come to him for help. Killing Joey would make me do that, did force me to do that."

Celia shook her head. "No, I know both men close. They not shoot from behind a tree and run off. They kill in open and declare it the American way."

"Then who shot Joey?"

"I not know." Celia stood up. "I do know you late for lunch unless we start getting you ready."

"How can I sit calmly eating lunch with that monster who ordered a man crucified?" Lizzie stood and gestured toward the window. "How can I eat while that man is hanging bleeding in the hot sun with nothing to eat or drink?"

"You must. You not want make Mr. Winters angry. You see what he do." Celia wrung her hands.

Lizzie walked over to the window and looked out at Gaston, who was bare-chested and wore tan work pants. He had not moved. He silently hung attached to the wooden wall glaring toward the main house. Lizzie wondered if he could see her looking out the upstairs window.

"I was so wrong about Augie," stated Lizzie. "I was warned he was dangerous but I wouldn't listen. Val warned me. Now I can't even reach Val. I tried again before going to sleep but again I got a recorded message."

"Don't tell me about use that phone. I not want know," Celia said. "If you get caught and they think I know. I couldn't stand what they do to me." Celia shook her head and cried. "I sorry I so weak."

Lizzie patted her on the shoulder. "You have every right to be scared."

Celia threw her arms around Lizzie and hugged her. "If they catch you with that phone you'll be crucified next to Gaston after they rape you. I don't see how you so brave."

After hugging Celia back, Lizzie broke from her embrace. "You're right; I should go to lunch with Augie. He respected me when I worked for him on Sanibel. Maybe I can reason with him about Gaston." She put her hands on her hips. Her eyes became hard. "And maybe I can find a way to get even with him for all this horror."

175

CHAPTER FORTY

Lunch

"You're late," Augie said as Lizzie entered the dining room.

She remained silent as she walked slowly to her seat.

Augie glared at Lizzie. "I expect people to be on time."

Lizzie smoothed her dress and sat. She immediately rose back up. The chair was wet. Lizzie took a cloth napkin from the table, shook it out, and placed it on the chair. She sat on the napkin. Lizzie picked up another napkin from the holder in the center of the table and placed it on her lap. It made her feel less exposed. "I'm here now."

Augie grunted and rang his little bell.

Lydia rushed in with a large soup tureen. She ladled the lumpy liquid into Augie's and Lizzie's bowls and then retreated.

Lizzie dipped her spoon in and raised it to her mouth.

"Hold on a minute: prayer," Augie said. "We must praise God for all he has done for us." Augie folded his hands and intoned, "Oh merciful God we thank you for what we are about to receive and we praise you for allowing us to move forward in our work to save the American farm."

Lizzie had not put down her spoon. She took a sip of the potato leek soup. "How can you pretend religion while you're torturing a man?"

Augie picked up his spoon. "What man?"

Lizzie waved her arm toward the outside. "The man nailed to the building."

Augie gave a dismissal wave. "Oh him; that isn't torture. He won't be there for more than eight or nine hours. I've stood in a field in the hot sun for longer than that without even having a building to lean against. It's an exaggeration to call that torture. It's an enhanced punishment technique."

Lizzie set down her spoon. "But his arms are clamped to the wall and stretched out. It must be very painful."

Augie shook his head. "You've been too sheltered, Lizzie. These Haitians don't feel pain like you or I would. That's why you have to be tough with them to get your message across."

Lizzie trembled with emotion. "What about the heat? It's summer. He could suffer sunstroke."

Augie chuckled. "Haven't you noticed; he's black. The sun and the heat don't bother black people. That's why they're black."

Lizzie stared at Augie. "You can't be the same person I knew on Sanibel Island. There you seemed concerned about animals, the environment, and people. Here you've turned into Mr. Hyde."

Augie shook his head. "Dear sweet, innocent Lizzie, you still haven't learned about life. We're all phonies living pretend lives. If you don't, people will see you for what you really are. We're all playing games."

Lizzie shook her head. "Don't you care anything about the environment? Wasn't anything about you on Sanibel real?"

Augie chuckled. "Ninety percent of those environmentalists would abandon their most cherished conservationist beliefs if those beliefs threatened their property values. They are for the environment because it is currently popular to be for the environment."

Lizzie frowned as she glared at Augie. "I can't believe my ears. You're a cynical monster."

Augie took a sip of soup, made a slight face, sprinkled some salt on the remainder, looked back over at Lizzie, shook his head, and laughed. "I'm a realist. But you're not cynical or realistic. You're the most dangerous kind of person, the type of person who screws up everything. You're an idealist, one of the ten percent. You really want to help the animals, help the people, help everybody. But look at you, you can't even help yourself; poor beautiful misguided Lizzie. It's you deluded bleeding heart reformers who really screw up the world."

Lizzie gaped at Augie. "You have no humanity at all, no empathy for the suffering of your fellow creatures."

"You don't understand maintaining control. That's the trouble with our society; everything is too lax. If they crucified some shoplifters in front of Wal-Mart there'd be a lot less thievery." Augie's eyes sparkled.

"You're crazy."

Augie laughed. "Lizzie, Lizzie, Lizzie, I'll tell you what. You can take that boy out there some water if you're so concerned about sunstroke." Augie gave Lizzie a benevolent smile.

"You'll open the fence for me to go out to him?"

"Hell no, that fence keeps the house safe. If you want to take that black boy water, you'll have to climb over the fence." Augie looked Lizzie up and down, leering. "That's something I'd like to watch you do, climb the fence in that short skirt." Augie wiggled his bushy eyebrows.

Lizzie stared at Augie, stunned to silence by his crudeness.

"Unfortunately," Augie continued, "I won't be around this afternoon to watch you tackle the fence. I need to go into town to do some shopping and then drop by Sanibel to get a little work done there, and visit the wife. Gotta keep her happy. Dinner might be late tonight."

Lizzie stood up. "What about the man crucified to the building?"

Augie scratched his head and looked puzzled. "What do you mean?"

Lizzie gestured out in the direction of Gaston. "When will you order him taken down?"

"When I get back. Or maybe I'll just leave him there as a message to anyone else thinking of escape."

"He'll die."

"Probably not."

CHAPTER FORTY ONE

Water and Woods

After returning to her bedroom, Lizzie looked out the window at Gaston, who hung limply from the metal brackets on his wrists and appeared to have passed out. Nobody else was around. All the guards and workers were probably in the fields.

Someone tapped on Lizzie's door, startling her. "Yes," Lizzie called.

Celia looked in. "Everything okay? Lydia say Mr. Winters angry with you at dinner."

Lizzie turned from the window. "I need a bottled water."

"Look in the nightstand by your bed. It a refrigerator."

Lizzie examined the unit. "I never would have guessed."

Celia spread both arms. "House full things and people aren't what seem. Be careful." She suddenly placed a hand to her mouth. "But I not say anything. I not know what you plan. I not even know you plan something. Good luck." She hurried out. Lizzie watched her go then opened the front of the nightstand. Inside the small refrigerator were waters, beers, some strawberries, and some cheese.

As Lizzie took the bottled water she realized she needed a wet cloth to cool Gaston's forehead. In the bathroom she found a washcloth. She then hurried back to the hallway door and opened it a crack. She listened carefully for almost a minute but heard no sounds in the hall. So she opened the door and stepped out.

Lizzie made her way cautiously along the hall, down the back stairs, and through to the back door. She crept on bare feet, hesitated, and listened for sounds of other people as she went. She didn't encounter anybody.

After closing the back door behind her and crossing a tiny landing, Lizzie descended steps to the narrow stretch of yard between the back of the house and the fence. The woods beyond the fence cast dark shadows over the backyard.

Lizzie dashed across to where the fence unhooked. If she hadn't already known the exact location she would not have found it in a million years. After quickly undoing the fence, Lizzie stepped through and then easily linked the mesh back together.

Sounds came from the back of the house. Lizzie hurried into the woods and hid behind a large cabbage palm, the same type tree she had been tied to on Sanibel.

After several moments of silence, Lizzie crept out from behind the palm and moved away from the fence into an area of grass, weeds, and very small bushes. She crept forward until she was adjacent to the corner of the fence but about twenty feet out from it. Still nobody in sight.

Lizzie ran full speed across the ragged, weedy grass. She held the water bottle in one hand and the washcloth in the other. Lizzie stopped when she was opposite Gaston. He looked ghastly up close. She approached him. His chin was slouched on his chest, his eyes closed. His arms hung from the two rusty brackets. Blood dripped where one of the brackets cut into his wrist.

"I have water for you," Lizzie whispered.

Gaston's eyes opened slowly as his head rose. He stared at Lizzie. *"Un Ange, un ange blanc,"* Gaston whispered. *"Est-ce que je suis au paradis?"*

"No, I'm certainly not an angel," Lizzie replied. "I'm Lizzie; I've brought you some water, *l'eau.*"

"Bon, Lizzie, J'ai soif," Gaston gasped.

Lizzie unscrewed the top from the Fiji water bottle and held it to Gaston's lips. He sipped.

Lizzie drew the bottle away. "Not too fast," she cautioned. She reached out her hand and touched his brow. "Let me put some on your forehead. It's burnt from the sun."

After spilling some water into the washcloth, Lizzie placed the wet cloth against Gaston's forehead.

"Ah, merci," whispered Gaston. *"Plus de l'eau, s'il vous plaît."*

Leaving the wet washcloth plastered to his forehead, Lizzie again put the water bottle to his lips.

Gaston drank deeply.

Holding the bottle with her left hand, Lizzie reached up with her right to pull at one of the spikes holding the bracket on Gaston's left wrist.

Gaston jerked his mouth away from the water bottle. "*Non, non,*" he exclaimed emphatically.

Lizzie drew her hand away. "Maybe I can pull the nails out."

"*Non,*" Gaston repeated.

"Are you afraid if I get you down they'll punish you more?" Lizzie asked.

"*Oui.*"

Lizzie nodded understanding and placed the water bottle back against Gaston's lips. Suddenly a door slammed on the far side of the barracks building.

Gaston's eyes widened. "*Vite! Depechez-vous!*"

Lizzie did not understand the words. Her high school French had been long ago. She did understand the terror in Gaston's voice. She dropped the water bottle and ran toward the opposite side of the building, away from where the door had slammed.

Just after turning the corner of the building, Lizzie heard a deep southern voice: "Where the hell'd that washcloth come from?" Then, after a pause, the voice said, "Damn, almost tripped on that fuckin' bottle. Who the hell's been here?"

Gaston did not reply.

Lizzie heard the crunch of heavy footsteps coming toward her. She backed down the side of the building until she came to a door. It was unlocked. Quickly she opened the door, entered, and closed it behind her.

The smell was almost overwhelming. Lizzie turned and looked along two rows of metal bunk beds. It was like a World War II training barracks from an old movie, except it stank and the mattresses on the beds were gray-stained with black splotches. The walls were discolored with mold and fungus and dirt. The ceiling was covered with leak stains and dark fungus.

A small amount of gloomy light was let in through the filthy windows at the far ends of the building. The side walls were solid wood, with no windows or doors.

Lizzie crept into the long room. She looked around in disgust. It was amazing people could actually live like this or that other people would force them to. She knew she must get away from the door she had entered before the man looking for her reached it. The floor felt sticky under her bare feet. She hurried down toward the other end of the building. Just as she reached the door at that end, she looked back and saw the shadow of the man through the filthy window of the door she had just come through.

Lizzie turned the knob. It turned but wouldn't open. It wasn't locked. It was stuck.

Lizzie looked back. The man was at the window in the door at the other end of the building. The filth of the window benefitted her. The man couldn't see in. So he couldn't see her standing at the other end of the long, dark interior. But he would see her as soon as he entered.

She shoved her shoulder against the door. It creaked then burst open. She stumbled out and quietly closed the door behind her.

Lizzie hurried along the side of the building until she was behind it. Then, as she ran out across dirt and weeds away from the building, her foot unexpectedly met empty air. She found herself tottering above a long slit trench. She twisted and threw her leg forward until her foot hit solid ground. She ended up straddling the ditch, looking down into a stinking mess of filth. It was obviously the worker's toilet. It exuded an unbelievable stench. No enclosure surrounded the ditch. They had to do their business out in the open, in public.

Lizzie swung her left leg across the ditch onto the side away from the barracks. She wobbled on the edge of the latrine ditch and then, waving her arms, recovered her balance and leapt free of the ditch. Decisively, she picked a relatively obstacle-free route and ran through thickening weeds and bushes toward the section of woods behind the fence at the rear of the house.

A fallen branch tripped Lizzie. She fell face down into leaves, weeds, and tiny sticks among low bushes. The fall knocked the air out of her. She lay still a moment. Looking back, she discovered her fall probably kept her from being discovered. A man with a rifle exited the barracks. The man looked around but apparently didn't see Lizzie where she lay behind the bushes. He had hard, lifeless eyes. She had noticed before, when Gaston was being tormented, that the guards all were expressionless, like they lacked souls or human feelings, like zombies or drug addicts.

She kept very still, hoping her black dress would help conceal her. She worried about the dress being so short and her legs being so white. She tried to scrunch her legs up under her.

The man with the rifle walked out almost to the latrine ditch. Then he turned and walked back around the far side of the building, the side where Gaston hung crucified. Lizzie hoped Gaston would not be punished further because of her attempt to ease his suffering.

After cautiously getting up and brushing leaves and small sticks off her dress and legs, she made her way into the woods. She stepped on some briers but they were only an inconvenience to her shell-hardened feet.

Eventually, Lizzie found a trail that seemed to lead back toward the rear of the house. After walking down that trail for several hundred yards, Lizzie came to a cross trail. She decided to explore and turned to the right, away from the house. This trail was narrow and winding. At times it almost vanished in the undergrowth. A short distance down the trail Lizzie heard a rattling noise. She stopped dead still. Directly in front of her was a huge rattlesnake. It stared at her and flicked out its forked tongue. Its rattle beat the ground as its head drifted from side to side.

Lizzie took one step back then looked around her. Beside the trail lay a rotten fallen limb. Careful not to alarm the rattler, Lizzie picked up the limb by its narrow end. She raised it, paused, and then brought the heavier end down suddenly with all the force she could muster directly onto the head of the rattler. The rattling ended abruptly.

Repeatedly, Lizzie pounded the snake with the limb. Then she tossed the branch aside, took a deep breath, stepped over the mashed remains and continued along the trail.

"Dumb snake," she muttered.

Lizzie followed the trail in and out between trees. After one final turn the trail was blocked by a high fence. This wire-mesh fence had a barbed wire extension on the top which stuck out away from the side Lizzie was on. This seemed curious; the fence was obviously designed to keep something or somebody out. Lizzie would have thought the fence was to keep the farm workers in, not to prevent entry into this hell-hole of a farm.

Looking up and down along the high fence, Lizzie noticed a sign. It read: "DANGER! Wild animals." The fence must enclose Aaron's animal clinic. All she had to do to save herself was climb the fence and find Aaron. But right now she felt ready to drop from physical and emotional fatigue. She was too worn out to climb the fence. The tension had gotten to her and finding Aaron might not be easy. She might get lost in the thick woods. She would try during the night or the next day, after resting and regaining some of her strength.

Lizzie made her way back along the trail. She passed the snake and the intersection with the side trail. She hurried on. Eventually, as she thought she would, she came to the edge of the woods behind the house.

Once again, Lizzie looked around carefully. Then she dashed over to the fence, unhooked it, squeezed through, rehooked it, and hurried into the house. She hesitated, wondering if she had been wrong not to leave now, to get away from this horrible place while she could. Who knows what might happen tonight?

Lizzie's mind was made up for her by the sound of footsteps came from the front of the house. She would not have time to get out without being seen. Lizzie turned away from the back door and dashed to the stairs to the second floor. She climbed without making a sound and snuck down the hall to her room. She threw herself onto her bed and fell into an exhausted sleep.

A rap on the door awakened her sometime later. It was Celia, looking concerned. "Mr. Winters very angry. He order you go to dining room now."

CHAPTER FORTY TWO

Accusations

Lizzie took her time preparing for dinner. She looked out the bedroom window. Gaston was no longer nailed to the barracks building. But bloodstains discolored its wall.

Lizzie took a hot shower and changed her dress before going downstairs.

Augie glared at Lizzie as she entered the dining room.

Boss Pigott was also at the table. He looked like he was enjoying a private joke. His bulging eyes burned into her and the edges of his mouth curled up in a mocking smile.

"You missed dinner," Augie growled.

Lizzie silently stood in the doorway a moment before casually walking to the table.

Augie's and Pigott's plates contained the remains of meals. Lizzie's plate was empty.

"Sit down," Augie ordered.

"No, I believe I'd rather stand."

Augie's eyes shifted to Pigott. Augie motioned sharply with his head toward the stairs.

Pigott stood ponderously and shoved his chair back from the table. The chair legs made a screeching noise on the wood floor. Pigott trod purposefully out of the dining room. Lizzie heard the stairs creak as Pigott climbed them.

"Somebody gave that boy water," Augie stated.

Lizzie focused her attention on Augie. She looked down at him. "What boy?"

"You know very well what boy." Augie's fat face turned slightly red as he raised his voice. "That boy who was nailed to the worker's quarters."

Lizzie nodded. "You've taken him down. I'm glad."

"Of course we took him down. We ain't dumb. When there's a shortage of workers you don't waste one; we were just knocking him back into line." Augie punched his open left hand with his right fist. "A little discipline is good for these people. He'll be back in the fields tomorrow. He tried to escape without paying what he owes for being brought here from Haiti. The crucifixion is a symbolic message to these people that until they pay their debts they're attached to this farm."

Lizzie tapped the edge of the table. "Keeping him prisoner is slavery."

"Oh crap, that's just a word." Augie spat, as he shifted around in his chair. "Listen to me close; depriving him of water was part of his punishment. Whoever gave him water defied me. Nobody defies me."

Lizzie shrugged. "At lunch you suggested I give him water. How could it be defying you to do what you suggested?"

"That was irony. Don't you know irony when you hear it?" Augie shook his head as though exasperated. His chins wobbled. "I suggested you give him water knowing there was no way you could get over the fence to reach him. I was suggesting the impossible, I was being ironic."

Lizzie leaned forward slightly. "Then why are you angry with me?"

Augie started to rise. "I realize now you must have got the water to him with help from the other side of the fence. You could have taken the water up to the fence and squeezed the bottle through the mesh to somebody over there."

Lizzie shook her head. "You can't prove that."

Augie now stood facing Lizzie with a corner of the dining room table between them. "All I have to prove is the water came from your room." Augie pointed toward the stairs. "If it did, your treatment here is about to change drastically. I will do whatever is necessary to discover who helped you. If you don't give me that name quickly, you will regret the day you came here."

"I already regret that day."

Augie pointed directly at Lizzie's face. "You have no idea how bad things can get for you."

Lizzie shrugged. "But you don't know the bottle came from my room."

Augie stepped behind his chair and grabbed its back for support. "I will soon. I sent Boss Pigott to search your room. If a water is missing, you better have the empty bottle."

Lizzie shook her head. She stared off into space regretting she had not escaped earlier. But she refused to give any outward indication of her inner despair. She wouldn't give the bastard the satisfaction. She looked down at her empty plate. "What about dinner?"

Augie laughed. "You're not eating a damned thing until I know you ain't a traitor. We got an opportunity here to save the American family farm. What I'm doing is God's will. Treason will not be tolerated. It's an abomination before God."

Lizzie tapped the side of her head. "You're crazy, completely Looney Tunes."

Augie waved his arms at her. "You're an abomination. You laugh at God. Leave me. Get out of my sight."

Lizzie turned and headed toward the stairs.

"Not your room," Augie yelled after her. "That's off limits to you until the search is completed."

"Can you play?"

Lizzie was startled by Boss Pigott's voice behind her. She had been sitting at the piano in the front room idly plunking at the keys and worrying about her situation. She did not want to think of what might lie ahead.

"No, I never learned," responded Lizzie. She turned and looked up into Boss Pigott's smiling face.

"That's too bad," Pigott said.

"Why are you smiling?"

Pigott's smile widened. "I've got some good news and some bad news."

"I could use some good news," said Lizzie. "What's the good news?"

Pigott continued smiling. "I'd rather tell you the bad news first. The results of my search of your room enraged Mr. Winters. He wants to see you in his office right now."

Lizzie stood up. "Where is his office?"

"In the back of the house, down the hall past the stairs. Don't worry about finding it, I'm taking you there." Pigott grabbed Lizzie's right arm and jerked her away from the piano, knocking over the piano bench in the process. He dragged her painfully from the front room into the hall. The enormous man pushed Lizzie past the stairs down a narrow hallway. She stumbled and he pushed her harder. Lizzie tried to resist but Pigott was much stronger than she was. She gasped out, "Please stop for a minute. Tell me: what's the good news?"

Pigott spun her around and grinned down into her face. Lizzie noticed some of his teeth were gold capped. Pigott brought his face down close to hers. His breath had a rotten smell, the smell of infection and bad hygiene, rotting fish.

Pigott licked his lips. "The good news is I'm gonna enjoy sloppy seconds."

He roughly twisted her back around and shoved her further down the dark hallway.

CHAPTER FORTY THREE

Evidence

With his left hand holding Lizzie by the back of her neck, Boss Pigott knocked with his other hand on an unmarked door at the end of the hall.

"Enter." Augie's voice was faint but firm.

Pigott pulled open the door and shoved Lizzie into the room. She tripped over a small flag-shaped rug and fell to the hardwood floor in front of an enormous carved oak desk. She banged her knee as she hit the floor. It hurt.

Large American flags on slanted poles filled two corners of the room. Framed high on the wall behind the desk was the single word: "BELIEVE!" Augie glared down at Lizzie from his leather executive's chair behind that desk. "Get her off the floor." The word 'BELIEVE' was directly above his head.

Pigott grabbed Lizzie's arms and pulled her up. He lifted her until her feet cleared the floor. The pain in her knee lessened. Augie suddenly smiled. "Keep holding her like that. She's the first natural blond we've had on the farm."

Lizzie realized her arms being held above her head had raised her short dress embarrassingly high. She struggled but it seemed to have no effect on Pigott. Augie's eyes sparkled out from the folds of skin around them.

"You're sick." Lizzie spat the words toward Augie.

"That's why I likes workin' fo' him," laughed Pigott, whose lifting of Lizzie seemed effortless, like she was weightless.

Augie became serious. "Let her down. I don't need to be distracted."

Pigott released Lizzie's arms. Her bare feet dropped to the floor. She maintained her balance in spite of a renewed sharp pain in her knee. Her arms fell to her sides. She smoothed her dress down.

"You want me to stay, Mr. Winters?" asked Pigott.

Augie made a dismissal motion with his hand. "Wait outside the door. I don't think I'm in any danger from her."

Pigott left, closing the door behind him.

Lizzie stood in the middle of the room, staring defiantly at Augie. The wood floor was cold under her bare feet. She refused to show him any pain or discomfort.

After shifting a Bible from the center to the side of his desk, Augie pointed to that center space. "What do you see there?"

Lizzie did not understand. "Nothing, I don't see anything there."

"Exactly," exclaimed Augie. "You don't see a bottle of water and you don't see a wash cloth. You don't see them because they're missing from your room. They weren't there. Can you explain that?"

"No," Lizzie replied defiantly. "It's your house. You expect your guests to keep track of everything in it?"

"You know damn well you took out that water and cloth." Augie yelled. He stood up. "I want to know who you passed them to."

Lizzie slowly shook her head. "You said earlier I gave them to Gaston."

"Who?"

Lizzie took a step forward. "Gaston, the man nailed to the building. Don't you even know the names of the people you torture?"

Augie turned red in the face. He pointed at Lizzie like a prosecutor exposing a murderer. "You passed them through the fence to somebody. I want to know who."

Lizzie firmly put her hands on her hips. "I did not pass them through the fence to anybody. I could pass a lie detector test on that."

Augie shook his head. "I'm really disappointed in you, Lizzie. I always thought you were an honest person. You know how I value honesty in an employee."

"You're not only nuts, you're stupid. I'm no longer your employee."

Augie dropped back into his chair. He was still shaking his head. "Yes, I'm really disappointed. And what makes me even more disappointed is this." Augie pulled open the drawer in front of him, reached in, and pulled out a cell phone. It was the cell phone Joey had lent to Lizzie before he was shot. Augie held the cell phone up like some sort of prize. "Can you explain this?"

"It looks like a cell phone."

Augie gestured upward with his eyes. "Boss Pigott found it hidden in your bathroom in a box of Kotex."

"I haven't used any Kotex since I've been here."

Augie waved the phone around. "Are you denying this is your cell phone?"

Lizzie smiled. "That's not my cell phone. Have you tried calling some of the numbers on the speed dial to ask whose cell phone it is?"

Augie gave a slight smile back. "You're trying to trick me into using this phone to notify somebody you're here. But you can't outfox an old fox. All I have to do is call my private line." Augie pointed to a phone on his desk. "Caller ID will tell me whose phone this is."

Augie opened the cell phone and began tapping numbers. But then he paused. "You sure you want me to do this? One last chance to admit it's yours. I hate liars."

Lizzie remained silent.

Augie tapped a couple more numbers. The phone on his desk rang. He ignored the ringing but looked at the small display screen on the phone. His expression was curious when he looked back up at Lizzie. "It says Joseph Caunteloupo. I know that name. He's a damned New York City Mafia gangster. How the hell did a Mafia chief's cell phone get in your bathroom?"

Lizzie took another step toward Augie. Her knee felt better. "Perhaps you should be more careful where you buy your Kotex."

Augie yelled as loud as he could, "Boss, get this woman out of here right now."

The door slammed open and Pigott entered. He grabbed Lizzie and started to drag her out of the room.

"Just a minute," Augie shouted.

Pigott turned Lizzie back around to face Augie, who dropped the cell phone into the center drawer of his desk. He used a key to lock that drawer and stuck the key ring into his pants pocket.

Augie pointed toward the second floor. "Take that woman up to her bedroom. Lock her in. I'm going to visit her later. After I've gotten my satisfaction you can fuck her all you want. My son will be thankful for whatever is left when I turn her over to him tomorrow."

"Yes sir, Mr. Winters, sir." Boss Pigott yanked Lizzie around and pulled her behind him as he left the room.

Out in the hallway, Pigott shoved Lizzie against a wall then stepped back and looked her up and down. "I do love my work. I sure do."

CHAPTER FORTY FOUR

Night Encounters

Lizzie couldn't sleep. She waited in fear for Augie's arrival in her bedroom. Plotting escape but discarding each plan, she tried to think of a way to defend herself or convince Augie to release her. Filled with dreadful anticipation, the wait seemed to stretch for hours. After first sitting in the chair beside the window, she began pacing the room. Then she settled briefly on the edge of her bed.

An eternity passed. Restless, she stood, walked over and looked out the door into the hall. Boss Pigott was perched on a metal chair just outside her room. He turned toward her and smiled, revealing his gold-filled teeth. "Mr. Winters'll be joining you soon. After that, it'll be my turn."

"I can wait."

"I'm not sure I can." His gold teeth flashed. He grabbed his crotch in an obscene manner and winked.

Lizzie slammed her door and hurried back to resume sitting on her bed. She despaired what was to come. But the most frustrating thing was the waiting. Action was better then sitting doing nothing. She decided to look around for an alternative, a chance to strike back.

After looking through everything in the bedroom, Lizzie walked over to the bathroom. She opened the drawer beside the sink to examine its contents.

Lizzie was back sitting on her bed when Augie strode in through the door from his bedroom. He wore a terry cloth robe with an image of a crown decorating his left chest. His robe bulged at the crotch.

Lizzie stood and faced her tormenter.

Augie pointed at her. "Take off that dress." Augie ordered.

Lizzie trembled, her hands clasped modestly in front of her. She did nothing.

Augie removed his robe. His erection wobbled like a metronome. His skin was a sickly white except for a rash covering his upper right leg and part of his belly. The redness of his erect penis contrasted to the whiteness of most of his paunchy belly.

Lizzie looked down. Augie was almost in range of her foot. But he turned slightly so any kick from Lizzie would hit the side of his leg. He smiled and shook his head. "Don't try it. I can read your mind."

Suddenly Augie sprang forward, reached out, and grabbed the front of Lizzie's dress. He ripped down. The fabric tore. The dress hung open in front, exposing Lizzie's breasts and everything else. "Now take the damned thing off."

Lizzie dropped her arms, letting the rags that remained of the dress fall to the floor.

"That's better." A wicked smile contorted his face. "Now be nice to uncle Augie. I've wanted this since that first day you walked into the Conservancy."

Lizzie didn't move as Augie wrapped his arms around her. His erection pressed against her naked skin just below her navel.

"Oh, Augie," Lizzie moaned as she rubbed his back with her right hand. She reached up with her left hand, shifted open the manicure scissors she had been palming, and stabbed one of the blades into his neck. She slit the blade upward trying to sever his carotid artery and his wind pipe.

Blood spurted from Augie's throat. His mouth fell open. His eyes stared unbelieving at Lizzie. She tried to pull out of his encircling arms. Blood was spurting all over her, drenching her. Lizzie wriggled sideways then pulled back. She got partly loose. She kicked up with her knee.

Augie gasped and released Lizzie, grabbed his throat, and stumbled across the room toward the hall door, tripping over his own feet and falling backwards. A loud cracking noise sounded as Augie hit the floor. Blood still spurted between his fingers which were wrapped around his wounded neck.

Lizzie scooped up her torn dress and ran into Augie's bedroom. She paused, looking around to get her bearings. His canopied bed was enormous. A large plaque on the wall above it listed the Ten Commandments. An American flag was in one corner, a Confederate flag in another.

Lizzie rushed to the door leading from Augie's room into the hall. She grabbed the handle with her free hand, but paused; afraid Boss Pigott would attack her the second she stepped out.

Augie emitted a gurgling scream for help.

Lizzie waited a couple seconds to give Pigott time to leave the hallway to assist his employer. When she opened the door, the hallway was empty. The chair Pigott had been sitting on lay on its side.

Naked, the rags of her dress in her hand, Lizzie ran down the hall to the rear stairs. A sound froze Lizzie in her tracks as she reached the bottom stair. A door opened to the left of the stairs. Lydia came through the doorway, saw Lizzie, stopped, gasped, stepped back and vanished as she slammed the door. The lock clicked.

Lizzie ran out the back door, quickly undid the fence, slid through, and then redid it, making sure she left no sign of her passage. Shouts came from inside the house.

Lizzie was deep into the woods beyond the back fence before she paused to put on her dress. Not much was left to put on; it was badly torn and hung open in front. The dark night was made darker by the gloominess of the woods. She looked around. Air plants, both bromeliads and orchids, hung from the sides of some of the tall trees. An extravagantly beautiful orchid bloomed about seven feet up one nearby tree.

Lizzie found a vine hanging from another tree. With a lot of work twisting it around, she was able to break off a section.

People at the house were yelling but they were too far away for Lizzie to understand them.

Images of Augie and of the blood spurting from his throat flashed before Lizzie's eyes. She shuddered at her close call as she tied the vine around her torso just below her breasts to hold her dress closed.

The noises coming from the vicinity of the house seemed louder and closer. Some people must have come outside after her. Lizzie dashed up the trail. She ran until she reached the fence with the sign warning about wild animals. Lizzie grabbed the wire mesh of the fence section immediately in front of her. The mesh was firm to her grip. She found she could pull herself up and then place a foot into the diamond pattern in the mesh. But the V shaped bottom part of the diamond severely hurt both her hands and feet.

Lizzie jumped down from the fence. She ran back to where she had found the vine used to tie her dress. Just off the trail a multitude of vines hung down. Lizzie jerked at the vines until she found several loose enough to pull away from the trees.

Footsteps scrunched on the trail she had just left. Lizzie dropped into the underbrush. The rustle of leaves and crackling of small branches moved up the trail until the sounds were directly adjacent to her. She peeked between the low plants she was lying among. A man with a rifle stood on the trail. He looked around and then walked on toward the fence. Like all the guards he had hard, dull eyes.

Lizzie remained still. A few minutes later the man returned. Again he stopped opposite where she lay. His image was faint in the darkness as Lizzie looked through a tiny opening at him. She hoped the vegetation and darkness hid her from his view. Lizzie didn't know how much longer she could hold her breath. But she couldn't just wait for him to notice her. Somewhere she had heard that a good offense is the best defense. Trying for absolute silence, her stomach pressed to the ground, Lizzie slid forward toward the man.

He pulled a walkie-talkie off his belt and held it up to his mouth. "This is Mark. No sign of her on the west trail." The walkie-talkie made static-saturated voice sounds. Lizzie moved forward quicker. Mark's listening to the walkie-talkie would block out her sounds.

"Okay, I'll come back in," Mark said. "How is he?"

More tinny voice and static sounds came from the walkie-talkie. Lizzie searched around blindly with her hands and found a thick, fallen tree limb.

Mark said, "Well, at least that's something." He clicked a switch on the walkie-talkie, clipped the device back onto his belt and turned away down the trail.

Lizzie leapt up and swung the tree limb like a baseball bat. It broke in half when it hit the back of Mark's head. He dropped to the trail without making a sound. Lizzie stood over him with the remains of the tree limb for a moment. When he didn't move she tossed the limb away. Then she knelt down and removed his gun and his walkie-talkie. She threw the walkie-talkie into the woods and then looked down at the gun in her hand.

The man on the ground at her feet wasn't moving. If she put a bullet in his head, he would never move again. He couldn't come after her later. Lizzie aimed the gun down at the back of Mark's head. But she did not pull the trigger. She could not bring herself to shoot a helpless person even if he was a slaver and a murderer. She had become braver and harder but not yet that hard.

But now that she was armed, she might be able to free the workers without going to get additional help. She ran back down the trail and turned onto the intersecting trail. Lizzie slowed down and went into a crouch just before coming into view of the barracks. She moved slowly forward in that crouch. Finally she stopped, using for cover the last tree before a stretch of clear ground between the woods and the barracks.

Disappointment swept over Lizzie when she saw three rifle-bearing guards. Guards who were off-shift must have been called back to duty to hunt for her. With additional guards on duty, this would be the worst time to try to liberate the workers.

One of the guards stood in front of the barracks door. The other two walked the outer perimeter of the fence around the house. As she watched, they passed each other in opposite directions. Lizzie decided she should hurry back before the slow-moving guard walking in her direction was adjacent to her trail.

Lizzie snuck away from the tree and crept back down the trail. As soon as she was out of sight of the guards, she ran back the way she had come. When she got to where she had hit Mark, her heart skipped a beat. He was no longer there. The broken limb was there. A blood stain was there. And the vines she had gathered were still there. But Mark was gone. She looked around. He could be anywhere. She saw no sign of him.

Lizzie picked up the vines and dashed back to the fence.

She sat down beside the fence and frantically began winding vines around her feet and hands. She must get over the fence before Mark returned with the rest of the guards. The wound vines formed a thick matting to protect her feet. She hoped the vines around her hands would provide protection like construction or gardening gloves.

Standing up again, Lizzie grabbed the wire mesh and once again began climbing. This time the strands of wire hurt only slightly, the matting of encircling vines protected her hands and feet.

At the top of the fence, Lizzie came to two strands of barbed wire mounted outward at an angle toward the wild animal area. She would have to get past the barbed wire before she could get over the fence. She reached out with her left hand and carefully grabbed a section of the wire. A barb stuck between the vines and pricked her palm. She pulled her hand back.

A sudden loud noise nearby almost made Lizzie lose her balance and her grip on the fence. Her heart fluttered with fear until she realized what she heard was the call of a barred owl. She steadied herself, breathing deeply.

Perched with her feet firmly in two openings in the mesh of the fence and her knees pressed against the fence higher up, Lizzie studied the situation. She pulled the gun out which she had shoved under the vine tied around her waist like a belt. She threw the gun over the fence. Then she undid that vine which also had tied her dress closed and contorted her way out of the dress.

Lizzie ripped the dress in half, wrapping one half around the barbed wire strand closest to her and the other half around the second strand. She wound it so it was thick enough to keep the barbs from pushing through.

Next, Lizzie removed the vines from her hands and wound them on the outside of the dress around the second strand of wire, providing an additional protective thickness above the fabric of the dress.

Lizzie moved her feet up almost to the top of the fence. She leaned out and grasped the protected section of the second strand of barbed wire.

The owl hooted again. Lizzie jumped, almost slipping off the fence. She was starting to lose her appreciation for owls, at least for this noisy one.

Lizzie raised first her left foot then her right foot onto the top rail of the fence. She was bent double, balanced precariously with her feet on that rail and her hands on the second strand of barbed wire a short distance above the top rail and a foot and a half in front of it. Her bare bottom was stuck up into the night air. She felt like some sort of circus performer or the female lead in a porn movie.

Pulling forward and down against the wire, lowering her head, and kicking out and up with her feet, Lizzie attempted to somersault herself over the barbed wire. A barb broke through the cloth from the dress and between the vine strands, tearing into her left palm. She released that hand's grip and found herself hanging from the wire by only her right hand. Realizing she was over, she let go. She dropped more than five feet and landed on a clump of Brazilian pepper bushes, which mashed under her. She rolled off onto bare ground.

Lizzie lay for several minutes waiting for the agony of broken bones. She ached all over but without any particularly sharp pain. Her knee still hurt from earlier but did not feel broken.

An unusually long series of owl hootings echoed through the pine wood.

As Lizzie rose, she bowed slightly. "Thank you, I thought I did well too."

Moving very tentatively, Lizzie looked back at the fence then down at her bloody left hand. It was not a deep cut. She clenched the hand into a tight fist as she glanced down at her naked body, glad it was a hot summer night.

Lizzie searched for several minutes for the gun. She couldn't find it. She concluded it probably was in a thicket of thorny plants which had already drawn blood without her even getting very far into it. She gave up on the gun and began threading her way between palms and palmettos, around Brazilian peppers, and other plants, all gloomy and shadowed by darkness. She could not find a trail and did not know which direction to go to find Aaron. She dare not yell. The guards from the farm might hear her.

Dry leaves crackled a short distance away. Lizzie stopped dead, listening.

Heavy breathing, like that of a large animal, came from beyond a clump of trees.

Lizzie edged away from those trees. She turned and ran, dodging in and out between trees and bushes. She heard crashing sounds in the vegetation on both sides of her as she broke out of the woods into a clearing. The bushes on the other side of the clearing suddenly parted as an enormous Bengal tiger pounced through, its fiery eyes locked on Lizzie. It crept slowly forward growling. The sound was so deep and pervasive it filled the woods, echoing between the trees. The sound pierced Lizzie's nerves. She shivered, suddenly chilled and terrified.

The tiger crouched directly in front of Lizzie preparing to spring forward onto her. It bared its fangs as it growled. Its ears were laid back against the sides of its head.

Lizzie stepped back.

The tiger glanced up behind Lizzie and hesitated.

Something slammed into Lizzie from behind knocking her to the ground. She felt hot fur all along her naked backside, heavy on top of her, pressing her into the ground.

The creature that had knocked her down let out a piercing screech. Lizzie felt a chill of terror through her entire body. She thought of the fabled wail of the banshee. She had never heard a stranger, more terrifying sound. She could feel the heat of the animal pressed against her back.

The tiger roared and clawed the air with one paw.

The animal on top of Lizzie again made the strange screeching noise, a sound which went through Lizzie like nails across a blackboard.

The tiger backed off uncertainly.

A rumbling noise sounded inches from Lizzie's right ear.

The tiger turned and ran to the edge of the clearing. It looked back, roared once defiantly, then disappeared into the undergrowth.

Lizzie was shaking all over. She did not understand why the animal that had knocked her down was not clawing or biting her.

A tongue slurped along the side of Lizzie's face, feeling like wet sand paper.

Lizzie slowly turned her head and found herself nose to nose with an old friend.

"Agnes!" Lizzie exclaimed.

CHAPTER FORTY FIVE

Aaron

"I know you're glad to see me, but I need you to lead me to Aaron," Lizzie told Agnes as the Florida panther energetically licked Lizzie's face and purred contentment. The animal's eager tongue rocked Lizzie backwards.

"I'm really glad to see you too. You saved my life." Lizzie hugged Agnes and petted her smooth-furred flank. She inhaled deeply and looked around; nothing but woods and darkness. Lizzie was sure that when her natural hair color grew back she would have more than one streak of white hair from her encounters with Augie and with the tiger.

Lizzie looked over at Agnes. She and the panther sat naked, side by side on sandy ground in a clearing surrounded by dark pine woods. Fireflies flickered among the trees. Lizzie swatted away a mosquito. She needed to get moving before the entire mosquito population found her, but the forest looked the same in all directions. As she stood, she placed her right hand on the back of Agnes's neck and gestured with her left hand. "Where's Aaron? I can't stay here. Agnes, I need you to lead me to Aaron."

Lizzie tentatively started walking toward the side of the clearing directly in front of her. Agnes ran up and blocked Lizzie with her body. Then Agnes scampered to another side of the clearing, looked back at Lizzie, and emitted a chirping noise.

Lizzie stepped over and patted the big cat's back. "Good girl, take me to Timmy."

Agnes gave her a questioning glance.

Lizzie shook her head. "Sorry girl, too many old TV shows, I mean Aaron."

Agnes slid forward into the underbrush, Lizzie walking beside her. Thorny bushes scratched Lizzie's bare legs as she moved through the woods with the big cat. Mosquitoes and no-see-ums clouded around Lizzie. She glanced down at Agnes. Fur protected the panther, but Lizzie was like a walking bloodbank. She removed her hand from Agnes' back and slapped at the little black dots affixed to her skin and clouding around her. Blood smeared, her blood. She tripped over a small rock sticking up from the ground.

Agnes stopped and stared at Lizzie as Lizzie picked herself back up.

"You're obviously taking the direct route," Lizzie told the panther. "That's hard for me."

Lizzie thought she saw the tiger stalking through the thick undergrowth beside them as they resumed walking. She pressed closer to Agnes's warm body.

They walked around a hammock, a slightly higher rise of land containing a thick mixture of plants, including red maple, gumbo-limbo, mahogany, and strangler fig.

After a tiring distance of bush wading, the undergrowth thinned. Lizzie and Agnes moved faster through an area of tall pines and short grass. Fireflies had thickened in this area, giving the jungle a fairy-tale luminescence.

A trailer appeared through the misty blackness. Aaron's Toyota Prius was parked in front.

Agnes walked Lizzie up to the trailer door then stopped.

Everything was quiet. The stillness, a few fireflies, and more than a few mosquitoes pervaded the clearing. The sounds of night in the woods drifted into Lizzie's consciousness; the whirring of crickets and the hoot of a distant owl, perhaps the same one she heard while crossing the fence.

Lizzie felt some of the tension leave her. She had escaped. Aaron would protect her. She might have to turn herself in to police but the worst prison would be better than the slave farm.

"OHMYGOD!"

Agnes had shoved her wet nose up between Lizzie's legs from behind.

Lizzie jumped forward and looked back at the cat. "Agnes, I've told you before not to do that. I'm not another panther."

Lizzie had been propelled by Agnes's cold nose to the door of the sleek metal trailer.

A click echoed through the woods followed by the sound of a motor. Startled, Lizzie stepped back bumping into Agnes. Lizzie put her hand to her chest to calm her nerves. She laughed when she realized she had been startled by the trailer's air conditioning going on.

Agnes cocked her head sideways, looking at Lizzie like she thought the female human was crazy.

"It's all right girl," Lizzie said as she petted Agnes again. "I've had a difficult night."

Lizzie rethought her situation. Contacting the local police might not be smart. She was still wanted for two murders and may have just killed Augie. She needed to contact Val. But now she no longer had his private number; it was in the cell phone locked in Augie's desk drawer. She should have memorized the number.

Agnes pushed against Lizzie, either trying to get more petting or trying to push Lizzie back toward the trailer door.

"Okay, I'm going," Lizzie said.

Lizzie looked down at her nakedness. Aaron would be glad to see her. She opened the trailer door and stepped up into total darkness. She felt around beside the door until she found a switch. She clicked it on and was blinded by sudden light. As her eyes adjusted she realized she was in the trailer's living room.

Aaron wasn't very neat. Piles of books and magazines competed with cardboard boxes, animal cages, and veterinary supplies for space on the table, sofa, and chairs. One of the cages contained a nervous rabbit whose nose urgently sniffed the air while its eyes darted one way then another.

Lizzie walked back through the kitchen. The sink was filled with dirty dishes. Aaron had always needed her to look after him.

At the end of a very short hall was a door. Lizzie opened it. She reached in, found a light switch, and flicked it on.

Aaron lay sprawled out on a full-sized bed which filled the trailer's bedroom wall to wall. He wore blue pajamas. His shirt was open exposing his scrawny chest. His arms were spread outward, palms up.

Lizzie studied Aaron's features. His mouth gaped and a whistling noise came from his pointed nose. He really was funny looking. Why hadn't she seen that before? Perhaps their shared devotion to animals or her desperation, meeting him just after leaving her asshole husband, had blinded her. Lizzie sighed, "Oh, Aaron."

"What? Who?" Aaron shook himself awake. He opened his eyes. "Lizzie? What are you doing here? I didn't expect you this soon."

CHAPTER FORTY SIX

Cat

"I need something to wear," Lizzie said, holding her hands protectively across her body.

Aaron propped himself up on his elbows and looked her over. "You didn't used to mind my seeing you naked."

Lizzie exhaled sharply. "I've had a difficult night, Aaron. Please don't argue. Anything will do. I don't mind being naked but I dislike feeling naked."

Aaron smiled and patted the bed beside him. "Come, lie down, I'll make you feel better."

"No, Aaron. Please; something to wear." Lizzie felt a chill.

"I don't have any female clothing." Aaron paused, looking thoughtful. "I do have another pair of pajamas."

Lizzie nodded. "That will have to do."

"I need to get into the hall." Aaron pointed behind Lizzie, who stepped back down the hall.

Aaron jumped up from the bed directly into the hall. He opened a closet door, rummaged around in a basket on the floor of the closet, and came up with a pair of blue pajamas covered with little yellow cartoon tigers.

"They're not washed," he commented as he handed them to Lizzie.

She ruffled her nose at them, feeling a surge of despair. But she had no choice. "That's okay," she said, taking the crumpled clothing which was stained and smelled of male sweat.

With one hand against the hallway wall for balance, Lizzie put on the wrinkled pajamas, which were far too long. Lizzie waddled into the kitchen, sat on a metal chair, and rolled up the pajama bottom legs so she wouldn't step on them. She also rolled up the sleeves.

"We need to get help," Lizzie told Aaron. "That farm, Augie's farm, I escaped from is..."

Aaron interrupted her. "How did you get through the animals?"

"Agnes saved me. A tiger looked like it was about to attack me. Agnes drove it away."

"You're lucky. Burning Bright likes to hunt. The only human she tolerates is me and I have to be firm with her. You didn't see a lion, did you?"

"No. How many animals do you have?"

Aaron shrugged. "Just three; but I'm negotiating to get more. Would you like some coffee?"

"I'm trying to tell you we need to get police or somebody to raid that farm."

Aaron made an exasperated expression. "Stop and think for a minute, Lizzie. Aren't you still wanted by the police?"

"Yes," she admitted.

"Then you need to calm down, have a cup of coffee, and think over your situation. Will you do that?" He stepped back, looking intently into her eyes.

Lizzie slowly nodded. "Okay, I guess I am frazzled by everything."

Aaron stepped over and put his hands on her shoulders. "Could you wash the cups while I make the coffee?"

"Okay." Lizzie looked at the disgusting pile of greasy plates and bowls in the sink. "I might as well do all the dishes while I'm at it." She wondered why Aaron kept avoiding her plight, why he didn't ask her what had happened to her on the farm. Why she had to escape over the fence. Why she was naked.

Aaron grinned. "That would be great. After the coffee, I'll introduce you to Catherine."

Lizzie shot liquid detergent into the water she was letting into the sink. "Who is Catherine?"

"Catherine's the lion. Don't use much water; it has to be trucked in."

"Why Catherine?"

"Because she's a cat."

"What's the name of the tiger?"

"Burning Bright."

"Why? Does she start fires?"

"She's got a fiery personality. The lion is more thoughtful. And, of course, Agnes is Agnes.

Lizzie was surprised she hadn't collapsed after the difficult night she'd had. She seemed to have gotten her second wind; probably all the adrenaline in her system from stabbing Augie, running from his men, and the encounter with the tiger.

After Lizzie finished the dishes, cleaned around the sink, and sipped some coffee, Aaron still didn't want to discuss the farm or her escape from it. He insisted they go outside to visit Catherine. Aaron led Lizzie past the back end of the trailer. Agnes followed behind them.

"I've put in a water trough and created a shaded area for the animals." Aaron pointed toward three large cages at the edge of the clearing. In front of the cages was an open tent, like large craft fair exhibitors use. A very low horse trough was at a right angle to the cages.

"The cages are only in case the animals need to be isolated," Aaron explained as they walked toward the tent area. "Also, cages will be convenient if we ever have to move. But usually the animals have the freedom of the land enclosed by the fence. You must have crossed that fence somehow to get into the animal shelter area. You also must have ignored the warning signs; that wasn't very smart... Ah, there's Catherine."

In the dimness Lizzie could just make out the shape of the female lion sitting on the ground in front of the middle cage. It was chewing on something.

Aaron continued walking toward the lion. Lizzie stayed behind him. The lion was not restrained in any way. Agnes had vanished.

"Don't worry." Aaron glanced back at Lizzie. "She won't hurt you when you're with me."

"She's still a wild animal." Lizzie edged further behind Aaron. Her hand was on his shoulder. She looked around his left side at the animal.

Aaron walked right up to the lion.

Lizzie looked down at the huge beast. It was chewing on a black human arm. The lion's paw, claws extended, held down the wrist. The two smallest fingers were missing from the hand. The lion's huge head was tilted sideways as it worked its teeth into the lower arm. The beast tore into the muscle. Blood stained the lion's nose, lips, and teeth.

All the breath left Lizzie.

"What did you do with the rest of that?" Aaron asked the lion, who responded with a low rumbling growl.

Lizzie's mouth fell open. She felt nauseous. She was shaking uncontrollably and backing away, like in a dream, in a nightmare. She felt like she was moving in slow motion, caught in quicksand, her mind fogging.

"I can't figure out what she's done with the rest of the man," said Aaron. "Yesterday evening, when I got back from my trip, she was happily munching on one of his legs. She's selfish; she hasn't shared with Agnes and Burning Bright. I've had to buy them food."

Lizzie doubled over and threw up. She staggered several feet toward the trailer, became dizzy, lost control of her legs, fell to the ground, and passed out.

CHAPTER FORTY SEVEN

Explanation

"But the animals wouldn't serve Augie any purpose if they weren't a real deterrent to escaping," Aaron explained. "And you must remember Augie gave me the land and is paying for the upkeep of the animals."

Lizzie lay on Aaron's bed. She was still in a daze. Aaron must have carried her there. He'd sat on the edge of the bed talking endlessly since she'd regained consciousness. He was trying to explain himself, trying to get her approval.

"Augie pays to get these workers to the United States. He pays for their room and board. They contracted to work off their debts to him. Some try to escape; try to avoid paying what they owe. The animals are intended to discourage escape. If the workers are properly fearful of the animals, the workers will fulfill their obligations and everything will work as it should."

"But that lion killed that man," Lizzie stammered.

Aaron nodded. "Yes, that's why I need the rest of his body. I'll take his head to Augie, who'll display it to the other workers. Then no more workers will try to escape over that fence; Augie's property will be protected and lives will be saved."

"But a man is dead." Lizzie still felt nauseous.

"He died a Christian death," Aaron exclaimed. "Like Jesus, he gave his life that others might live."

"He didn't give his life." Lizzie sat up in the bed. "He was murdered."

"Don't be silly. A lion can't be a murderer."

"No, you Aaron, you're the murderer." Lizzie pointed directly at him, her finger almost touching his skinny nose. "You put the lion where it could kill someone."

"Oh Lizzie, Lizzie, Lizzie, you're so naïve." Aaron shook his head emphatically. "I didn't bring that man into the animal compound. I tried to discourage him. I put signs up every ten feet warning about wild animals. I put barbed wire on top the fence. No jury on Earth would convict me of murder."

Lizzie was shocked at this attitude from a man she thought she knew. "Don't you feel any guilt for that man's death?"

Aaron stood, chin up and arms akimbo. "No, I don't feel I've done anything wrong. I've saved wild animals from mistreatment, nature's most noble beasts. I've helped maintain the security of the farm. My father approves of everything I've done."

"Your father? What do you mean? What does your father have to do with this? Do you mean your father in heaven? Are you referring to God?"

"No, my father: Augie."

Lizzie stared at Aaron, speechless.

Aaron smiled. "Yeah, Augie's my dad. He's trying to make up for all the years he neglected me. He owes me a lot. Augie had an affair with my mom. That's why nobody on Sanibel could know I was his son. God only knows how his wife would react. Social status is everything to June. Her husband having a bastard son by another woman would hurt that status."

Augie's your father?" Lizzie was dumbfounded.

"Yes, of course. Did you think he'd just give all this land to a stranger, to somebody who'd only worked for him a few months?" Aaron sounded like he thought it should be obvious.

Lizzie paused thoughtfully then murmured. "You were always confiding everything to Augie, asking him for advice."

Aaron spread his hands open. "You should have figured out Augie and I were related."

Lizzie looked him up and down. "You don't look very much alike. Your mother must have been very thin."

"My mother suffered through difficult times. She was an angel."

"Are you saying Augie abandoned your mother and you?"

"He's trying to make up for that now."

"How?" Lizzie glared at Aaron. "By getting you to kill people for him?

"Augie is good to me. He gave me this land." Aaron waved his arms out to encompass the surrounding woodland. "He's buying animals for me and providing for their upkeep. He promised to give me you as my wife."

"He did what?" Lizzie edged closer to Aaron.

"Promised you'd be my wife," Aaron held his hands over his heart. "Mine

205

exclusively; protected on the farm. In the outside world men are always around you. On the farm you'd be kept away from other men. You'd be mine alone."

Lizzie laughed and shook her head. "Yes, of course, I'd be yours alone after Augie and Boss Pigott both rape me."

"My father raped you?" Aaron leaned forward over the foot of the bed toward Lizzie.

"He tried," she spat. "I stabbed him in the neck and escaped."

Aaron drew back. "You killed my father?"

"I don't know if he died. I hope he did." Lizzie smiled. "He was spouting blood all over the place when I left him."

Aaron looked agitated. His hands shook. He started to turn away then turned back. "We need to go over to the farm right away. I need to know how dad is."

Lizzie shook her head. "I'm not going back there."

Aaron pointed, sticking his skinny finger in her face. "Yes you are. We need to see how Augie is. We need to get you in a secure place."

"No way." Lizzie tried to jump up from the bed.

Aaron intercepted her. He tackled her, knocking her back onto the bed.

They struggled, rolling over each other; Lizzie trying to escape, Aaron trying to hold her down. Lizzie elbowed Aaron under the chin stunning him long enough to fling herself from the bed. But as she ran into the hall, Aaron leapt off the bed and tackled her.

They slid together into the kitchen on the slick trailer floor. Lizzie pulled herself up holding onto the edge of the sink. Aaron's skinny arms were wrapped around her lower legs. Her pajama bottoms were slipping down.

Lizzie grabbed at the drying basket beside the sink. She pulled a butcher knife from it.

Half turning, Lizzie held the knife blade in front of Aaron's eyes. "Let go or I'll cut you."

Aaron froze.

Lizzie brought the blade against the bridge of Aaron's nose. Blood trickled.

Aaron released his hold on Lizzie's legs. He stood up slowly and backed away with his arms spread open. Lizzie held the knife aimed at his throat. She edged around the small kitchen table and inched back into the hall, pulling her pajama bottoms up as she went.

Aaron followed her. "Be reasonable, Lizzie, you have no place to go. I'm the only one who wants you. Everybody else thinks you're a crazed murderer. I've tried to protect you. I even killed that old man so you wouldn't soil yourself with someone inappropriate for you."

Lizzie gasped, but then turned and ran. She dashed through the living room and slammed open the trailer door. The tiger stood immediately in front of her, its front paws on the trailer doorstep, its bright eyes fixed on Lizzie. The tiger opened its jaws, exposed its fangs, and growled.

Lizzie, startled, dropped the butcher knife and turned around to flee from the tiger. She faced Aaron, who had run up behind her.

"It's Burning Bright's dinner time," Aaron said as he let loose a roundhouse punch which hit Lizzie in the jaw.

She crumpled.

CHAPTER FORTY EIGHT

Tied Up

When Lizzie revived she was on her back on the bare ground in front of the trailer. Aaron had pushed her legs up to her chest and was tying her wrists together behind her legs. She was immobilized in the fetal position.

Aaron had changed into blue jeans, a western shirt, and motorcycle boots. Lizzie was still wearing Aaron's pajamas with the little cartoon tigers.. The rays of the rising sun stabbed between pine trees. A thin mist hung in the air. It was morning. Lizzie saw no sign of the tiger. "Are you binding me up for tiger food?" she asked Aaron, who tied an unnecessary multiplication of knots.

"No, of course not, I love you. I'm making you secure for the ride to the farm." Aaron pulled a knot painfully tight. "We have to go around the outside on the public roads. There's no route directly across country." He held up a finger. "Don't move. I'll be back in a moment."

Aaron walked away around the end of the trailer. Lizzie lay on the ground struggling against her bonds and cursing to herself. A loud shout of "no, no, back" bellowed from the other side of the trailer. Several minutes of silence followed. Then came two loud bangs. A few moments later Aaron reappeared carrying something wrapped in newspaper.

Lizzie, lying on her side on the ground, tried to turn her head to see what he was carrying. She felt dizzy.

"Catherine didn't want to give me this," Aaron said. "I had to be stern with her."

Aaron strolled over to his Prius, tossed the package onto the floor in back, and then opened the front passenger side door. He turned, walked back, and squatted down beside Lizzie. "I always remember when I'm lifting something to squat rather than bend over. That way I use my legs to do the lifting. It saves my back."

Aaron placed his hands under Lizzie's shoulders and under where her hands were tied behind her knees. He rose up and grunted. "I think you're heavier. Are you pregnant?" He plopped her back down.

Agnes crept around the side of the house and stood staring at Aaron. She cocked her head sideways as though she considered him strange and maybe embarrassing.

"I couldn't be pregnant," Lizzie responded.

"No, you're wrong," Aaron insisted. "After I caught you naked with that man in your apartment, I realized I not only had to get rid of him, I had to find a way to bond you to me. So when we had sex in the hotel the day after that man was killed, I poked holes in the end of the condom with a pin." Aaron smiled. "So you could be pregnant."

"You wanted to get me pregnant against my will?" Lizzie strained at the ropes binding her wrists. They didn't loosen.

Agnes bounded over to Lizzie, who had tumbled onto her side, and sniffed at the ropes.

"Sure… I knew you wouldn't agree." Aaron lowered his face closer to hers. "But I also knew a baby would hold us together, bind you to me in a family. All I've ever wanted was a family, a real American traditional family."

"The acorn doesn't fall far from the tree," Lizzie snorted.

"What do you mean, Lizzie?"

"You're as nutty as your father."

Aaron furrowed his brow, and then smiled. "I'll choose to take that as a compliment. A family, we'll have a real family."

"I'm not pregnant," Lizzie murmured.

"Not important." Aaron was still smiling. "We have plenty of time to work on it."

Lizzie felt like screaming. She felt like clawing his eyes out. But bound immobile in the fetal position, she was helpless, at least for the time being.

Agnes licked Lizzie on the cheek.

Aaron knelt down and picked Lizzie back up. He carried her to the car, followed by Agnes.

When he got to the car, Aaron stood for a moment looking in. "This isn't going to work. I can't sit you up in that bucket seat with your arms tied behind you, you couldn't hold on, you'd tilt over at every curve. I'll have to lay you on the back seat."

Aaron sat Lizzie down on some low prickly plants, opened the Prius's back passenger side door, pulled the fold-down seats back up to the raised position, picked Lizzie back up, edged her into the car head first, and then pitched her onto the back seat. She landed on her back with a thump.

As Aaron was closing the back door, Agnes squeezed past him and jumped up onto the front passenger seat. She sat staring at Aaron, her tongue hanging partly out.

Aaron waved at the panther. "Out, Agnes, come on girl, get out."

The large cat looked at Aaron like she had no idea what he wanted her to do.

Lizzie called out weakly from the back seat. "Let her come with us, Aaron. You know how much she loves to go for a ride."

Aaron stood for a second looking at Agnes. "Maybe you're right, Lizzie. They'll be angry with you at the farm for stabbing Augie. They'll want to punish you; probably severely; maybe lethally. I wouldn't want anything to interfere with our wedding plans so I'll oppose any punishment that would leave you dead or with lasting scars. I might need Agnes's help."

Lizzie thought she'd be the one to need Agnes's help. But she wasn't sure whether Agnes would help her or Aaron or would just stand there trying to figure out what the humans were doing. Lizzie wished she had some sausages.

CHAPTER FORTY NINE

The Return Ride

A complicated gate system was built into the fence at the exit from Aaron's wild animal woodlands. An enclosed area stretched for more than 20 feet beyond the first electronically controlled gate. A long pit within that enclosure was covered by numerous loose posts laid at a right angle to the road. The Prius rumbled over the posts.

"I adapted cattle guards," Aaron explained to Lizzie as the car bounced across the posts. "A car's wheels go over them with no problem. But anything with legs, such as a cow or a tiger, would slip between the posts. If an animal were to get past the gate, its natural animal sense would tell it to stay off the posts. So it couldn't get out. If it was dumb enough to try to walk on the posts, the cattle guard would trap the animal, might even break its legs. We can't have an animal escape. Safety always comes first."

Lizzie snorted, "That's a bunch of shit. But I must admit you did a lot of improvements in a short time." Lizzie pulled at the ropes binding her. It only seemed to make them tighter.

Aaron glanced over his shoulder at Lizzie. "Dad provided lots of free labor."

Aaron used a universal remote to open the second gate and the Prius drove out onto the narrow public road.

Lizzie thought back over what Aaron had said earlier. Her breath caught in her throat as she stammered, "I'm curious, what did you mean when you said you killed an old man?"

Aaron glanced back at Lizzie and smiled. "The old guy you were living with in that house behind Bowman's Beach. I shot him. You were there but you didn't see me. I kept down, kept hidden."

"You shot Joey?"

"I didn't know his name."

"His name was Joey. You killed Joey?" Lizzie shouted.

"That was my intention."

"He was my friend. He was a wonderful man. You're a goddamn son-of-a-bitch. When I get loose I'll kill you." Lizzie struggled harder against the ropes tied around her wrists but it only made them bite into her.

"I did it for you," Aaron said as his Prius reached the corner of the farm property. He turned left onto the larger county road which led toward the farm entrance road. "Your relationship with a man that old was inappropriate. If people found out, it would have embarrassed you. So I shot him. I did it for you."

The turning of the car had rocked Lizzie back and forth on the seat. She was silent for a moment. Then she asked, "How did you find his house? How did you find where I was when the police couldn't?"

The Prius approached a grisly old man limping beside the county road. The ragged old-timer stuck out his thumb in the conventional hitch-hiking motion. But both his finger and his jaw dropped when he saw Agnes riding like a human on the front passenger seat.

Aaron ignored the hitchhiker and glanced over his shoulder again at Lizzie. "You told me about the old man. You said he'd saved you when you ran into that other guy, what's-his-name, the guy you were later naked with.

"Clete."

"Yeah, Clete, the ass-hole." Aaron returned his attention to the road as he veered the Prius in at the entrance to Augie's farm. "You told me the old guy with the machine gun lived in a house back behind the beach, an isolated house. I remembered that. I figured you might run to him since he saved you before. I figured right."

"So you murdered him."

"It was for your benefit." Aaron looked over his shoulder at Lizzie. He had stopped the Prius in front of the first of the three gated fences on Augie's farm.

"That's crap," Lizzie hissed at him. "It's all for your benefit, for you and your insane jealousy. Ever since finding me with Clete you've been a jealous lunatic. You were border-line nuts before. I should have seen it. But I was on the rebound and was vulnerable, wide open for the first loser who came along. Seeing me with Clete knocked you over the edge. You've completely lost your mind with jealousy. You didn't have very far to go. Insanity runs in your family."

Aaron smiled at Lizzie. "You've never understood how precious you are to me. You've never really understood me. Eventually you'll learn, I'll teach you, and then we'll be happy together forever."

Agnes looked back and forth between Lizzie and Aaron as they talked. Neither one had anything for her to eat. She smelled blood and stuck her head between the seats to sniff at the newspaper wrapped package.

"No, girl," said Aaron, reaching over and pushing at the panther's neck. Agnes looked at Aaron. He shook his head no. She whined and turned toward the window. Aaron lowered the window so Agnes could look out at the farm and be distracted from the meat smell of the severed arm.

Lizzie pounded her feet against the door of the Prius and screamed at Aaron, "You're nothing but a murderous brute."

Aaron laughed. "You're too quick to judge me. I was subtle getting rid of Clete."

"You did what?"

"I let dad know that Clete told you he was involved in illegal alien smuggling and that the people running the operation were a danger both to him and you, particularly if you showed people his picture on that video you shot. I pointed out to dad that Clete would only have gone out of his way to warn you if he was some kind of cop and he would only worry about people seeing his picture if he was an undercover cop."

Lizzie stopped pounding her feet. "Couldn't he have just liked me?"

"It didn't matter; with dad's paranoia any hint the guy was a cop was enough to seal his fate. Dad believes he's on a mission from God to save the American family farm and anything, including an execution, is justified by that divine mission."

"You don't believe that crap, do you?"

Aaron looked back over his shoulder at Lizzie. "I just believe I need you, that you are my soul mate through all time, and that I will have you even if I have to lock you behind impenetrable fences forever."

Aaron clicked a remote attached to his belt. The gate in front of the Prius squeaked open.

Agnes stuck her head out the passenger side window watching the movement of the gate.

CHAPTER FIFTY

Arrival

Aaron drove the Prius up the circular driveway to Augie's farm house. He stopped beside the steps of the wrap-around porch.

Celia and Lydia, clad in their French maid's uniforms, ran from the house to greet the new arrivals. However, they halted, standing side by side on the porch motionless like beautiful ebony statues, when Boss Pigott walked up behind the Prius. Pigott smiled and licked his lips as he caught sight of Lizzie hog-tied on the back seat. He bent down to the right front window to speak to Aaron.

Agnes shoved her face out. Her nose collided with Boss Pigott's nose. She sniffed at him. Boss Pigott frantically back-pedaled, his arms flailing. He lost his footing on the loose gravel of the driveway and sat down hard on the second step of the porch stairs. The entire porch shook from the impact.

Celia and Lydia ran down the steps to help Pigott up. But they froze when Agnes snorted several times. The two young women looked at each other and then turned and ran back up into the house, colliding as they squeezed through the doorway.

Aaron lifted himself out of the Prius and walked around the front of the car. He stood gazing down at Pigott, who was looking past Aaron at the panther.

"How's dad? Is he okay? Is he here?" Aaron asked.

"You can't have that animal on the farm," Pigott growled, pointing at Agnes.

Aaron leaned forward over the enormous farm foreman. "Mr. Pigott, I need to know about my father. Forget about Agnes; she's in the car."

"Mr. Winters is still in the hospital in Naples." Pigott struggled to his feet.

Aaron took a step back. "How is he?"

"He lost a lot of blood, but he's getting better. They'll release him later today." Pigott was keeping Aaron between himself and the car. "Can't that panther get out through the window? He's half out already."

Aaron looked around. "She's a she. She probably could get out, never has though." Aaron smiled. "If they're letting dad out of the hospital he must be okay."

"He can't talk very well; she stabbed his voice box. Also she must have pushed him or something 'cause he fell and broke his leg." Pigott gestured toward the back seat of the Prius. "Mr. Winters'll be very imaginative punishing her. It should be fun."

Aaron looked serious and shook his head. "Just so he remembers she's going to be my wife; I wouldn't want her badly hurt."

"That's between you and him," Pigott said. "Course I wouldn't mind a shot at the pretty little thing myself. I'm due a turn. We was scheduled."

Aaron stepped up to Pigott, pointing a skinny finger at the foreman's huge chest. "She's mine. This isn't a matter of taking turns. Remember your place here."

Pigott laughed. "I been here a lot longer than you." He knocked aside Aaron's arm, placed a large hand in the center of Aaron's chest, and pushed him back. "I suggest you keep your skinny little ass out of my way." He smiled and pushed Aaron again. "I do admit you got a right to worry, little man. Once a woman been with Boss Pigott, she ain't likely to be interested in puny little you."

Aaron reached back, opened the door of the Prius, and stepped aside.

Agnes bounded out, ran up to Pigott, stuck her nose in his crotch, and sniffed. She backed off, shook her head, and sneezed. Then the panther ran around Pigott, who stood petrified. She ran up the steps and onto the long wrap-around porch.

"She likes to explore a new place," Aaron told Pigott.

The farm manager was visibly trembling, even though he tried to act as though nothing had happened. "I gotta get back out to the fields."

Aaron gestured toward his car. "Where should I put Lizzie?"

"She's in the bedroom next to Mr. Winters' bedroom." Pigott stepped around Aaron and backed away as he spoke. He kept his eye on the porch. "It's the bedroom with bloodstains on the floor." Pigott was still trembling. "I'll send somebody to guard her."

"Thanks, but I'll put Agnes in with her. Agnes will keep her safe until Dad returns and we can get everything straightened out."

"I wasn't thinking of protecting her," Pigott responded. "That crazy woman don't need no protecting. The guard's to keep her from escaping or from stabbing anybody else, like you, maybe."

"Good idea. Listen Boss, I'd prefer we get along better." Aaron walked up to Pigott. "I'm sure to be spending more time here; some day dad will turn all this over to me."

Pigott snorted and started to walk away. But then he turned and asked with a sly smile, "Would you like to come with me, since all this is gonna be yours some day?"

Aaron shrugged apologetically and gestured toward his car. "I've got to carry Lizzie in, get her settled."

"That's about what I expected." Pigott glanced back at the porch nervously as Agnes ran along it, her claws clattering on the wood floor as she dashed back and forth from one end to the other. Pigott took a couple additional steps away from the house.

"You might want to change before you go back out to the fields," Aaron suggested.

"Why?"

Aaron pointed at Pigott's pants. "Because you wet yourself when Agnes sniffed your crotch. That's why she sneezed."

Pigott looked down at his stained pants, mumbled, "It'll dry," and stomped off up the road toward the gate leading out to the fields.

Aaron opened the back door of the Prius and then pulled at Lizzie until she plopped out onto the white gravel driveway, the back of her head bouncing off the side of the car. Lizzie grunted, suppressing a scream. Her head felt numb.

Aaron knelt down, picked up Lizzie's tied up torso in his arms, and carried her up the stairs to the porch.

"You're sure quiet," Aaron said. "Penny for your thoughts."

Lizzie remained silent.

Agnes clattered back down the porch and looked up at Aaron and Lizzie, eager to learn what her next adventure was going to be. It was early but it was already one of the most interesting days Agnes had ever experienced.

Aaron struggled to hold onto Lizzie and open the front door at the same time. "Where are the damn girls who help visitors?" Aaron finally got his foot wedged behind the door and pulled it open. He used his shoulder to hold it.

Aaron shifted Lizzie in his arms and smiled at her: "Isn't this romantic; the groom carrying the bride over the threshold?"

CHAPTER FIFTY ONE

No Cat Food

Aaron carried Lizzie up to the bedroom she had escaped from the night before. He tossed her onto the bed, which had been made. Blood stains still splotched the floor.

Agnes explored the room, poking her nose into everything, and then vanished into the bathroom.

Aaron began untying Lizzie "I'm going to go back and get some of my stuff. This will be our room until I can get dad to give us something better." He looked around. "Although this is a lot nicer than the trailer, I'll have to stay there part of the time to feed the animals and check on whether they've been hunting. I know you'll miss me." He bent down and suddenly kissed Lizzie. She turned her face quickly so that the kiss landed on her cheek not her lips.

Lizzie turned her face back and spat at Aaron.

Aaron pulled his face back so the spit just missed. He shook his head. "You'll calm down when you realize I'm right. You need me; you know your body misses mine." He leered a smile and winked at Lizzie. "Quit trying to think all the time and let your natural passions lead you."

Lizzie snarled, "When I get free I'm going to cut you into little pieces and throw those pieces to your precious lion."

Aaron quickly and carefully undid the final knot from Lizzie's wrists and jumped back. "Somebody will be guarding the door until you calm down and get your head right." He hurried out. The lock clicked.

Lizzie rubbed her wrists, trying to get her circulation going. She slowly straightened her legs, cramped from being scrunched up against her chest for so long. She placed her bare feet on the floor. She didn't feel well at all.

Agnes ran in from the bathroom. Lizzie petted Agnes as the large cat rubbed against her leg. Lizzie was still wearing the pajamas with the little yellow tigers. "Are you hungry girl?" Lizzie asked. She slid up the bed and opened the nightstand's refrigerator. After popping a strawberry into her mouth, she held some cheese out for Agnes, who sniffed at it and turned away.

"You can't be too particular girl; we're prisoners." Lizzie got out a bottle of Fiji water, and held it in front of Agnes, tilting the water into her mouth. The panther slurped it up.

A metal chair made a scraping noise as it was unfolded outside the bedroom door. Lizzie knew the sound from her previous incarceration.

Lizzie ran her hand along Agnes's furry flank. "We're in this together girl."

The panther put her front paws on the bed, raised the front half of her body, and licked Lizzie's cheek with her wet abrasive tongue.

"Good girl, I knew I could count on you. Now I've got to figure out how to get to that cell phone and call Val. We need rescuing and we need it fast."

Agnes emitted a soft whimper.

Lizzie's back hurt from being tied up and tossed around. But there was nobody she could turn to for help; no doctor, no nurse, no caring person – she was all alone. In spite of that, she had no intention of letting pain, or Augie, or Boss Pigott, or Aaron or anybody get the better of her. She didn't know what she would do but she knew she'd never give in to the bastards.

A knock sounded at Lizzie's bedroom door.

Lizzie called out "Yes?" The lock clicked. The door opened partway. Celia peeked in. "I've got lunch. Is okay? Where animal?"

Lizzie looked around. "She must be in the bathroom. She won't bother you."

"I not come in if that thing can get me."

"I'll close the bathroom door." Lizzie walked over to the bathroom, leaned in, and found Lizzie looking into the toilet. She said, "Sorry, girl, this will just be for a couple minutes," and closed the door. Lizzie called out, "It's okay, she's locked in the bathroom."

Celia cautiously stepped into the bedroom. She was carrying a tray which she sat down on the nightstand beside the bed. Celia hugged Lizzie tightly. "I'm sorry your escape fail."

Lizzie shook her head. "It was a horrible night. But at least I learned what I'll find in that direction."

"Will you try again?" Celia drew back and looked into Lizzie's eyes. The two women stood in the middle of the bedroom.

"I'll never give up while there's a breath left in my body, even if it kills me. What about you? What about the workers?" Lizzie gestured toward the outside. "You live in unending horror. How can you stand it?"

"I, we all, have fear." Celia trembled. "They punish all thing. Mister Winters crazy. They kill people. Old people they not need, they kill. Everybody very afraid."

Lizzie placed a hand on Celia's arm. "I know people have been killed. The lion killed a man the day before I tried to escape. It's been eating him a part at a time."

"Oh no," Celia exclaimed. She stepped back, her eyes wide open, horrified. She put her hand to her mouth. "Ben, Lydia's brother, try escape two days ago. It must be him. Oh *Mon Dieu*. Poor Ben."

Lizzie took Celia's hands in her own. "I'm sorry about Ben. Don't you see this can't continue; you can't keep dying one by one. The workers need to stand up for themselves, revolt."

Celia drew in a deep breath. "There is talk. Everybody getting desperate. I think all take is one spark to light revolt. But what about you?" Celia squeezed Lizzie's hand. "You will be punished for trying escape. Mr. Winters usually crucifies people caught escaping. He enjoy it because it cruel and it in Bible."

Lizzie shook her head. "I don't know what they'll do to me. Whatever it is I'll not give in. I'll stand up to the bastard. They're waiting for Augie to return before they decide my fate, until then I'm locked in this room."

"He'll be here in a couple hours," said Celia. "He released from hospital this afternoon." She hugged Lizzie again. "I hope what they do to you not too bad." Celia silently looked sympathetically at Lizzie for a moment. Then she shook her head. "I sorry but now I must go make everything perfect for Mr. Winters return. I already cleaned his room" Celia leaned forward and whispered in Lizzie's ear. "Nobody told me to re-lock his door after cleaning." She pulled back, looking into Lizzie's eyes. "But now I here too long. People wonder why I take so long deliver one tray." Celia broke from Lizzie's embrace and rushed to the door. She turned and said, "Goodbye. I pray I see you again." Celia was crying as she left the room. The lock clicked.

Lizzie walked over and opened the bathroom door. Agnes stepped out, looked up at Lizzie, looked around the room, sniffed, and bounded over to the nightstand. Lizzie hurried after the panther but was too slow. Agnes pushed her nose up under the edge of the tray, which toppled, sending a plate of food onto the floor. A mess of butternut squash, green beans, Polish sausage, onions, and peppers splashed over Augie's blood stains.

Agnes pounced on and quickly devoured the Polish sausage.

"Hey, that's my lunch," Lizzie yelled. Agnes, still chewing, turned and looked at Lizzie.

Stepping carefully to avoid squishing the food underfoot, Lizzie made her way over and petted Agnes. "They didn't make a lunch for you."

Agnes sniffed at the squash, green beans, onions, and peppers. She turned away from them.

Lizzie chuckled. "There's no middle ground with you; you either attack food or turn your nose up at it." Lizzie looked at the mixed conglomeration squished into the carpet. "I'm like you. I'm starving but I'm not going to eat that mess. Come on girl; let's find the kitchen and the cell phone."

CHAPTER FIFTY TWO

Cellular

Lizzie had no problem opening the door to Augie's bedroom. It was unlocked just like Celia said it would be. Lizzie held the door open to allow Agnes to follow her. The panther ran back and forth sniffing the new territory. The large cat jumped up onto the huge canopied bed and snuggled down.

"You can't rest now," Lizzie called to Agnes. "Come on girl, we're looking for food."

At the word 'food,' the panther's head popped up from where it was resting on her front paws. She jumped from the bed and ran over to lean against Lizzie's leg. The big cat drooled onto Lizzie's bare foot.

Lizzie slowly turned the knob on the door to the hallway. She opened the door with extreme care and was about to peek out when Agnes lunged past her and sniffed at the crack in the doorway. Her throat rumbled.

Giving up caution, Lizzie threw open the door and stepped out.

A man sat tilted back on a metal chair in the hall beside the next door down the hall, the door to Lizzie's bedroom. Lizzie recognized him as one of the men who oversaw the farm workers. He had a pistol in a holster on his hip. A rifle was propped against the wall beside him.

The man had a plate balanced on his knees. He had a knife in one hand and a fork in the other. He had just cut a piece of Polish sausage. It was speared on the fork poised halfway up to his mouth. The man turned his head, mouth open, and stared at Lizzie.

"Look girl, sausage, food." Lizzie patted Agnes's rump with her left hand and pointed at the man with her right hand.

Agnes sped down the hallway and leaped toward the sausage and the man.

The panther's jaws closed on the Polish sausage. Her flying body knocked over the man and his chair with a resounding crash. The remnant of the man's meal splashed onto the floor beside him. Momentum carried Agnes past the man. She turned and ran back, stuck her nose into his scattered food, and ate the rest of his sausage. As the panther ate, she was straddling the man, who was motionless except for a violent trembling which went up and down his body in waves.

Lizzie ran over, pulled the pistol from the man's holster, and grabbed his rifle.

"Stay, girl," Lizzie yelled as she turned and ran toward the back stairs.

Frantically glancing around, Lizzie paused at the bottom step. On her right was the door Lydia had looked out from when Lizzie was escaping the day before.

The clatter of claws rattled the wooden stairs. Agnes bounded down beside Lizzie and looked up at her with eager yellow eyes.

Lizzie realized it had been dumb to ask a cat to stay. She stepped across the narrow hall and put her hand on the door handle. "I think this is the kitchen, girl."

Agnes, panting and salivating, sniffed rapidly at the door.

"Apparently you want to go first." Lizzie opened the door and Agnes sprang into the room. A woman screamed. Pans and plates crashed. It sounded like somebody was throwing crockery around the room.

Lizzie turned away and, still carrying the pistol and the rifle, walked down the hall to Augie's office. It was locked. Thinking back to numerous movies she'd seen, Lizzie aimed the pistol at the door lock and fired several shots. Pieces of door flew away as bullets shattered the lock and surrounding wood. She pushed at the door. It opened.

Lizzie entered Augie's office, shutting the door behind her. She ran to Augie's desk, leaned the rifle against the ornately engraved mahogany desk, and dashed around to sit in Augie's leather executive chair. She tried to open the middle desk drawer. It was locked. One shot from the pistol demolished that lock. She pulled out the drawer, picked up the cell phone, and speed dialed Val's private number.

After four rings, the phone was picked up. A recording of Val's voice said he was not there and the caller should leave a message at the sound of the tone. When the tone sounded, Lizzie exclaimed, "Oh, Val, damn it, where are you? Aren't you ever in your office? I'm at Augie's farm. They plan to torture me. I need help. Please come fast. Please get this message."

Running footsteps in the hall stopped outside the office door. Lizzie hurriedly hid the open still-connected cell phone behind a large Bible on the desk.

The office door banged open. Aaron charged in, his eyes wild. Lizzie reached for the pistol sitting in the center of the desk.

"Don't," Aaron ordered, pointing a gun at Lizzie. "I don't want to hurt you."

"Is that the gun you shot Joey with?" Lizzie asked. She had raised her hands and was edging toward the right side of the desk.

"You mean the old man you were shacking up with?"

"Yes, Aaron, the old man, my friend Joey."

Aaron glanced at the weapon in his hand. "Yeah, this is the gun. But I don't want to shoot you Lizzie. What are you doing in here?"

Lizzie moved around toward the front of the desk. She wanted to distract Aaron away from the cell phone. She pointed at the regular phone at the other end of the desk from the hidden cell phone. "I was trying to call for help, call the police. But you were too fast for me."

Aaron shook his head. "What would you tell the police, Lizzie?"

"I was going to tell them you talked Augie, Mr. Winters, into having that policeman kill Clete."

"Oh, my dear, sweet, innocent Lizzie, they wouldn't have believed you."

"But it's true."

"Of course it's true. But you don't have any evidence." Aaron stepped closer. "You need to go back to your room now, Lizzie. Augie would go berserk if he knew you'd gotten out. Will you come peacefully or will I have to get rough?"

Lizzie threw up her hands. "I'll come peacefully. I'm worn out."

Aaron waved his pistol, motioning Lizzie toward the door.

She slowly walked past him, secretly happy at getting every word of his confession recorded on Val's answering machine. But that wouldn't do her any good if Val didn't get the message, if he didn't come to rescue her, or if she was dead when he finally did come.

Lizzie stepped out into the hall followed by Aaron. Agnes met them at the bottom of the stairs. The large cat's snout was covered by a white creamy substance which could have been pudding, whipped cream, or cake batter. Agnes's tongue came out and slurped in some of the white gunk.

Aaron directed Lizzie toward the front stairs, prodding with his pistol up against her back. Agnes followed behind them, still licking her lips.

As Aaron, Lizzie, and Agnes reached the stairs, the double front doors at the other end of the entry hallway were slammed opened by Lydia. She was followed by Celia, who pushed a wheelchair containing August Winters. He was slumped in the chair until he saw Lizzie. He suddenly sat erect. "Stop," he yelled in a high soprano voice, which sounded like Truman Capote.

Lizzie and Aaron halted dead in their tracks. Agnes bumped into the back of Aaron's scrawny legs.

"You emasculated dad's voice," Aaron whispered to Lizzie.

Winters frantically waved at Celia to push him over to Aaron and Lizzie. His crazed eyes looked up and down Lizzie's pajama-clad body then settled on her face. His left arm rose to point directly at Lizzie's face. "You tried to kill me. But God protected me and now has delivered you back into my hands, proving once again that God is on my side."

Winters' arm dropped to point at Lizzie's crotch. "She's wearing the wrong clothes. Remove them."

Nobody did anything. Everyone stood immobile.

Agnes looked around at the frozen people as she licked the remaining clumps of white stuff off her lips and whiskers.

"But dad...," Aaron objected.

"You dumb fool," Winters screeched. "Pull off her pants..."

"But she'd be bare below the waist," Aaron pointed out.

Winters' eyes brightened. He smiled. "Yes, exactly."

Aaron still held Lizzie's arm with one hand. His pistol was in his other hand. He shifted from one foot to the other indecisively but did nothing.

"Push me to her," Winters ordered.

Celia pushed the wheelchair up to Lizzie. Winters reached out and roughly jerked down Lizzie's pajama bottoms.

Lizzie slapped Winters hard and was following through to backhand him when Celia pulled back the wheelchair.

Agnes leapt forward into a crouch. She hissed at Winters.

Aaron bent down and restrained Agnes, holding her under the neck and stroking her throat.

Lizzie's pajama bottoms pooled at her feet.

Winters rubbed his cheek where Lizzie had slapped him. He slowly looked Lizzie up and down. The right corner of his mouth twitched. He placed a hand in his lap and stroked himself. "Crucify her tomorrow at reveille dressed as she is now. All workers must watch. You must watch, son. You must learn to be tough, to be a real man."

"Dad, I..." Aaron started to speak but was interrupted by Augie, who screamed, "Take her away now." Winters pounded his fist on the arm of his wheelchair.

Aaron hesitated.

"Now," Winters screeched.

Aaron pushed Lizzie toward the stairs with his gun hand as he led Agnes with his other hand. Lizzie tripped over the pajama bottoms but caught herself by grabbing the banister.

Aaron stepped on the edge of the pajamas. "Step out quick," he urged Lizzie. "Dad's so angry he's turning red."

Lizzie stepped out of the pajama bottoms and hurried up the stairs.

August Winters leaned back in his wheelchair. He laughed looking up between Lizzie's legs as she ascended the stairs.

CHAPTER FIFTY THREE

Wedding Plans?

"Your cutting my father's throat seems to have affected his mind," Aaron said as he pushed Lizzie toward her room. "That high voice must really trouble him. He prides himself on his manliness. I'm worried about him. He's become strange. He seems obsessed by you."

Lizzie looked back over her shoulder. "You don't think he was strange before?"

Aaron pushed her harder. She almost stumbled. "He's not used to a woman getting the better of him." Aaron looked unusually glum. "I'm worried he won't be himself again until you're dead."

Lizzie's room was already guarded. A serious-looking man sat on a metal chair in the hallway. It was the same chair but a different man from earlier. Both men had the dead eyes Lizzie previously noticed on the guards. She wondered if they all were on drugs. When the man saw Agnes, he stood up and casually strolled a short distance down the hall, holding his rifle at the ready.

As soon as Aaron opened the door to the room, Agnes bounded toward the bed. She leapt onto it, snuggled down, stood up, turned 180 degrees, snuggled down again, and closed her eyes.

Lizzie sat on the edge of the bed. She placed a pillow in her lap.

Aaron stood in front of her, still holding the gun, still aiming it at her. "I need to talk to dad, get him to be reasonable. In his current mood he might permanently damage you. That would not be a good beginning to our married life."

"I'm going to kill him," Lizzie stated. "Any chance I get, I'll kill him."

Aaron laughed. "Don't be ridiculous, Lizzie, you're not the violent type."

"I didn't used to be."

"But Lizzie..."

"He's put me through too much."

Aaron shook his head. "I understand why you feel that way. But things will just get worse if you remain obstinate. Dad has never backed down once in his life. Maybe if you apologized to him he'd go easy on you."

Lizzie glared at Aaron. "You're as crazy as he is."

Aaron inhaled deeply then let the breath out, as though exasperated. "I'm on your side, Lizzie. I don't want dad to hurt you. But if hostilities continue you're bound to be unhappy in our new home. I realize relations are often difficult between a new bride and her father in law."

"After I kill him, I'm going to kill you." Lizzie stood up. She continued to hold the pillow in front of her.

Aaron raised his weapon. "You've forgotten I have this gun."

Lizzie took a step toward him. "I don't care."

Aaron backed away. "This is probably not the best night to start our honeymoon. I'll sleep somewhere else tonight. But first I'll talk with dad."

Lizzie glared at Aaron as her former boyfriend walked over to the door to his father's bedroom. He jiggled the doorknob. It wouldn't open. "Good; it's locked. Dad would really go ballistic if you escaped again. I'll be back later to let you know how things are."

Aaron backed out through the door to the hall.

Lizzie sat back down on the bed. She petted Agnes and placed the pillow she was holding beside Agnes's head. "We'll make it through this, girl; just keep your spirits up."

Agnes opened one eye, looked at Lizzie for a second, closed the eye, shifted her head onto the edge of the pillow, and returned to sleep.

Lizzie and Agnes were left alone for several hours. Agnes slept peacefully. Lizzie was too nervous. She brushed her teeth, took a long, hot shower, and applied makeup.

She threw the pajama top in the little trash can in the corner of the bedroom. She didn't care what Augie said or did, she would never wear that obscene top again.

Lizzie picked out a white dress from the closet and put it on. It was short but at least it covered her, more or less.

The sun was descending into twilight when a knock sounded at Lizzie's door. It was Celia with dinner. She peeked in. "Is that panther in the bathroom?"

Lizzie stood. "No, she isn't. It's about time you quit being afraid of her. Agnes wouldn't hurt a flea."

"She wouldn't?" Celia asked, opening the door a little further.

"Well, actually she would hurt a flea. Agnes hates fleas. But she wouldn't hurt you."

Celia looked around cautiously. "Are you sure?"

Lizzie gestured for Celia to come to her. "Get in here, Celia, and quit being a baby."

Celia cautiously looked at Agnes, who still slept on the bed. "She's so big."

Lizzie shrugged. "She's harmless."

Celia crept in and placed a tray of food on the nightstand. A lump of chicken salad was surrounded by a variety of fruit pieces; orange and grapefruit predominated.

Lizzie looked over the meal. "You don't have anything there for Agnes."

"Mr. Winters not happy panther in his house. You sure that thing won't hurt me?"

Lizzie smiled and shook her head. "No, she won't hurt you. But she won't be happy at the lack of food for her. Food and sleep are her two favorite things."

"I'll look in the kitchen later; see if I find something for her."

"Did you hear that, girl," Lizzie said, turning and petting Agnes. "Celia will get you something to eat later."

Agnes opened her eyes. She looked up at Celia, opened her mouth wide, and yawned.

Celia stepped back. "She has such big teeth."

"Come here," Lizzie said. "Let her smell your hand. She's just like a house cat, only a little larger."

"A lot larger," said Celia, nervously sticking out her hand.

Agnes sniffed the offered hand then licked it.

Celia drew back her hand. "Icky"

"She tends to drool."

Agnes stood up and jumped from the bed, landing beside Celia. She licked the house servant's hands enthusiastically. Celia was frozen on the spot.

"You must have gotten food on your hands," Lizzie said. "Pet her."

Celia reached a shaking hand up and petted the top of Agnes' head. The large cat rubbed against Celia's leg.

"She likes me," Celia exclaimed.

A gunshot rang out.

"Oh no," Celia cried. She raised her hands to her mouth. "Mon Dieu."

"What is it?" Lizzie asked.

"It might be Lydia," Celia sobbed. "I told her that skinny man Aaron maybe brought Ben's arm." Celia repeatedly shook her head and gasped, as though she could not catch her breath. "She loved her brother. She went crazy. But I hope she not do something stupid." Suddenly Celia smiled. "Or maybe she all right. Maybe she shoot Mister Winters."

Lizzie stood and grabbed both of Celia's arms just above the elbows. Lizzie forced Celia to look her in the eyes. "You must do something, Celia, you and all the other workers. You can't let this horror continue."

Celia inhaled deeply. "But what can I do?"

Lizzie pulled Celia closer. "Talk to the workers; convince them to take action."

Celia wiped her eyes and nodded her head. "I have been too much coward. I will sneak to barracks tonight. I will talk to everybody. Tomorrow will be the day. Tomorrow we will stand up to them. Tomorrow we will free ourselves or die trying."

"Good," Lizzie said. "I'll do what I can to help."

Celia turned and walked to the door. Agnes followed her.

"No, here, girl," Lizzie said.

Celia looked at the panther as Agnes turned back to Lizzie. "I hope your big cat on our side too." Celia opened the door and quickly exited.

Lizzie knelt down and petted Agnes. "I hope Celia doesn't forget about your food."

Agnes licked Lizzie's face.

"I also hope the workers don't wait until after I'm crucified to revolt." Lizzie sat back on the bed. The panther jumped up onto the bed with Lizzie, lay down beside her, and purred.

CHAPTER FIFTY FOUR

Crucifixion Eve

"LOOK at the sleeping beauties," Aaron said as he prodded Lizzie awake with his pistol. Lizzie's arm lay across Agnes.

Lizzie turned over, sat up, and rubbed her eyes. "What time is it?"

Aaron backed away a couple steps. He held the gun at his side. "It's only a little after ten. Nothing will happen until around dawn."

"Does he still plan to crucify me?"

Aaron spread his arms in a pleading gesture. "Lizzie, I'm sorry, I tried. I talked to him. Dad can be really stubborn."

"So what now? Have you given up?"

Aaron gestured toward the other bedroom. "He's gone to bed. There's nothing I can do until morning. I certainly don't want to wake him."

"You woke me."

"You're different. And he's angry enough at me already. I would have thought my saving his life would have made him listen to me. But no, he's too bull-headed."

"When did you save his life?" Lizzie slid off the bed and stood up. She smoothed down the white dress.

"Earlier tonight." Aaron pointed at the dress. "Dad won't like that. He said to stay in the pajama top."

"I don't give a fuck what he says," Lizzie spat.

Aaron shook his head slowly. "Oh, Lizzie, Lizzie, Lizzie, that attitude will only get you in deeper trouble. I'm trying to build a long term relationship between us."

Lizzie stood hands on her hips staring at Aaron. She took a step toward

230

him. He raised the gun slightly. "How did you save Augie's life?" Lizzie repeated.

Aaron shrugged. "At dinner; that girl, the waitress, what's her name?"

"Lydia?"

"Yes, Lydia. She went crazy." Aaron waved his arms around and made a face to indicate craziness. "She started screaming and pulled out some kind of butcher knife and was lunging at Dad to stab him." Aaron shrugged. "So I shot her."

Lizzie's eyes went wide open. "You shot her?"

Aaron smiled and held up his gun. "Yes, I've gotten real quick with the gun, just like a genuine old time cowboy. I've been practicing. You'd think Dad would be grateful. He seemed more upset by her betrayal then appreciative of my saving him. She was his favorite."

Lizzie couldn't believe what she was hearing. "You shot Lydia?"

Aaron stared at Lizzie for a second. "Yes. He should have been more appreciative. I did it for him."

"You're pathetic, stupid and pathetic." Shaking her head, Lizzie walked away from Aaron, then turned and stomped back. "Did you ever get around to asking Augie to go easy on me?"

"Yes, right after I shot that girl, what's her name again?"

"Lydia."

"Yes, Lydia; after I shot Lydia I pleaded your case. I thought Dad would be particularly willing to do me a favor then. But he just looked kind of sick. He went to bed without even finishing dinner and you know how he loves to eat. It's going to be an early morning tomorrow. I need to get Agnes secured somewhere and get some sleep. Move over that way." Aaron gestured with his gun for Lizzie to move away from the bed.

Lizzie stepped aside but watched for any opening which might allow her to grab Aaron's gun.

Aaron went to the bed and nudged Agnes.

The Florida panther opened an eye, looked at Aaron, hissed, and then closed the eye. She snuggled down more in the bed.

"Well, uh, I guess she can sleep here." Aaron turned and headed to the door.

"Wait a minute," Lizzie said. "What about Lydia? Is she okay? How badly was she hurt?"

"Oh, she's definitely dead." Aaron held up his gun. He patted it and smiled. "My gun's more reliable than anything else in my life, certainly more reliable than you. Also, after I shot her, Boss Pigott cut off her head so we can display it to the workers tomorrow."

Later that night, Lizzie was awakened by Agnes bounding out of bed.

Bleary-eyed, Lizzie rolled over to see Celia standing with her hand to her heart. "Mon Dieu," Celia exclaimed, her legs trembling.

Celia had dropped a plate of food onto the floor at her feet. Agnes was devouring sausages and part of a pot roast.

"She not wait."

Lizzie sat up. "Agnes doesn't have very good table manners when she's hungry."

Celia carefully walked around the panther, who was enthusiastically chomping on the meat. As Celia sat on the bed beside Lizzie, she took Lizzie's right hand in both of hers. "Everybody really angry now. What happen to Lydia may be straw that broke elephant's back."

"They know about it?"

Celia nodded. "I sneaked out and told them. I also told them about Ben."

Lizzie gripped Celia's hands tightly. "So they will do something now, before I'm crucified tomorrow?"

Celia shook her head. "Not tonight, they too tired."

Lizzie placed an arm around Celia's shoulders. "Well then tomorrow morning, when they are all gathered together to see me crucified; will they revolt then?"

Celia slowly shook her head. "I not sure. They angry but they angry before." She squeezed Lizzie's hand. A tear ran down Celia's cheek. "We see what happen tomorrow."

Agnes licked the plate, which now sat empty on the floor. She stood, turned, and came over to the two women. Agnes sniffed where Celia's hands held Lizzie's hand. Agnes licked the joined hands.

Some time later, after Celia left, Lizzie crawled onto the opposite side of the bed from Agnes, laid her head on a pillow and immediately went to sleep.

Agnes opened her eyes, looked at Lizzie, rose up, went over beside her, lay down leaning her cat body against the human body, sniffed at Lizzie, whimpered, closed her eyes, and went back to sleep.

CHAPTER FIFTY FIVE

Nailed

Voices from beyond the inner fence, from the crucifying area, awakened Lizzie. Dim light filtered through the windows. The sun was on the verge of rising, bringing a pale dawn light. Sleepily, Lizzie looked around. Agnes was not on the bed.

Lizzie sat up, turned, and placed her bare feet on the floor. She was nervous but felt rejuvenated. Her backache was gone. She thought her tense muscles must have finally relaxed. She had heard somewhere that condemned people on death row sleep well the night before their execution.

She rose and hurried to the bathroom. On the way she picked her white dress up off the floor.

Agnes was slurping a drink from the open toilet.

Lizzie gave Agnes a push. "I need the bathroom, girl. I'll only be a few minutes." She patted the panther on the rump and the large animal slowly walked into the other room. Lizzie shut the bathroom door.

"It's time, Lizzie." Aaron's voice came through the bathroom door. "Dad wants you downstairs now."

Lizzie was applying makeup. She couldn't find the nail scissors. "I'll be right out."

"Now," Aaron yelled. "Dad's in a bad mood, a strange mood. Don't make him wait."

"Okay."

Lizzie applied lipstick that looked like congealed blood and slipped on the white dress.

When she came out of the bathroom she found Aaron kneeling to pet Agnes with his left hand. His right hand held the pistol which seemed to have become a permanent attachment.

Aaron looked up at her. "Dad won't like that dress."

Lizzie smoothed down the front of the short dress. "I don't care what he likes or doesn't like."

"Why won't you wear what he wants?"

Lizzie gave him the finger. "Fuck you."

"Oh, Lizzie. Can't you even give an inch?" Aaron looked distraught. His hands shook. "Don't you see both your life and our marriage are at stake?"

Aaron shoved Lizzie from her room toward the stairs. Agnes trotted at their heels. The rifle-carrying hallway guard followed behind the panther, far behind the panther, as they all trooped down the front stairs. Lizzie recognized him as Mark, the guard she hit on the head in the woods. A bandage was wrapped around the top of his head.

At the bottom, Aaron turned to the guard. "Watch her while I tell Dad we're ready."

"Yes, sir."

Aaron hurried down the hall toward August Winters office.

Lizzie knelt and petted Agnes. "I hope we both get out of this alive, girl."

Mark stayed as far away from Agnes as possible in the narrow space near the base of the stairs. Lizzie looked around. The guard's fear of Agnes made her think now might be the time to make a run for it. She stood up and motioned to Agnes. "Come girl."

Lizzie began walking forward. But Agnes didn't follow.

Mark raised his rifle, pointing it at Lizzie. "Stop right there. You almost killed me out in the woods, so it wouldn't bother me none to rid the Earth of both you and your animal."

Lizzie stopped. Her lack of any weapon, Agnes's failure to follow her, and the sounds of several people coming from the office put an end to Lizzie's plan. Celia pushed the wheelchair carrying Winters, followed by Boss Pigott and Aaron.

Winters pointed at Agnes like Charlton Heston parting the Red Sea. "Get that animal out of this house."

"Uh, yes, uh, yes sir," Mark, who was standing against the far wall, replied. He took a step forward.

Agnes made a rumbling noise in her throat.

Mark stopped.

"If you can't get that beast out of here, shoot it or I'll have you shot."

Winters had a Forceflex trash bag in his lap. Lizzie shuttered, thinking what the bag must contain.

Aaron edged around the wheelchair. "I'll take her out. Come on Agnes, let's take a walk." Aaron petted the panther's head, gestured toward the front doors, and then walked to those doors. Agnes hesitated, looking up at Lizzie, who leaned down, patted the panther's rump and said, "Go ahead, girl, go with Aaron." She didn't want to risk Agnes getting shot.

Agnes trotted across to the door, her claws clicking on the wooden floor. Aaron followed her out.

Boss Pigott quickly stepped around Lizzie and went to the door.

"Take the bitch out," Winters growled at Mark, who stepped over to Lizzie, grabbed her right arm, and pulled her toward the door. She did not resist.

Boss Pigott watched Lizzie walk across the entryway toward the door. His eyes swept her from head to crotch. Pigott stuck his arm out and stopped Lizzie when she reached the door. He whispered in her ear. "We gonna have some fun while you nailed to that wall."

The workers, approximately forty tattered men and women, grumbled among themselves in Haitian Creole. They had been herded to the side of the clearing opposite the barracks building's bloody wall. The plantation house fence was behind them. Blood from Gaston's crucifixion and from the torture of other farm workers stained the wall they faced. Gaston himself stood near one of the guards. The guards held rifles and watched the workers.

Aaron and Agnes were the first to reach the area between the workers and the wall. Several workers and one of the guards moved further away when the panther arrived. "Madre mia, una pantera," a guard exclaimed.

Boss Pigott and the guard from the house dragged Lizzie into the clearing and shoved her down onto the ground directly in front of the workers. Pigott's immense body towered over Lizzie. She looked around, eager for any opportunity to make a last ditch effort to save herself.

The ominously silent farm workers glanced nervously at each other; eyes meeting briefly. Gaston took a step backward so he was slightly behind the guard standing beside him. Other workers shifted positions. Lizzie hoped they were preparing to act.

"Damned bumps," croaked Winters as Celia pushed his wheelchair over the uneven ground. He held the closed Forceflex bag on his lap. Celia maneuvered him around until he was next to Lizzie, facing the workers.

Winters tossed the bag down beside his wheelchair on the opposite side from Lizzie. Winters leaned toward Pigott and whispered, "Nail those to the wall on each side of her."

Pigott nodded but made no immediate move toward the bag. He stayed beside Lizzie, one hand gripping her arm.

Winters looked around from worker to worker, waiting until all eyes were fixed on him. "I see the looks in your eyes," he growled. "Be warned: any rebellion will be dealt with severely. We can't have class warfare, don't listen to the Communists and the Socialists among you. The family farm is all important to this country and to the world." He gestured toward Lizzie with his right hand. "This woman rebelled. You are about to see what happens to rebels. This woman has defied God by trying to assassinate me. I proclaim her guilty of attempted murder and of attempted escape. She is sentenced to be crucified. The crucifixion is to include the spear wound suffered by our savior. May her soul rest in peace."

Everyone in the silent crowd looked at Lizzie. The silence was broken by Aaron suddenly running forward screaming, "No; you promised she'd be my wife. You can't kill her. I love her. Give her to me. Please father, please give her to me." He fell to his knees in front of Winters.

For a moment Winters glared at his son, then he growled, "Do you dare defy me; dare question my orders?" Winters pointed at Aaron. "A son defying his father; violating the commandment about honoring thy father and mother."

Aaron stood up, his skinny body towering over his wheelchair-bound father

Winters' pointing arm followed Aaron. "If you think my punishment of that whore of Babylon is too terrible, wait until you see what I inflict on you. Being a relative brings more responsibility, not less. I cannot tolerate weakness."

Aaron pulled his gun from the waistband of his pants and stuck it against Winters' head just above his ear. "Sorry, dad, I want my wife, so I can't let you kill her. She leaves with me now."

Guards started to raise their rifles but Winters waved for them to lower their weapons. A smile spread across Winters' face. He opened his hands in a conciliatory manner. "Of course, son, I hadn't realized how much you loved her. Take her." Winters gestured toward Lizzie then dropped both hands to his lap. His right hand slipped under his lap blanket.

Still holding the gun on his father, Aaron edged over to Lizzie. "Come with me. We don't need Dad for our wedding. We'll elope."

Lizzie jumped up, turned and ran toward the fields. At the edge of the nearest field Lizzie stopped, turned, and yelled to the workers. "Be brave. I'll return with help." She turned again and ran into the field.

Winters eyed his son. "Looks like your girlfriend plans to elope without you."

"Wait for me," Aaron yelled toward Lizzie as he withdrew the gun from beside his father's head. "Sorry dad, you know I wouldn't really have shot you. Goodbye. I hope someday you accept my choice of a wife. She's really nice if you don't get her angry." He turned and ran after Lizzie.

Winters pulled an Uzi machinegun from under his lap blanket and fired, striking Aaron repeatedly in the back, tattering his shirt with streaks of red. Aaron staggered then fell onto a mound of dirt at the edge of the fields. He twitched slightly and then lay still.

Winters looked around at the guards and then over at Boss Pigott. "You're all completely worthless. Do I always have to do everything myself?"

Boss Pigott ambled over to Winters. "He was your son. Family stuff has always been too complicated for me."

"He ceased to be my son when he defied me. Now get that bitch Lizzie. Bring her back to me. Think you can do that?"

"Shouldn't be difficult." Pigott smiled. "The inner fence is locked. She can't get back to the house. She also can't get out past the middle fence. She'll be somewhere in the fields and she don't know the fields. Mind if I have some fun with her before you crucify her?"

"Don't take too long."

Pigott trotted off in the direction Lizzie had run. His heavy footfalls echoed off the side of the barracks.

The workers watched Pigott depart. A couple gave covert nods to each other. One gave a thumb's up sign. Another whispered to the man beside him. That man nodded.

Winters looked around at the workers. "While we have a few minutes, let me tell you again why the American family farm must be saved and why anybody who fights my efforts to save the family farm is both unpatriotic, a Socialist, and defying the will of God. George Washington was a planter, which is just a fancy word for farmer. Thus from its beginning our country..."

Agnes had run behind the barracks and hid at the sound of the loud banging noises. She cautiously came out while the man in the rolling chair barked at the others. She ran over to Aaron's body and sniffed, then nudged him with her snout and, when he didn't move, whined softly.

Agnes looked up at the man making all the noise while the other people stood silent. Her mistress had vanished.

A man at the back of the crowd suddenly jumped on the man beside him, one of the men carrying the noisy sticks. Other people in the crowd began fighting.

Agnes sniffed at a black bag on the ground. It smelled interesting. She clomped onto it with her jaws and dragged it off behind the barracks building. She hid it among some bushes. Then she ran back out into the clearing.

A strange vibrating sound came from beyond the orange groves on the other side of the farm.

The man who had been barking with the high voice was pushed away in his wheeled chair by the woman who had petted Agnes last night. Agnes thought about going with them. But she sensed the man didn't like her. She couldn't understand why. She hadn't done anything to him. Another loud noise sounded and Agnes decided to get as far away as possible. She dashed off toward the tomato fields.

Lizzie ran between rows of low lying tomato plants trying to reach the woods behind the house.

"Stop now or I'll shoot," Boss Pigott yelled from the edge of the road bordering the fields. He held a pistol and was gasping for breath. His enormous stomach wobbled with each inhalation.

Agnes crept up behind him.

Two helicopters suddenly appeared beyond the distant orange trees. They swept low across the farm. The noise was deafening, throbbing, vibrating the earth.

Lizzie threw herself onto the ground.

Agnes ran around in a circle.

Pigott stood, hands on hips, watching the copters.

Coming in only a few feet above the ground, the two copters flew over Lizzie, Pigott, and Agnes. The large machines headed toward the barracks building, where they descended spreading clouds of dust, engine sounds suddenly changing from a high pitched deafening roar to a steady swish, swish, swish as men jumped out just before the copters touched down.

Through the dust, Lizzie, who was lying on her stomach, could see men in ICE jackets jumping from the copters. Each man held a weapon. Some fired as they jumped.

When she looked back away from the helicopter invasion, Lizzie found herself staring at dirty boots. Boss Pigott stood over her. "Don't bother getting up. I gonna enjoy you right there on the ground."

An explosion shook the whole farm. Flames and smoke shot up from behind the orange trees, near the outer fence gate.

"Looks like I don't got a hell of a lot of time," Pigott straddled Lizzie sitting his weight down on her rear end. He opened his belt and began unzipping his pants. Lizzie tried to stand. Pigott pushed her back down.

"You don't gotta move," Pigott panted, "I gonna take you from behind." He stood with a booted foot in the small of her back. "Just gimme a second to shuck my pants."

An explosion shook the ground as the gate in the second fence flew into the air. Parts of the fence peppered the fields as a Buick Le Sabre roared through the gap made by the explosion. A dust cloud swept behind it as the Buick raced down the dirt road between the fields.

Pigott pushed himself down on top of Lizzie. Her back made a popping noise. Pain radiated through it. She felt his huge erection pushing up between her legs as his arms wrapped around her waist and neck.

The Buick skidded off the road and headed across the tomato field toward Lizzie and her rapist. But it was too far away. He would be in her before the big car reached them.

Out of the corner of her eye, Lizzie saw Agnes. The big cat was watching Pigott shove himself down on top of Lizzie but was doing nothing. It suddenly occurred to Lizzie how to get Agnes to intervene. At the top of her lungs, she yelled, "Food."

Agnes charged.

A sudden additional weight crushed down on top of Lizzie. Her back popped again and her pain was swept away by a vibrant feeling, a surge of energy. Her face was pressed into the dirt.

"What the hell," Pigott screamed. He tried to push himself off Lizzie. "Help, help," Pigott gasped into her ear.

Pigott's body suddenly flew off Lizzie.

The Buick had stopped a few feet away.

Lizzie rolled onto her side. She saw Agnes jumping around pawing and nipping at the half naked Pigott, who was stumbling backwards, trying to push the panther away.

Pigott had dropped his gun. Lizzie picked it up and aimed it at the huge farm foreman. She laughed, partly from relief, partly because Pigott looked so funny; his face contorted in fear, his whole body shaking, as he stumbled, his pants down around his ankles. "Don't worry, she won't hurt you. She thought we were playing and just wanted to join in." Lizzie looked down at the gun in her hand. "I'm the one who might hurt you." She leapt to her feet, suddenly feeling like a million dollars.

"Hey Lizzie, you got spunk." Lizzie recognized the New York accent of the voice coming from behind her but she couldn't believe her ears. Joey was dead. She had seen him shot. She turned and looked incredulously at semi-retired mobster Joey Caunteloupo, unbelievably alive.

Lizzie forgot all about Pigott and Agnes as she squished through mashed tomato plants to reach Joey. She placed her free hand on his shoulder. "You're real. How can you be? I saw you killed. I saw you shot to death."

Another man got out of the front passenger side of the Buick. Two more men emerged from the back seat. All three looked like football linebackers. All three held guns and all three smiled at Lizzie.

"You gotta learn to check a pulse before you assume a guy is dead." Joey grinned at Lizzie.

Lizzie still couldn't believe he was standing there in front of her. "But you were shot in the chest."

Joey shrugged. "I gotta lotta experience being shot. My body's used to it. Though this time was worse than most."

"Hey, Joey," the man standing behind Joey interrupted. "She ain't got no pants."

Joey looked down at Lizzie. "No she don't. Lizzie girl; do you know you don't got no pants on?"

Looking down, Lizzie realized her white dress had been ripped to shreds by Pigott's rape attempt.

"I got a jacket she could wrap around her," said one of the men standing on the other side of the Buick.

Lizzie had moved her hands down to cover herself. "I would appreciate that."

The man tossed a light cloth jacket across the car. Lizzie caught it and wrapped it around her waist, tying the arms together to hold it on.

A scream came from behind her. Lizzie looked around. Boss Pigott had tried to run. Agnes had knocked him down again and was standing over him licking his face.

"I oughta introduce you to the boys." As Lizzie turned back, Joey pointed in turn to the three men. This is Jay, over there is Jack, and that's Jose'. They're the three J's."

"That's us," the three men chorused as they smiled and nodded to Lizzie.

"They're the field operatives of the Southeastern regional office of the insurance division of the organization I used to be associated with. I thought they might be helpful since their work involves using a lot of explosives, accelerators, and other flammables."

"We was happy to do something different, something to help out Loopy Joey," said Jay, the man who had thrown Lizzie the jacket.

240

"Yeah, I'm missin' my kid's Little League game, but I told the wife it was for Joey and she understood," added Jack. "I'm not sure my kid understood. But, hell, he'll learn what's important in life: friends, respect, values."

"I'm amazed you're okay," Lizzie said to Joey. "I was so depressed."

"I'm fine," Joey assured her. "I had to spend a lotta time in the hospital. Every time I opened my eyes somebody was sticking a needle in me. Val was there most every day. He's a good friend."

"So that must have been where he was when I kept trying to call him."

"Yeah, he finally got your messages. He put together this raid. I insisted on joining it. He didn't think it was too appropriate my boys coming along on a raid by Immigration and Custom Enforcement, but I pointed out he could be creative in his reports."

"Where is Val?" Lizzie asked.

"He was in the lead helicopter. He must be in the middle of that fire fight." Joey gestured toward the battle by the bunkhouse.

With the shock of seeing Joey, Lizzie had blocked out the distant sounds of gunfire.

"My God he could be shot," she exclaimed. "We need to help him."

"Yeah, we should." Joey turned to his companions. "Jack, Jose', why don't you secure that guy? Put him between you in the backseat."

"Can't we just shoot him?" Jack asked.

Joey shook his head. "No, we're part of a federal government raid. We have to behave as if we were the law."

"You been gone too long if you think the law don't just shoot people," commented Jose'.

Jack and Jose' started walking toward Boss Pigott but then stopped. "What about that big cat?"

"I'll get Agnes," exclaimed Lizzie. She ran over and pulled Agnes off Boss Pigott. "Come on girl; let's go check on all the excitement over there." Lizzie patted Agnes on the head and pointed toward the firefight.

Lizzie and Agnes ran together across the field toward the fighting men. Gunfire had decreased to just an occasional pop.

"Wait for us," yelled Joey, as Jack and Jose led a stunned Boss Pigott to the Buick.

Lizzie, continuing to run, looked back and held up the gun she had taken from Pigott. "I can't wait. I've got to make sure Val is okay."

CHAPTER FIFTY SIX

A Confrontation

Lizzie ran as fast as her legs would carry her toward the groups of struggling men and the now-silent helicopters. The jacket tied about her waist flapped around her legs. She reached down in passing and grabbed a ripe tomato from its bush and ate it as she ran.

Agnes bounded along ahead of Lizzie. Things sure had been exciting the last couple days. Agnes hoped the fun would continue.

Joey's Buick sped past Lizzie, crushing tomato plants as it crossed the fields. A limb loaded with oranges and part of a gate were caught in its grill.

Out of the corner of her eye, Lizzie saw Mark, made obvious by his bandaged head, separate himself from the fight. He dragged an anemic-looking boy of about six or seven with him as he snuck behind a tractor parked beside the first field, the field Lizzie was crossing.

Lizzie stopped running and dropped to the ground between rows of tomato plants. Mark came out from behind the tractor. He held a pistol to the head of the child as he dragged the boy toward the woods and the inner fence. He ran along the outer perimeter of the fence until he disappeared where the fence went around the back of the house.

Lizzie looked over at the other guards, farm workers, and ICE agents. Some were still fighting. Others were backing away from Agnes, who looked like she wanted to join the tussle. Joey's Buick had arrived but the doors were still closed. Nobody else seemed to have noticed Mark and his small hostage.

Lizzie jumped up and ran after them.

Lizzie slowed down when she reached the trail behind the house which led to the fence enclosing the animal compound. Mark must have taken the boy down that trail. He could not have safely gone anywhere else. If he had continued along the fence he would have ended up back at the fight. Lizzie moved carefully down the trail. She knew the dead-end at the animal compound fence would at least delay Mark and possibly turn him back.

She glanced down the intersecting trail when she passed it, but saw nothing. She passed the spot where she had knocked out Mark what now seemed like years ago.

Finally, up ahead, she saw Mark standing with his back to her, looking up at the fence. The boy was at his feet crumbled in the fetal position, trembling and sobbing.

Lizzie silently snuck up behind them.

"Ain't no way I can get you over this fence if you won't stand up, you little bastard," Mark growled. "So you brought this on yourself." He extended his pistol toward the boy's head. "Sayonara."

Lizzie dashed forward and stuck the gun she had taken from Pigott against the back of Mark's head. "Not so fast. Let the boy go."

Mark didn't move, didn't flinch. He chuckled. "Looks like we got us a Mexican standoff and we sure don't want to get us both killed. So why don't we put our guns away?"

"Mexican standoff?" Lizzie replied. "No way, Jose. That's when two people have guns pointed at each other. Nobody's got a gun pointed at me."

"I can take care of that, bitch. Cause I know you don't got the balls to pull your trigger." He raised his pistol away from the boy's head and started to swing it toward Lizzie.

She pulled her trigger.

The gunfire and fighting were over by the time Lizzie and the boy got back to the crucifixion area. She paused to catch her breath. The boy yelled "papa" as he ran over and threw himself into the arms of one of the farm workers. The ICE agents had separated the workers from the guards and were watching both groups. Some of the agents were using straps to bind the wrists of the guards and putting hoods over their heads. Some workers helped tend the wounds of other workers.

Joey and his men were finally emerging from the Buick, keeping their distance from the federal agents.

Val ran to meet Lizzie. The two came together at the edge of the field like a couple running toward each other in an old television commercial. They embraced awkwardly. Each still held a handgun. Lizzie realized she should have ditched hers. But it seemed to have become a part of her hand, lending a feeling of security.

Lizzie's kiss was passionate. She groaned, need and yearning pulsating through her. It had been too long.

Agnes ran over, growled, and then ran around the couple. She tried to stick her snout in between Lizzie and Val.

"Oh my God," Val exclaimed.

"Ignore her," moaned Lizzie, reaching down to push Agnes away as her lips again merged with Val's. Sweat poured down her face. "I knew you would come to save me," Lizzie whispered.

"I've missed you terribly," moaned Val as he raised his free hand and stroked her hair.

"Get a room," yelled one of the ICE agents. The others laughed.

"We'll have to continue this later," Val said as he drew his lips away from hers. "We have ambulances and local police on the way. I need to finish securing the area."

They reluctantly drew apart. He looked down at her. "You're wearing somebody's jacket around your waist."

Lizzie blushed. "I didn't have any pants."

Val's brow furrowed with concern. "The jacket's all bloody."

Lizzie shrugged and smiled. "That's okay, I'll get it washed off."

Val looked her up and down. "Are you wounded? Are you bleeding?"

Lizzie's smile brightened. "Forget about it. The blood's not mine."

Val took her free hand. "You have been through hell."

Holding hands, they walked toward the others.

Agnes trotted along beside them, looking around eagerly. New stuff kept happening.

Even though they were being guarded by federal immigration agents, the workers were happy, laughing, talking rapidly in Creole, and slapping each other on the back. They never thought they would live to leave the farm.

The uninjured guards sat silently on the dusty ground.

Joey spoke briefly to Val, who then sent an agent to extract Boss Pigott from the Buick.

Lizzie looked around. "Where's Augie?"

"What?" asked Val.

"August Winters; he's not here. He was here when I ran off but he's not here now."

Val looked at the gathered farm workers and guards. "Damn it, you're right. Where could he be? We'll have to initiate a search."

"Only one direction he could have gone." Lizzie turned and ran toward the far side of the crucifixion barracks.

"Wait," yelled Val, "I gotta turn over supervision here. Only take a second."

Lizzie ignored him. She ran around the end of the building and saw Augie ahead, his wheelchair stopped at the edge of the latrine ditch.

Celia was on the far side of that ditch. She took a step backward.

"One more step away from me and you're dead," screeched Augie. "Rebellion and desertion is punishable by death. Come back here now. NOW."

"No, please, I not take any more. I need look for my son." Celia fell to her knees. She cried and held up her hands pleading.

"Big brave man," yelled Lizzie, "running away like a coward at the first sign of trouble and then threatening a terrified, unarmed woman."

Augie spun his wheelchair around to face Lizzie. Behind him, Celia jumped up and ran off into the woods.

Augie placed his hands on top of the Uzi machinegun in his lap. "I need a hostage to get out of here. You'll do, come here, now, this minute, or die."

Lizzie walked slowly toward Winters, holding Boss Pigott's pistol at her side.

Augie looked her up and down. "I'm taking you out of here with me. Then I'm going to prosecute you and all these other people for violation of private property and for destroying the American family farm. I have worked for years to prove..."

"Listen you idiot," Lizzie interrupted, "haven't you noticed I also have a gun?"

Augie laughed. "Are you kidding, Lizzie. I know you. You're a weak, cowardly female; good for only one thing. Now drop that silly gun and push me out of here."

Lizzie hesitated a second thinking and then dropped her gun.

"That's better," said Augie, "now push me over to those woods. I have a secret exit. Nobody gets the better of me, I thought ahead for a day like this."

Lizzie walked around Augie's wheelchair, keeping enough distance to avoid being grabbed. She came up behind the wheelchair and slowly turned it around.

"Good," said Augie, "After we get out of here I'll consider commuting your sentence when I get my farm back."

Lizzie pushed Augie forward.

Augie pointed off to the right. "No, down toward the far end of the ditch. Go around it, toward the woods."

Lizzie laughed. "Dream on, you bastard." She tilted the wheelchair forward.

Augie screamed as Lizzie dumped him into the shit-filled latrine ditch.

Lizzie stepped to the edge of the latrine hole and looked in. Augie's shoulders and head floated above the stinking mess. His face had been splashed with stinking dark liquid. His hands slipped as he desperately tried to grab the sides of the hole to pull himself up.

"You're dead," Augie screamed. "You don't realize how much political influence I have. You can put me in jail but I won't stay there. I'll be out on bail in a day or less. I've got money for the best lawyers. I'll never be convicted of anything. Then I can resume God's work of saving the American family farm. God has given me that mission to…"

"Oh shut up," said Lizzie. She turned away, walked over, and retrieved Boss Pigott's pistol from where she had dropped it.

"You can tell me to shut up but those are only the weak words of a lowly woman, I will continue to proclaim God's will," Augie shouted. "Nothing can stop me."

"This can." Lizzie aimed the gun at Augie's head and fired three shots. Red stains spotted the brown mass surrounding Augie as his head exploded.

Lizzie looked around, wondering if she might have become too hard, might have overcompensated for her previous fear and harmlessness. Nobody was in sight. But she heard yelling and the sound of running feet near the far end of the barracks. Lizzie dropped Pigott's gun into the latrine hole and fell backward away from that smelly ditch. She carefully caught herself and eased herself to the ground. As she lay there, she concluded that too hard or not, it might be best now to appear weak.

Val ran up beside Lizzie, followed by Joey and several ICE agents. "Oh my God, my poor sweet Lizzie," exclaimed Val.

"Check her pulse," interjected Joey.

Val knelt down beside Lizzie and gently took her wrist. "She's okay. Strong pulse. I don't see any wounds."

Lizzie stirred. Her eyes fluttered open. She smiled up at Val. "What happened?"

"You must have fainted." Val put a hand to her forehead.

"Augie threatened me," Lizzie said, her voice weak.

"You poor thing." Val looked around. "His wheelchair is over by that ditch. Someone take a look."

A couple of the ICE agents ran over, looked in the ditch, and then stepped back covering their noses. "He isn't going anywhere," said one of the agents.

"Except to the coroner," interjected the other. "Sure glad body recovery isn't part of our job description."

"Or examining the crime scene. That'll be the local sheriff," added the other.

"Crime scene?" asked Lizzie.

"Looks like he's been shot," said the first ICE agent.

"Oh," whispered Lizzie. "I must have fainted."

"Don't worry," said Val, "leaning down and kissing Lizzie on the cheek. I think we've all learned not to suspect you of anything. That recording of Aaron you put on my answering machine cleared you. All charges have been dropped."

"I told you she couldn't hurt a fly," added Joey.

"I'm so happy." Lizzie smiled up at Val. "Let me see if I can get up."

"I'll help you." Val placed a hand under her arm and helped her to her feet.

Lizzie shook her head as if clearing it. "I'll be all right."

An ICE agent came around the building from where the farm workers and farm guards were being held. "The local sheriff's people are here," he yelled to Val.

"I need to talk to them," Val told Lizzie. "Will you be okay for a few minutes?

"Sure, go ahead. I'm okay. You have a lot to do and I need to catch up with Joey on what happened to him."

"Okay, but first. You must know that I love you." Val tenderly kissed Lizzie before turning and running off with his men back to where the workers and guards were held.

Joey smiled knowingly at Lizzie. "So you don't know who shot Augie?"

"I didn't say that." She smiled back at him and winked. "All I said was that I fainted."

"Didn't I notice you had that big guy's gun in your hand when you ran after Augie?"

"Anybody looks for that gun will have to go through a hell of a lot of shit." Lizzie smiled.

Joey glanced over at the latrine ditch. "I think staying with me rubbed off on you," Joey laughed. "Come on, babe; let's go join the others. I gotta get out of here. Too many cops around for me."

As she walked back, Lizzie saw two ICE agents walking a handcuffed Boss Pigott towards a helicopter. Lizzie ran over to them. "I was disappointed,"

Lizzie said to Pigott, "I thought someone with such a talent for the piano might have a good side buried in him."

Pigott stopped and laughed sadly. "That's what mom thought. That's why she forced me to practice; thought it would help me spiritually."

"Get moving," one of the ICE agents ordered. Pigott ignored him.

"Did she finally give up on you?" Lizzie asked.

The agents pulled at Pigott but he didn't move. "No, I gave up on her; so she died."

"What?" Lizzie was startled. "Are you saying…?"

"I ain't sayin' no more. See you some day when you don't expect me, you sexy little thing." Pigott grinned, raised his eyebrows, and wiggled his tongue at Lizzie. "Okay boys I'll go with you now."

Pigott let the agents lead him off to a helicopter.

Lizzie stared after them for a moment, shuddered, shook her head, and then walked over to Val. She gestured around at the farm workers. "These people have suffered terribly. They don't deserve further suffering."

"I'll do everything I can," Val assured her.

Joey joined them. "I might be able to help. This looks like a nice farm. I can see myself as a farmer. I've been bored silly sitting around doing nothing and the boys won't object to me farming. They ain't interested in that, it don't compete with nothin' they got their fingers into. Maybe I can work a deal with Winters' widow for the farm, make her an offer she can't refuse. So I'll need these farm workers and I can guarantee good working conditions. I'll put in modern air conditioned living facilities."

"How can you make a success of a farm and pay good wages and have good working conditions, all at the same time?" Lizzie asked.

"Easy; I gotta lotta influence with a whole lotta Italian restaurants and grocery stores. They'll pay me what I need for good fresh produce. So it'll work out great for everybody."

Lizzie shook her head. "Except those stores might have to pay a little more than they'd have to if they weren't influenced by your organization and could shop around."

Joey grinned. "Hey, I knew you'd learn something from being around me."

"I'm not so sure you're a good influence," Val said to Joey. He turned to Lizzie. "I'm going to have to keep you close to me so you don't come under any other bad influences."

"How do you plan to do that?" asked Lizzie.

"By marrying you."

Lizzie stared at Val open mouthed. "Yes, yes, oh yes." She threw herself into his arms. "Oh Val," Lizzie reached up on her tippy toes and kissed him.

Val embraced her tightly.

Something in addition to Val was pushing between Lizzie and Val down below. They tried to ignore it but it was persistent. They pulled apart and looked down.

Agnes looked up at Val and Lizzie. She had the plastic Forceflex back in her jaws.

Lizzie realized what it was and instinctively backed away.

Agnes dropped the bag at Val's feet and looked up at him. Her eyes were eager and she was panting.

"Uh, what am I supposed to do?" Val asked, nervous about a Florida panther standing less than a foot away, but aware that Lizzie loved the animal.

"She likes you," Lizzie told him. "She's offering you a gift."

"I should open it then."

"No, don't."

But Lizzie's warning was too late. Val knelt down and opened the Forceflex bag.

"Jesus Christ," he exclaimed.

"She was the kitchen serving girl," Lizzie said. "You'll need that for evidence."

Val closed the bag and stared at Lizzie. "You have been through hell."

Lizzie placed a hand on Val's chest. "It's been difficult. But now that you're here, I'm safe and everything is wonderful."

Val took her in his arms. "My dear, sweet, innocent Lizzie."

CHAPTER FIFTY SEVEN

What Happened Next

Val had to send for a government car from the U.S. Coast Guard station at Fort Myers Beach. Agnes had refused to go anywhere near the helicopters and Lizzie had refused to leave without Agnes.

Collier County sheriff's cars transported Boss Pigott and the uninjured guards to jail.

Ambulances removed the injured guards and workers. Hearses removed the dead. Nobody could figure out how a guard found dead on a trail in the woods got shot. Some speculated a stray bullet must have hit him.

The uninjured workers would stay at the farm with an ICE guard, at least for that night.

Some discussion was required before Val, Lizzie, and Agnes could get seated in the government car. The Coast Guardsman refused to let Agnes sit with him on the front seat. There wasn't room for three in front and Val and Lizzie wanted to sit side by side. So Val, Lizzie, and Agnes all sat in back with Agnes on the right and Lizzie in the middle. Even though Lizzie had introduced Val to Agnes, Val did not feel comfortable sitting beside the large cat.

"The police didn't show any interest in me," Lizzie commented. "So you were right, all charges were dropped."

"Just keep your nose clean. As I told you, that recording you made of Aaron confessing convinced the Sanibel police and the state attorney of his guilt. I forwarded it to them." Val smiled and took Lizzie's hand in his. "More good news; you were worried about the farm workers being sent back to Haiti. That won't happen for a very long time. They have to remain in the United States as witnesses in the murder trials of Boss Pigott and the guards."

"Will they be free to work?"

Val smiled and nodded. "I'm sure Joey can get them put in his custody."

"So everything is perfect." Lizzie snuggled up against Val.

"Only one problem: what are we going to do with her?" Val gestured toward Agnes, who was looking out at the scenery along Route 82, the road from Immokalee to Fort Myers. A red shouldered hawk swooped across the road in front of the car. Agnes ignored it.

"I don't know," Lizzie replied. "We can't leave her unprotected."

Val shook his head slowly. "We certainly can't take her to Atlanta with us. I don't think Delta Airlines would want a panther on board."

Lizzie nodded. "There's some sort of wild animal shelter out on Route 31 but I wouldn't want to see Agnes in a cage."

A sign beside the road read "panther crossing next seven miles, only 30 left, drive carefully." The driver did not slow down.

Val touched Lizzie's arm. "What about you? Will life as the wife of a customs official be enough for you?"

Lizzie smiled. "I might be able to help you investigate things. We could be like Nick and Nora Charles."

"If I'm The Thin Man does that mean that Agnes is Asta?" asked Val.

Lizzie laughed. "She's more intimidating and more of a pussycat."

Lizzie could see herself as Nora Charles. But there was one obstacle. Val had apparently forgotten that Lizzie was still married. The divorce process might take time, which was all right with Lizzie. She hadn't known Val very long; the relationship needed a test drive. Lizzie looked forward to living with a law enforcement official. She could see herself backing him up. She resolved to get her own gun.

Lizzie's thoughts were interrupted by Val asking her a question. "Will you miss beaches and sun in Atlanta; miss your conservation work?"

"I think I could find something to do there. The Georgia branch of the Nature Conservancy protects over 267,000 acres and monitors gopher tortoises. Also there's a group called AWARE, the Atlanta Wild Animal Rescue Effort, which has a seven acre natural habitat wildlife center. I would probably have to work as a volunteer before I could get a paying job. But I do have experience."

Val looked at her suspiciously. "When did you do this research about Atlanta?"

Lizzie shrugged. "Back at Joey's house on his computer; when you were there."

Val's brow furrowed. "But I hadn't asked you to go to Atlanta with me then."

Lizzie gave him her most dazzling grin. "It doesn't hurt to be prepared."

Val raised an eyebrow. "I thought asking you to go to Atlanta was my idea."

Lizzie chuckled. "It was your idea. I just decided to study it before you had it."

Agnes suddenly growled and shifted back and forth. She stood on the seat, her rear end almost in Lizzie's face.

"What's wrong with her?" Val asked.

"I'm not sure," Lizzie responded. "She always seems to get upset on this stretch of highway. I think it's where she was hit by the car."

Agnes was scratching at the window with her left front paw.

"Driver, pull over," Val ordered. "She might need to go to the bathroom."

The sedan pulled onto the slightly slanted, grassy shoulder of the road, near a sign reading "10 acres for sale." Lizzie pushed Agnes's rump out of her way, reached over, and opened the door. Agnes bounded out and ran a short distance back along the road. She emitted a high piercing howling noise. It sounded like the scream of a woman in terrible pain.

Lizzie slid along the seat and got out. She leaned back in and said to Val. "I've never heard her make a noise like that before. It's different from the noise she makes when she challenges another animal."

In the distance, from the woods across the road, a distant echoing screech answered Agnes's call.

Agnes howled again, yowwwl, yowwwl, yowwwl, and started to cross the road, almost getting hit by a car, which swerved out of the way at the last moment. She backed up to the side of the road and emitted another howl.

The answering panther's caterwauling was closer now.

Agnes waited until all cars had passed, which took a while because they were all slowing down to look at her, and then she bounded across the road and off into underbrush. She reappeared in a clearing in thicker woods beyond the roadside bushes and underbrush. Agnes paused beside a lone cabbage palm, looked back at Lizzie, made a mewing sound, turned and ran through a gap in the multitude of thin white trunks of partially denuded trees which made up the forest stretching out of sight to the south toward The Everglades. She did not reappear.

"Well, I guess that settles that," said Val as he emerged from the car.

"She's back with her true love." Lizzie put an arm around Val's waist.

"He waited for her and he'll always protect her." Val kissed Lizzie on the cheek.

Lizzie rolled her eyes skyward.

THE END